THEODORE'S WORK IN PROGRESS
Copyright © 2022 by Chelsea Lauren

ISBN 978-1-7324643-8-4

Cover Design by Brittany Evans

Edited by Represent Publishing

THEODORE'S
WORK IN
PROGRESS

THEODORE'S WORK IN PROGRESS

CHELSEA LAUREN

REPRESENT PUBLISHING

To all those tirelessly fighting to make the world better:
Thank you.

I see you.
I hear you.
I'm trying to be you.
Please, promise to take care of you.

PART ONE

T - 5

October 2

"Hi, guys, if you're new here, I'm Theo. Last year, my parents were murdered by police on October 10th at Majestic Park in Creston, NY for protesting the construction of a factory being built on the park. The factory still wants to tear the park down to put up their cancer-causing building, and the police officers are pleading, 'Not Guilty' to murder. This park is sacred to the surrounding neighborhoods as it's the only space big enough and clean enough to grow up on. Not only would the park disappear for children, but it would contaminate the Earth and the thousands of people in the radius. Please join me in the fight to get the factory shut down and to prosecute the police officers in charge of killing six individuals that day. Links are in my bio and follow for more updates."

One

I have approximately eight minutes to cook my omelet and be in my car, a situation that shouldn't have presented itself if the damn stove worked on cue. Even the lighter my uncle swears always does the trick isn't working to ignite the flame. I grab the oiled skillet and throw it into the kitchen sink, smiling as it clangs against the silverware from my brothers' breakfasts.

"Glad I brought breakfast."

Jonah, my boyfriend, is holding two sandwiches at the front door. His cheeks are flushed from walking a couple of blocks to my house. A slight shiver courses through him. I make a note to grab my jacket for the brisk autumn morning.

Jonah grins, his hazel eyes glowing as he crosses the kitchen to meet me. I guess today is a good day. Last night ended in an argument with Jonah and me, but I've learned those feelings are only temporary, and it's best not to bring them up the following day.

"Sit. Have breakfast for," he glances at the wall clock, "six minutes and five seconds."

I want to smile at that, but my frustration is still lingering. My uncle said that he'd get the stove fixed for real this time. It's been seven days since he mentioned it.

Jonah sits on the bench side of my kitchen table, and I sit at the head, right next to him. He presses a kiss against my lips—he tastes like peppermint toothpaste. I won't have time for that this morning.

"Five minutes and forty-five seconds." He winks before tossing over a handmade egg sandwich, still warm and wrapped tightly in foil.

As I unwrap it, steam drifts out of the foil, reminding me of how kind his family is. There is no way this came from Jonah's cooking. The last time Jonah *actually* cooked me eggs, he spent the day soaking and scrubbing the pan repeatedly, threatening to toss it in the trash. Then, he claimed to hate eggs in general, but he only hates *his* eggs.

"My mom had a feeling today was bacon day," he says before taking a massive bite from his own sandwich.

I laugh at that; my shoulders finally relax for the first time this morning. It is almost always a bacon day to his mom, but I sure as hell won't complain. With just one bite, my frustrations simmer, and all I want to do is forget my anger with my aunt and uncle.

Except, I can't. The stove is just one more appliance broken in my childhood home. My parents were never wealthy, but from what I've overheard about my parents' will, my aunt and uncle did get a portion to help take care of us if we were minors when they passed. If we weren't, the money would be divided between my brothers and me.

"Do Laura and Jeffrey know the stove is acting up again?"

I give Jonah a side-eye over my sandwich. His intentions are good, but sometimes he asks redundant questions.

"Noted." His voice drops an octave, his eyes laser-focused on his sandwich. "More breakfast in the morning. I can do that."

Except, I don't want him to do that. It's just one more thing for him to take care of as he's switched roles from boyfriend to caretaker. I know he resents me for it even though he says he doesn't.

"T - 2 minutes. Shall we head out?" Jonah's wrapping up his foil, taking my trash along with his as I shove the last piece in my mouth.

The clock reads 7:25 am—just enough time to drive to school and be a few minutes early to homeroom.

Grabbing my backpack and jacket, I make sure Jonah tosses the foil before we both head out of the house into the overcast weather and into my car.

Most days, we try to carpool to school. Sometimes it doesn't work well if I rush to my parents' agency or Jonah decides to stay after school. But for the most part, Jonah can walk to my house in the morning, and then I drive to school and drop him back home before going to work.

"Tonight, you're coming over for dinner and studying, right? After you check-in at With Love?" Jonah asks when we're halfway to school.

With Love is my parents' non-profit agency that serves my county. It focuses on helping secure homes for the homeless, guaranteeing food for families, helping foster children get adopted, supporting foster parents, and ensuring people can get crisis intervention if needed. My parents started it from the ground up when I was only ten. Now, it's grown into a massive force. At the moment, I am planning the annual fundraising event.

"Yeah, I'll leave at six. I have to do some things to promote the trial, but I'll do that at your place?"

"Sure, after we study. You need to pass this test, Theo." He sighs.

I choose to stay silent instead of fueling the fire. He acts like my physics grade is detrimental to him. I've already harped that this test is minimal to my parents' deaths getting justice. Besides, who assigns a test a few weeks into the school year that can make or break your cumulative grade?

"I'll be fine. I have time for it all," I say.

That's part of why I keep such a meticulous planner. From the moment I get up, I plan my entire day. Like, how long each chore my aunt assigns me takes to the amount of time I can shower and how many hours my eyes can close long enough to try and appear rested.

"You need to schedule some time to relax." His monotone voice is back. Like clockwork, my shoulders tense.

I pull into the parking lot at the perfect time. A minute longer, and we'd rehash our argument last night. Apparently, I prioritize the wrong things, do too much, and don't spend enough time just relaxing. Except, he doesn't understand that he can embrace the silence when he relaxes. When I relax, I relive the day my parents were murdered.

T - 4

October 3

"Coming to you from the With Love agency this afternoon. The event is two weeks away, so we are in final crunch time. I can't wait to announce who our vendors will be! They will be announced tomorrow afternoon. We have a fantastic raffle this year, and our speakers are out of this world. Tickets are still available for purchase. All funds go directly to the foundation. The ticket gets you into the event, where the food, drinks, and speakers are all included. The only additional cost is to enter the raffle. If anyone has any questions about the agency or the fundraiser, ask them below, and I'll answer them later tonight. Thank you for all your love and support."

Two

Five of us are in the conference room of With Love working on the annual fundraiser. The money goes toward our intervention resources, stocking up our food pantries, and giving prospective foster parents the support and opportunity to learn more. Throughout the year, we have smaller, more focused events. However, this fundraiser is my favorite and our most important. Without my parents around this year, I commandeered myself as the head coordinator—with board approval, of course. It helps that I have six years of experience planning these events with my parents.

The bland conference room is hardly recognizable, with mounds of boxes, decorations, and scattered chaos. All of these boxes need to be transferred to the event space after taking inventory of what we have saved from years before. Every fundraiser before this seemed a hell of a lot more organized than it is now. But this year is the first year without my mother or her right-hand woman, Ellie. They were impeccable organizers.

Despite board approval, I still have them watching my

every move to ensure my word means something. I need to go above and beyond to show the board that I can be a leader and that I am capable of delegating, which means getting all the forms signed and permits paid on time. It's one step closer to proving to the board that I can take over the agency once I turn eighteen—in just over six months. Someone on my team dropped the ball, though. There are no donation forms in my stack of papers.

"Who was in charge of getting all the donation forms signed?" I raise my voice, standing up. My chair wobbles behind me as I look up at the four volunteers scattered throughout the room.

If these forms aren't complete, I'll be late for my study session with Jonah. My shoulders grow tense as Jonah's words shoot through my mind, *"For someone always on time, you're always late for me."*

Katie, the receptionist at the agency, covers her ears. "Jesus, lower your voice. You were responsible. You're *always* responsible." Her eyes roll at her laptop, not even having the decency to make eye contact with me.

"I thought—" I flip through my planner, glancing at all the cross-outs, scattered words, and different colored pen ink. I delegated the forms only a few weeks ago.

"It's a shame you're not as organized as your mother."

My hand stops searching at her words. She has no right to talk to me—

Delegate Donation Forms. The only thing not checked off my planner three Tuesdays ago.

"Shit," I mutter. *How the hell did that get past me?*

I check the last couple of weeks in my planner; every other thing was crossed off. That Tuesday, Jonah asked me for help with some college applications. I was running late with the fundraiser, but I chose Jonah over completing my tasks at With Love. I cannot repeat history.

Alejandro, a friend and a fellow volunteer, crosses the room to me. He's organizing the decorations for the event. His brown skin is highlighted with the glitter we had for children to use last year. Even some specks made it to his top bun.

I glance at my phone, mentally calculating how long it would take to get all the forms signed and delivered by tonight *and* only be a few minutes late to Jonah's. The board needs to approve it all tomorrow.

"Theo, I mailed them out," Alejandro says. "You left them one night after saying they needed to go out, so I sent them. I just haven't had time to touch base with the vendors. I'm sorry I forgot to tell you."

I let out a breath, flipping back to today's date in my planner. In a bright red pen, I had written, "Are donations set in stone?!"

My phone rings, vibrating across the table, Jonah's picture popping up. I ignore it, placing it in my back pocket. The list in front of me is too long to get distracted. I still have a half-hour before I should be at his place.

Alejandro sits next to me, scanning over my once-neat handwriting in my planner. It may be only Monday, but it's already covered in scribbles.

"Is there anything else I can help you with? I'm happy to take something off your plate." Alejandro scratches the side of his face, leaving more glitter in his trail.

"Decorations are fine." I give him a smile before I close my planner. A few text messages vibrate in my pocket. I wish Jonah would understand that distracting me only makes me later. "Thank you, Alee."

He salutes with a smile and heads back to organizing

decorations with his father. Every year, Alejandro and his father decorate the community hall and make it look stunning. His father also hand-carves signs for all the businesses that have a booth. Alejandro and I had a few classes together in high school, but it wasn't until he started volunteering at With Love that we started a friendship. Now, I'm not sure what I would do without him in my life.

Okay, Theo, you've got this. I just have to figure out how to collect forms from all different locations across a couple of towns and not have my boyfriend be frustrated that I am once again late.

"Theodore Montgomery?" a voice asks from the doorway of the conference room.

Glancing over, two tall, polished men walk into the room. Both smiling, they lock eyes with me. There's a vague recognition, but my head isn't sorting through my files fast enough.

My eyes zone in on the paper the guy with a groomed beard is holding. *Please, please, please let it be the damn form.*

Walking over to them, I clear my throat and offer my hand. "Theodore," I greet.

"Caden." The one without the paper shakes my hand.

Jackpot. But can it be? The owners of Isabella's Coffee traveled from Maine to New York?

"And this is Ben. We are the owners of Isabella's Coffee."

I breathe in, giving a closed-lip smile as I try to calm my mind. Isabella's Coffee is a company praised for its outspoken owners, incredible treatment of employees, and outstanding quality of coffee and service.

"It's an honor," my voice shakes as I speak, but they both smile reassuringly.

There are only a few Isabella's Coffee shops in the Northeast. We have one about forty-five minutes away near Majestic Park. Alejandro and I try to go and support them whenever we do events at the park. Ben and Caden have donated time and raised money for numerous events, marches, and charities throughout the Northeast, some even for ones I've attended, but I've never met them.

"It's an honor to meet you, Theodore," Caden says.

My knees grow weak, so I lock them tight.

"We've heard about the Montgomery family's impact in New York, and we've been supporting the trial, but we really wanted to team up. When we heard about this event, we knew we had to say yes," Benjamin tells me as he hands me the signed donation form. "We don't want to keep you, but the two of us will be running the booth. It's an important event for us, so we want to be there in person."

The donation form crinkles in my palm. Our big-name donors will be here in person. I urge my stomach to remain calm; the last thing I need to do is faint or double over. If I mess this event up, I may lose their donations forever.

"G-great. I look forward to it. If there's anything you two need, just email the agency, and we'll get on it."

"Actually," Caden starts, "would we be able to post a quick video with you? We don't need to post it until you announce the donors, but we would love to support this event on our page, too."

My heart literally skips a beat at their request. I plan to make videos with all the donors at the event but didn't think about making videos beforehand. We still have a few tickets left to sell. This could help our online donations too.

"He would love to," Alejandro says, jogging to the door, saving me from my awkwardness—always. "As the voice behind the camera in all his videos, let me take it for you guys."

I look over at Alee as my body begins to overheat. Alee raises his brow, ever so slightly, boring his muddy eyes into mine. Telepathically telling me to calm the hell down. I do a quick body shake before I stand between Caden and Ben, quickly running my hands through my knotted curls.

Caden hands his iPhone over to Alejandro. Sweat starts to build up under my pits at the proximity to both Caden and Ben, whom I respect so much. While Isabella's Coffee has been around for nearly ten years, it started becoming more than a coffee shop in the past four years.

Alejandro has his angle and nods toward us as a "go." Caden starts speaking.

"Hey, guys! Our week is officially made. If you've been following our stories over the past couple of weeks, you know we've been talking about the Majestic Park trial in New York and the courageous activist Theodore Montgomery. He has been working diligently to spread the word. We won't go into detail here as we've got everything saved in our highlights, but we had the pleasure to meet *the* Theodore Montgomery today."

I do an awkward wave and put on my social media smile. *"The"? Surely, I'm not that special.* I inhale, breathing out a controlled breath as Ben starts speaking.

"Today, though, we aren't talking about Majestic Park. Instead, we are so honored to be a part of an event With Love, his parents' agency, is hosting. Theodore, can you tell us more about it?"

Shit. Shit. Shit. Uh. Ben nudges my back to speak. I grin way too big. I grip my hands, crinkling the donation form, to keep them steady.

"Hi, friends! Theo here, coming from the With Love agency. We are hosting a fundraising event that helps intervention services, foster children, the homeless, and more throughout the community. Thank you for the love and support on this page. I'm a fan of the coffee shop, so I've been lurking on Instagram. I'd say I'm the lucky one here to have Ben and Caden donating their time and coffee to my parents' fundraising event."

Ben interjects.

"Speaking of, tickets are on sale for this incredible event. Come support Theodore and the amazing families in his community, and while you're there, come to our booth and say hi! Info for tickets and donations are linked in our bio."

We all wave goodbye, and then Alejandro hands the phone back to Caden. I let out another slow, controlled breath of relief. My heart is definitely going to break my rib cage.

"Thank you! That's great," Ben exclaims. "Our DMs have been filled lately with how to help out on your parents' trial. This, I think, will make things a little more attainable for some people," Ben says.

"Thank you." I feel heat rise to my cheeks. This is entirely unexpected.

While I talk about my parents' trial every day on social media, people rarely talk to me about it in person unless it's

Alee. It's like a taboo subject. People either don't believe the police should be convicted, think I should just get over my parents' murders, or they just don't know what to say.

The three of us exchange phone numbers so they can contact me about the event before the two of them leave, and I'm left standing awkwardly at the door.

Looking down at the donation form, it's now moist from my clammy hands.

"That was amazing!" Alee exclaims, placing a hand on my shoulder. "That's definitely what we needed to sell the last bit of tickets."

Another text vibrates my pocket, shaking me from the moment. I smile at Alejandro and nod before taking my phone out of my pocket. Of the numerous messages that came through, only one is from Jonah. The rest are from my aunt demanding me to clean the kitchen, living room, and bathroom when I get home. I know I have chores to do when I'm home; it's a daily cycle of the toxic environment I was shoved into. But the reminder of each and every thing that needs to be done increases the pressure on my lungs. I shove the phone back in my pocket and rush over to my spot in the room to gather all the paperwork I have with me into my bag.

I'm about to run out of the conference room when Alejandro is right next to me with his own bag.

"Let's go get signatures and promo videos," he suggests.

I have ten minutes to get to Jonah's with four pit stops in between.

"Brilliant idea," I say, and we run out to the parking lot.

To say Jonah is frustrated when he opens his front door is an understatement. He's walking away before I'm inside. It doesn't matter that I'm carrying his favorite food from Lucy's Cafe or the ginger beer he is obsessed with. While I didn't make a pit stop for either because Lucy's Cafe is one of our donors catering the event, I'm still two hours late.

"I already ate." He crosses the threshold into the living room, disappearing from sight.

I kick the door closed behind me and jog through the dark kitchen to catch up to him.

The bright lights of the living room cause me to squint. Jonah already looks deep into his homework; it's sprawled over the coffee table. An empty pizza box is next to his backpack.

"I'm sorry. It's just I had to pick up all the donation forms because I forgot to ask someone to do it."

"You forget a lot these days—like responding to my messages." Jonah collapses on the couch with a huff, curling his legs underneath him.

I place the food containers and ginger beer on the opposite side of the coffee table and sit on the hardwood floor.

"You knew I had a couple of hours at the agency today. There's still so much to do. And I got stuck at each place for a lot longer than anticipated today. Everyone wanted to talk to me about how excited they were, and then Alee and I decided to film videos with each donor because Caden and Ben—" I lift a ginger beer out of the pack and twist off the top.

"So you spent time with Alejandro when you said you'd be done by six?"

His words have my hand pausing before I can taste the ginger beer.

"Alee and I were working. So yes, I spent time with him. You had your opportunity to volunteer with us; you still do. You just choose not to."

I take a sip, trying to regulate my breathing. It's the same goddamn fight over and over again. He claims I spend too much time volunteering or going to events or protests, and I swear he doesn't lift a damn finger. Have I gotten busier since my parents' deaths? Yes, because I have the trial and their fundraiser. But ever since the day I could sit on my father's shoulders, my life has always been about volunteering and protests.

Bringing Alejandro in as ammo is rare, though. I thought we got past the jealousy a few months ago.

He grabs a bottle of ginger beer and settles back onto the couch.

"I'm not trying to fight with you, Theo." He leans his head in the palm of his hand, elbow resting on the arm of the couch. The eyes that shined bright for me this morning are now dull and exhausted. "I'm disappointed you didn't have the care to text or call me that you're running late. The world doesn't revolve around you and your schedule." He sighs. "Just study for the test, and then maybe we can hang out."

The hunger pangs that screamed at me only minutes before at the smell of this lasagna have now solidified. There's no greater failure than being a disappointment.

"I already studied, but I left out my notes in case you need help," Jonah says.

"Thank you," I mumble.

I want to tell him more. I want to apologize and go into further detail on why I was so late—again, and why he doesn't have to worry about Alee, but he's halted the conversation.

Without a glance toward me, he stands up and heads down the hall, closing the door to his art studio. I open up my planner and squeeze it into today's column: *Talk to Jonah*. He has important deadlines too.

My pen drops as I answer the last question to a practice test Jonah had, of course, created. A quick review of the score shows I got a seventy-two. *Good enough. Passing is passing at this point.*

My phone reads 10:13 pm by the time I pack up my backpack. There are a ton of notifications I have to sort through, but I don't have time. At 11 pm, my aunt will text me, telling me that I'm past my curfew, with another reminder to clean the house. I shouldn't hang out with Jonah, but I'm in a lose-lose situation.

Living with my aunt and uncle hasn't been the most comfortable journey. We still can't get past our differing views, particularly the one where they believe my parents got what they deserved. To say they've always been radically different from my immediate family would be an understatement. I'll never wrap my head around why my aunt and uncle were in my parents' will instead of Sam and Ellie, their best friends.

But I digress. There is still one thing left in my planner for today. Hopefully, Jonah's cooled down.

I find him in his bedroom, lying on his bed. His hair is wet and a little shaggy on top of his head. He doesn't look over at me when I walk into the 'organized chaos' he calls his room, but he shifts under his white comforter. His eyes are drawn to his phone, looking at a photo of us cuddled together on my back porch.

I make my way over to the bed and sit, tapping his shoulder with my own. He moves, and I crawl under the comforter, interlocking our feet. I lean into him, focusing on the picture.

It was taken on October 9th last year. My father was known for his incredible barbecuing. My parents, Sam and Ellie—basically my godparents without the responsibility of the will—Jonah and his parents, and then my twin brothers, Jack and Timothy, were all there.

Jonah and I were so good that day. We were still carefree teenagers; the world hadn't touched us yet. It was one of those weekend afternoons that felt like the universe was providing happiness for us. Everyone was joyous. A copious amount of wine was consumed by the adults. Jonah and I even had the chance to sneak away and make out while everyone was distracted. This photo was taken right after we had crept back down, goofy smiles on our faces as we fell onto the wooden swing on my back porch. Ellie had snapped the photo and sent it to us. I didn't know at the time that it would be the last good memory I had. The following day was the protest, and a few days after the funeral, Sam and Ellie disappeared from my life, too.

I don't realize tears are streaming down my face until Jonah nudges my shoulder. He places his phone down. When my eyes clear, his are filled with sympathy, making me want to either punch him or curl up underneath the sheets. I need a distraction to keep myself from spiraling. This is the longest I've relaxed in over a week.

I blink a few times before clearing my throat. "How was your day?" I ask. "Tell me three good things."

Jonah usually starts the conversation about three good things when I'm stressed or beginning to spiral, but "Mission: Talk to Jonah" involves actually asking about him first.

He hesitates, flipping his phone around on his lap.

"I had breakfast with you." I can feel the fight in him between giving in or holding onto his frustration. His shoulders want to sag into mine, but he keeps shifting upward.

I nudge his shoulder, grinning. "That's a good start to the day. I do appreciate that."

His face relaxes as he looks over at me. Not quite a smile yet, but the green in his hazel eyes start to shine.

"I aced my English presentation on *Macbeth*." This gets a slight twinge of his lip. I forgot about his presentation. He enjoyed the play and wouldn't shut up about it all last week.

"And . . . " I drum roll on the comforter with a big smile on my face.

He sits up for this last one as he flushes. "I started my art portfolio today."

"Ah!" I yell, wrapping my arms around him. He steadies us from collapsing into the wall before hugging me back. It's a light hug, but the feeling of his hands on my skin is comforting, regardless. "That's incredible. What did you do?"

"A charcoal portrait. It's not finished, but I figured out a theme, and I'm really excited about it. It'll be tight, but I think I can finish the portfolio in time."

Jonah has an art portfolio due in November for an internship in England. It would be a summer-long program, and if he did well in it, he'd have access to one of the best art schools overseas. It's an incredible opportunity that he knew about before our senior year began; fear, I think, has kept him from starting.

I release the hug just enough so my hands rest on his shoulders, and I can look him in the eyes. "I was going to hound you about that today."

I don't tell him that I forgot to write it down, and if it

isn't written down, it barely passes through my mind these days.

Darkness flashes through his face before he sighs and lets go of me.

"I know. I haven't felt inspired. But I just let myself feel when I got home. And well, it all just kind of came naturally," he says.

I know better than to ask him what his theme is. He's very secretive about his art, another reason it's taken him so long to start. I'm partially to blame. He likes to help consume my downtime when there is any. And if he isn't with me, which is quite often, he's usually stressing about how I overwork myself. I'm not ignorant to the fact that it hinders his life. Though, I'm choosing to ignore that his inspiration tonight likely has to do with his frustration toward me . . . but I can play that role if it helps his dreams.

"Well, I'm proud of you."

"Thank you," he whispers. Jonah settles back into position before looking up at me expectantly. "Your turn. Three good things."

"Uh, I got an A on that history essay even though I demolished the American History textbook by stating actual facts and not what the government wants us to know."

He laughs, a genuine pure laugh that covers my skin in goosebumps. His round eyes, now bright with life, finally look at me—his boyfriend—not the person he's annoyed with or the grieving boy.

"When we finish this conversation, we'll throw on *Parks and Rec*, and we'll cuddle."

"That's cheating; that hasn't happened yet. What if I say you have to leave and can't hang out?" He raises his brow. "That would alter the course of your night and could no longer be a good thing."

I don't falter. "Seeing you is always a good thing."

It's true. Even on our hardest days, my most stressful nights, or when Jonah just doesn't understand my grief, he's the person I want to see. Jonah is still here after all this time, and that says something.

He blushes. I've broken him down; we're a team again. "Okay, I can't argue with that."

I press my lips against his, enveloping him in another hug. Jonah's muscles relax underneath my fingertips.

"You still have number three," he mumbles against my lips.

Disconnecting our lips, I remain in a hug. "The owners of Isabella's Coffee came into the agency today and said they'd be at the event."

"Whoa." Jonah pulls back, his eyes widening, allowing me to see all the hues of the greens and browns. "They really signed on to donate?"

Most of the donations are from places my parents have worked with for years. Isabella's Coffee was my addition, and we honestly weren't sure if they would.

"Not only donate, but they are volunteering their own time." I smile; my cheeks ache with all the grinning I've done with the video promos.

A smile graces his face now. He gives me a quick peck. "That's amazing, Theo. I'm really proud of you."

I swallow the compliment, shifting in his arms. "I'm sorry I was late."

He just nods, slowly maneuvering us to lie in his bed. Jonah nestles his head in the crook of my neck and wraps his leg over my waist.

"Oh!" I exclaim. "Gimme your phone; maybe they posted it." He hands me over his phone.

I click on the Instagram app before searching Isabella's Coffee. They told me they'd wait until I announced it on the With Love page, but I was on such a high when Alejandro and I were filming the other videos, that I gave them permission to post it tonight. Selfishly, I wanted the video so I could watch it over and over again.

"Caden and Ben wanted a video with me, which is what inspired Alejandro into coming with me to pick up the donation forms, so then I could make videos with everyone."

He doesn't respond, but it doesn't matter because, sure enough, a video preview is posted in their stories, directing us to the static post. I click on it, my heart racing at the sound of Caden introducing me. The excitement coursing through my body overpowers the fact that I look like a literal train wreck in the video. My thick, brown curly hair is flying in different directions after a long school day and running the mile in gym class. There are bags under my eyes from the maybe three hours of sleep I had the night before. And my olive skin looks pasty and dry from the copious amounts of coffee I've consumed instead of water. I try to ignore the fact that I'll look like this for all the videos, but there's no time to re-record.

"That's really amazing, Theo. I am happy it's all coming together." His voice has become more monotone, and I'm about to ask what is going on, but my alarm blares through the room, reminding me I have to leave in two minutes to be home before eleven.

Jonah lets out an audible sigh and rolls away from me toward the wall.

"I'm sorry," I whisper. I jump out of bed, run my hands

through my curls, and give him a quick kiss on his head before rushing to the bedroom door.

Just as I'm about to shut the door behind me, Jonah speaks up. "I'm not upset with the fundraiser, Theo. I'm upset that I went from being the most important thing in your life to literally being penciled into your planner for you to remember that I exist."

My second alarm reminder rings, and I close the bedroom door, swallowing the lump forming in my throat.

I should go back in and talk to him. I should ignore what my phone says about the time, ignore that my aunt will lose her shit if I'm not home by eleven, ignore the laundry list of chores that never ends because my aunt and uncle despise me. But I can't. I can't disrupt the schedule. Because if I disrupt everything now, then tomorrow will make me more anxious. There isn't enough time between school, my parents' trial, my parents' foundation, cleaning, and sleeping.

The house is pitch black when I arrive home, but I get to work on the written list on the kitchen counter. I'm responsible for the sink-full of crusted dishes, despite only putting a skillet in there all day. I have laundry baskets to fold in the living room for the entire family; I have to wipe down and mop the entire kitchen and living room, and then finally, by the time 2:00 am has rolled around, I make my way up to my bedroom, thankfully down the hall from the other two bedrooms.

After filling my diffuser with lavender (something Jonah was adamant about me trying), I curl into bed and go through my notifications. Emails from different websites and networks remind me that I need time tomorrow to answer questions about the trial. With a quick tap into my calendar app, I set a reminder before diving into the rest of the notifications. There are comments from social media, a text from Alejandro telling me that Isabella's Coffee posted the video, and one other text message from Ellie.

Sam and Ellie moved to Colorado after my parents passed. They said the deaths of their best friends and running the agency was too difficult on them. They moved to be closer to Ellie's mom. I haven't forgiven them for abandoning me a couple days after my parents' funeral instead of helping me or fighting for me. Likely, my aunt and uncle would have been fine with Sam and Ellie being my guardian. But Jonah says that they have to grieve in their own way.

Regardless, Ellie follows my socials and every-so-often checks in with me. Sometimes, it seems like we both lie in our messages, so we don't worry about the other. Despite everything, whenever her name pops up on my phone, my body relaxes. She used to be my person before I started dating Jonah. She was the one I could always go to, and she wouldn't tell my parents a thing. She used to joke that I abandoned her when Jonah came into my life. I never realized that there would be a day when I wouldn't have her.

I open her message and grin at the excitement.

Ellie: *THEO! Look at you go. You got Isabella's Coffee as a sponsor? Best upgrade ever! I wish I had asked for that coffee instead of my terribly brewed coffee last year. And your socials? Boy, you're famous!! Sam and I are so, so, so proud of you. We are almost ready to come back home. I promise we will soon. We miss you terribly. It looks like you are doing just fine without us, though. We love you so much.*

My hands shake as I reread her message a few times.

She's never once mentioned coming home. *Home.* They are just visiting Colorado. It was never permanent.

I write her back a thank you and a miss you. As the tears start to brim from her message, I distract myself by filming different videos for social media. There is no way I can sleep now.

Most videos answer questions from those who asked about the event earlier today. Some videos are about the trial, reiterating that we will find out if the police are convicted this coming Friday. I highlight a few different things people can do. I also mention the protest this Thursday at the park, the last final plea to convict the officers who killed six people. The final thing I do is schedule the videos I took with the donors today for them to be released every few days leading up to the event in two weeks.

As I'm falling asleep, I receive a text message from Jonah.

Jonah: *Stop posting. Go to sleep. It'll all be here when you wake up.*

I roll my eyes, put my phone on airplane mode, and curl into my comforter. I always forget he gets notifications that ding on his phone when I post. It used to be cute until he started using it as a way to track me.

T - 3

October 4

"Hi, guys, I wanted to give you some info on two incredibly important events this week. Most of you know, but for those who don't, we have a protest at Majestic Park in Creston, NY on Thursday. The verdict on my parents' trial is Friday at the courthouse in Creston. The protest is hosted by me and my best friend, Alejandro. We will be there from 10:00 am until however late we need to be. I'll be making three speeches. Most major news networks will be broadcasting these if you can't attend. We urge you to spread the word, show up, donate money to those helping us, and be angry as hell. All the info to help join the fight is in my bio. If all you can do is share this message, that's more than enough. Thank you for all your support. Let me know if you have any questions."

Three

My morning started without breakfast, even though Jonah said he'd continue to bring it. Instead, he never showed up, delaying my commute to school. Naturally, like clockwork, a more detailed chore list was waiting for me this morning that I somehow had to fit into the next two days. Not only that, but to not fall behind in school, I have to stay after and complete assignments that I'll miss on Thursday for the protest and then Friday for the verdict. All in all, not a prime day to be running on two hours of sleep.

My social media blew up from overseas overnight, though. My one positive of the day. By the time I'm halfway through school, my million followers have turned into two million. I'm not sure if the followers have to do with Isabella's Coffee or because the trial is on the news again as we get closer to the date. Either way, it's helpful. I caught a clip this morning of a news station highlighting my social media. While I never gave them permission to use my videos, at least I'm getting some money from all the views, likes, and followers.

The positive responses from my phone throughout my

day and rereading Ellie's message are what get me through because Jonah is actively ignoring me. We had our physics test this morning, and he didn't look at me. Alejandro adds to my stress with a bombardment of texts about the fundraiser and trial.

By the time I make it to the ninth period, the extra period of the day, my lungs are tight, my head aches, and if I move too quickly, the room sways.

My English and history teachers are working with me to ensure I don't fall. I ignore the fact that I'll be missing physics for two days because I'm fairly confident I failed today's test, and I don't need it to graduate. Plus, my English and history teachers actually care about my well-being. While they won't be taking off work this week, they have supported me and have tickets to the fundraising event.

After spending the period catching up on work, Alejandro meets me in the classroom I'm in.

"Hey!" he greets, taking a seat next to me as most other kids who stayed after filter out. "So ignore the panicked voicemails I left you about the table and chair crisis. My dad will help us figure it out. I want you to go home and relax."

I narrow my eyes at him because while he's concerned about me, he often doesn't say it. Yes, I need sleep. Yes, my eyes burn from the strain, and I'm nearly ready to snap, but this is my responsibility.

"I would like for you to stop taking advice from Jonah," I say as I put my bag on my back. "If Jonah is concerned about me, he can actually talk to me."

"We are both concerned," Alee rushes as I start to walk out of the classroom, and he jogs to catch up. "It's just there's a lot happening in the next few days, and I've seen your schedule, and I saw your post times last night. Take the night off."

My phone rings in my back pocket, and I take it as an excuse to get out of the conversations, but of course, it's my Aunt Laura calling.

"Yes?" I sigh as I answer.

"You're so disrespectful, Theodore. I need you home in thirty minutes to watch your brothers. I don't care whatever lib-tard thing you have planned for the night. Your uncle and I need to go out. You also need to clean the entire house. We will be having guests this weekend for a party."

My stomach drops at the mention of a party. Not only is the trial verdict on Friday, but the anniversary of my parents' deaths is Monday.

"No," I say, trying to swallow with my dry mouth. I've never said no to them before, but *this* is disrespectful.

"Tell me no one more time and watch how fast you lose everything you've ever created. You and I don't agree, but I turn a blind eye to your homosexuality—"

My feet freeze in place. Alee's hands steady my shoulders as I start to sway.

"—and you hanging out with that brown boy. I see the vile lies you spread across the internet. Do not forget I can end you in a second." The line clicks to an end.

My aunt and I have gotten into some pretty heated arguments, but those stopped nearly nine months ago when she put me in my place, letting me know that I had a roof over my head, heat, and food. Similar to this sickening, bone-chilling tone, she told me that she'd take that all away from me too. She said she'd turn a blind eye to my *lifestyle* as long as I did everything she asked. While a part of me didn't believe she could legally refuse me shelter, she has locked me out enough times that I try not to risk it.

When my aunt and uncle moved in, I quickly developed a system where I rarely saw them. I volunteer, protest, host events, and go to school, filling every waking hour of my day. I return home when she's in bed, and I leave the house after she has. It's worked almost every day for those nine months—and when school isn't in session, and I can't do anything else, I spend my time with Jonah or Alejandro.

"You okay?" Alejandro asks.

I blink, swallow, and force a smile on my face. "Yup. I'll take you up on relaxing tonight. Text me if you need anything."

"Are you—" Alee starts, but I wave him off and jog toward the school exit.

Jonah and Alee know that my aunt and uncle suck, but only based on their human rights views, not because of their threats. They've only seen them interact around my brothers, who they put on a good show for.

My aunt and uncle are dressed up when I open the front door. My uncle is in a three-piece suit, and my aunt has a floor-length golden gown on. Where the hell they are going looking like that on a Tuesday night baffles me, but fewer questions, less arguments.

"There's a list on the table of everything that needs to get done. There's pizza in the oven for the boys. We'll be back late tonight. I expect everything to be done before then. Absolutely no guests," my uncle explains.

I can already hear the video games blaring from my brothers' bedroom. At least they'll be easy.

It's when I hear my aunt and uncle shut the front door, and I go into the kitchen that I know I have a rough road ahead. One, there are only two personal pizzas in the oven, so they didn't even cook for me. Two, while the list is technically one page, it is filled back and front with intricate tasks, like cleaning the window sills and the ceiling fans. Thankfully, it's a compilation of the list I saw this morning.

I quickly eat a bowl of cereal, my only meal for the day, and start to film a video in the silent kitchen.

"Hey, guys!

You all are unbelievable. I can't believe I reached over two million followers this morning. I appreciate every single one of you. Not only does it brighten my day to be able to talk to you all and make videos, I know it's helping many other people. I am not the only person who has lost someone like this, and I'm so grateful I can say I have so many friends loving and supporting me. I'll respond to some comments soon, but first, I've gotta be a responsible teen."

I wave bye to the camera, quickly upload the video, and clean up my mess all before bringing the pizzas up to my brothers and getting a start on the chores. I assume I have approximately six to seven hours to make the entire house spotless, even though it'll likely be a mess before their party, anyway.

Jonah tries calling throughout the night, but I don't have time for him to explain why he chose to ignore me all day. After two calls from Jonah and no emergencies from Alejandro, I silence my phone and listen to a new episode about the trial from my favorite news podcast.

I even filmed a "watch me clean" video loop to add to my social media. Some followers don't understand how I do everything in a day. Some followers claim my family must be rich and I don't have regular teen responsibilities. Some followers don't even realize that it was my parents who were murdered. So every once in a while, I twist what my aunt and uncle make me do into content that I get paid for.

I had a job previous to my parents passing at a local cafe, but I couldn't keep up with it this past year. But when Alejandro told me I could make money off of social media, I signed up and started posting videos about everything I do. All the money goes into a savings account to help me move out when I'm eligible for a lease in April. The money isn't much at the moment, but it's only increasing. The money from my parents' life insurance is in a trust fund that I'll get periodically after I'm eighteen, too.

By the time I'm checking off the last thing on the list, my uncle's car pulls into the driveway. I dash up the stairs and immediately into my bedroom to avoid them. It's nearing midnight, and sleep is catching up to me, but I spend the next few hours completing homework and responding to comments on my videos.

At this point, insomnia has kicked in.

T - 2

October 5

"I get this question a lot. How the hell do I have time to do chores, go to school, protest, volunteer, have friends, have a boyfriend. I can tell you that I keep a meticulously scheduled planner. I can tell you I'm laser-focused. The honest truth is, I sleep about two to three hours a night. I skip meals some days. I have people who back me up, but I likely am not who they need me to be. And the real, disgusting truth? If I'm not filling every single second of my day, all I remember is my parents' murder. If you were in my shoes, it'd look like you were the most productive person on the planet. Want to know a secret? I wish, for a day, I could escape from this world, shut down,. Not be the teen whose parents were murdered. Instead, I am a loving, kind, and energetic teen. I miss who I used to be, but that person died with my parents."

Four

"It's going to be okay, Theo. It's okay. We'll all be okay." My mother cries, sinking to the ground as she holds my forearm tight.

I collapse with her, placing her head in my lap.

Another round of shots go off, and we both look forward, startled. My father runs toward the police, screaming, shouting, crying.

What's the damn 101 emergency care we all practiced and memorized before each protest? Protect and care for each other before reacting.

"It's okay, Mom. You're going to be fine." I rip my t-shirt off through the lie, crumbling it in my hand before applying pressure to the wound right below her heart. I'm not a doctor, but she won't survive if the police don't leave immediately.

The tear gas still burns my eyes as I try to blink through the fog, smoke, and tears.

Five shots. Pew. Pew. Pew. Pew. Pew. They all went off as the teargas covered the entire area.

Through all the screaming and crying, it's hard to focus. My pressure becomes shaky as my mom starts to tremble.

Name things, Theo. Focus.

My dying mother is in my arms.

My father is nowhere near.

I'm surrounded by dead and wounded bodies.

My heart is breaking through my ribcage.

"I love you, Mom. We'll get help. Hold on. It's okay. It's okay." My tears drip on her sweaty face, trailing down and combining with her own tears. Her eyes are closed, but her breathing still comes in slow waves. Her trembling is minimal.

Please, oh please, let this not be real.

"Theo, my baby, me and Daddy are so proud of you," my mom rasps.

"Theodore! Your father!"

There's a grasp on my shoulder, someone else sinking to their knees.

"Oh, Theodore. Fuck. Fucking shit."

I stare in front of me. Watching as the police hit the inno-cent protestors with batons. Another round of teargas swells my eyelids.

We were here protecting a park. A park for children to roam and grow up. A place to smile and laugh and connect with family.

A park that the government wants to destroy for a massive factory that'll pollute the air, spread carcinogens, and affect future families.

My Future.

Gasp.

"Theo! Theo, it's just another nightmare."

When my eyes open, I see specks startled by the rage of energy and lifting of my torso. I'm drenched in sweat. I went to bed with a t-shirt on, but as my vision clears, I see my sweaty t-shirt crumbled in my fist. I'll be trying to protect her until my dying days.

"Theo, breathe. You're not there. You're here with me," Jonah says. He cups my cheeks, turning my head toward him. The coolness of his hands sends shivers down my sweaty body.

I don't make eye contact with him, but I mimic his breathing, closing my eyes briefly before they dart open and look off into the distance. Sometimes shutting my eyes too close to an episode causes it to come back.

My body collapses in his arms as the breathing starts to calm me, and we are both horizontal on the bed.

"It's okay, Theo. You're safe here."

Safe. I don't even know what safe means anymore.

My groggy mind begins to clear, and I push away, forcing myself to sit up. "It's not just a nightmare, Jonah. I stopped being safe the moment my parents were murdered."

I step off the foot of the bed, thankful I still have my sweatpants on, and haphazardly pull my gross t-shirt over my head. My body sways slightly.

I don't know why or how he's here, but he isn't welcome.

Jonah's loud sigh comes from behind me as I gather my belongings for the day. If Jonah made his way up here and woke me from a nightmare, I'm running late.

"That's not what I mean, and you know it."

"Then you should start saying what you mean." I glance over toward the bed at him. He is fully dressed for school in jeans and just a red t-shirt, but a piece of his short brown hair is sticking up out of place. His eyes look tired, but there shouldn't be any reason he didn't sleep last night. "Why the hell are you here, anyway?" I ask.

I gather my clothes for the day, getting ready to hop in the shower.

"You didn't answer my calls last night," he says, and I can't contain my eye roll. "I was worried about you."

"You chose to ignore me yesterday!" I let out a sardonic laugh. "You must have been real worried."

"Alejandro mentioned you got a phone call at school and you seemed put off. So yes, I became worried."

"So you invite yourself over to my house? *Inside* my house?" If it wouldn't take time to clean up the mess, I'd throw my clothes across the room at him.

"Up until a year ago, I used to be a member of this household." His tone is sharp as he stands from my bed, crossing his arms. "So yes, I used the key my parents have and opened the door."

When my aunt and uncle moved in, they made it clear that if they didn't see Jonah, they didn't know what I was doing. To avoid issues, I just told Jonah that my aunt and uncle didn't like people over, and I always offered to go to his house. Besides, Jonah knows how homophobic they are. There is no reason to be uncomfortable here if we don't have to be. It's rarely been an issue between us. This is the first time he's mentioned point-blank that he used to be at my house all hours of the day. His parents used to eat dinner here some nights just to see their son.

"I have to go. My day is packed." It's not a lie; my planner is jam-packed. But really, I'm just frustrated that he thinks it's okay to disappear on me, but I can't have the same decency for space.

I'm halfway out of my bedroom door before his hand is on my shoulder.

"Can we at least drive in together? Talk? I'll wait while you shower."

"No, I don't want to talk." I shrug off his shoulder and head to the bathroom.

"Okay, okay. Tonight, can you come over for a Marvel movie? No talking, just cuddling and Marvel?"

I pause at the door and turn to look at him. His eyelashes perfect his round eyes today, like a damn puppy dog, and if he's offering Marvel . . . our favorite company of all time.

"No talking. I'll be there at eight." I then slam the bathroom door behind me.

The rest of the day consists of much of the same. I stay late for school work again. I go to the agency to help with finalizing speaker times, securing tables and chairs, working on a few new video promos, and then I send out reminders about the protest tomorrow.

By the time I'm walking up to Jonah's house with some subs and iced tea, it's just before eight. The first time I've been early to see Jonah in a long time.

When he opens the front door, the beaming smile on his face shows he noticed the time. He doesn't know that I set twelve really annoying alarms in order to get here. Or that I did actually place him in my planner. All that matters is he thinks he's first on my list tonight.

I kick off my shoes and drop my backpack by the front door.

"I think we should watch *Guardians of the Galaxy* tonight. What do you think? Some good 80s playlist with some light-hearted laughs?" Jonah says as we walk through his kitchen.

He's grabbing plates out of the cabinets and some napkins for us to head upstairs.

"And watch a movie where his mother dies right in the beginning?"

Jonah turns away from the cabinet, his face flushed. We've seen it countless times together. I'm really just busting his chops that he'd choose that movie this week.

"Shit! I'm sorry. That was insensitive." He pauses, tapping his fingers on the countertop. "We could bring it to something more generic, like *Iron Man 2* or more intense battles with *The Avengers*."

I shrug. "Doesn't matter. As long as we watch a movie and eat, I'm good. I just don't want to think anymore."

"Deal." He puts the plates and napkins down on the counter and takes a few tentative steps toward me. Jonah wraps me in a hug, pressing a kiss against my lips.

With an inhale and exhale through my nose, I relax into his hug, wrapping my own arms around him, the sub bag hitting the back of his legs.

He pulls away from the kiss, and I lean my head into his shoulder. I don't know what is happening between the two of us and how long we can continue this hot and cold, but he usually knows what I need at the end of the day, and I fear losing that.

For the better half of ten minutes, we stand in each other's arms. The silence is better with him. It's as if I can see my filing cabinets close for the night with each passing moment.

We finally make our way to his bedroom, put on *Guardians of the Galaxy*, and curl up on our makeshift couch. One side of Jonah's bed rests against the wall, so we pile pillows against it. It allows us to sink into the cushion for movies and curl up in his down comforter. We often get into petty arguments about who leaves the nest if we forget something.

"Sometimes I wish I could be transported to a new planet," I mumble once my sub is finished and I'm picking at the slivers of lettuce that fell onto the plate.

"Why?" Jonah shifts next to me, but I keep my eyes on the movie.

"Because I don't want to live in a country that aided in my parents' murder."

Jonah chokes on his sub. He sits up, placing his plate on the bedside table. He still has a quarter of his sub left. "The entire country didn't aid in that." His voice brings shivers down my spine.

"Are you kidding me?" I laugh, putting my plate on the bed so I can match his stature. "The police and wealthy rule this country. There's no equality. My parents fought to make sure children could have a school and park to grow up in without dying from poison, and they got killed for that." I untangle myself from the comforter. "*Of course*, the country is involved." I pause the movie and climb off of his bed.

"But what about the good people? Those fighting, like your parents did? Shouldn't they count for something? *They* are part of this country. They need more good people to help."

"I don't always want to be a good person!" I shout before I take a shallow breath, covering my face with my hands. Adrenaline courses through my blood as I start to pace back and forth on the small path his bedroom provides. Tears burn my eyes, and I force them to stay in. I don't want to be a sobbing mess in front of him. Not now. "I don't want to be the youngest awarded activist in New York. I don't always want to make the world better for people who don't deserve it, Jonah."

He moves himself to the edge of the bed, hands gripping the comforter. His eyes watch my every move.

"The good people cannot just disappear from the fight."

I halt mid-step. My breath catches as another weight is added to my shoulders, and I narrow my eyes, looking over at him. It doesn't matter that his brain is scrambling or his eyes are shifting, creating a game plan. He knows he misspoke.

"Maybe you should learn to lift a hand, too," I mumble.

In a fell swoop, I grab my plate and I'm out of his room. Even before my parents' deaths, I didn't have tolerance for people who told me to keep fighting when they barely lifted a finger. Jonah hasn't been to one protest for the trial. Not a single fucking one. No one understands the pure exhaustion of it all, and when it's your parents you're fighting for? I'd give anything to have the privilege to never lift a finger again.

I jog down the steps and run into the living room. I'm almost through the threshold to the kitchen when I hear Jonah slide around the corner.

"Theo, stop."

I do stop, momentarily. Just long enough to see his parents now relaxing in the living room. They look at each other, likely questioning whether or not they should intervene.

I offer a smile and wave my hand. "Have a good night, Rebekah and Dan."

I proceed to the kitchen, grabbing my backpack before I slip my shoes on. I'm turning the door handle when Jonah's damn hand grips my right shoulder. "Th—"

"Jonah!" I swing around on one foot, stumbling slightly as my bag catches the handle. My heart pulsates in my neck, and I can feel my one vein popping out. "Stop."

Jonah glances at my vein, and he takes a few steps back. The best part of me wants to fix it. I know Jonah's faults, and I can help him through them. I know the vocabulary. I know how to be a better boyfriend, a more patient boyfriend. But the worst part of me always wins; it interweaves with my wires, stretching and splicing them, mixing up words and meanings, short-circuiting when happiness enters the scene.

"Let's talk about this. I didn't mean that. I'll come to the protest tomorrow."

That's. Not. The. Point. I close my eyes and take a deep breath. If I educate my followers each day, I can take a moment to reeducate my boyfriend.

Opening my eyes, I let out my breath. "Jonah, you'll never understand the weight I feel until you lift a finger yourself. The pressure to be good has tripled this past year. I'm the son of two dead activists, two very impactful people in our region—in our fucking state. Where will Theodore end up? That's been the question. You know where I'd like to end up? Trading my spot for my parents because they did this whole 'changing the world' thing way better than me. If you show up tomorrow, show up for those murdered by police. Don't show up for me."

Without a kiss or a hug goodbye, I walk out, letting the screen door snap closed behind me. It may not be better at home, but at least I can lock myself in my room and pretend the world doesn't exist for a bit.

By the time I make it back to my house, there are a few text messages from Jonah. In situations like this, when Jonah misspeaks, or he's insensitive, he usually apologizes profusely. Then he explains what he should have said in person. It's pretty standard and predictable. Instead of reading them, I click to open the messages and close them out, erasing the notifications.

Actions speak louder than words.

When I make it to the front door, I search for my house

key inside my bag. All I need right now is a hot shower, my bed, and my diffuser—block out the world until Alejandro picks me up for the protest.

As soon as I turn the knob for the door, I immediately get the chain lock's restraint.

Goddamnit.

This usually only happens when I ignore their orders, but today, they never called me, and it isn't past 11:00 pm. Likely, I messed something up on the chore list yesterday. This would probably be considered child abuse if anyone found out, but our meetings with the lawyer are few and far between.

"Fuck you!" I scream, slamming the door as loud as I can with the chain. I do it a second time, just for good measure, hopefully waking them up.

I trudge my way to the backyard, slamming the fence behind me, too. Wake up the damn neighborhood for all I care. Alert the police. I'll tell them to their face how their department killed my parents.

I toss my backpack in the grass outside of the porch. I could attempt the backdoor, but it's usually locked, and there is no key. When my aunt holds a grudge, she's thorough. I'm just grateful it isn't winter yet. The first time this happened, I woke up to snow falling.

As I lay back on the cold, damp grass, I look up at the brightly lit sky. One deep breath in and out, and I know I'll be back in my element soon.

The skies aren't as bright as they used to be, the air pollution has significantly gotten worse as I've grown up, but it's still enough to imagine I am Star-Lord's friend on a new mission, and no one can take away that fantasy of mine. Not now, especially not this weekend.

It might seem silly to imagine that I could escape to

another planet, disappear for a bit, and have a break from the world. I don't want to forget what happened, nor do I think deep down that I want to stop helping others, but *fuck*, am I tired. I just need a few days where I'm not responsible for anyone or anything.

Or maybe I don't even need to escape, but if there was a parallel universe where I'm me, but living a different version of my life . . . maybe one where my parents actually stay alive?

Could there be a world without chaos? Or does no chaos result in chaos?

"Mom? Dad?" I whisper in the silence. The cold front is coming in, massive pure white clouds start shifting across the sky.

A shiver escapes me, "I need you."

T - 1

October 6

"Morning, guys, I apologize for my appearance. I'm exhausted and tired, and rundown. I can't pretend to lie about that. Today's a big day. One of the biggest days we've had. I'm going to get ready for the protest in just a moment. Thank you for the incredible love throughout the week. And all the followers. This morning I'm nearly up to three point five million. Absolutely unbelievable. I won't be running my account today; Alejandro will. He'll be posting updates throughout the day. Please share, please be loud, and if you're at the protest today, come say hi. I love you guys."

Five

I make my way inside the following morning at the crack of dawn. I climb through the kitchen window carefully so I don't wake anyone. I tried to climb through at night once and found my aunt waiting for me, which led to a punishment. Now, I choose to break in when I know they are in their final REM before their alarm.

In twenty minutes, I shower, dress, and gather my belongings for the day. Just ten minutes shy of my aunt's and uncle's alarm. I pick up coffee for Alejandro and me and then drive to his house. The original plan was for him to pick me up, but I'd rather not wait around and potentially run into my aunt and uncle.

He's already in his car when I pull up to his driveway, so I quickly grab our coffees and my belongings before we are on our way.

We exchange short hellos, but if he's anything like me today, we are both bundles of nerves. Alejandro must feel the buzzing tension between us and turns the Hamilton soundtrack on as we make our way onto the highway. It's been the saving grace of keeping us motivated throughout this year. The spring felt like there was space to breathe, like I was making a difference, not weighed down by death. And then, as summer hit and fall started rolling in, the impending year anniversary, trial, and annual fundraising event started suffocating me.

In just over a week, it'll all be over with. I'll be able to breathe again, but that means it's been 365 days since my parents were murdered. And that number isn't something I'm ready to witness yet.

As soon as "My Shot" comes on, I join him in singing along. This is our one and only shot at this. This last final push has to go well.

Alejandro's long, curly hair bounces on the top of his head in a bun as he sings, and for the first time all week, there is space to breathe. I inhale all the air to get me through today. It's safe here in this bubble. I run my hands through my curls, trying to tame the air-dried look that's happening; I'm in desperate need of a haircut.

Alee turns the volume down just slightly when the song ends. "Are you ready for the speeches today? I hear CNN will be there."

My stomach twists at the mention. We have been trying to get CNN involved for a while, but they never sent a reporter to one of the protests or events. We have been able to get on the radar of all the other major news networks throughout the year, though some, like we imagined, didn't go in our favor.

"Yeah, all good." I force a smile. "It's good. It'll be good." I wipe my hands on my black jeans before clenching my knees.

His dark brown, nearly black eyes hold mine for a moment before looking back at the road. "It will be what it will be. If tomorrow doesn't go well, we figure it out. Okay?"

I swallow the lump forming in my throat. My night-mares have progressively gotten worse leading up to the decision, much of why I've worked until three or four in the morning. The fact that it's only four days to the year anniversary has made it all the harder. The timing is impeccable.

"Right. It'll be okay," I lie.

The truth is, it won't be. It will never be okay because nothing will bring my parents back from their untimely deaths.

Forty minutes later, we pull up to Majestic Park. The construction of the factory is still on hold. The verdict about the police is tomorrow, and then later in the month, there will be a renegotiation of the construction. Honestly, it's disgusting that people are still considering the idea. With the year we've been given, some volunteers, Alejandro, and I have spent as much time as we can hosting events at the park. Not protests like today, but events for families. We've planted flowers and created some sports programs and childcare all at the park. Those who didn't care about the park before now do. They are mostly people within the region, but some people throughout the state and country have helped as well. All events are funded with donations sent to my parents' foundation—all in memory of them and the four others who passed. While I don't have much contact with the family members who also lost someone, we did all come to an agreement that instead of starting another donation fund, it made sense that the county got the bene-fits through With Love.

It doesn't matter how much good I do at Majestic Park or how often I step foot on this grass; it suffocates me each time. My chest aches most of the time, and by the end of the day, I'm exhausted beyond belief, but with each event, I show back up. The only thing I refuse to do here is allow anyone to step where my mom died in my arms. I never got to see my dad. The last memory I have is of him running toward the officer who shot my mom. I was escorted out by some of my parents' friends when my mother died. When my dad needed to be identified, they deemed me too young and called my grandmother all the way from California. Now, my mom's spot is a memorial for her and every individual who passed.

Alejandro interlaces his arm with mine once we exit his car, and we walk toward the park together. I don't know what I would have done without Alejandro holding me up this year. He let me grieve for a week before he encouraged me to fight for this park and for my parents—reminding me it's what they would have done. Through the deepest of grief, he continued to be my force. Never once leaving my side.

Jonah never really understood my activism. When we met at age twelve, he volunteered here and there with me to become closer friends, but he never volunteered to the extent that I did. When my parents were alive, it was okay that Jonah didn't attend everything because I started to learn how to separate my life between helping and relaxing. But this year, my worlds meshed, and there was no room for Jonah to not understand my lifestyle and the importance of it. Therefore, our relationship became more complicated—especially because Alejandro has been involved since day one. Alee is not at my level of don't eat or sleep, just fight, but he's close. He's been my biggest cheerleader, and he assists with my social media, helping me bring attention to the events at the park, the other protests in the state, and the annual fundraising event happening next Friday.

All of a sudden, Alejandro is in action once we've reached the center of the park.

"And Alee is back with Theo for this very important day. If you're in the area, please join us at Majestic Park. If not, comment below on whether or not a protest is happening in your area! We need as much love and support today as possible."

Alejandro pans the camera around the area, showing off the various people who are starting to show. Everyone is milling around, signs in their hands, warm beverages being consumed. The stage I'll be giving my speeches on is still being set up. While I've hosted the protests, still being in high school proved to have complications, so a few people were in charge of organizing and setting everything up.

"If you can't attend an event and are unsure of how to help, you can donate to the link in this video or share our content on your pages. The more eyes, the better! I'll be recording the event the entire day, so keep a lookout on mine and Theo's pages."

Alejandro stops recording and immediately uploads it. Sometimes he gives our content to a friend who edits these really amazing videos, or he practices his editing skills, but today that's not necessary. Just the basic information is the most important.

We wave and say hello to people as we head closer to the stage. I try not to read any of the signs created because I know from past protests that while things need to be said, I need to have a clear boundary and space between this being a protest and this being strictly about my parents.

I catch sight of a coffee trailer and stop immediately in my tracks. I assumed that a lot of people just picked up drinks on their way in. How the hell had I missed that Isabella's Coffee would be here? And with a tiny trailer, no less?

I pull Alejandro to a stop, and all he does is grin. "Surprise," he whispers.

My eyes bug before a smile consumes me. Not much gets past me, as I'm a control freak, but this is a lovely surprise. Especially the sign that says "Free coffee. Donations to With Love only."

I jog over to the truck as some people pull Alejandro away to talk. The space to breathe returns again for a brief moment. It isn't even ten in the morning yet, and their donation jar is overflowing.

"Caden!" I greet as I stop jogging. Just having them here has me on such a high. It's him and two baristas I recognize from the local store. They are only serving brewed coffee and tea, but the gesture is incredible.

"Hey, Theodore, I hope this surprise is good." Caden steps out of the trailer, coffee cup in hand. The trailer is the size an SUV could pull. I didn't even realize they had one of these. What a game-changer for events.

"A great surprise, thank you." I smile, and it might actually reach my eyes.

He hands me the cup with a grin. "Not coffee, because you likely don't need it at the moment, but some mint tea."

"Thank you." I hold the cup close to my lips, letting out a breath as the steam warms me. It's not a cold October day, but it's brisk enough for long sleeves and sweatshirts.

"What else can I do to help?" Caden asks. "It's just me and our baristas. Ben is back home. But can I talk on social media? Do you need any help with your speeches? Will you need any food?"

I glance around at the park. In just a few moments, my alarm is going to go off, telling me it's 10:00 am. It's even more packed than it was when I walked over to the trailer. I see Alejandro up on the stage, talking to the coordinator. News trucks are all lined up on one side of the park, but I see cameramen and boom operators set up in front of the stage.

"Keep doing what you're doing. This boost for people will help a lot." I open my arms, and he steps in for a hug. "Thank you," I whisper before I step away.

As I walk toward the stage, I blink away the tears in my eyes. There are students I recognize from school, some of my past teachers, a lot of friends and acquaintances my parents have made throughout the years, foster parents are even here. I spot Alejandro's parents on the side of the stage, waiting for him to come down. They've been unbelievable. They were never close to my parents outside of volunteering for With Love, but they've helped me immensely throughout the year. Always made sure I left their home well-fed too.

Hidden in the middle of the crowd, I see Jonah and his parents. He's not looking for me and he's not on his phone, he's talking to people around him.

I let a few tears fall. I don't know whether I want him to find me. If I want him to acknowledge that he's here. Or if I hope he remains in his own space, taking in his surroundings, and heads home without saying hi.

Both scenarios have my chest tight, my hands gripping my tea to keep from shaking. I don't win in either scenario.

My alarm goes off in my back pocket, and I immediately silence it. I do a quick body shake, careful not to spill my tea, before I turn my video on, camera facing me, for one last update before the day blurs past me.

"We've made it, friends. I see a ton of you here with me today, and I'm overwhelmed. In a good way, in a sad way, in an unbelievable way. I wish I didn't know all of you, if I'm honest. Or, I wish I knew you all under different circumstances. But we're about to begin. If you're here, Isabella's Coffee is giving away free coffee and tea today, so go check them out. They are accepting donations on behalf of my parents' foundation. I'll be giving a speech in just about fifteen minutes, and then we begin."

I post the video on social media and then find Alejandro. In a minute's lapse, he looks at his phone and then finds me in the crowd, and I grin. A nod of his head, and we both meet each other halfway.

My morning speech begins the protest, which is mainly a summary of what'll happen during the day, who will make speeches, and a massive thank you to each and every person who has shown up physically, financially, or by word of mouth.

Throughout the day, I interview with the press, talk with the families who also lost loved ones that day, talk with families who have lost loved ones in similar situations, and do the second of my three speeches. Some of the other family members affected speak on the stage, and even the mayor of Creston urges us to continue the fight. Alejandro films the entire day. No doubt by tomorrow morning, not only will there be so much content available, but he will have an edited video too. It looks like we may even reach four million followers today.

By the end of the night, I am shattered. The sun has set.

We're now lit with cell phone flashlights and park street lamps. The stage has proper lighting, coordinated by the news networks, to have clarity on their broadcasts. One final speech, and then I can try to crash until tomorrow.

I walk up to the podium on the makeshift stage at the end of the night. The park is still filled with barely a section of grass available. Every national network has arrived to hear stories and film the protest. It isn't looking good for tomorrow, nor have the Blue Lives Matter people disappeared; they've chanted over our peaceful protest all day. But I can't let them distract me. Their goal is to have us stumbling—failing.

I look out from the podium, and I spot Alejandro and his family in front of me. I don't see Jonah. I haven't since earlier this morning. The park is packed, so it makes sense I can't find him, but my exhausted brain has me questioning whether I actually saw him at all. Isabella's Coffee is still here, serving drinks. A bakery even came midday to help with food donations, but they are now long gone.

I close my eyes at the podium, allowing the silence from my crowd and the chants from the Blue Lives Matter people to overwhelm my senses. When my breathing regulates and my ears hone in on the silence more than the chanting, I open my eyes to begin.

"We came peacefully," I start. "We came with signs and research. We came with peaceful chants. No one had a weapon. No one was armed. No one attacked any person of power. No one fought back against the police. The police arrived with their SWAT team. They tear-gassed us. They antagonized us. Once the tear gas fogged up our area, they shot at us, and we couldn't see. They continued to follow people and beat them when people backed down. All over a factory. Six people died. Two hundred people were injured.

All because a factory wants to tear down a park in an area that needs it most. I lost my parents at sixteen. My brothers were only eleven. They already lost their biological parents, and mine adopted them. Gave them a loving home, and they lost their second parents all before becoming teenagers. The six individuals were parents, children, grandparents, and friends. All lost in a moment. All because of money, power, greed, and pollution. We need to make a change. Those involved in the deaths and injuries need to be prosecuted. This can't keep happening. Innocent people cannot keep dying because someone in blue believes they are superior. No matter how tomorrow goes, it isn't the end. We are just beginning."

Cheers erupted throughout the park, silencing the opposing crowd. The cell phone flashlights cause a strobe-like effect throughout the park, and suddenly, I grip the podium to steady my balance. It's almost all over.

The heat from the studio lights burn into my skin, stomach acid twists and bubbles inside me, my clammy hands grip and slip and shake on the wooden podium. While I'm falling apart from the inside out, I hope what's being shown is leadership.

"Thank you to everyone who has shown up. Everyone who has donated money, time, and energy into getting to tomorrow. We've created a better park, a better community, and while none of this will bring back those six individuals, it can help save someone else. Thank you and be safe."

Despite my speeches being complete, I'm not done for the day. I'm escorted off the stage by some of my parents' friends. I'm handed water to drink before hugs are given. I feel like I'm being passed from person to person before I make my way to some news outlets for the last interview. It's getting late, the temperature is dropping, and my skin aches—no longer only my muscles and bones, but just the touch of my skin stings. Everything I've been fighting for comes to an end tomorrow morning, whether for good or bad. But I've fought 355 days for justice. I mourned for seven days before Alejandro stepped in and helped place the grief and anger toward good.

What happens when it all ends?

Who am I?

Alejandro joins me for the interviews. More so being my shoulder to lean on, quite literally, as I'm asked over, and over, and over again what it was like to hold my mother, what it was like to hear the shots and be tear-gassed, how I was handling activism with being a senior in high school. The answers are all over the internet. All over social media. But everyone always wants them for *their* publication versus taking and crediting another source.

"That was incredible!" Alejandro exclaims as we climb into his car two hours later.

I'm half-asleep in the passenger seat the moment his car starts to roll. The dash says it's 12:03 am. We need to be back in Creston at the courthouse before 10:00 am.

"It was good. We did good," I say softly. I shut my eyes, allowing the rhythm of the car to lull me just slightly. If I don't sleep, I can't be haunted by nightmares.

"People are hopeful. The police have to get convicted after today."

"We'll see," I mumble.

"How can you not be more psyched about today? You did amazing, Theo. Stop for a moment and acknowledge how good you did." Alejandro has a playful attitude. He's always looking to brighten the day. But his tone shifts, and when it shifts, it goes into a lecture that I don't want or need to hear. He may be a relatively new friend, but he claimed his stakes hard.

"Alee, please stop." I lift my head, which feels like a thousand pounds, and look over at him. "I'm exhausted. This has been almost a year in the making. I need to be realistic right now. And that means that I need to sit with myself for the next ten hours, sick to my stomach, on the verge of vomiting, while maintaining my anxiety enough to show up tomorrow, to be the face that people want and need from me, all while not crumbling."

"Okay," he says softly. "Am I driving you to Jonah's or home?"

"Home."

I never heard from Jonah. I checked my phone right before we got in the car. I checked his social media, too—but it's just his art page. No videos or updates or shares from anything today. I hope my vision didn't fool me, and he showed up on his own.

I squint my eyes shut, blocking the tears that threaten to fall. Today was one of the most important days of my life. He should have been by my side. He should have helped me through those last interviews. He should have held my hand and given me hugs when I was struggling throughout the day. Even if he did show up, I'm not sure he can be forgiven.

"Are you guys okay? He's been messaging me a lot recently about things he should be able to ask you."

"I don't know," I whisper, swallowing the lump in my throat. I turn my head toward the window as tears slide down my cheeks. Running Alee's words through my head, I make a mental note to question him at another time about his conversations with Jonah. From what I know, Jonah resents Alee for spending so much time with me, but come to think of it, they both had me take a 'day off' this week. Some weird collaborative effort I didn't think much of.

"Do you want to be okay?" he whispers.

"I d-don't k-know." I curl up in the front seat, turning my entire body toward the passenger window.

Closing my eyes, I see my mother hovering in front of me, brushing my tears away, telling me it's going to be okay.

T - 0

October 7

"You all . . . are unbelievable. I'm sorry you can't see me. My lights are off. I'm about to crash. But the support today . . . I'm overwhelmed. I'm exhausted. I hate to say that I'm happy? I shouldn't be happy about this, but you guys, my goodness. I'm at a loss for words. I don't know where I'd be if I didn't have this platform, this fight, those supporting me. I wish everyone had as much support as me. Tomorrow or well, in just a few short hours, the decision will be made. I don't know what happens if it isn't good. I may have to disappear for a little bit. But I'll be back. You guys deserve it. Thank you, and see you in the morning."

Six

"Theo. Theo, babe. Focus on my voice." Jonah's voice fights through the popping in my ears. I try to blink away the blur, but I squint my eyes shut, trying to rid the searing headache between my brows.

I have to open my eyes and focus. Name things, visual things I can see. All I know is I'm in my bed. I'm drenched. I'm freezing. And I feel like I'm about to pass out.

"Theo, the feeling isn't real. You're stuck in it. You're not in the present."

Tears escape my eyes, tracing down my dry skin. Jonah places his forehead against mine; his skin is cool against my steaming forehead.

"Feel my pressure." He kisses my lips. "Feel my kiss." His hands wrap around my shoulders, and he pulls me against him, so he is spooning me. "You're coming down from an anxiety attack. You'll feel better soon."

Jonah tightens his arms around me, creating pressure, allowing me to feel his deep inhales and long exhales. I follow suit inhaling through my nose and exhaling through my mouth. I don't know when I started the attack or when

Jonah got here. For all I know, it could be well past my alarm.

Wait . . . he isn't a part of today's plan.

"Court begins in two hours," he whispers in my ear. "Let's get you calmed and fed, and we can head out."

I try to relax in his arms as my mind spirals, trying to remember the conversation where he said he'd be here today, but I get distracted with his gentle words in my ear. He's whispering to breathe in, count to four, and breathe out for four. My favorite moments are when he tells me my next steps. He knows when my breathing shifts or my body tenses. He can usually decipher the tone of voice I'm using in my head to talk to myself.

"I've got everything bagels with cream cheese downstairs, and we'll stop at a coffee shop on our way. My parents took the day off and are going to meet us at the courthouse too."

I nod against his back, blinking back oncoming tears. There's a vague memory of seeing him yesterday, and I make a note to ask him about it, but I only have the energy to sink into his love. The only fight on today's agenda is my parents' fight.

My phone chimes on my nightstand, and Jonah shifts on the bed to grab it.

"It's Alejandro." He hands me the phone, and I quickly swipe open the message. "Why does he think you'd need a ride?" His voice is monotone again.

"Why are you reading my messages?" I shoot back.

I hate the tone that's immediate—for both of us. It's a rhetorical question; he always reads over my shoulder. I do the same for him. Jonah's annoyance with Alee doesn't make sense if Jonah's been reaching out to him. It seems to be underlying jealousy. Though it's Jonah keeping himself from attending everything Alee and I do. There's nothing between Alee and me, never will be. He has told me numerous times that I'm not his type, to the point it's sometimes insulting.

"Just . . . why wouldn't I bring you to the courthouse this morning? I am your boyfriend."

I sit up and sigh, grateful that my breathing has gotten slightly easier. The weight of his arms falls to the bed, and I start to crawl off toward the foot.

"You're assuming that people would think that," I start, "as they should, as I used to. Now? Now, I assume the worst."

My feet hit the cold hardwood floor, and I jump to the area rug in front of my dresser.

"My life isn't consumed 24/7 with activism like yours is. I support what you do, but that doesn't mean I want to be at all your events. I have other things to do," Jonah says.

I nod, biting back a laugh. He's right, in the most ignorant of ways. He does have a different life, and he has hobbies, like being a phenomenal artist. He used to share things on social media until his art portfolio became more important and his social media became strictly professional.

I yank open drawer after drawer, pulling out clean boxers, dark blue jeans, and a purple and white speckled short-sleeve button-up. I'm not going to have time for a shower this morning.

"Having other things to do is cool when it's literally about anything else but my parents' trial. *That's* where I need you the most. In fact, this past year, I've really needed you more than ever, but it seems all you want to do is pick fights with me."

He's sitting up on the bed when I glance back at him

before quickly changing. We've never gone farther than handjobs, but we often change in front of each other.

"Let's just focus on today. I'm not here to fight. I'm glad," he swallows so audibly I have to roll my eyes, "that you have a friend who looks out for you too."

Once I'm dressed, I walk over to my full-length mirror hung on the back of my door. After Alee woke me when we got to my house last night, I couldn't fall back to sleep until around four. The bags under my eyes are thriving this morning. My eyes are bloodshot, and my curly hair needs a haircut, product, and a good detangle, but all I have time for is a quick thread of the fingers. I rub my eyes with the back of my knuckles, hoping the pressure brings some blood to my olive skin.

Jonah wraps his arms around me from behind and rests his chin on my shoulder. His lips tickle my neck before pressing in for a kiss. When I open my eyes, he gives me a smile. His hazel eyes don't shine like they usually do, but it's the pity smile I've grown used to.

"I was there yesterday," he whispers. We hold eye contact as he continues, "You were really amazing. I'm sorry I didn't go with you."

I squeeze his hands that are interlaced at my belly.

"I know. I saw you. I'm sorry too."

We have a peace that I'm nervous about breaking, but today, the time restrictions are too tight. I push his hands away and grab my backpack and cell phone. The air between us is cold. We're walking on a tightrope.

I make sure to find his glossy eyes before I say my last words. "I'll be riding with Alejandro today. If you want to go, go for the trial. You've lost your chances showing up for me," I whisper.

He nods, and the two of us silently make our way to the

kitchen. There are chore lists left and right, and the kitchen is a mess. I've blocked my aunt's and uncle's numbers for the next two days, but they had the decency to leave the door unchained last night. They'll likely make my weekend a living hell, but it's nice to know there is an ounce of care in them right now.

Like Jonah said, there are two wrapped bagels on the kitchen table. Alejandro pulls up outside. I grab a bagel and walk out the door, leaving Jonah jogging after me, asking me to stop.

"Hey!" Alejandro greets. "I'm sorry, Jonah. I don't have a coffee for you. Are you joining us today?"

"I—" Jonah hesitates.

"You and I will be going together," I interrupt, eyeing Alejandro. He glances between Jonah and me before nodding.

"I brought over breakfast. Thank you for taking Theo." Jonah hands his bagel to Alee and gives us a wave. I make eye contact with Jonah, offering him a small smile before he turns and walks down the street.

Alejandro doesn't ask about Jonah, and I don't offer any information. I'm not even sure what happens now. In a way, I think I may have ended us.

I try to eat pieces of my bagel, but I mainly drink my chai latte from Alejandro. I use the drive to play a few videos I've been tagged in that people created about the entire trial. Some are from yesterday, some are from the entire year. My feed mainly shows support for the trial, but I know it's biased from the algorithm. It's America; the likelihood of those in blue getting convicted isn't high.

"Holy hell, we've made it past four point five million!" I exclaim when I focus on the count.

"It's wild, right? We hit four million when we got home

last night, but the world was awake. People love watching you, Theo. They trust you. They believe in you. They are all rooting for you."

The weight of the world is literally on my shoulders. Everyone is watching. Some want me to win. Some want me to fail. Some just don't want me.

The small amount of food in my stomach churns, and I wrap the bagel up, placing it next to my feet. The last time I had a proper meal with nutrition was the sub at Jonah's the other night. My body is already shaking, and my breathing is at max capacity. There hasn't been a moment to settle from my anxiety attack this morning.

A message comes through from Ellie right as we pull up to Majestic Park.

Ellie: *Hey you. No matter what happens today, we will figure it out. You have done everything you could. We are so proud and devastated that you've had to do this. You know we've been fighting from a distance with you. We promise today isn't the end. We will call you after the verdict. We love you so much.*

If I make it through today, it'll be a goddamn miracle.

I START TALKING ONCE ALEJANDRO NODS HIS HEAD. He started recording on my phone once we met the rest of Alejandro's family at the courthouse. The area is packed— and controlled by police.

"We've made it. Today is the day we've been fighting for. Just less than a year to date. Court is in session, and we should know any minute now."

My stomach gurgles and my eyes search for a place to sit. I can't stand in this rare October heat and wait. Yesterday, a sweatshirt was good. Today I'm sweltering in a short-sleeve button-up.

Regardless, I cannot be told good or bad news on two feet.

"No matter—"

Tears fill my eyes as I think about the sentence I want to say. It does matter what happens. The country is watching, and if these police officers get away with murder, other police officers will look up to that. My parents aren't the first to die at the hands of the blue, and they, unfortunately, won't be the last.

Alejandro shoves the phone at his dad's face, and he's over to me in a minute.

"Let's find a place to sit. You can update people later," he whispers in my ear.

I look over at Alejandro's dad, and the phone is still in position, but he nods. Alee has trained his dad's reporting skills well.

"I'll be back shortly with an update," I say before Alee is leading us through crowds.

Most people here know my face—I recognize many of them from yesterday. We push through "We are thinking of you," "I'm so sorry for your loss," "We are here for you." As we walk, some phones are in my face, and Alee stops us when we are close enough to the courthouse steps, right in front of the police roping off the area. They all stand straight, watching the surrounding crowds, weapons hidden. I know there is a hidden SWAT team on the ready. I know these police officers are armed with weapons. They are ready for the worst, the fucking irony of the entire situation.

I start to sway, and Alee's hand tightens on my shoulder, steadying me. I pretend to have x-ray vision, analyzing what exact weapons might be underneath each police officer. After my parents' deaths, I spent a god-awful amount of time watching videos of police officers gearing up to see what just their average uniform consisted of.

My vision starts to blur as more people crowd in, pressing us against the rope they have set up. Step over the rope, and you're likely arrested, if not worse.

The rope digs into my skin, and I grip it with my fingertips. I don't miss the shift of one of the police officers. They are all wearing sunglasses, though, and I can't tell who they are watching.

No one in Alejandro's family was there the day of the protest. Otherwise, they'd understand that this exact location is the worst place to be standing. I'll be able to hear the verdict anywhere in this radius. I don't need to be directly standing in front of an officer who can kill me in an instant.

Though, the worst part of me wants to stand here if this goes violent. I have a duty to protect those around me who have made this entire trial possible. I have to protect every person who has supported me because I couldn't protect my parents.

"Theo." Alejandro has me jumping. His voice is next to my ear as the noise around us gets louder and louder. "We should be safe. Take a few deep breaths. The police won't get violent at a trial about police brutality."

I'm not sure I believe a word of what he says. I think they expect it to get dangerous here if it doesn't go the way the crowd wants. Why wouldn't it? I'd be insulted if everyone just disappeared after all this time.

The crowd is silent in an instant. Only a few "shhs" before those disappear too. There's a ringing in my ears, and the small guy on the courthouse step gets smaller and smaller with each breath I take. Alejandro squeezes my hand, gripping my fingers between his.

"You're okay, Theo."

I lean back against Jonah. I don't know when he got here or if it's really him. But his words are in my head, and someone's chest is a steady fall back. My legs tremble, and I can't see the little man on the steps. The sun has grown dark, and I shiver. Hands rub up and down my bare arms as sweat or tears drip from my face.

I need to sit. I have to sit. There's a lodge in my throat that I can't swallow. I lean forward, heaving.

"Good morning, Creston. For the charge of murder in the first degree, the jury has found the defendants Officer Manson, Officer Jans, and Officer Jeffers not guilty. For the charge of—"

Darkness consumes me.

PART TWO

Seven

"Theodore Montgomery." I hear my name before my body regains the ability to . . . move.

There's no chanting, no movement. Just silence. Something is tickling my bare arms. I'm not on the pavement. I'm not sweating in the heat, but there is light. My head has a gentle throb, as if I fell a while ago.

What the hell is happening?

My fingertips graze the area. I'm in . . . grass? The individual slices of grass filter through my fingertips. I inhale; the air feels like a crisp autumn day cleansing my lungs with one breath.

"Open your eyes, Theodore."

Open my . . . oh.

Blinking my eyes open, the sun burns my retinas. I wince, immediately squinting my eyes.

"Oh shoot, sorry." There's a rustling in front of me that sounds like the opening of a bag before something hard touches my hand. "Wear these. They are vitaglasses. You'll need them for a few days."

A few days? Do I have a concussion?

I instantly put the glasses on. After a few seconds, I attempt to open my eyes again. I don't know what vita-glasses are. These seem like sunglasses. Even so, the sun is still excruciatingly bright; the sky looks white with the brightness. Despite the cool air, the heat from the sun is intense.

I lift up on my elbows and come face to face with a sun-kissed guy around my age. He's kneeling in front of me. Blonde semi-crewcut. His crystal blue eyes sparkle, and his smile is intoxicating. It'd be welcoming, if not terrifyingly close to me.

I look down at my hands, twisting the grass between my fingertips. It's soft and green, not a single strand of brown grass. It is autumn, isn't it?

I vaguely remember being at the courthouse, but . . . this isn't that.

I twist my body, looking around me. Everything is flat save for an enormous mountain range a few miles away, and on the opposite side, there seems to be a town. Ahead of me lies one single red domed, hobbit-like building. Not a single cloud disrupts the pale sky—that I can see.

I must have hit my head really hard because I don't remember any of this.

Unless . . . holy hell, did I die? Did I confront the police?

My eyes dart to the guy's. "Am I in Heaven?" There's a jolt in my heart at the thought.

If this isn't Heaven, then a stranger is staring at me. He definitely is not from my school—I'd recognize those eyes anywhere. He doesn't have bags under his eyes or any stress wrinkles. Not even a single bump of acne.

"Hi, I'm Flynn," he greets. "You're not in Heaven."

"W-where am I?" The throbbing grows as panic sets in.

I glance at my surroundings. I don't even know how to escape.

"Welcome to Otium."

I whip my head toward him. "Ot-what?" I sit up straight. I don't know about an Otium.

This guy Flynn sits back on his butt, giving me some space. He adjusts a black backpack next to him.

"Ot-i-um. The planet we are on. You've traveled here from Earth. You're ninety years into your future timeline."

I can't help but laugh at his insanity. *Ninety years? Not a chance.* Time travel only exists in the Marvel Cinematic Universe. If time travel existed in my time, I'd use it to go back to the past, not some futuristic . . . prairie?

"Am I alive?" I ask.

"Yes. You are very much alive."

My chest tightens at that, and my eyes burn.

I haven't made it. I'm no closer to my parents than I was yesterday. If I'm not in Heaven, maybe I'm dreaming. I haven't slept well this entire week, nor have I eaten much.

I close my eyes, thinking back to what happened on Earth. I can barely hear the verdict in my head. I don't remember reacting before my world went black.

I open my eyes again, and Flynn smiles. There's a weird relaxation that courses through my body, unclenching every muscle. His smile grows.

Who is he?

"This is going to take some time to wrap your head around," he says gently, and I narrow my eyes. "I won't bombard you with information until you're ready." He clasps his hands on his lap and just . . . waits.

Well, I'd like some *information. I have to have head trauma.*

I pinch my bicep and then my forearm. I slap my cheeks

back and forth, willing myself to wake up. "Come on, Theo. This is stupid. Wake the hell up. You didn't actually want to be on a new planet." The result only irritates my exhaustion.

I stand up, wobbling slightly. Once I gain my footing, I pace back and forth. The grass doesn't even crunch beneath my feet. It softly folds, slowly popping back up when my foot removes itself. It definitely isn't autumn here. But aren't other planets supposed to be bizarre? Entirely different from Earth? Why does he look like a human? Have we gotten the alien species wrong?

How can I prove this is a dream? Prove that I can just open my eyes and be back in the nightmare that is my life.

My . . . my phone. Yes. My phone. I can just call someone or look at the date. Or Google effing time travel!

Reaching into my back pocket, I find it's empty. *Shit! It was in Alejandro's hand.*

"May I ask what you're looking for?"

He's standing now. Flynn is dressed in form-fitting maroon pants, a white button-up t-shirt, and loafers that don't really go with his outfit. He towers over me, though, with what seems like perfect posture. I can already see from where I am that I'll have to look up to meet his gaze with my five-foot eight-inch frame.

"My cell phone. But it isn't on me."

His mouth opens in an "ah!" and he nods his head. "My planet may have figured out time travel, but your phone cannot connect calls to your home planet." His cheeks have a pink haze to them as I watch his lips twitch.

"Okay, smartass." I close the distance between us, standing up as straight as I can. I was right. He towers over me with at least another four inches. "If I'm definitely on a new planet, why am I here? Why me out of the billions of people on Earth? And how the hell did I get here? I don't see any spaceships or portals."

All I want in my life is some solid sleep and peace. Not a new problem to deal with.

"You've been chosen as a candidate for the Otium Initiative. You are one of 601 people who have traveled here for the initiative. 570 people have completed the program before you. You are in the last cycle of this year."

I blink before swallowing the saliva in my mouth. Apparently, my brain is forgetting my simple motor functions.

Time travel has been happening while I've been alive? That, or I'm writing a brand new sci-fi film in my dreams.

"As a part of the Otium Initiative, you will go through a series of workshops and life experiments to see if it's possible to help change and guide humans into a more sustainable, loving, and kind group of people." He pauses as if he's trained to give me a moment to process, but his eyes dance, and he shifts on his feet.

I have to admit, this sounds incredibly cool. If it's a dream, I need to live this out. If this is real life, I have no time in my life for it. It's already jam-packed; my planner needs a planner.

But who am I in a few days' time? The trial is over, my parents' anniversary is in two days, the fundraiser is in seven. All meaning . . . my fight is coming to an end.

"You and many others from all over planet Earth did, in fact, enter a portal, but the portals disappear at the click of a button." He grins, lifting his wrist. He's wearing what looks like a sleek black smartwatch. His index finger presses a button, and then he flicks his wrist to the right. Like a goddamn magic wand, a portal opens in front of us. The oval shape glittering gold like in the movies—it looks like I could walk right into the abyss. "Pretty incredible, huh?"

"Yeah," I breathe. How many times have I watched a Marvel movie, wondering what it would be like to time jump? And now, whether real or make-believe, it's in front of me.

I take a step forward. I can step right into the abyss. All my worries, fears, and stresses, they could disappear, right?

Would it bring me closer to my mom and dad?

The portal disappears. I lock eyes with Flynn; his expression is neutral. The air vanishes from my lungs. If I want out, I have to get that watch.

"Portals can be very dangerous if not programmed properly," he says.

"What makes your planet qualified to mess with mine?" I ask, crossing my arms.

"We are the remainder of what was left on Earth." His demeanor straightens, and a more clear, customer-service-esque voice appears.

I pause my movements. *Remainder?*

"In your near future, Earth becomes uninhabitable. I'm sure you already see those effects. People in your lifetime had to develop technology to get somewhere new. There weren't many who made the journey, and it was a struggle to begin on a new planet, but now we are starting to thrive."

He pauses again as I sit back down on the ground. *Yes, Earth is having climate issues, and we are searching for a new planet to live on. That planet is Mars, though. Not Ot-fucking-whatever.*

"This isn't Mars?"

Flynn sits cross-legged in front of me again and shakes his head. "Nope. From my understanding, it didn't have everything humans needed."

Note to self: do more research into Mars.

Okay, Theo, think. How plausible is this? Marvel makes movies about multiverses. And there are conversations about other planets and life. You're not ignorant enough to believe humans on Earth are the only humans that exist.

"Our goal is to go back in time and get more humans onto this planet. Greed, hate, wealth, and poverty were a lot of why Earth failed. So we've established a set of workshops and experiences that we believe can help change that. The idea is that the mentees go back to their homes, help do more good, and inspire those in smaller community settings. When the time comes to go to Otium, our mentees will be on the ground helping adapt those on Earth to the change."

None of this makes sense. The more he speaks, the more questions I have, but I'm not even certain how to form them. Did people come in years ago? Do they all get transported to the future? To now? Will I experience Otium at seventeen and then be back again in a few years as my same self with this same person in front of me? Or will time have passed, and Flynn will be way older?

A wave of uneasiness courses through my body. I pull my knees to my chest, gripping my forearms as I try to steady a sway that wants to take over.

Name things, Theo. Focus. This is likely a dream, and you're overcomplicating it. Let your mind rest instead of controlling your dreams too.

I inhale, taking note of my body. I should be way more anxious than this, and that is making me anxious. But the throbbing in my head has disappeared; my chest is no longer tight . . . while my exhaustion is so deeply ingrained, the rest of me feels alive.

No restricted lungs. No clammy hands. I don't feel scared by his words. Just confused.

Suddenly, Flynn is shaking his body, similar to how I'd move if I needed to restart and shake something off. "I'm sorry. You're confused and overwhelmed. I'm messing this up. I probably sound like a robot. There's just so much they want us to say and pauses to take that I haven't gotten the whole introduction down to a science yet. I'm trying to memorize everything, and I get lost in it. I promise, it's pretty great here, and if my friends heard me right now, they'd be making fun of me."

I catch his eyes, and his own posture relaxes in front of me. He has friends here. They'd be making fun of him—in a friendly way, presumably. He's nervous he isn't doing his job correctly. That's all normal.

What is his job? If it's a kidnapper, he's pretty shitty at it.

"Okay, okay, okay," I say, trying to process what's in my head. I don't think I care how I was chosen or why, but have I just entirely disappeared from Earth?

Would anyone care if I was gone?

"What happens now?" I ask. Seems a bit silly to ask the person keeping me trapped here how to move forward, but if I'm not in a dream, I do have a life to get back to, a schedule to complete. I have videos to make, letters to write, people to be angry with. I even have an event to run.

"Now, I lead you to Olive, the town you'll be staying in. You'll have a welcome meal, learn more about Otium and the initiative, get to know the other people here, and then be shown your room."

I blink a few times. The meal will likely be a drug to make me submissive and do as they say. I don't know what I wanted his answer to be, but that isn't it.

"Okay, um." I swallow the spit lodged in my throat. "I'm sure your planet is aware of the term consent?"

His eyes light up at the question. "Well, yes. Of course. We take it very seriously here."

"Right," I draw out, looking between him and that hobbit-like building. A train just appeared behind it. It's possible I can outrun him, get on a train, and . . . get lost on a planet? *C'mon, Theo.* "Okay. Well. No."

He tilts his head. A single line forms on his forehead. "No?"

"No. I do not consent." *Is this guy serious?* "Send me the hell back home."

His eyes bore into mine. They don't darken into anger, and he doesn't use his frame to hover over me. In fact, he's still sitting peacefully, but his smooth skin does furrow at the brow.

Take consent seriously, ha.

"I'm afraid I cannot do that. It is my responsibility to bring you to the town center. We have had members leave, but we ask you to stay for the meal in exchange for your trouble. You'll see the town you will live in, and often, after you eat, meet the other candidates, and learn more, you'll likely choose to stay. But the decision is yours after dinner."

A meal for my troubles? This place has to be fucking kidding me. They can kidnap me, tell me they know consent, *feed* me, and then tell me I can go home?

I have got to still be dreaming. Maybe I hit my head on the pavement, have a concussion, and this is just a new nightmare. While it's not welcome, it's a better nightmare than my parents' deaths.

"We have bikes to ride into town. We don't use cars here because they ruin the environment. We only have electric trains that get us to different geographic locations." He points to the building behind him.

The train is leaving the station at a slow, steady pace

before it picks up speed. I have to admit, it looks sleek and a hell of a lot nicer than anything New York has.

"The hydrogen trains are used for longer distances. Each train station is about a mile away from the main town. So to get to and from, we bike. I assure you, we have a smooth journey." He turns toward a couple of bikes that are lying on the ground.

Hydrogen trains are amazing, and those already exist. Could it actually be possible that there's a place that wants to do good? That wants to take care of a planet? That has faith in humanity—somehow—that instead of moving forward, they've created a program to help backward?

Or do I just so desperately need to believe in humanity?

"We should be heading to town now." He starts walking to the bikes about fifty feet away.

I should panic. My body should be having some internal conflict, gearing up for an anxiety attack. Maybe adrenaline is calming me.

He's halfway there before he faces me again. "You can either choose to join me, or you can remain in this field. Just know that if you don't follow me, you'll be spoken to by someone else. They'll continue to filter through people until you come to the welcome meal. Selfishly, I hope you don't do that because it doesn't look very good on me, but it is your choice. Time travel does take a toll on the body, though, and this bike ride will have you begging for food once we arrive."

I've seen enough movies to know that this isn't how safe, fun adventures begin. And to believe that I haven't been drugged during this journey yet? I don't remember the last time my body didn't ache, my lungs felt relaxed, and my heart didn't race. If I am already drugged, I'll defi-nitely be starving, ready for my next hit that's undoubtedly in the food. That's probably how they get everyone to stay.

Bad news for me? I'm already starving. It feels like forever since I've had my last meal.

He sighs when he doesn't see me moving. "I understand this is weird and strange, and I am here to answer any and all questions. Once we eat, you'll know more. But can I be candid for a moment?"

I nod my head when his shoulders slouch just slightly, and he runs his hand through the mop of his crewcut.

"If you stay in Otium, I will be your mentor. I like to believe that I'll grow on you, and you won't choose a new mentor. We'll likely become friends."

Presumptuous much? I restrain myself from rolling my eyes. *I don't need more friends.*

"With that said, you're my first mentee, and I've trained really hard to be able to work with you specifically. It would really, really suck if I failed at my first job."

His words jumble in my head. *To work with me specifically?* I don't know what that means, but I know how it feels to try so hard for something and fail at it. I just did that. I just failed at the biggest thing in my entire life. Can I live with knowing I willingly made someone else fail?

What is waiting for me back home? Failure, for sure. But devastation. My breakup. My awful home. I still have six months until I can move out of my aunt's and uncle's guardianship. Time away from them would be great.

Is it really the worst thing in the world to accept a meal and a bike ride with a cute boy? Someone actually being vulnerable and asking for what they need?

"Question," I say.

He makes his way to the bikes, lifting one off the ground. "I do believe I'll have an answer." He steadies a bike against his waist before leaning to lift the other into a standing position.

I tentatively walk toward him. "Do you guys have strangers here?"

He laughs, offering the other bike to me. I place my hands on the handlebars to steady it. Maybe I can pretend this is just a dream and ride a bike through a beautiful meadow—enjoy the break from my anxiety for just a moment.

"Of course. We don't all know each other. The difference between here and Earth, though?" He locks eyes with me, a gentle smile gracing his lips. "We don't fear our strangers."

I've really lost it now. So desperate for a semblance of peace, I've conjured up a beautiful utopia.

Eight

The meadow is stunning. Flynn explains that this geographic location is called the Flatlands, and he lives in the town of Olive. Aside from every morsel of grass being bright green instead of brown, the area is covered in wildflowers of varying shades of pinks, purples, yellows, even blues. We bike on a well-groomed red dirt path. It seems as if two to three bikes could fit the width. There is not a single paved road in sight.

As we bike, it truly is just the two of us. He informs me that the animals live more in the Forest and Valley, preferring the water and food options over the Flatlands. Occasionally, he says there are wild bunnies or even some dogs and cats that roam, but we haven't come across any. Flynn's tone completely changes when he talks about his area. His welcome speech is apparently complete, allowing his personality to shine through.

"If you choose to stay, I cannot wait to show you my favorite places, have you taste the incredible food, and introduce you to different events here!" Flynn smiles, standing up as he pedals his bike. "Our area is a really fun place to live, and knowing what I know about you, I think you and I will get along really great."

I choose to ignore the questions of how and what he knows about me. It's almost comforting in a strange way to have him be so excited.

"And we can travel to the other populated locations whenever we want, so if you happen to not like Olive, your free time can be spent elsewhere. I imagine you'll miss the mountains within time."

"How long is the initiative?" I ask. I'm not sure I want to know the answer.

"I'll allow the leader to explain all that because we're here." He gestures in front of us. "The town center."

More reddish domed, hobbit-like structures form a circle from the dirt path. Directly in the middle of the circle, on the grass, is what looks like a farmer's market. The center is packed with people, not only selling but buying.

"Hey Suzie, how's Renee?" Flynn asks as we slow our bikes past an older woman with long pin-straight pink hair.

"Aren't you sweet, Flynn. Renee is doing much better." Suzie waves before she heads into a shop.

Flynn hops off his bike, and I follow suit. A few other people pass us as we make our way to a bike rack. Flynn knows every person by name, always asking them how they are and how someone else is before they walk away. He's in his element now; the energy radiating off of him is electrifying. It's reassuring to see how lovely these people are. This seems like a real community. I'm almost exhausted by the generosity.

Only a few people around us are wearing vitaglasses. Flynn said I'd need to wear these for a few days, but how does my body adjust to the light . . . a new star?

"Flynn! I'm so glad you made it back." A tall, wellpostured woman with dark wavy brown hair and bright, wide eyes comes walking toward us. She's in a sleeveless, fitted dress with an apron around her waist. There's a familiarity she exudes.

We park the bikes in a bike rack before Flynn gestures toward me. "This is Theodore Montgomery."

I give her a small smile. Her golden eyes assess me from head to toe before a gentle smile appears.

"This is Andrya, the leader of the Flatlands," Flynn informs me. "And like I said before, if you choose to stay, I'll be your mentor."

His mother is the leader of the Flatlands? She barely looks older than thirty with her minimal wrinkles, and she has no bags under her eyes. Her skin is practically glowing.

"If?" The woman's calm expression becomes perplexed. Her shoulders grow rigid as she knots her hands in the apron.

"*If,* Mother."

The smile Flynn gives her twists my stomach. Not out of fear, but satisfaction? He isn't always a ray of sunshine to others. Something isn't right, though. The energy between the two of them as they challenge eye contact has my hands growing sweaty. It's all fun and games to follow, whatever this is—escape home for a little bit, but that was with the assumption that I had a choice.

Andrya nods, relaxing her posture before a slow smile appears on her face again. "It's a pleasure to meet you, Theodore. Let's introduce you to the others, and we can all eat dinner. We will then tell you more about Otium."

My stomach rumbles. The last time I had a full meal was two nights ago at Jonah's. I haven't had the stomach to consume anything more than coffee and a few bites here or there. Last I knew, it was Friday mid-morning, but I could be living an entirely different day. Time has to operate differently here. That's what space movies say, right? One day on Earth is multiple days or months for another planet?

I look over at Flynn for confirmation that this food can be trusted. Suddenly, he is the more trustworthy one in this situation. Andrya, just like any other leader, has something up her sleeve.

He gives me a smile with a nod. "C'mon, Theodore. You do not want to miss this pasta."

At the word pasta, my stomach growls again, loud enough that Flynn laughs beside me. I may be on another planet, but at least they still have pasta, and I seemingly have an appetite for once.

Flynn starts to walk away from the bike rack, and I pause, looking back at it. "Don't we have to lock these?"

Flynn looks over at me, his bright white teeth shining back at me. "Not at all. Oh, and close your mouth when you walk. You don't want to know the insects that'll go into your mouth. I told you, we don't have bad strangers here."

With a wink, he walks ahead, gesturing with his hand to follow.

I run to catch up, trying to rid my brain of what could possibly fly into my mouth. To be clear, any insect is terrible.

While we walk along the pathway, I can't help but eye all the little shops of knitting, pottery, clothing, and paper supplies. There are food shops and little niche hobbies that would never survive where I live. My town used to have stores like these, but as rent rose, most turned to work-from-home or closed up shop completely.

We arrive at a path that goes left, right, or straight. It seems like the main dirt path to the rest of the community. To our left is the largest structure I've seen; a two-story rectangular building with the same curved architecture and reddish exterior as every place we've passed. The path seems to lead to multiple smaller structures too. Oak trees are scattered in both directions—thankfully—otherwise, my New York heart wouldn't manage all the flat land. Flynn turns right, and I jog to catch up, but the straight path seems to lead to larger buildings.

Slightly off the path, there's a long picnic table with an umbrella that fits the length of the table. Flynn heads toward it. There's another building a few feet from the picnic table, all with outdoor seating. About a dozen people are already at the picnic table, looking up curiously at my arrival. None of them are wearing vitaglasses, but the same glasses I'm wearing are on the table next to their plates.

"We have our final guest. His name is Theodore from the United States," Andrya introduces me. "Theodore, this is Amalia from France, Zhang from Hong Kong, Kwaku from South Africa, Abella from Spain, Elias from Germany, and Oscar from Ireland." She points to each individual who waves when called.

Next to each guest, another person is sitting next to them. "The seven of you have been chosen for the Otium Initiative. We keep an eye on individuals throughout Earth who can either protect the human race or help improve it. Our plan is to educate a few people from Earth every few months, so we can continue to make Otium better."

Flynn taps my arm and leads me over to an empty space at the picnic table. We both take a seat while his mother continues talking. She repositions herself to the head of the table as someone else starts to fill up plates.

I pull the glasses off once under the shade. My eyes can finally tolerate the light.

"This is our welcome dinner," Andrya says. "While you

all agreed to come here today, this is a voluntary program. After dinner and our introduction, if you do wish to leave, we will escort you home." She makes eye contact with every other volunteer except for me.

I glance over at Flynn, but his eyes are focused on his mother. Who agreed to come here and how? Did I agree to something that I didn't read because I've been running around too much? Or did Alejandro sign me up for something that he forgot to mention?

Panic sets in. It's doubtful she's telling the truth about allowing us to leave. How can there be a program to time travel if time travel doesn't exist?

"Throughout dinner," she continues, "we will discuss everything that will happen over the next three months."

Three months? Oh no, no, no.

One of the guys holds up their hand, and she asks him to wait.

"You will be here the entirety of the program. Each person will have a program that best suits their needs. It will be a minimum of twelve weeks. Your mentor, the person who greeted you out of the portal, will be your point of contact throughout the program."

This is far too intricate for my brain to rationalize that this is a dream. I have to be here in the flesh. Otherwise, if I did have a panic attack, it rewired my brain, thinking I'm at some Hogwart-esque invite-only, yet I'm Harry entirely out of this loop.

I look over at Flynn, who now flashes me a smile. Despite starting to feel overloaded, I can't deny that his smile helps calm the wave of nausea passing through me. Those blue eyes too . . . something about him is so familiar— just like his mom. Except, she brings nerves, and he provides comfort.

"Before I begin discussing more of the program, let's dig into dinner. The one thing that seems to be entirely loved by all cultures is pasta. So we've made our homemade tomato sauce with a twang of Otium spices and fresh rice spaghetti. Please enjoy."

Forks scrape across plates before I can even pinpoint mine.

How long have these people been waiting for me to arrive? Is it possible that we all came through different portals in different directions or did we all come through the same one, at the same time, and I was the only stubborn one?

I open my mouth to apologize, but no one is looking at me. Everyone silently eats their food. I'm never late for anything. Well, I'm always late to Jonah's but not for events. An uneasiness settles in the pit of my stomach as my planner flashes in my mind.

I scheduled my parents' trial day to a T. Regardless of what the verdict was, I knew I'd need a plan. Now the entire day has gone into shambles. I'm on a foreign planet. Late to my kidnapping. Does anyone know I'm missing? Am I living two lives, or did I just turn to dust?

My head is lightheaded at all the bizarre situations I've seen in time travel movies. It's never discreet or secretive. They always cause chaos. Time travel causes a ripple.

"So," Flynn starts, interrupting my spiral as he slurps spaghetti before continuing, "what state are you from?"

For someone who knew my name at a time portal and his planet has chosen me, somehow, someway—how would he *not* know where I'm from?

He gives me an awkward smile at my deadpanned face. "You have a file with this information, yes, but I would like to know from you. Have a genuine conversation."

I swirl some pasta on my fork. It twirls just like the

gluten-free rice pasta my mom used to eat. Hopefully, it tastes similar. Though, to have a welcome meal be spaghetti and tomato sauce? A planet that knows time travel can do better than that.

"I'm from New York, but not the city, if you know there is a difference."

He chuckles, showing me his chewed spaghetti sitting on the back of his tongue. "I might be from another planet, but the planet we originated from *was* Earth. I know about New York City and the rest of the state. Most major cities worldwide are studied in-depth here as a model of how to build a more sustainable life. For example, no location on Otium will have a cluster of people similar to New York City."

After everyone has eaten a few bites of pasta—including Flynn and Andrya—I decide to take a bite. And holy hell, is this the best thing I've ever tasted. The spaghetti might be made with rice, but it was cooked so that olive oil, Italian seasoning, and garlic are all wrapped up in every single noodle. I mix the tomato sauce more into the pasta to try another bite, and each taste bud is electrified. Each flavor is fresh. The pasta tastes handmade; the tomatoes taste like they were just picked today; the spices don't taste like they've been on a shelf since I was three.

"It never gets old watching someone from Earth try our pasta for the first time. There's a reason this is our welcome meal. Such a simple dish hooks you in and convinces you to stay."

Instead of answering him, I devour the dish. If it is drugged, I am already going to be affected by one bite. Might as well just enjoy the entire thing before I pass out, and they put me in prison or whatever other awful plans they might have.

Maybe this is what it feels like to have a last meal. Your taste buds ignite. The simplest meals taste like expensive gourmet dishes because you know this is the last time you'll eat something—forever.

"Dude. You look like you saw a ghost. You okay?" Flynn asks.

His plate is almost empty. He is scraping up the last few remnants of his own pasta. That has to mean something, right? Everyone's dish was served from the same massive bowl. There is no way it was poisoned. The mentors and leader would eat from a different pot if that were the case. Unless, of course, it is something they are immune to. Something this planet did to their bodies, like an antigen that the average human body doesn't have?

I let out a breath. *I've watched too many movies.*

I shove pasta in my mouth before mumbling a "fine" and giving him a closed-mouth smile.

Each person is carrying on a different conversation, yet they all speak English in their specific accent, but of course, they do. Only Americans are unintelligible, monolingual people—well, many Americans.

Am I the only one freaking out here? Everyone seems to be eating and socializing as if this isn't the most bizarre situation they've encountered.

HELLO. WE ARE ON ANOTHER PLANET.

Andrya waits until we all finish eating before she starts her presentation right at the table. She lifts a black rectangular device that's similar to a smartphone but one that actually fits in your palm and is just a few centimeters thicker. The interface lights up, and she taps a button, pointing the device to the empty space behind her. There's no projection screen, but in an instant, an Otium Initiative logo appears, like a hologram, but the logo isn't see through.

It blocks the trees and buildings behind it. This is a technological advancement I've only ever seen in a Marvel movie. All the candidates seem pretty intrigued.

A hand rests gently on my shoulder. "The video is going to provide you with a massive overload of this planet and program. I'll be here to answer any questions, anytime you have them," Flynn whispers, his breath tickling my ear.

Shivers run down my spine, and I create space between us. Flynn's fingertips leave my shoulder, and a feeling of loss washes over me.

The presentation starts entirely in 3-D, but I can't seem to focus on it. Flynn is mere inches behind me, creating a sense of excitement coursing through my nerves. I can focus on the images flashing on the presentation, but not Andrya's words. Some sort of destruction of planet Earth, followed by an image of a purple, speckled green, and a reddish planet, presumably this one. Stunning aerial views—of hopefully Otium. Violet and deep purple oceans, green valleys, tall mountain ranges, and red deserts. As I start to get intrigued by the landscape, images flash of building homes and bigger buildings. All of the structures are built with the red dirt formed into a strange material. It reminds me of paper mache and wet sand. The windows are oddly shaped; the homes are domed and imperfect. Andrya's talking too fast. Explaining too much. Each picture has me questioning a hundred things in my mind. I can't process being on another planet; nonetheless, process the picture of Earth destroyed like some alien planet in a Marvel movie shot it to pieces.

A star larger but more blinding than the sun starts to set as the presentation comes to a close. I have to shield my eyes from the light as it seeps under our shade. The market around us is packing up for the night. In front of us, dessert is being placed on the table—bowls of white-looking ice cream. So far, I don't feel weird or confused in the sense that I was drugged. Just very uneasy about where my next few hours might take me. My lack of concentration on the presentation and Flynn's shoulder brushing against mine have me flustered and confused.

"Now," Andrya continues, "as we close out this meal and start to eat our vanilla bean ice cream, I ask you to question whether you're willing to test out this program. Once you're in it, you have one week to decide it isn't for you. When that week passes, you'll have to stick it out until the end. We do this because we need to trust your full confidentiality. We have to be careful with how we manipulate the past, present, and future. Within a week, you will not have enough information to concern Earth. Once you finish the program, you'll have enough to disrupt Earth's flow and concern citizens, but you'll have the knowledge and willpower to not do so."

"So." Flynn nudges my side. My spoon clangs against the clear glass bowl. "Wanna still leave?"

I open my mouth to speak, but I close it. Whenever someone asks me to attend an event or protest something, my stance is always yes. But I'm exhausted. I'm tired of fighting with no giveback. I just wished I could escape to another planet, but really, Starlord never had peace in space. He had to continuously fight for others too.

Is it better to escape here and learn in a place that is promising me a better way to fight back home? Or do I go back toward the dark stormy cloud of New York, watch as my parents become forgotten, a factory destroys a city, and I lose the only boy I've ever loved.

Flynn picks up his bowl and turns his body toward me. "What questions do you have?" He scoops some ice cream and devours it with the top of the spoon on his tongue.

"What happens when I'm here? Andrya said this was a voluntary program, but I didn't volunteer. Has my body disappeared from Earth? Are people searching for me?" My heart starts to race at the idea that I'm now a missing person. The last thing I remember is being at the courthouse, surrounded by people, people who wanted my reaction after the verdict, and I suddenly vanished?

Did anyone notice?

"Everyone has a different situation. You're hospitalized. You're safe, but—"

"I'm what?" I scream, struggling to get myself off the picnic table. Instead of climbing out, I kick Flynn's knee by accident. "No. No. No." My mind flashes to the last time I was in the hospital, waiting for my grandmother to identify my father. "I cannot be in there."

Did they put *me in there!?*

Flynn blinks at my outburst, and his eyes dart to his mother's as all conversations stop.

"Theodore," Andrya says. "You and I have more to discuss separately. You are safe. You are protected."

WHAT DOES THAT MEAN?

I want to scream, punch, throw, hit. Something— anything at all. Let the chaotic energy in my system escape.

She has no apology. They should understand the severity of my situation if they know who I am. Every volunteer here should be concerned that I have no idea what's going on.

I didn't choose this.

The spaghetti churns in my stomach, ready to burst through my esophagus at a moment's notice. This is turning into a nightmare whether I'm dreaming or not.

My sight narrows as the silence continues. The bile threatens to rise again as my body begins to tremble. I need to remain present. I have to name things, focus, divert this attack. It's just like the courthouse.

Forehead soaked in sweat, clammy hands, nausea that has me . . . I tip backward, hitting the grass beneath me.

"Flynn," I hear.

I don't know who says it, and I don't know why. But before I know it, I am lifted. Through my speckled vision, I see the bottom of Flynn's chin. His perfectly smooth, narrow chin.

My body is weak; I can barely lift my arms. I don't have the strength to fight off this control.

"I'm here to protect you, Theodore."

I feel myself calming in his arms. My eyes close as the light disappears over the horizon.

Nine

Silence is all around me. No diffuser hum, no lavender essential oils consuming my senses, no arguing from my aunt and uncle. Just silence. I'm not at home. This mattress forms around my body. Softer, warmer. The comforter envelops me like one of my mother's hugs.

It's dark when I open my eyes aside from a flickering flame that is coming closer to me.

Blow it out now, I think, rubbing my eyes. *You know what Mom and Dad used to say about candles.*

They hated them; they feared a fire would burn down everything they built.

I'm shattered. As if I wasn't actually just sleeping. The flame comes closer, illuminating a silhouette. It isn't either of my brothers, Jack or Timmy . . . it's . . . Flynn?

Flynn? How do I know a . . . oh. Flynn.

"Hi." His voice is soft as he hovers over me. I can just make out glossy eyes and his pure-white smile. "You've been out for about thirty minutes. This is the apartment you've been assigned if you choose to stay."

A rush of memories come to the forefront of my mind.

This is real. I can't sleep within a dream. If I stay in Otium, I get an entire apartment? This could be my opportunity to live independently . . . but at what cost?

I sit up, repositioning the pillow against the wall for more comfort, and I bring the blanket up to my chest. The comforter here is similar to the one I had when I was in middle school. It was massive and down, a size too big for the bed I was in. Enough to cocoon me up and away from the world. Mine from middle school got destroyed by my brothers in a terrible bike ride extravaganza they pulled. After that, I gave my mom a hard time with each new comforter she suggested before she got frustrated and told me I had to use an old one from our attic.

With the candle, I can only make out shapes in the room. My twin-sized bed is up against the back wall. There are two doors, one to my left and one directly in front of me, right next to a kitchenette with two countertops and a fridge. Along the right wall, there's a two-person sofa and a desk with a carved wooden chair. A studio apartment is what he meant to say; regardless, it would be my space.

"We are," Flynn pauses, and I direct my attention back to him. "I'm sorry for how your human body was left on Earth. Your time jump from Earth was insensitive. I will have a conversation with my mother about why she did what she did, and hopefully, I can get answers. Most people who come here have chosen to. From what I know, a select few people, like you, do not choose until they get here. Usually, a newbie like me wouldn't be assigned a case like yours. For, I guess, obvious reasons. We mess it up." He takes a deep breath, trying to steady the shaking candle in his hands. Wax drips down the long stem.

"This job is very important to me," he continues, "and I wanted to be the best mentor you could have. I am supposed to protect you, make you comfortable, answer your questions, and be a friend. I haven't done any of those. But I would like to try again . . . if you can trust me, that is?"

If I'm not the first person they've kidnapped from Earth, then they should have an awareness of comprehension, processing times, and kidnapping techniques.

The last thing I remember on Earth was the verdict. It's plausible I've been hospitalized for an anxiety attack—before Otium extracted me. Even more likely that I attacked the police, and they failed at bringing me to my parents. But if Otium actually hospitalized me . . .

"I'm sorry." His voice is barely a whisper, but it's enough to break through my subconscious. "I reread your entire file. I understand why you panicked at the word hospital. I still have information to get from Andrya, but I didn't want you to wake up alone."

"Do you know if I was hospitalized before Otium extracted or if Otium is responsible for my hospitalization?" I ask.

There's something about his voice and his stance. He's shifting from foot to foot, and his shoulders slouch; he's nervous. From the beginning, he hasn't been a leader. How can he lead me to be better for my community?

"All I know is that my mom said this was her opening. I overheard the conversation. As mentors, we only know so much, but I will try my hardest to get answers."

My brows furrow. "What does your mom mean by her opening?"

"I don't know, but I will find out." The candle switches hands, and pressure fills my chest with each second it isn't on a steady surface.

"Do you know why I was hospitalized? Or at least what my family and friends have been told?"

His eyes close as he breathes in. I watch closely as he keeps them closed, holding his breath before he finally exhales ten excruciatingly long seconds later.

"I don't know," he says, making eye contact with me. A pang hits my heart at his honesty, and his hand reaches toward me before he pulls it back to his side.

"What do you know?" I ask softly. I should be angry and pissed, but his vibe tells me that he doesn't like the position he's in either.

His eyes search my face, and I give him a slight nod—if he's even asking for permission.

"You may not believe it, but I was thrown into today, too. You were always going to be my first mentee, but you were supposed to volunteer after you turned eighteen. I was notified this morning to cancel my day and prepare for your arrival. I should still be overseeing two programs before I have my own mentee to advise. So, while your extraction was abrupt and seemingly careless, there has to be a reason behind it."

Suddenly, he leaves my side of the bed. My lungs deflate as he crosses the room, but not because he walked away and finally put the candle down. Something is strange about this entire thing. How can even my mentor be in the dark?

Logically speaking, if there is a planet trying to better themselves from the mistakes of Earth, they would be seeking out activists. I've been recognized by New York State. *Logically*, it isn't so far-fetched that I'd be a prime candidate. I'm young but nearly legal to go off on my own and do the dirty fight. But what was so crucial that they couldn't wait until my birthday to recruit me. How the hell do they even recruit people to another planet without alarming humans?

Flynn pours what looks like water out of a pitcher. Before he comes back to my bedside, he flips on a light switch. A ceiling sconce gives a dim haze throughout the room.

The interior walls are made of that reddish-clay exterior. It's not painted or wallpapered. There's a handmade flow to the room that feels whimsical. The desk and countertops are built out from the wall like clay was morphed to connect them.

"These buildings are so different from New York." The material curves instead of precise 90-degree edges. It honestly feels homier—a perfect place to come nestle after a stressful day.

"They are cob houses. The only type of housing we have on Otium. There is a desert on Otium where the sand makes the perfect clay-like mix for these structures." His slender frame relaxes, and his face becomes more animated as he talks about his planet. He knows this information. "It helps make homes fire-resistant and temperature controlled. They are eco-friendly too."

"They seem really cool," I offer with a smile, and his smile matches my own. And they do seem really cool. Intricately designed, yet the artistic feel of the construction worker. Jonah would be inspired.

Flynn hands me the glass of water. "Have some water; it's been a while."

I take the glass, immediately distracted by the beautiful air-brushed pattern of mountains on it. There is something written very small, right at the bottom of what looks like snowboarding trails. It says Belleayre Mountain.

My eyes blur. I haven't been able to snowboard for years. When New York gets winters now, they are too frigid. Everything turns to ice, or the temperature is warm like spring. The year before my parents passed away, there were only one or two days that were prime for spending the money to board, but we already had events we were attending. We didn't know that was our last chance.

"We try to customize everything for our guests. We like to be able to make each guest's apartment something that they can call home." Flynn sits down on the floor, adjusting a throw pillow beneath him. With his height, his shoulders are above the bed. "If you look around the room, you'll notice more about your life."

My stomach twinges. *More about my life?* This glass is a personal memory of mine. How long have they been stalking me? I haven't snowboarded in three years.

"I did not give consent to being stalked."

His spine straightens. It feels like he's about to turn into a robot again; give me some bullshit, monotoned response. Instead, he looks over, his eyes searching my face. I want to answer for him that he "doesn't know," but from how his face lit up about the cob homes, I get the feeling that he isn't used to not knowing things—similar to me.

He squints his eyes, takes a breath, and then slouches his shoulders again as his face neutralizes. "We do what we do for the better of humanity."

The robotic finality of it. No argument to be had. They actually believe that stalking is okay.

"How is everything customized for me if my extraction was spontaneous?" I raise my brow.

"I don't know why, but I do know that these have been customized for a while. Yes, they threw your room together fast today, but like I said, I've been prepping to advise you. I guess the design team has too."

What makes me so fucking special?

I narrow my eyes, searching the room for more

customizations. There are two plaques hanging above the desk. My breath catches. They look so similar to the two plaques hanging in my own bedroom. I climb out of bed, walking toward them. One represents my parents' activism in my county. The other represents my activism—the highest honor for a freshman in high school. I was, and still am, the youngest person in my region to advocate change.

My blood starts to boil as my shoulders tense. If I find out that anyone actually went into my room and took my plaques to just make it *homier* here, I'm going to flip.

"Those plaques are mainly the reason you're here. You've made some real strides in New York." Flynn's voice calms the anger coursing through my system. My fists are tight against my sides as I analyze them. "They aren't real," he offers, but I hesitate to let out my breath. "Well, they aren't the original. We carved them here."

They aren't real. I repeat to myself. Finger by finger, I release my fists.

I don't know about this place, but Flynn seems to be honest, even if he doesn't know anything. I have no reason to believe he's lying.

I let my right-hand index finger trail over the carvings. Tracing over my parents' names. The job is impeccable, really. Everything down to the exact hue of the plaque is the same.

These are the reasons I am here. My goal was to be as good as my parents had been. I was always right by their side, saving the world one day at a time. We were unstoppable—until the police stopped us. Day in and day out, I've worked myself to the bone to try and continue my parents' fight, to become the person they wanted me to be despite grieving. They would have pushed forward. They would have done everything to get me justice if it were me who died instead of them.

I owe my life to them.

"This room only has some replicas of what you have or have had. Nothing was picked up directly from Earth."

I nod. I wanna crack a joke like, "Didn't pick up anything but me," but I refrain.

As this planet becomes more transparent, it also brings up hundreds of more questions. My brain can't catch up with sorting between what I need to know, what I want to know, and what happens if I actually am trapped.

Truth is, I'm damn well curious about this place. I mean, who wouldn't be? I've literally been talking to the universe about wanting to escape to a new planet. If what they say is true about helping create a better planet, I owe it to my parents to stay.

It doesn't make sense, though. If a planet like this exists, NASA should know about it.

I walk over to the couch and see a collage of photographs. Something I've always wanted to do at home but never got to. Most are pictures of my parents and me helping at their agency or attending an event. There is one photograph of my parents, my brothers, and me. Our last Christmas card. There's a picture of me in elementary school snuggling between Ellie and Sam. I trace both of them. They said they were coming home soon, and now I'm gone. There are even a couple of rare photos with Alejandro, Jonah, and me, but oddly, there are no individual photos with either of them. Just specific to us volunteering at my parents' fundraising event. The one that happened last year right after their deaths and the one previous. Our expressions make it easy to determine which year is which.

A knot starts to form in my stomach. In the midst of the

year, I had forgotten that Jonah helped with my parents' fundraiser. So why, when I'm the one in charge, did he decide to walk away? Decide he didn't want to fight anymore?

I take a seat on the couch, tucking my legs underneath me. Every photograph was chosen for a reason. Out of my entire camera roll, those aren't the pictures I'd choose to define my life.

Step one, get all the *logical* information.

When I look over at Flynn, he's now standing. A device similar to Andrya's is in his hand, yet his is thin like the iPhone. A screen projects above it, showing what looks like a message thread.

"When did humans move to Otium?" I ask, and his head instantly jerks up, finding me across the room.

"They started thirty years in your future," he says, glancing back at the device, typing something into it.

I do some quick math in my head, trying to work this out. How hasn't NASA discovered a planet that we will be moving to in just thirty years? We've been discovering Mars for over forty.

"So humans have been on Otium for sixty years?"

He glances over at me again and gives me a warm smile. "Exactly."

I wanna ask him if I made it to Otium. If I have a life or family here that I could visit, maybe confirm all this. But I stop myself short. If time travel is anything like the movies, I don't want to cause any more ripples. Even if I did travel to Otium, I'd be over a hundred. I'm definitely dead.

Flynn tucks the device in his back pocket before crossing the room. He takes a seat next to me on the couch.

"I don't want to rush you, but we have a meeting with

my mother. She wants to speak about your situation, and we need a decision on whether you choose to stay or go home."

My stomach plummets. It's now or never. I nod, standing up, and Flynn follows suit. I twist my hands together in front of me. There's no simple solution. Though, my gut says jump. It says I'll regret the decision if I decide to leave now. But my mind tells me that it's insane to trust anyone here, at least without asking a good series of questions.

"Let's go talk to my mom, or well, Andrya. All of us can get on the same page, you can ask any questions you have, and then a decision will be made."

I just nod again. If I open my mouth, I'll either vomit or make the wrong decision.

Ten

Flynn and I walk along a dirt path away from the apartment building toward where his mother's office is. The fresh, cool air filters through my lungs, cleansing any fear still rooted in my body.

Stars light up the sky in various sizes and patterns, though, like the sun, none compare to the light that lit this planet earlier. There is a soft white that rims the horizon. The majority of the sky is now a deep purple with some blue hues and a hint of maroon. It's absolutely breathtaking.

"Does it ever pitch-black here?" I ask.

"This is the darkest it'll ever get. It's nice because we rarely need any additional light to walk outside. Depending on the season, it'll remain dark like this for ten to thirteen hours."

I like the way he speaks. His even, silky voice calms my body. Maybe he doesn't have all the answers I want, but when he does, he's thorough.

The town center, where the markets were, is behind us. As we continue on the path, we are soon surrounded by the hobbit-domed homes I saw at a distance earlier. Different paths lead off the main one, giving way to rows of houses. While these homes are small, they all have a vast backyard. Every home seems equally spaced apart from its neighbor, but each is uniquely designed. Some are more square, others are oval. Some are two-story with balconies; others are one-story with wraparound porches. I can't pinpoint faces, only shapes, voices, laughter, and music in their backyards, but it seems the community is still awake—for whatever time it may be.

Flynn directs us immediately to the right at the end of the path. He's kept silent, sometimes glancing down at his device and typing away on it. It seems some things haven't changed in the future. While I'd love to be bouncing this experience off of Alejandro or Jonah, it's been a nice break from my phone. Though, I don't even want to imagine the amount of notifications clogging my screen.

As I look ahead on this new path, it leads to a home twice as large as the others. It's a two-story with two balconies and a wraparound porch. Compared to the others here, this home is extravagant. Nicer than most homes in my community.

"That's where I grew up." Flynn points at the home.

I roll my eyes and instantly blush at my judgment. Thankfully, Flynn is looking ahead. *Of course*, the leader has dominance still, even in a society trying to create a better world. While messed up, it oddly feels comforting to know that not everything has changed.

Unlike leaders in the United States, this house sits in a neighborhood with homes surrounding all sides. While there is a fence to the backyard, it's just an average four-foot picket fence. Not blocking out any privacy, in fact, there's a welcoming stone path up to a double front door.

"Though I don't live there anymore. I live in your building. The upstairs is for mentors, and the first floor is for the mentees. My mom wants me to stay at the house, but I prefer my space and some distance from her leadership."

"How old are you?" I ask.

We slow our pace. The front porch has a light on right above the door. I wonder if it's because we're coming or if it signifies when the leader can be bothered.

"I'm eighteen and four months on Otium, so roughly eighteen and seven months on Earth." We stop two houses away, and he turns to me. "Time operates a little differently here. We have calendars with years, months, and days similar to Earth. The days and years last longer, though. On Earth, you have 24 hours, 365 days, and a 12-month calendar. We have 28 hours, 420 days, and a 14-month calendar. Every month is 30 days."

I nod, trying to sort through the math, but my brain shuts down with math equations. There will be no way I can try to sort through time travel without them just giving me information—information I just have to trust.

When I don't answer, we start to walk again. It's not that I don't want to acknowledge his explanation; I'm just crashing fast. I still haven't had a full night's sleep in over a week.

Flynn waves at a few people we pass by—all around our age. It seems that the people here express more of themselves through their appearance versus the house they own. Eccentric hairstyles, hair color, clothing, piercings, and tattoos. While we've passed some people who seem to just want to fit in, it almost seems like "fitting in" causes you to stand out more.

Every person who greets Flynn also greets me—by name. I keep my head forward and my arms crossed. They shake beneath my pits. There are two options: Flynn is excited about advising me and told his friends my name. Or everyone knows everything about everyone here, even the newcomers. Neither option suits me.

"We are asking a lot of you." I jump as Flynn starts speaking again. We're now standing in front of his childhood home. "The transition period isn't easy, but don't be afraid to ask questions about us and this planet. I'm an open book. We have nothing to hide."

Of course, I want to know everything, but they are already hiding something. If they weren't, Flynn would have all the answers. This situation needs patience. Something I struggled recently to have on Earth, but here, it feels like something is coursing through my blood, reminding me to be patient and just allow the answers to come forth.

They could have drugged me. That extra water could have been another sedative. I mean, how did I pass out before? Was it from the food, exhaustion, or just shock? I feel fine, but Marvel has dealt with some wild serums before that Otium could have concocted in real life.

As we walk up the stone path, suddenly, it hits me. I don't care about my fate. If I did, no matter what they said, I'd want to be back home. If I did, I wouldn't have been disappointed that I wasn't in Heaven. I don't think I have a choice, though. They can allow me to leave, but they've already tracked me down and transported me through time. I'm in a hospital bed on Earth. If I say I want to go home, who says they can't stop my heart.

The situation perfectly presents itself. The only option is to go along with what they want. Once I sort out what is really happening on this planet, I can either learn to work with them or work against them.

We pause in front of Andrya's yellow front door—Flynn's childhood just inside. There is a sign on the door:

All are welcome when the light is on, but please knock first. If the light is off, we will see you tomorrow. If it's an emergency, ring the bell.

"Your mom takes emergency hours at her house?" I blurt the question out before I realize I asked a question.

Flynn laughs as his hand grasps the doorknob. "Of course, she's the leader. If someone needs something that isn't a medical emergency, it's her job to help."

Right, totally normal. I roll my eyes. *As if anyone in America could just knock on their leader's door without being arrested.*

"Ready?" Flynn asks, nodding toward the door. "Remember, there is nothing to fear. We want you to be happy."

I refrain from laughing, though my eyes sting. It feels like forever since I've been happy.

"Okay," I whisper instead.

I should smile. I want to believe him, and I want to trust him. At the bare minimum of this bizarre experience, it has been so long since I've trusted someone new. I used to be able to let my guards down at the drop of a hat, my gut letting me know when I felt safe and secure, but now, even though my gut says to stay, I'm second-guessing it.

Flynn swings the door open. I thought the "please knock" would still apply to us, considering he doesn't live here. But he gestures inside, allowing me to walk through before shutting the door behind him.

"My mother works from home. She always wanted to be close to her children while working. Something her mother prioritized here because her mother did so on Earth."

"Hey, Flynn." A middle-aged man comes down a wooden staircase in the center of the home.

Similar to my room, the interior of this home has furniture flowing with the walls. It seems like one seamless, handcrafted design. To my left is a kitchen, where the cabinets form from the wall. To my right is a long, dimly lit hallway. Shoes and jackets are hanging in this room, and there are two couches with some bookcases built into the walls.

"Hey, Dad, this is Theodore. I'm his mentor. We're here to meet Mom to discuss some things."

His father's eyes light up, but not toward me. He's looking at Flynn. Flynn shakes his head ever-so-slightly, and his dad's excitement reduces to a friendly smile.

Open book, my ass. What the hell is going on?

"Hey, Theodore, I'm Jay." His father holds out his hand, and I straighten, giving him a firm, slightly clammy shake. "I'll brew some tea. Mom's in her office."

"Thank you." Flynn hugs his father quickly before he gestures for me to follow him.

"What are you hiding?" I blurt as he leads me down a long hallway. My pace slows as photographs of his family are hung all over the walls. I could spend so much time standing here, analyzing it all, puzzling his life together. I wonder if people were able to bring important possessions with them here and if any of these photographs are from Earth. Most of the photographs are too vibrant to have been around for so many years.

"I promise it's not important," Flynn says.

We reach a closed door, and Flynn, again, doesn't knock or wait to be let in. He just opens the door. I'm hoping he was messaging his mom to tell her we were on the way instead of being disrespectful, barging into her office.

"Theodore! Welcome," Andrya greets with a smile. "Give me one moment."

She is behind a standing desk with two screens projected from two black devices sitting on her desk. Unlike the 3-D presentation earlier, this is a square 2-D projection. I can't see through them, though, like I could on Flynn's.

She writes something down in a folder open on her desk before she closes it and files it away in one single, five-drawer filing cabinet. On the wall behind her, there's a document naming her the leader of the Flatlands. Other than that, the walls are bare. Two sofa chairs sit in a corner between the door we came through and another door to my left.

Andrya types a few things onto one projection before they both disappear. "Okay." She lets out a breath and gathers her hair into a ponytail. "What a day." She smiles, her eyes crinkling. She grabs one of the devices and walks around the desk, closing the space between us. Her hand rests on my arm. "Theodore, dear, I do apologize for earlier. On behalf of myself and the town of Olive, welcome to Planet Otium. I've been eager to meet the infamous Theodore Montgomery, and now you're finally here."

Infamous. I haven't accomplished that much in my lifetime.

"Nice to meet you, too, Mrs. Andrya?" I offer a handshake, but she pulls me into a quick, gentle hug. The hug alone warms my body, and as I sink into it, my gut tells me that it's okay here. I'm safe here.

"Andrya is just fine, dear," Andrya says before she hugs Flynn and kisses his forehead.

His grin is genuine, not sheepish embarrassment because he's a teen and his mother showed him affection. When they part, Flynn walks over to the closed door. "Let's go into the living room. We all need some rest," Flynn offers.

I mouth a "Thank you" to him. I don't know if he can

read me quite yet, but my legs are yearning to remain in one location for at least twenty-four hours.

"Absolutely." Andrya grins, opening the door and gesturing for us both to walk through. "Let's have some tea in the living room and talk."

Flynn rests his hand on my mid-back and guides me through the door. I nearly stumble into the room as his pressure warms my body. And this living room . . . it's cozy as hell. A large maroon L-shaped couch sits in the middle of the room, looking directly at a rose-colored wall. I imagine something television-like is placed in that area somehow—similar to how her device projects. A carved wooden coffee table with a glass top sits in front of the couch. This wood must be common to the area as it's what my desk chair is also made from, as well as the bookshelves in their foyer. Five glossy white coasters rest on the glass, all spaced evenly apart. The only lights in the room are in the ceiling, and they seem to be dimmed. Just like the hallway, photos of the family are throughout the room. These are all framed, including a large canvas of Flynn, Andrya, his dad, and a teen girl. She's nearly identical to Flynn, the biggest difference being her wavy auburn hair to his blonde crew cut.

Andrya walks around my frozen frame to sit on the couch, and a woman, who looks a little older than me, with short jet-black pin-straight hair, walks in through an arched doorway with a tray of mugs. Flynn's dad follows behind her with a teapot and a grin.

Flynn's hand rests on the back of my arm as I watch Andrya place a large coaster down for the teapot.

"Theodore," Flynn whispers.

I look over at him. Those crystal eyes of his search my face.

"While Andrya is my mom, it is my job to advocate for

you. My mom is doing her job right now, and I am doing mine. I promise to be honest with you if you promise to ask for what you need. My mom will push, but you hold the power here. Otium needs you more than you need Otium."

"Theodore," Andrya calls. I glance over at her, and the young woman is smiling next to Andrya. "This is Lana, my assistant. Lana, this is Theodore."

Lana's piercing green eyes stand out against her stark pale skin. They shimmer at the mention of my name.

I give a small wave. I've already forgotten half the names here. I'm really only interested in learning more about this initiative. If I stay, I can remember names later.

"Let's sit," Flynn says, guiding me over to the couch.

The moment my body meets the couch, I'm enveloped in it. If they could just leave me here for a day to rest, that would be lovely. I force my body into an upright position; otherwise, I will fall asleep.

Lana hands Flynn and me steaming mugs of tea before she sits on the couch with Flynn's parents. The smell of lavender and chamomile fills the air as the steam rises up and warms my chin.

"So, Theodore," Andrya starts. She blows some steam away from her mug and looks over at me. "I want to talk a little bit about how time works here, about where you are on Earth, and really, the most crucial for us is to talk about how important it would be for you to stay here and go through the program. After all is said and done, a decision will have to be made. Does that sound okay?"

For some reason, I look over at Flynn for confirmation. He places his hand gently on the middle of my back, giving me a small nod.

"Y-yeah," I swallow. "Okay."

I don't want Flynn's hand to move, but it drops between

us on the couch. I need that added support his warmth provides, as if transferring confidence in me with just a touch.

"As you briefly saw in the video earlier, Otium is a democracy. A better, more improved version than on Earth now. This does provide some complications with those volunteers that do not come from democracies. But when Otium was established, we collectively decided that if democracy is run well, it succeeds.

"Each leader of Otium meets and makes arrangements about the planet together, like the United Nations. We have five geographic locations, three of which are established with residents. In those three locations, we have a few towns, depending on the population. For example, Olive is a town in the Flatlands. Those three locations each run an Otium Initiative. While there is a general guideline of workshops that every volunteer participates in, the experience is customized for each volunteer based on the country they are from, who they are, and what they advocate for.

"The Otium Initiative is 99% a volunteer program. However, there are a select few people, like you, who Otium specifically wants to work with, and we haven't perfected getting those specific people as volunteers before we have to extract them." Andrya stops speaking to take a few sips of her tea.

My mind is operating in sloth-mode. It all makes sense to me, except for why I'm more critical than any other volunteer here.

"I sincerely apologize for your hospital stay," Andrya continues, "though I do want to be clear that we did not put you in the hospital."

I glance over at Flynn, and he looks just as intrigued by this information.

"You were in an altercation with a police officer at your parents' trial."

I grip my mug tighter, inhaling as hot water splashes onto my skin. This time I feel Flynn's eyes on me, but I don't have the courage to see if he's shocked by this news or if he's just checking in. To be fair, *I'm* not shocked.

I sink back into the couch. I have no memory of the altercation. I'm not sure if I want a memory of it. Nothing's changed, though, just like I thought. It doesn't matter if we were at a trial for police brutality; the police still came after us.

"The police officer didn't harm you, but you had a panic attack. It was so severe, and in a public space, EMTs had to evaluate you and escort you off the premises. When you were being assessed at the hospital, we stepped in. The hospital staff ran tests and determined you'd stay overnight for evaluation. You were severely dehydrated and exhausted that likely they would have kept you for observation even without the panic attack. You aren't allowed any visitors right now, which buys us time and allows for an empty hospital bed. We have a staff member from Otium stepping in as a travel nurse, pretending to give you fluids. However, you did receive some fluids before we extracted you. Regardless of your decision, you have to be conscious in your hospital bed by early tomorrow morning. We will make sure you receive proper fluids before visiting hours begin."

"Why don't I remember this?" I ask. This seems quite chaotic for my mind to not have a single memory.

"You blacked out on the scene, and at the hospital, they gave you a cocktail of fluids to ensure your levels evened out, and you got proper sleep; that's where we stepped in. Your family and friends know that you were admitted for a panic attack and exhaustion. You will be evaluated by a psychologist regardless of if you stay on Earth or come to Otium." Andrya gives me a motherly eyebrow raise. It reminds me of Ellie when she would try to discipline me if she caught me doing something I shouldn't. "Either way, we recommend counseling."

Jonah's been harping on me to see a psychologist since the day after my parents passed. I've lost count of how many times I've said no.

"If you do choose to participate in the Otium Initiative, you will inform your family and friends that you'll be entering an inpatient program for grief therapy. This will allow you to disappear for a bit. We know therapy has been up for discussion in your life, so we feel like now, it would be the perfect time to enroll after such a severe attack."

What. The. Fuck.

This is insanity. Knowing Jonah has mentioned counseling? We haven't been *discussing* it. I've refused it. And even if I do need it, there's no way in hell my aunt and uncle will sign off on it. They are wildly against any form of therapy. It's part of the reason I have refused to go, because I can't have that conversation with them, and I can't have Jonah fighting my goddamn battles.

Flynn places his hand on my leg, holding it down. The other begins to shake uncontrollably. My tea wavers in the mug, scarily close to overflowing and spilling onto me again.

"Breathe in." It almost feels like his words are in my head, but it has to be that he's just close to my ear. Leaning into me. Applying pressure onto my leg to calm it.

The tea is out of my hands as my vision blurs. My burning, clammy hands immediately reach behind my neck, pushing me forward. Flynn's knuckles press into my chest. It's the only way to calm me in this position; my head leaning forward, chest against my legs, my eyes looking at my shins—well, if they are ever open.

"Theodore." His voice is coming in front of me. Similar to Jonah.

Jonah knows how to handle this. It's his place and not Flynn's. Every single move Jonah does, Flynn is now replicating it as if he watched a reel of my anxiety attacks to learn how to handle mine.

I don't know when his hand left my leg, but the moment Flynn's hands grasp the sides of my head, I shiver. There's a coolness where it left. His thumbs massage my temples. I want to collapse into it, succumb to the comfort, but it's not safe here. It's not home. It's not . . .

"You're safe here, Theo."

. . . Jonah.

My body bolts up, and I shove Flynn away from me.

"Screw you!" I spit. My face is saturated with tears. My pants are soaked with snot.

How dare Flynn try to use my comforts. How dare he know those private, immediate moments between Jonah and me. How much do they know? How much have they seen? When does it all start and begin?

"I'm sorry. I'm sorry; that was too much." He tries to stand and recenter with me, but I brush past him.

"Screw all of you."

I take off into a run back through Andrya's office and down the hall from which I came. I don't have anywhere to go, and I don't know where to go. While I can navigate my way back to the building I believe my room is in, I don't know the room number or if I need a key.

I collapse mid-step, tumbling down the five stairs they have leading up to the front door. Rolling, I stop headfirst into this damn fresh grass. I grip a handful, ripping it up from the soil or whatever magical substance is below it. I keep ripping it up, throwing it just millimeters away. I can't even demand to go back to Earth because I know that I'll mess up some time/future paradox without the proper departure information—even if they claim I won't. They need to give me a strict script because if I tell Jonah or Alejandro that I dreamed about this, they will drag me to therapy. My aunt and uncle may even agree because of my "insanity."

I can feel Flynn's presence. His shifting feet. Cracking of his own knuckles. The awkward silence between the time you *know* someone is there and when they actually make themselves present.

"Please don't run."

"I'm trapped." I snap. "Where do you expect me to go?"

He sighs loudly before his body drops down next to mine. I throw the clump of grass I have in my hand and look up at him.

"I'm sorry. For a lot," Flynn starts. "The main thing is making you feel like you're a hostage. And the second thing, my mother. I don't know what this is like for you. We get training on how to be a mentor and how to deal with certain situations, but we don't really know. We can't. Even with volunteers, their transition is tough. Our practices can seem invasive—" I raise my brows at him, and a soft laugh escapes his lip. "*Are* invasive. However, we justify it because of the end result. But we need to remember that people on Earth haven't been living on Otium. Where you are now, Otium just got discovered. We can't possibly expect you to really understand our motives—at least within the first week— nonetheless, mere hours."

He grants me silence. The sounds of the community are now silent. No cars driving or screeching, no dogs barking up the neighborhood, no more laughing in backyards. I can't even hear grasshoppers chirping. It's so quiet I can hear the ringing in my ears.

Flynn isn't looking at me. Not staring me down, demanding an answer. Instead, his gaze is up toward the sky. The deep periwinkle sky with thousands of new stars and likely new planets. Otium has to be in another solar system. It's possible that I missed this discovery with the hectic year I've had.

I lay down in the grass, allowing the tension in my body to disappear. I'd give anything to be lying in my backyard, looking up at the stars, thinking about my parents and where they'd be right now. Thinking about . . . Star-Lord and getting the ability to uproot his life on another planet.

Internally, I let out a scream of frustration. I want to squeeze my eyes shut, forcing back the tears, stomp my feet, and slam my fists into the ground. Have a proper tantrum, lose control for just a moment in time. When did I stop being a kid?

"I want to be alone, and I need to sleep. Can I at least do that?" My voice is barely a whisper.

My body's shutting down. *Am I a hostage?* Maybe. *Will I ever get out of here?* I'm not sure. All I know is that I need sleep to navigate the blurred lines.

Eleven

A knock startles me. Last night, the moment my head hit the pillow, I was out—fell asleep in my jeans and now-disgusting button-up. Usually, complete silence is a fantastic time for my inner voice to come through. Naturally, the voice is also silent on the night I'm desperate to overanalyze.

The knocking persists. Kicking my legs off the bed, I stand up. A train definitely ran over me last night. My head is pounding. My eyes start to water, blurry from the gunk in my water lines. I jog across the room before I have to witness one more excruciatingly loud knock.

I unlock the door, and before it's even halfway open, I can tell it's going to be a mistake.

"Good morning, Theodore!" Flynn's smile is too bright. The smile of someone who greets you with loads of espresso—lucky for him, his hands are full.

"Morning," I mumble, grabbing a travel mug from him and a glass container.

I am not a morning person. The only thing that motivates me out of bed is the constant go, go, go of my planner.

Fuck. My parents' fundraiser. I can't stay in Otium when the fundraiser hasn't happened because if I'm not there, it could fail, and if it fails, then the funding for the agency is tight, and I can't take over the agency with a lack of funds when I don't know what the hell I'm doing, and—

"How are you this morning?" His words slice through my thoughts.

My breath catches, mid-thought, and I cough. Flynn opens the blinds in my room. It's still dark outside, possibly a tad brighter than it was when I went to bed. No wonder I still feel like shit.

I take a deep breath in. I can panic about the fundraiser when back in the hospital bed. Right now, I need to focus on making sure what they said was real. Bright side, I wasn't murdered in my sleep.

"How many hours have I been asleep?" I ask as I sit down on the couch. I take a sip, closing my eyes and moaning as a chai latte with oat milk hits my tongue. *This is a benefit of them knowing everything.*

"It's been a little over six hours since I left you."

I nod, nursing my drink. That doesn't give me an exact time, but if I have to be back on Earth in morning Earth hours, then it must still be the middle of the night here.

I rub my eyes, hoping to get the sleepies out without diving for them in the mirror. Flynn sits down on the couch, turning toward me.

"We need to eat and walk toward the portal in a few minutes. We can't risk someone walking into your hospital room with your bed empty."

Blood drains from my face, and I rest the cup on my thigh so I don't spill it.

"Lana, from last night," Flynn continues, "is one of the people who travel to the United States on behalf of our candidates. She's a certified travel nurse and will take over as your nurse in the hospital. If you find yourself alone with her, feel free to ask her any questions. Your time in the hospital will be hectic, though, as you'll have to be discharged in the evening."

They've thought of everything. More time is good. Any time with my phone gives me the opportunity to research Otium's discovery on Earth.

"How am I supposed to make a decision?" I ask, distracting myself by popping the lid on the glass container. A breakfast wrap is inside. While it looks delicious, this decision curbs my hunger.

"Do you care about Earth?" His professional tone is out. We aren't friends.

I turn toward him, opening my mouth. *Of fucking course I do,* I want to snap. *Just because I'm hesitant about Otium doesn't mean—*

He raises his hands up before I have a chance to mutter a word. "I'm just asking questions to gauge your answer."

Oh.

"Do you care about Earth?" He tries again; this time he sounds nonchalant, like it isn't an intense question.

I swallow and nod.

"Do you care about doing the right thing?"

I nod again.

"Do you feel like you must try to make a difference in whatever way you can?"

"I try," I sigh, leaning back against the couch. "I don't know how much I have left in me, but I want to live up to my parents' impact."

"Take this as the opportunity to be able to do better. For yourself. For your family. Your friends. Your community. Don't think of this as a global issue. Think of your community and the change you can make once you've been provided with the right skills and can teach everyone back home."

"How am I supposed to trust that you all are telling the truth? You've extracted me from my planet and have stalked me for years. For wanting to be better, it doesn't seem like trust is a big factor."

This silences him. There isn't a rebuttal. His eyes glaze over, the wheels begin to rotate in his mind. He has no text-book answer for this.

Maybe they don't always mess up as badly as they have with me. Or perhaps other people are a lot less trustworthy than they should be, or maybe their lives are bad enough that this is an escape. But I can't just up and leave my fight with no good reason or truth behind their words.

"I want to believe you," I continue. "Otium sounds incredible. I want to believe that this place is real. That this has been the escape I've begged for."

"But?" His question is quiet as he takes a sip of his own drink.

His eyes lock with mine, and a wave of calm ripples through me with a nod of his head.

"What if this isn't everything I need it to be?"

Twelve

The light is blinding on my closed eyelids. There is no sunlight. No fresh air—instead, the air smells toxic. An incessant beeping in my ear is a clear reminder that I'm not in my bed. The blankets are used and thin. The sheets cool to the skin. I'm homesick for a place that hasn't felt like a home in a year.

And it hits me like a ton of bricks. My consciousness is clear. I can see the two worlds vividly in my mind. I have no memory of traveling back to Earth. One minute I was admiring the portal, and the next, I'm waking up in a hospital bed.

A hand squeezes mine tightly. It's soft, moist. Squeezing it back with my own, my fingertip grazes the slight bone out of place on his middle finger. Jonah is here.

"Theo?" His voice thick with saliva.

I squint my eyes shut before letting them open slowly. The fluorescent lights have me yearning for that damn candlelight.

"J-J—" My mouth is dry as if I haven't talked in days, despite knowing I spoke right before going into the portal.

Jonah's puffy eyes shine with fresh tears.

"Hi, you." His hand grips mine tight. "How are you feeling?"

Like a train wreck. There's pressure in my head, no doubt from the amount I cried in my "panic" state. The aftermath of a migraine is here. My eyes are puffy, my cheeks still dry from tears. All the typical side effects of a panic attack, all my energy sucked out by anxiety. My limbs are weaker than usual. If I have the same body on Earth and Otium, I don't understand why it feels so different.

There's a tray of food and a cup of water on a table that can swing toward me. Behind the table is Alejandro, on the other side of my bed.

"Hey, Theo," Alee says softly with a wave. He sits up in his chair, putting his phone on his lap.

I let go of Jonah's hand, reaching for the cup. My hands are unsteady, gripping the plastic, making sure it doesn't slip. I make a mental note to ask Lana about the effects of time travel. I bring the straw to my lips and finally take a sip of the room temperature water.

Holy shit, this water is awful. I force myself to swallow the liquid. I like to believe hospitals have high-quality water, but I'm not sure anything will taste as crisp and pure as the water I had last night on Otium.

"Are you in pain?" Jonah asks.

I rest the cup on my leg over top of the shitty blankets.

"No pain. Just exhausted."

"That sip made it seem like your throat was sore," Jonah says.

Because I had incredible water on an entirely different planet.

"Just dehydrated. All good." I try giving him a small

smile, eyes darting over to Alee to help him feel included. I don't miss the silent communication between the two.

"The nurse said you were severely dehydrated. Have the fluids overnight not helped?" Jonah, the ever-present caretaker, asks.

They probably would have if I actually had my entire dosage.

I don't know how I'll keep these two worlds separate. If something as simple as water tastes different, I imagine the rest of the food does too. A simple bowl of spaghetti last night had me over the moon, and my breakfast wrap this morning was filled with the freshest vegetables—no doubt because of the water on Otium.

"I'm sorry I didn't keep track of your water intake at the protest, Theo," Alee says, his voice thick with guilt.

"How are you both?" I question, changing the subject. I try to narrow in on Jonah's face, his bloodshot eyes and sunken frame. His hair is greasy, the natural wave matted down from running his hands through it.

If Andrya is telling the truth and they didn't place me in the hospital, this is the first panic attack that hospitalized me. The only one Jonah hasn't been able to help me out of.

"Better now that you're awake." His face barely forms a smile; it's painful and tight. "You really scared me. I've never seen you react like that. Not only was it the worst panic attack you've had, but you were pretty threatening to an officer." Jonah raises his voice. "Were you trying to get yourself killed?"

He punctures my lungs with his words.

"Jonah," Alee sighs. "Please."

I glance over at Alejandro, who looks just as bad, if not worse, than Jonah. Alejandro has reason, at least. He's been working around the clock on this trial. His bun is puffier than usual, flyaways sticking out in different directions.

"No. I need to know." Jonah's gentle, honey-like voice is gone. It's been often missing these days. Replaced with frustration and disappointment. "The police are right outside that door, waiting to question you. Waiting to fucking charge you. For assaulting a police officer, Theo!"

I choke on my breath at his words and rising volume. I know I was in an altercation but to be charged? If they want to press charges, I will be charged as an adult.

The beeping on my machine picks up its pace, and Alejandro's hand grips the pressure point on my hand, between my thumb and forefinger.

"What were you thinking?!" Jonah screams. His voice reverberates in my ears.

"Jonah!" Alee raises his voice. "You're not helping." He lowers his voice and moves his hand to hold mine entirely. There's a crease in his forehead that wasn't there a few days ago.

My eyes blur as I look between the two of them. Alee has never talked back to Jonah, letting my arguments with Jonah be my own. Something happened in the time I was admitted to now that doesn't look good on either of them.

Most of my indecision on Otium was because I didn't want to leave them behind, even if I did end things with Jonah. Maybe it's best if I do leave. Alejandro can rest, and Jonah can be rid of me once and for all.

"I was there, you know," Jonah continues. "I showed up," he repeats. Like he wants praise for supporting me. "I was about to tell you I was there, but then the announcement was starting. I didn't want to interrupt."

My stomach clenches, and I can feel my lungs start to restrict. This feeling had become a norm, something I lived with every minute of the day. On Otium, I had only been anxious twice. I didn't recognize the extreme difference until this exact moment. This insufferable feeling has me questioning if I did have a death wish.

Jonah watches my machine. My daily life is on display for them. I grip Alejandro's hand, looking directly at Jonah.

"You should have been there from the beginning." My words betray me as they waver.

"I have been there from the beginning!" Jonah's eyes fixate on my hand in Alejandro's, his biggest insecurity festering in his head. He massages his hands over his face, leaning back in the hospital chair. "I kept you alive after your parents died. Helping you out of panic attack after panic attack. *You* were the one who left me."

"Because you haven't been there for me!" I yell, throwing my hands in the air.

The disgust in his voice has my mind shutting down, retreating, disappearing into my shell. If Lana is here, if I actually have the decision to go to Otium, I choose now. I ignore the incessant beeps of my heart rate and the searing pain in my forehead.

"I was on national TV, Jonah! I was making speeches. I was fighting for the last bit of hope my parents had." Letting out a breath, I drop my shoulders as fresh tears trail down my face. "I needed you, and you weren't by my side."

A soft tap on the door interrupts us. Lana, from freaking Otium, opens the door and starts walking toward us.

I try my best to keep my face straight, tightening my jaw to keep it from dropping, when all I want to do is let out a sob of relief.

I don't want to be here. I don't want to be around Jonah's anger and my family's anger and watch Alejandro become a shell of a person like me. I can't—my chest heaves as the sob rips through my throat. I tuck my feet in, wrapping my arms around my knees and resting my head atop them. My body shakes, my forehead hitting against my kneecaps in the rumble.

Alee's arms wrap around me briefly before I hear, "I'm sorry, Theo," whispered in my ear. Seconds later, a door slams.

"Theodore, are you okay?" Lana's voice is calm and melodic. "They both left."

I lift my head, trying to control my breathing. She almost looks angelic, her pale skin porcelain glows as if her presence on Earth only makes her more stunning. Probably because we have poisonous water and fucking stress.

Lana takes a seat next to me, where Jonah sat. "How are you feeling? Was the transition back here okay?" She watches the heart monitor as the beeping starts to slow.

I work myself through a series of controlled breaths, but I can't get Jonah's voice out of my head. The anger and resentment. If I leave, that'll be our last interaction for three months. I gasp before burying my head in my knees, focusing my eyesight on the blurred cream blanket.

"Can I get you anything?" Lana asks. The pads of her fingers type away on an iPad in her hand. Andrya wasn't lying about her being a nurse. "I cannot give you any more of the anxiety supplement, as the doctor wants you to be evaluated first. But I can answer questions or get you some tea? You still have a psych evaluation, and you have to talk to the police. After both of those, a decision will need to be made. You have to be discharged in a few hours to either Otium, the inpatient program here, or home."

I turn my head to rest my left ear on my knees and look over at Lana. I don't fit in at home right now, but if I can't get justice for my parents, I'm not sure I qualify for Otium.

"How do I fit into Otium's plan?" I ask.

"We didn't dive in a lot last night, but your program will be geared toward grief therapy versus the original program of the Otium Initiative. We want to help you before we ask you to help us."

"Why?"

"Your well-being has a butterfly effect on everyone around you, Theodore. You're a force of nature."

My cheeks warm at her compliment, but I don't feel worthy of it. Not even my boyfriend thinks I'm doing amazing things.

"I shouldn't tell you this until Andrya is ready, but I think you need it for your decision. Your situation is unique, as is your family. Andrya tried to recruit your parents when the Otium Initiative first started, but it was only two years into your parents' agency. They didn't want to step away or leave you and your brothers. Andrya then wanted to recruit your entire family. We had the plans all set; your parents seemed intrigued by the idea again. But the timelines didn't sync before the protest happened. Andrya's mission changed again. Originally, we wanted your family to help the future of Earth. Now, she wants Otium to help you. The volunteers from dinner yesterday? They are still on a mission to help Earth. They applied, they had interviews, and they were chosen. They have situations set up, so no one questions them being MIA for a few months. Your program is different. The volunteers will all be in a program together, and you'll be one-on-one with Flynn. We'll gear you up to help save Earth if that is the mission you want, but before that happens, we will take care of you."

What the hell. My parents knew of Otium. Or knew of this internship.

I try remembering if I saw any weird mail or pamphlets

throughout the years. I wonder if they were unsettled or excited about the idea of a new planet. If they did know about another planet, they did a hell of a job hiding it.

"Why didn't Andrya lead with that? Or try to recruit me the way she did my parents?" It doesn't make any sense. Lead with my parents wanting to be there, and I would have agreed in an instant. No second-guessing. No worrying about anyone here.

"I don't know why. The original plan was to recruit you when you turned eighteen. The moment she saw you in the hospital, she panicked and extracted. This has been a special case of hers for five years. You will have to discuss with her as to why that is."

Flynn's statement about me being eighteen checks out. If they happen to be lying, at least their stories are the same. Lana's phone in her scrub pocket beeps. She checks it quickly and then walks to the end of my bed, picking up a clipboard.

"The police don't want to wait anymore. They need to ask questions, and then your psych evaluation will be after that. Are you okay with that?" Lana asks.

I give her a meek smile because I don't have a choice. I haven't had a choice in much lately. Otium will be my choice—and even that feels tarnished.

Thirteen

One of Ellie's hands massages my scalp as the other clasps my right hand. My eyelids clench shut, trying to block out the room and focus on Ellie's comfort. Sam and Ellie somehow made it here in the chaos that is my hospital room. It's an added weight of having to figure out why they are here and how, but Ellie's fingertips soothe my overstimulation. Allowing me to fall into a lull before I lose it.

"Mr. Henning," Lana's voice is stern, talking to my uncle.

I haven't had a moment to breathe. It's been chaotic between the police investigation, the psych evaluation, and my uncle storming into my hospital room with my aunt, brothers, Sam, Ellie, and Lana in tow.

"With Theodore's prior history," Lana keeps her voice raised, "his parents' deaths, and this current incident, we deem it medically necessary for Theodore to participate in an inpatient therapy program. The police confirmed that if Theodore completes the program, they will drop all charges."

They'll do what? I don't even know what happened.

My investigation with the police was a blur of anxiety. They kept watching my heart monitor increase with every question they asked. That only made me feel more suspicious. They asked me to tell them what happened yesterday, but I had no memory, which gave me more anxiety, thinking I was lying to the police. It was such a mess that the woman officer, who didn't ask a question, ended the investigation. She handed me some tissues, told me not to worry, and shoved the other, angrier officer out the door.

I didn't have a chance to blow my nose before my psych evaluation started. The therapist and I could hear my uncle causing a fit in the hallway as he waited to come into my room. He just wanted to rage about how much of a "fucking idiot" I was and how therapy is a "crock of shit." If Otium didn't have a say, I probably would have been recommended inpatient care just for my physical panic reaction to hearing my uncle speak.

If Lana is telling the truth about the charges, though and Otium is approved as proof, I have no choice but to go. I can't afford to be charged as an adult.

My uncle huffs. "We can't afford counseling," he says.

It's a complete lie, but nothing new. My brothers and I barely see an ounce of his income. If anything, my brothers get more.

"We already have Theodore's insurance, and it covers most of the inpatient care. It would just be a couple hundred out of pocket," Lana informs him. My uncle barely holds back an eye roll.

"I can cover it!" I yell, finally opening my eyes.

Ellie's grip tightens on my hand. Everyone else in the room jumps, looking over at me as if they forgot I existed. I don't know why Otium is asking for Earth money, but my uncle isn't standing in my way if they need it.

"I have some money saved, and I'll get a job when I get out," I press on.

My aunt and uncle don't know that the couple hundred can be paid for with my social media.

"We will cover it, Theo," Sam offers, walking over to Ellie and me. He places his hands on her shoulders, looking down at me. He has a thick ginger beard now compared to his scruff I'm used to. His smile doesn't get lost in it, though. "This isn't something you should have to worry about. Go to therapy and just worry about therapy. Everything else will be sorted by the adults." Sam then eyes my aunt and uncle.

My aunt already shut herself down, as she often does when my uncle gets riled. She's been furiously texting away on her phone most of the visit, no doubt updating her gossip crew on how much of an inconvenience I am. I try to remember that my mom had faith in her. Apparently, she was a different person before my uncle came into her life. Now his backward thinking and control keep my aunt subdued and complicit.

My uncle laughs, gesturing to my brothers to get up. He looks between Sam and Ellie. "If you two want to come and save the day after you abandoned him, be my guest. I refuse to pay a dime for this counseling or ridiculous hospital stay."

My aunt, uncle, and brothers are almost out the door when my uncle turns back to me. "You're all about wanting to save the world, and you can't even save your goddamn self. You're pathetic."

My uncle storms out of the hospital room, my aunt and brothers following in tow.

Lana makes eye contact with me. "They need to sign papers before they disappear. Have you made a decision?"

She hasn't specifically said Otium, but just the brief

mention of something we're both hiding from Sam and Ellie has my hands growing clammy.

Now or never, Theo. Now or never.

"Yes, I'm going to therapy."

She narrows her eyes just slightly, and I confirm again with a nod. Her green eyes brighten before she dashes out the door.

"I'm proud of you," Ellie says, combing through my hair. "We are so sorry we left you. Things got really difficult, and it felt like we didn't have a choice. We didn't realize how much that might have hurt you."

I pick at the blanket covering my legs. I'm not ready to hear their apologies. Apologies that are conveniently timed with my downward spiral. Like the spiral is what made them recognize their abandonment.

"We will be here when you're out," Sam adds. "After treatment, if you would like to live with us, you're more than welcome to. We will figure it out with Laura and Jeffrey."

"And you will not use a dime of your own money to cover the hospital costs," Ellie chimes in.

I focus on the blanket, flicking a pill of thread with my finger. I'm afraid to open my mouth, to ask questions. I want to know, but I don't. If they had a great year, a good year even, disappearing from here, I don't want to know. Not now. At least not in the mental state I'm in.

It's my turn to disappear now.

Lana kicked Sam and Ellie out a few minutes later. We said our goodbyes, or they did. It seems on par with every person in my life to have an awful separation. In three months, everything will be different. Brighter. Happier. Lana escorted Sam and Ellie to finalize the hospital bill and said she'd be back to discharge me.

Before she comes back, I grab my phone that was charging on the bedside table. I scroll through the nightmare of notifications. Texts from people I barely know, social notifications of followers sending direct messages, emails upon emails of people checking in, news outlets wanting stories, notifications about the fundraising event. I swipe it all away to open Google.

In just under five minutes, I learned that a new planet *was* discovered out of our solar system in a parallel universe. NASA said while they are still investigating Mars, they have started investigating this new planet that already seems to have more potential. There is no name. But their image of this planet is the exact image from the video Andrya showed—just more pixilated. The reds, purples, scattered greens are all on a round planet. There are a few different land masses, but similar to how Earth used to be, there are fewer and larger masses.

They confirmed it is smaller than Earth, and they are tracking its days and rotations around Vita, what they've named the star that lights Otium—and the five other planets they've discovered in that solar system. Otium is the most similar to Earth in NASA's discoveries so far.

I place my phone facedown on my chest as I process the information. It's real. I'm going. Whether the morals of the planet are good or not is something I'll have to learn. But they wanted my parents. My parents were interested. And like the multi-verses in Marvel, this is my opportunity to be my own superhero.

I open my camera roll, scrolling through my photos until I reach the one I need. The picture of my parents and me at Majestic Park the day they died. We had our organized t-shirts on and posters at our feet. Sam and Ellie were supposed to be there that day, but Ellie wasn't feeling well, even though she was perfectly fine the day before at our last family barbecue. They weren't even there for me that day.

"Theodore?" Lana asks, opening the door. She walks over to my side, iPad in her hand again. She quickly checks my vitals. Her pastel green scrubs are wrinkled, and her hair is now in the tiniest ponytail at the base of her neck. "Before we head back to Otium, is there anything else you'd like to know?"

Oof. Where do I even begin?

She takes a seat next to me once she's finished with the iPad.

"You said that Andrya tried to recruit my parents. But can you tell me why? I know we're activists, but so are thousands of other people."

She studies me for a moment before situating herself cross-legged in the chair.

"Personal connection. I can't tell you names, so please don't ask. But friends of your parents had a baby, and that baby is Andrya's mom."

Friends of my parents.

"Andrya is trying to create more of a personal connection with her past as the Otium Initiative grows. When she found out your parents passed, she knew she still wanted you to help, but as the year went on, Andrya thought it would be best if we offered you help first."

I don't know whether I should be flattered or creeped out.

"When was or is Andrya's mother born?"

"Five months ago."

Most of my parents' friends are closer in age to them. They wouldn't be having children now. My eyes shoot to Lana, and she holds up a hand. There is only one possible answer.

"Let's move on."

But if it's them, that can explain so much. Is it possible they know about Otium, that they went there too?

"Theodore, please ask another question, or we will head out." Lana's tone is stern as she fidgets with a smartwatch on her wrist—just like Flynn's.

I sigh. I can dig more on Otium. What I can't do is help my brothers, no matter how ungrateful they may be.

"My brothers need to get grief counseling, too. I can't be transported to another planet and leave my brothers behind."

Lana is silent as her brows furrow. "Your brothers aren't eligible for the Otium Initiative."

"No. They need help here. To actually grieve my parents' deaths and work through my aunt's and uncle's trauma. If I'm supposed to come back to Earth to help change it, it'll be a hell of a lot harder if my brothers aren't getting healthy too."

Lana nods and pulls a device out of her pocket that's similar to what Flynn and Andrya had. The screen doesn't turn into a hologram as she types into the device, nor is it projected. "We will wait to see what Andrya says." Lana shakes the device like she's letting me know a message was sent.

In the meantime, she goes over the Otium Initiative. When I go back, I'll have the same room in the apartment building. Everything will be covered when I'm there. I clarified about the money conversation from earlier, and Lana said the money was only needed to cover this hospital cost— which Sam and Ellie already paid for. I will have group counseling with the other members, but like she said earlier, most of my training and lessons will be with Flynn. He is my mentor for the entire three months. Because I'm still in high school, I do have a curriculum to complete that will already be a part of my schedule. It's schoolwork that would be given to me in a normal inpatient program. It'll be completed through the Otium device and sent through their technology to get it back to my school. The planet to planet connection is confirmed when Lana's device beeps, and Andrya approves the counseling, saying that she will make sure it happens.

"Anything else you need before we head out?" Lana asks.

"Ten minutes of privacy?" I ask, and she glances at her watch.

"Ten minutes. No more." With that, she walks out.

I flip the camera on my phone, so I'm looking at myself. I'm utterly disgusting and in desperate need of a shower. It's almost repulsing that Flynn saw me like this. My gross matted and tangled hair, my splotchy, greasy skin. I even have a few pimples forming on my chin.

I don't have time to do anything about it, though. I press the red record button.

"Hi, everyone, it's been a wild twenty-four hours. I'm not entirely sure what's happened, but I just want you all to know that I am so grateful for the support you've given me this last year. All the time and money that's been donated has been out of this world. I never in a million years thought I'd have so many people in my corner.

With that said, I am signing off for a bit. I am going to therapy to take care of myself and process this past year. I don't know if or when I'll be back, but I wanted you all to hear it from me first.

Keep peacefully fighting. Take care of yourselves. And I love you."

I send the video to Alejandro, asking him to post it for me. I also update him that I'll be in therapy for a few months. I tell him I love him and that I'll see him soon.

I contemplate calling Jonah, but instead, opt to just send a text message:

To Jonah: *Thank you for being my caretaker, but we need to officially end this. I'm sorry. I'm sorry we've lost sight of who we were supposed to be. I'm going to therapy. I'll be gone for three months. Maybe we can talk after. Maybe you'll have moved on. Either way, I love you and I wish you the best. Take care of yourself.*

Soon after, I'm discharged. Lana plays the role of rolling me out of the room in a wheelchair, going on a maze of the hospital before she pushes me into an empty room.

The dark room is instantly lit with the click of the remote, a rectangular golden portal appearing. There is no seeing the other side through these portals like Marvel's Endgame. Instead, it looks like vibrating, electric golden pixels spiraling. Studying the portal is eerier this time, as I truly have no memory of stepping foot into it to leave Otium. Once a body part reaches in, do I get sucked away?

"Are you ready?" Lana asks, reaching out her hand to help me up from the wheelchair.

I stand with her, but now it's real. I doubt the one-week rule works for me. I'm signed up for a three-month program regardless of what planet I'm on.

"We have to go, Theodore. We don't have time."

Within a second, she steps toward the portal, her foot disappearing beyond. Once she entirely vanishes, my body jerks forward, and I'm sucked into the abyss. Lana is nowhere around me. She isn't holding my hand or in the distance. I 100% do not remember this experience. I try to reach out as my skin stretches back against my face at the pressure. I'm not sure if I'm falling upward or downward, but I don't have control. I can't reach out. It's a silent void of nothingness around me. Despite the look of electricity, there isn't a single sound of static.

Fourteen

"Welcome back, Theodore."

A wave of warmth trickles through my body at the sound of his voice. I open my eyes, greeted by the light of vita and Flynn's smiling face. He's sitting in front of me as if he has been waiting for this moment since I left. For all I know, he has. His hand holds out vitaglasses that I gratefully put on.

I inhale the wonderful, crisp, fresh air and let out a long exhale. Starting to feel woozy, I lay back in the grass. The sky is again nearly white with no cloud coverage. The soft stems of grass curve around my body, tickling my bare skin. Before I left my hospital room, Lana had a fresh pair of clothes, jeans and a black t-shirt, for me to change into. She even gave me a moment to wash my face.

I focus on the sky, watching as we rotate, similar to how Earth did. The thoughts in my mind start to relax. *I made it, Mom and Dad. I'm going to make you proud.* The thought brings tears to my eyes. They wouldn't have considered this situation if it weren't safe. My gut tells me this is right.

Flynn lies beside me, shielding his eyes from the vita.

"You have blue skies on Earth, right? Are they ever this vibrant?"

"Vibrant? Your sky is white." The warm air and silence try to lull me to sleep.

"Right." He lets out a breathy laugh. "I'm sorry I'm not better prepared. Your eyes will adjust to this planet in a few days. Then you'll see we've got spectacular violet skies."

"Why can't I see them now?" That sounds incredible. It makes sense why there was so much purple on the planet picture. I wonder if the ocean is purple too.

"Humans on Earth can't see the violet light; their eyesight can only process up to the blue light. However, there is a vitamin in our soil that seeps into the plants we eat and allows us to see violet. It's been studied, and it's good for us. I've never known anything different. My grandparents do, though, and they talk about how Otium looked when they first arrived, and then, how majestic it was when they started eating proper meals."

"That's cool," I say.

I wonder how long it'll take me to wrap my head around everything here. Everything that happened in the past few days. I'm five seconds away from asking to go to my room, but if I do, I likely won't come out. I'm my own cheerleader on this planet. I don't have Alejandro motivating me forward. I don't have Jonah dragging me out of bed, shoving food down my throat, making sure I stay hydrated. If I lock myself in my room here, I'm done for. There is no saving—only crippling depression.

Flynn rustles beside me, and my body tenses. I'm not ready to move, nor am I ready to have any serious conversations. Flynn doesn't say a word, though. As time passes, my heart rate anticipates that he'll open his mouth at any moment while my eyes wrestle with drowsiness. It's enough to send my body into a full-blown panic.

I don't dare turn my head to see if he is looking at me. I don't want confirmation that I'm being watched. But if I am, he's sure to see the sweat outlining my face. Even my t-shirt isn't enough to keep my body from overheating on this spring-like day. The vita is strong.

A humming sound causes my body to convulse. The hum doesn't miss a beat. It maintains a melody that I can feel through my bloodstream. A wave of heat followed by a coolness travels through my veins, giving me the strength to prop myself up on my elbows and look over at Flynn.

His eyes are closed; there's not a crease on his face—total relaxation. In rhythm, his chest rises and falls. I'm captivated by the movement of his Adam's apple as the melody overwhelms my senses. If he's aware I'm watching him, he doesn't make it known.

I allow my body to fall back onto the grass and take in the melody. Closing my eyes, I succumb to the sound. Allowing the rhythm to enter one ear and out the other. I clench my fingers and toes, unclenching each one until I fall into a cycle of deep breaths.

I don't know how long we lay there, side-by-side. Long enough for me to know that sleep won't come—or well, I won't allow it in an open field on a new planet.

Opening my heavy eyes, I sit up and look around at the vast flatland not overtaken by houses and commercial buildings. This will now be my home. A place I can breathe fresh, clean air. A place where I can hear the slight breeze tickle my ears instead of being drowned out by a horn or garbage truck. A place where those who are angry or I've made angry are in an entirely different universe. Far away from my spirals and their chaos.

The humming stops. I tilt my head toward Flynn. His eyes are open now, and a smile forms on his lips.

"Pretty peaceful, huh?"

I nod. I don't trust my words to keep the peace.

"Would you like to stay here a while longer? Or would you like to settle in?"

I contemplate the scenarios. Settling in doesn't necessarily mean I'm alone, but it does mean the start of this initiative program. If we remain out here, far enough from the town, maybe we remain in limbo. Not living my Earth life, not learning a new life. Just being.

I look down at Flynn, and he sits up, dusting his hands off from the ground.

"Say what's in your head," he says. "One thing you'll learn here is that we try to say what's on our mind because we learn not to be nervous about the outcome."

I refrain from raising a brow because I'm pretty certain he was nervous the last time I saw him. Instead, I give him a light laugh. "Can we just be? I don't want to be Theo, the activist, right now. I want to be Theo, the boy who needs a moment."

"Absolutely." Flynn grins, jumping up and reaching out his hand. "The only requirement today is that you try to relax and enjoy yourself. May I show you one of my favorite places?"

I open my mouth to argue because I never specified no town.

"I promise there are no people. Just me." His smile grows as he lifts his brow.

I wonder if my pet peeves and anxiety intricacies are in my file. It rattles me that he can learn about me through a file. I'd rather he ask me personally, but that didn't work yesterday, and honestly, I probably wouldn't share much.

"Sure." I give him a small nod, taking his hand to help me up. I sway a bit, and his arm on my elbow steadies me. I don't know how long we were lying there, but long enough for me to remember that I didn't stand when I arrived, nor did I really stand back on Earth.

"You okay?" I just nod, and with a grin, he walks past me, over to our bikes, just a few feet away. "We have to get to the train because this place is in the Valley."

My heart skips a beat in excitement, and I try to hide my smile. Another location isn't what I anticipated. Though, I'm psyched to go toward a location that looks more similar to New York.

The bike ride is a good half-mile away in the opposite direction of the Valley, but I don't think I'd have the energy to bike all the way there.

Once at the station, we store our bikes and wait for the train to arrive. In one swift "swoosh," the train silently comes to a stop a few minutes later. No screeching engines or wheels rattling on the metal. No one else enters or gets off when the three train doors open. We have one cab entirely to ourselves.

Flynn pulls out his device, taps a button, and a holographic card appears. He scans it on a machine inside the train twice. When I have space to think, I'll need to ask him about money here. As he pockets the device, the doors close, and the train zooms faster than the Metro-North. I imagine it's a similar speed to the Eurostar, if not faster. What seemed like miles away is only a few minutes.

As we step off the train, a few people get on, waving and smiling as they do, before the train leaves the track again, heading back toward the Flatlands.

The two of us leave the station; each minute of silence makes me appreciate Flynn more. Every step brings us closer toward this valley, with mountain ranges easily exceeding peaks higher than any mountain in the Northeast of America. I would love to snowboard down one of the peaks—if they even have snow here.

The farther we walk, the more uneven the ground gets. I'm sweating by the time I see a body of water. Every step, every breath of the fresh grass and moist air, makes me feel more at home. A small part of me is disappointed that my time here is located in the Flatlands.

"So this is the town of Laurel. They have the highest population. Most people settled in a location similar to where they came from on Earth. However, some ventured off—like my family. This," Flynn gestures toward the water with two mountains on each side, "looks similar to the pictures I see of where my great grandparents lived in New York."

He never shared that he was from New York when I mentioned it the day before, but it makes sense with the new information from Lana. While my parents have friends in other states, his great-grandparents are likely from my town. I don't think I can share that information, though. He told me he didn't know why I was special, just that I was.

"Is this a river or a creek?" I ask, trying to divert my mind. The water is shallow enough that it's crystal clear.

"The Laurel River," he says. "It's quite vast, traveling through the Valley and beyond. We are at the beginning, which is why it's more narrow. There are sections that are too wide to swim across. This river supposedly reaches the ocean, but a portion that most have never traveled to. East of the Flatlands, we have the Oceanic location. Pacifica, where there are sandy beaches and a ton of oceanfront living, is another popular town. Otium is filled with bodies of water, but a lot is relatively unexplored because of our population."

To our far left of the river, a family of deer roams, eating the grass, and a flock of birds fly above. I pause to watch the deer. The first wildlife I've seen since I've been here. Flynn did say they lived here more than the Flatlands, but it's still somewhat startling. Their antlers are more curved here, and their coat is a darker brown.

"My grandmother wanted to get more into farming and crops when she moved here, so they settled in the Flatlands. I really think I would have liked it in New York, though. I find myself in the Valley quite often."

"Would you consider moving?" I ask, hopeful we may spend more time here.

We reach scattered rocks nestled at the beginning of the river, and Flynn stops walking.

"Possibly, but becoming a mentor in the Valley is harder, and because I didn't grow up in this location, I'd have more hurdles in my way. As a mentor, I feel like I'm a part of something bigger than myself." He points toward rocks. "C'mon! It's this way." He jumps onto a rock and hops effortlessly from one to another, crossing the river and making his way to a sturdy rock slab. "Just be careful. Some of the rocks tend to move on you."

Tentatively, I step upon each small rock. At home, it was usually dirt and a groomed path I hiked or walked. It was rare that I encountered loose rock—at least where Jonah and I have ventured. The last rock slips beneath me, twisting my ankle, threatening my gravity. Flynn grips my elbow, pulling me forward and onto the flat rock surface.

"One last bit, and we are there." His hand moves from my elbow down my arm, clasping my hand. He doesn't even look behind him to smirk or raise a brow, wondering if it's okay. It's almost as if he doesn't recognize a handhold could be seen as something entirely different from just helping lead the way.

My mind flashes to Alejandro holding my hand, and Jonah's implications. *Oh.*

I focus my attention on the ground below me. The air becomes overwhelmingly moist as we walk along a rock wall embedded in the mountain. Trickling water grows louder with each step. We finally stop in front of a pitch-black cave entrance.

I grip Flynn's hand tighter as he leads us inside. "Is there any light in here?" I ask, taking off the vitaglasses. There doesn't seem to be any crevice letting in light.

"Yes. Stay still." His hand leaves mine as he walks over wet rock slabs.

My eyes refuse to adjust in the dark. It isn't until there is a flicker of light in the corner that I can see fragments of the small cavern.

The candlelight illuminates Flynn's smile, his eyes bright with excitement. He holds out his hand, steadying the candle in his other. "Be careful. While the rock in here is still, it is slippery sometimes."

I apply more pressure to each footstep, being cautious. The candle barely highlights the dripping limestone surrounding us. It's impressive that I haven't hit my head on any yet.

In elementary school, we visited a cavern. There was an entire tour dedicated to the history of the cavern and washing off small rocks to take home as souvenirs. I want to take the candle and discover the depths of this one. There is something more intimate about this space, not being surrounded by a tour guide or other children. This cavern, I imagine, is relatively untouched.

"Here, take a seat." Flynn tugs my hand down a little, and I sit beside him on a bench-level, cold rock surface.

He begins to rustle around next to me, and suddenly three more candles are lit. He kneels on the ground, dumping out a stash of what looks to be snacks from a backpack.

"Come here often?" I smirk.

I kneel on the ground in front of me, sorting through the pile. There are different cookies and chocolate, even some sort of paper carton drink. What's more fascinating is the fact that none of the cookies or chocolate are mass-produced. They are all in glass containers like my mom's Pyrex containers.

"I try to. No one else has discovered it—at least, no one messes with my stuff. When I do make the trek, I want it to be enjoyable."

There's a stack of magazines in a woven picnic basket to my right. My curiosity gets the best of me as I maneuver my body closer. They aren't *just* magazines; they are first edition Captain America and Spider-Man Marvel comic books.

"Holy shit. These made it all the way from Earth?" I exclaim. I've always wanted these.

He's immediately right next to me, grinning wide. "You like Marvel?"

I have to laugh. He's got no idea what Marvel truly is.

The thought has me pausing. *What must it be like to live in the wake of Earth?* From my impressions, he hears and sees what Earth was like; the people here try to emulate a healthier version of it. But that's all it will be, a different version.

"I love Marvel. Especially Spider-Man. He's my favorite." I start to flip through the first edition of Spider-

Man. I used to read the comics when I was in middle school, but I haven't since I started high school and life became more hectic. However, this isn't a comic I've ever gotten my hands on. "How do you have this?"

"My grandparents were massive Marvel nerds, as they like to call themselves. They had a keepsake box of things that they desperately needed to bring with them if they ever moved—or, well, traveled to a new planet."

His grandparents. His grandmother, who was born this year, will grow to love Marvel. My mind tries to process what set of my parents' friends love Marvel. Only a few come to mind.

The dripping water focuses me. I loosen my grip on the comic books.

"You really should keep these in a dry place," I say.

"I just brought them here earlier today, anticipating bringing you here. I was going to ask if you liked Marvel—thought it might be a good conversation starter. But yeah, I'll bring them back tonight. Unless you'd like to have them while you're here?"

I almost dropped the comic books at his suggestion. This poor boy has no idea what he's holding onto, keeping them in a damp cavern and then offering them up to a stranger?

"Do you have movies from Earth here? Or, well, do you ever watch movies or television?" I ask.

"Yes, we have quite a collection of movies and television shows from Earth."

I smile, flipping through the Spider-Man comic. At the very least, if I'm ever homesick, I have the movies and these comics.

"Suggestion," I start, giving him a smirk. "If you mentor

me on life and Otium, may I mentor you on Marvel, and why you're a fool not to cherish these?"

He laughs but nods. "That's exactly what I was hoping for. My parents like Marvel as much as any other movie—but don't really understand the hype. I've always wanted to get a take from someone who truly loves them. Like, why, out of everything, did my grandparents find these important to transfer to a new planet?"

I gently place the comic books back in the picnic basket, cringing at the idea of them sitting in here a moment longer. After all these years, a damn cavern can't be the end of them.

I sit back on the cool floor against the bench. Flynn joins me with a container of chocolate.

"What's the story here? Why is this your favorite place?" I ask as he opens the container. Circular mounds of what looks like dark chocolate stare up at me.

Flynn takes a chocolate and then offers me one. I wait for him to eat his first.

"I feel like there is so much pressure sometimes to create this perfect world where nothing goes wrong. Sometimes I just need a break from it. Don't get me wrong, I love what I'm doing, and I'm passionate about the Otium Initiative, but I think striving for perfection creates unwanted chaos. I don't think perfection exists." He pops the chocolate in his mouth.

"If your world was perfect, my introduction to this planet would have been executed differently," I offer, taking a bite into the solid piece. The chocolate melts in my mouth. *This* is heaven.

"Case-in-point." He gives me an awkward smile. "I apologize again. I had a long talk with my parents, asking why my mom handled things the way she did. I didn't get any information aside from program updates, but my mom did apologize. She really didn't want you to be extracted like that, but said she didn't have a choice."

Lana's secret weighs heavily on my chest. If Andrya isn't telling Flynn the truth, I most certainly can't.

"You don't have to answer," he continues, "but was being home okay?"

I look over at him as he glances down and inspects the other snacks before locking eyes with mine. Being home was disastrous.

"It was okay," I say, adjusting my t-shirt over the slightly too big waistband. I hesitate to give him more than that.

He offers me another chocolate instead of a verbal response. I appreciate his moments to end a conversation and not push for more. It's something I used to be awful at. I can't even say I'm good at it now. I just haven't had the energy to pry more out of my friends—especially when they've taken over that role.

We share chocolate back and forth until we've finished the glass container. While the pasta was something incredible, I have to admit that the chocolate in my hometown is better. While these melts in your mouth, my hometown chocolate is creamier, and I always have it with peanut butter filling.

After the chocolate depletes, I take one of the candles and give myself a tour of the cave. It is quite small—nothing in comparison to where I went on school field trips. But it is quaint. There is even a small running stream that continues past where the cavern allows us to travel. On a school field trip, we went to one cavern where we had a boat trip into the cave, but nothing like that could work in this space.

Flynn lays down on the rock floor while I walk around and observe. He only mentions facts here and there when I arrive at a specific part of the cave. Questions keep bubbling up in me to ask, wanting to know more about him and his life, but I force them away. I like silence. It feels comfortable and safe.

As I make my way back to Flynn, my stomach growls. He pulls out his device. The screen lights up, but this time, it doesn't hover in the air.

"It sounds like it's time for dinner!" Flynn sits up and starts to gather the snacks back into the backpack.

"What time is it?" I'm not sure if the answer will help me, but some semblance of a schedule is needed. After having a schedule dictate my every move for nearly a year, my brain feels foggy and disconnected without one.

"Six in the evening," he says as he reaches for the comic books and puts them in the backpack, too.

I left the hospital around seven in the evening. Now it's nearly ten Earth time, and I'm just about to eat dinner. This time change is nothing like traveling to another country, but it'll take some getting used to.

Fifteen

The restaurant Flynn takes us to is only a few minutes away from the cavern. It's right at the beginning of where the town truly begins. A few structures—same reddish clay—are in immediate view before the town expands outward. The population has to be bigger here just at how this town is constructed. All dirt roads, though, these roads lead to more streets than it seems Olive has.

As we get closer, everyone around us speaks Spanish, and mariachi music floats through the streets. The area is vibrant, filled with laughter, music, and cheers. A few people greet Flynn and ask him how his mother is as we pass by, though they switch seamlessly to English. Flynn responds to each person with a big friendly, politician smile, cheery voice, and fluent Spanish. He may not believe in perfection, but he seems to have the personality down pat.

We immediately get a table at this small, brightly lit restaurant—the first restaurant I have come across. Colorful lights line the low wooden fencing around the property. Mariachi music is coming from a live band in the corner of the restaurant. There are around fifteen tables, all within the fencing. No coverage for precipitation or vitalight. A tiny domed structure has "Casa Mendoza" hanging in front of it. It looks just big enough for a kitchen and a bathroom.

A few of the tables are taken by people who look around our age or are just a little older.

"You speak Spanish?" I ask, picking up the menu on the table.

"Yeah, mostly fluent in Spanish, Italian, and French, but I've also picked up enough German to communicate. Pretty bad at Mandarin, but I'm learning."

"Wow. That's impressive." I'm genuinely amazed. Though, I shouldn't be. Accept others, make them comfortable, and learn from them, right? That's what helps make the world better? "I'm almost fluent in Spanish, but that is more of a necessity for me," I offer. I wouldn't be able to volunteer in my area without being able to communicate with half the population.

"You'll be one step ahead here if you're already proficient. We try to learn multiple languages from a young age to be able to understand everyone and make everyone feel more at ease. We aren't all fluent in each other's languages, but it's the effort that counts."

I nod and look down at the menu again. I'm not ready to discuss programs yet. The menu is in Spanish, and this place serves authentic Mexican food. Don't get me wrong, I love Tex Mex as much as anyone in America, but you can never beat the real thing.

"So, are there many restaurants on this planet? It doesn't seem like Olive has any," I ask, taking a deep breath as a waft of onions, cumin, and coriander surrounds us. To be fair, I have no idea what Olive has.

"Olive has its restaurants all on one side of town. You haven't been over there yet. There are four in Laurel, plus the communal eatery. Olive has two, and we have the communal eatery as well."

"Each location gets to decide?"

"Yeah, each town decides what is in their community. There is a majority vote. So this restaurant had enough people wanting it around, so it was built by the community."

"Huh."

I try to imagine a community in the United States that would come together and build a business they weren't going to make a profit on. They are few and far between.

"And you pay?"

"With something like paper money? No. We have a point system. It's based on good deeds. Ideally, we all have the same amount of points to spend. The leaders follow the point system, too, which holds them accountable for their own good deeds. If a leader loses too many good points, they are removed from their position, regardless of election time.

"While it isn't required to have a job, many still do. Though people only have jobs they enjoy. If you are employed, you gain points by doing your job. You can earn additional points for doing good deeds for the community. For example, I get a specific amount of points for being your mentor. If my friend needed help building something and I offered my time, I'd also get extra points. The idea was to create a system that was fair but still motivated people."

"And what about those who can't work?"

The waiter greets us with a grin and places water glasses on our table before walking away. I immediately gulp the water down. I hadn't realized how parched I was, but the chocolate, time travel, and our trip here apparently took a lot out of me. Oh, and the awful water I didn't drink much of on Earth.

I glance over at the waiter to see what he's up to, and he holds up a pitcher, giving me a nod.

Flynn takes a sip before he speaks. "You mean elderly, disabled, or those with medical conditions?"

I nod, and as I do, the waiter is refilling my glass. I thank him before taking another few sips of water.

"Whoever wants a job can have a job, and the job will be catered to whatever needs a person has. With that said, everyone can do something nice for someone, right? While it may look different for everyone, no matter if you're elderly, disabled, or have a medical condition, there is always some sort of way you can bring good into the world."

"So, it's a motivation for people to be nice to each other? As humans, we lack compassion without reward?" I tilt my head.

While I'm hesitant about the idea that some people don't get left behind somehow, the idea makes sense. We *do* lack compassion. Humans without motivation wouldn't have a thriving society.

"For a lot of people, yeah, the extra motivation of points does help. Just like any system, we have tiers. It's inevitable with the human species. But we don't have poverty like on Earth. Those who choose not to work or don't work often do more around the community to make up extra points. For the elderly, there are two factors. They get a base amount of points for the good deeds they did in their lifetime, and then they can continuously earn points by doing good deeds. For those with medical conditions or disabilities, who cannot work or don't like the job opportunities offered, there is a stipend, and then their good deeds get added to this. Every year, the stipend is reconsidered. If you were deemed by the community to not be kind or helpful, you would lose the stipend. Same with any person. If I choose to be an asshole and the community votes, I will lose a significant amount of points."

I'm hesitant to believe that the stipend is actually anything better than what the United States offers for unemployment or disability. The word can be used, but that doesn't mean the points reflect a similar job wage.

"We have luxury here too, like anywhere else, but that also costs more points. But everyone has the ability to gain those points. The idea being if you're a luxurious person and want to showcase that, you're likely one of the most helpful people around too. The system was originally created to weed out those who somehow made it to Otium on false pretenses."

I need to dissect the program more because there has to be something wrong with it. It could start out with the best intentions, but so did FDR's social security plan for retirement, and that's money I'll never see even though I have and will pay into it again. And what happens when someone is tired from a day of work and then sees someone collecting points without having done anything? I don't have an issue with it, but many Americans have been quite vocal about unemployment benefits.

The waiter interrupts my thought process, asking for our order. I order the only thing I recognize I've had before in Spanish: tacos callejeros de verduras con frijoles. Flynn requests the same.

"How are the points calculated? What is considered a good deed? Can I say that your coral shirt really brings out your eyes and get points?" I ask. The countless questions spiral through my mind.

He looks down as he blushes. I wasn't lying with the compliment. His coral button-up really does bring out his blue eyes against his tanned skin. I hope that I can walk away with golden skin like his—though that may be suspicious coming back from "therapy."

"Compliments like that do get you points, but very minimal. That's the bare basics of being a nice person. It's an honor system. At the end of each week, you report how many compliments you gave someone. One compliment is a tenth of a point."

"And how many points is this meal?"

"5 points for this dish. The most expensive thing on this menu is 10 points."

I nod, doing the quick math in my head. Fifty compliments for one meal that can be pretty steep. Though, it's easy to just throw around compliments, especially in an honor system.

"The thing with compliments is they are often the most suspicious. At a community vote, if your morals were questioned and people found out you've been saying compliments left and right without meaning, it will be questioned."

That all makes sense. "How much to help build a home?" I ask. A home seems like the ultimate gesture.

"Depends. The average one-story home can give you up to 50,000 points."

That's a lot of tacos.

"And the average job? Like our waiter. What does he get for being here?"

Flynn glances over at the waiter, who is laughing at another table. He's even pulled up a chair to sit with them.

"Does he get any points deducted for not doing his job?" I ask. How unprofessional to sit down and stop working.

"Why would he get points deducted?" Flynn asks, and when I look at him, his brows are furrowed.

"Because he's not paying attention to the kitchen or customers or cleaning the tables? He's socializing with what seems like his friends on the clock." This would never fly in America. Waiting tables can be one of the most stressful jobs.

"Is there anything you need? Would you like a different drink?" Flynn asks.

"No, I'm fine. Don't change the subject."

Flynn laughs, sitting back in his chair. "I'm not. Everyone is fine and satisfied. The waiter doesn't need to do anything right now, so he can relax."

At that, the waiter checks his device in his apron and jumps up, walking toward the building. Within a minute, our plates are delivered. The waiter asks us if we'd like anything else, if it all looks exactly how we wanted it, and when Flynn says we're great, the waiter walks away.

Flynn grins at me, and my shoulders deflate a bit. My Americanism is getting to my head.

"The waiter will get points deducted at the end of the week if he does something he shouldn't. Like, if he ignored that our food wasn't ready, then he wouldn't be doing his job. But he stopped mid-conversation to deliver our food, checked in with us, and is now checking on the other tables. We don't assume the worst in people from the get-go."

I look down at my plate, focusing on the vegetable street tacos in front of me. My bad habit is always assuming the worst in everyone recently.

We sit in silence for a while, eating the tacos, which are just like I imagined, absolutely incredible. Every single flavor is prominent. The corn shells aren't bland or flaky. There isn't too much onion, nor are the beans overcooked. I'd order another round, but I don't have control over my points.

Speaking of points, I wonder if I will have control of my own or if my entire time here is controlled by my presence with Flynn. He said he hopes we become friends, but how can we be friends when he's paid to be near me?

"Are you working now, or is it a good deed to make sure I get fed?" I ask once my meal is finished. For the first time in a while, I don't feel famished.

Flynn rests his chin in his fist, his elbows on the table. His eyes focus on me for a moment. "Both."

I sink back in my chair. That's not the answer I wanted, but that is my reality. I wasn't brought here to make new friends, to replace my damaged life.

"It was my job to make sure you arrived safely," he continues. "I was a friend showing you my favorite place. It's a good deed and something a friend should do to make sure you eat."

Cool. Sounds like another complicated, exhausting friendship.

"You said I was your first student?" I ask. Maybe he doesn't understand the balance either.

He smiles with a nod, sitting back in his own seat. The waiter removes our plates and refills our water.

"My first solo mentee, yes. While in training, I helped two mentors. A total of four people in the initiative so far. Though our time together will be different from my training."

Because I'm so goddamn special, I'm sure. I think back to what Lana said. Everyone else is in a specific program together, whereas Flynn is my go-to person. It makes me wonder if those mentors have less responsibilities than Flynn—even more downtime. Like now, does he want to be spending his time having dinner with his work responsibility instead of hanging out with his friends?

"Different because you're also my babysitter?" I blurt.

There's a flicker of confusion on his face.

"Have you brought the other people here?" I don't know why my voice sounds strained as I ask the question. It really shouldn't matter. It's just a goddamn meal. But I don't want to be looked at like a burden or a good deed, nor do I want to be watched over like I can't take care of myself.

"Not on the first night, but throughout their time, yes. This is one of the best places on Otium. I took you here tonight because you're here for more of a personal experience. We wanted you to get settled. Today, the others in the initiative started their program introductions, but your timeline is different."

I don't want to be different, I want to scream. My mind is jumbled and confused. I need sleep. I need alone time. I'm frustrated, and a part of me doesn't understand why. I want to know why my parents were going to come here and what the hell *my* program is about. If I'm extracted for my activism, then I don't want to have a personal experience here. I want to fight instead of having a mentor who talks about friendship, but I have to because it's interlaced with responsibility and payment. I don't want to wonder when Flynn is a friend and when he's in charge. I want a friend I can truly lean on, open up to, heal through.

"I never asked for this," I mumble. I'm depleted by the words leaving my mouth.

Flynn leans forward, resting his forearms on the table. "I know," he says softly. I feel his sincerity as we lock eyes. He's empathetic, and I hate it. "I want to be able to do whatever I can to help this transition." He reaches his hand across the table. "I need you to lean on me and be honest about what you need, or this time here will be miserable."

His fingers swipe mine before I yank my hands back, placing them in my lap.

The rush of electricity from his touch has my blood boiling. I want to believe them and fall right into his trap, but he's still the son of the leader.

"I'm sorry." His hand retracts, and his Adam's apple bobs with a gulp.

I need comfort and safety, but right now, it's just a reminder of what I've lost.

"We didn't make a great impression, and we will fix that. I promise. But also remember, Otium is doing you a favor."

A favor? Bull-fucking-shit, they are doing me a favor.

I'm lightyears away from my support system. I'm away from my followers who have supported me. I'm missing my parents' fundraiser for the first time. Andrya had the opportunity to bring my family here—a situation that could have saved my parents' lives, and they didn't.

The realization has my body swaying. My stomach drops. I push myself away from the table, my chair screeching behind me.

I take off running. I despise running with my entire being, but I have to get away from here. I contemplate going back to the cavern, sitting on the cold, uncomfortable rock to breathe through the anxiety rising within me. But Flynn will find me there.

I hit the cavern without him following me. I don't know if it's because he's giving me space or if he's caught up paying for the meal. But I take the opportunity to pause for a moment and breathe deep. I may be fed and hydrated, but my exhaustion has my legs heavy.

I see the path we took earlier, just barely sectioned off in the grass, signifying a path to the train station. I could just jump on the train and ride the entire—*fuck, I don't have points.*

"Theodore!" Flynn's voice has me breaking out into another run, following the path to the train.

He's a fucking track star. Note to self: never believe I can outrun him. He's in line with me before I can process how to speed up or slow down. My lungs clench as my throat aches for water. I try to swat him away, get him to back off, but his hand grasps my arm, and we both come tumbling to a stop, face first in the grass.

I cough as the grass tickles my skin and fills my mouth. I try to turn over, but the effort has me gasping for any particle of oxygen I can find.

"We need to get you into shape." He chuckles.

It takes everything in me to not kick him. Instead, I settle on a glare. We aren't racing for fun. This isn't a laughing matter.

"Better yet, maybe not. I may need to catch you again." There is no difficulty in his words. *How the hell is he breathing normally right now?*

I remain silent, trying to steady my breath. I use my limited energy to huff into a seated position.

"Why did you run away?" he asks, taking the backpack off his back. He opens it and searches through it.

I muster all the spit I can in my mouth and swallow hard to moisten my esophagus. I clear my throat as he tries to hand me a reusable water bottle, but I swat it away. "O-Otium is not doing me a single favor." I try my hardest to lace my panting with anger.

Flynn has the audacity to furrow his brows. As he opens his mouth, I push myself to stand, wheezing as my legs strain.

"My choice to be here was taken from me when I was

threatened with the options of Otium or get arrested. Now I'm separated from my brothers. I lost my boyfriend. I don't have my best friend. I was kidnapped to a planet that claims they have my best interests, but I know it's manipulative. I don't have a choice to walk away after I'm healed. For a planet who has the ability to track me for at least five years, they also have the ability to end me at a moment's notice."

I offer Flynn a pause to interrupt me. Tell me that's not true while I catch my breath. He sits there silently. His arms draped around his raised knees, just listening.

Rage vibrates through my veins. I want to shove him, force the energy out of my fingers, but instead, I clench my fists.

"Why does everyone else have the opportunity to volunteer here? To have ample warning before they travel to another planet? Even my parents were going to have time to process it all!" I scream. "So why me? Why is my situation so desperate? Is your mom trying to make up for not rushing my parents? Make up for their fucking deaths? She probably could have saved my parents' lives if she just extracted them at a moment's notice!" I gasp for air, leaning over with my hands on my thighs. I need that water bottle he gave me, but I'm too stubborn to reach for it.

My heartbeat pulses through the veins in my neck. Jonah often steps away when my one vein pops out; Flynn doesn't even flinch. He just seems confused.

"Your parents knew about Otium?" His words are soft. He drops to his knees, sitting cross-legged, his spine straight.

My thoughts stop in their tracks. *Shit. Shit. Shit.*

"Theodore, what are you talking about?" He raises his voice.

I shake my head as I sit back down on the grass. I work through my breathing exercises. Inhale, hold, exhale.

He grabs his device out of the backpack and furiously types away on it. He doesn't have the projection up, so I can't decipher what he's doing, if he's researching or if he's telling on me.

"I don't have that information in my file," he whispers after a few minutes. "I'm supposed to have all the important info in my file." He looks up at me, but his face is hard to read. "I'd say this is pretty freaking important."

I nearly reach forward to smooth the wrinkle between his brows, not wanting his skin to remember this frustration or confusion.

"Theodore," he starts, his tone stern. "I need you to tell me what you're talking about."

I look down at the grass, gripping the soft strands between my fingers, trying to rip them out of the soil.

"Your great-grandparents were friends with my parents. Word is, your mom is trying to learn more about your family and family friends. Your mom tried to recruit my parents— my entire family, even—but the timing never worked out. I'm angry because I was just uprooted with no care at all for my life. If my parents were just uprooted, I wonder if they'd still be alive."

My glossy eyes meet his own. It may have always been in the cards for my parents to die. Otium might not have changed that. It could have just interrupted the time I got to spend with them. But it's possible that shift could have changed the course of their life.

"You know my great-grandparents?" His voice wavers.

"D-did," I clear my scratchy throat, "you not just hear what I said?"

He waves his hand in the air. "Yeah, yeah. Definitely, but you know my great-grandparents?"

"I don't know!" I yell. "No one will tell me who they are."

"Samuel and Ellie Eddenburg," he whispers.

Their names suck the breath out of my lungs. I lower myself to lie flat on the ground, looking up at the darkening sky. I like that I can see the deeper purple hues. The stars in this solar system are starting to shine through. I can't wait until I can see the violet sky in the daytime.

I had a feeling Lana was talking about Sam and Ellie. They were my parents' closest friends. They worked with my parents. They volunteered with my parents. They introduced me to Marvel. They often came to protests except for *that* one.

Except that *one. Holy shit.*

Tears escape my eyelids as I mesh Lana's information with Flynn's. Andrya's mother was born five months ago. Meaning Ellie was pregnant the day my parents died, which is likely why they weren't at the protest. They knew. They were being cautious.

They never fucking told me, though. I just saw them. I've talked with them this year. I follow them both on social media. Not a single peep about a child.

For years, Sam and Ellie tried getting pregnant. They even told my parents that they'd adopt if they weren't pregnant by January that year. IVF worked in their favor.

"You know them," Flynn interrupts my thoughts. His voice is grave as he lies beside me.

How am I supposed to go back to Earth, knowing this information, knowing they lied? They want me to live with them. Live with them and a baby? *Andrya's mother?!*

I just lived through the worst year of my life, and they welcomed a new life.

"How long have you known them?" Flynn whispers.

"My entire life," I breathe. "I always considered them my aunt and uncle, except they disappeared when my parents died, and my real aunt and uncle got custody."

I massage my eyelids with my knuckles, trying to stop my tears. A memory of when I was eleven flashes through my mind.

"Uncle Sam!" I yelled, running down the staircase. I skidded to a stop in the kitchen when I saw Sam, Ellie, and my parents sitting at the kitchen table. "You remember when you told me that I was going to be a cousin?

"Theo—" my mom said.

"I know I didn't react so great, but I started thinking about it, and I can teach my little cousin everything you've taught me. And I know it'll be a few years from now, but when you introduce your baby to Marvel, can I please rewatch everything with you? Give them all the hints and clues like you did for me?"

My mom's hand gripped my arm, and she pulled me backward, pushing me down onto her lap. "Theodore, we need to—"

"You can absolutely do all of that, Theo. We wouldn't have it any other way," Sam said softly.

I looked over at him, grinning widely. I had to start a list of all the things I was going to teach this baby in just a few short months. But Sam was crying. His eyes were red. I looked over at Ellie, and her hands covered her face, leaning into Sam's shoulder.

"What's going on?" I whispered.

Ellie uncovered her tear-stained face and looked at me. "We lost the baby."

Sam and Ellie had their first miscarriage when they were thirty. I had reacted poorly to them telling me they were pregnant. I got jealous, thinking that I'd lose them.

Every time after that, I reacted better. I got more excited with every announcement too, but each time ended in a miscarriage. My gut wasn't wrong, though. I did lose them this past year when the pregnancy stuck. I missed something I had been by their side for. But after six years, they finally had a child—a child that gave them a grandchild who is a leader on a new planet.

The thought weighs down on me, squishing every last morsel of breath from my lungs. It's like the universe didn't think I had enough pressure, enough will to fight. Like the weight of the world I've felt was nothing compared to every step forward from here.

I may be gaining a sidekick who can help make changes with me, but our end game, the holy grail of hope, just got far more challenging.

"This whole situation makes more sense now," Flynn's words cut through my thoughts.

Silent tears still stream down my face. I'm not sure they'll stop anytime soon. I'm wavering on the tightrope of diving into this heaviness or yanking myself out of a closing tunnel.

"I knew you were special," he says. "I knew rules were being broken in the program. The moment I started school to become an advisor, my mom told me my first mentee was already chosen, that I had a high-profile case, and that it was crucial for me to do well in my studies. I didn't know who it was until this past year, but I still didn't understand *why* you were important compared to any other candidate. Most mentors don't have their first solo mentee until they are twenty. Now, I'm finishing up my studies and mentoring you.

"Despite recent actions, my mom wants to make you comfortable and hopes we become friends. I think part of why I'm your mentor is because she thinks we may get along well. She spoke about your case with such care—yet anxiety, too. I think that might be why there were so many hiccups in getting you here. While eavesdropping a few months ago, I heard my dad question why it was so important for you to be here. My mom said that she had one duty in all of this, and that duty was you."

I suck in as little air as I can from the pressure on my lungs. Usually, I'd be on the verge of a panic attack. Instead of panicking, my body has started to retreat.

All I know is that I need to get Andrya alone. I have to know why Flynn isn't aware of this, and if I've messed up some timeline by sharing this secret? Being here has to change the outcome of my future on Earth.

I sit up, pressing my hands on the grass in front of me, leaning forward as my stomach twists. My elbows shake as I try to maintain my balance.

What have I gotten myself into?

Sixteen

A knock wakes me up, and I immediately know it's Flynn. It's the same knock-kn-kn-knock as the other day.

By the time we made it back to the apartment building last night, I could barely stand. My body was sore from running and lack of sleep. Flynn hobbled me into the building. I wanted to explore my bedroom further, maybe try out the cool-looking shower, but all I had energy for was peeing and collapsing on the bed. It was around nine at night, A.K.A. one in the morning on Earth.

I vaguely remember Flynn telling me that I'd get a tour of Olive today and my schedule. Honestly, I've never been more excited about having a schedule again. With the onset of information, I need some sort of focus and direction.

I roll out of bed as his knocks become more persistent. Finally, I'm swinging open the door, leaning against the frame. I feel a little more rested, despite the fog settling into my mind.

"Good morning!" he greets, and my eyes squint at the

sound. Flynn's smile is too bright, and his hands aren't holding caffeine this morning.

"Morning." I trudge over to the couch and take a seat.

"How are you doing this morning?" he asks as he takes it upon himself to open my curtains, letting the light stream through.

I shrug. Today is day one of the next three months. I'm sore from running, but my eyes don't ache as much as they have the past few days, and the pounding in my head is gone. I am starving too.

"Hungry?" Flynn plops himself onto the couch next to me as I nod. "I'll introduce you to our communal dining that is available for all meals and snacks. Then we'll start our tour. Sounds good?"

"Shower first?"

"Of course. There are some clothes in your dresser. We can get more this week. Everything you may need is in the bathroom, too. Also, there should be vitascreen in your cabinet. It's crucial you use that while on Otium. I'll wait here." Flynn makes himself comfortable, kicking his legs up once I stand, careful to leave his feet off of the couch. He pulls his device out of his pocket and starts tapping away.

The dresser is filled with the basics. Some boxer briefs, t-shirts, a pair of jeans, and some chino shorts. I grab black chino shorts, boxers, and a white t-shirt. It's similar to my wardrobe at home, which has come quite bland over the past year.

The bathroom is small and has a shower built from the wall with the clay. There's a waterfall showerhead, though, and a touchscreen machine in the wall that sets the temperature, dispenses shampoo, conditioner, and body wash. My cabinets are filled with a couple towels, an electric razor, vitascreen (their sunscreen), and some curling product for my hair. It's been a while since I've taken the time for my appearance, and today won't be the day I try new products on my hair, but I'm intrigued. Also flattered that they thought I've grown facial hair already.

When we're en route for breakfast, Flynn leads us toward the town center, past the welcome dinner picnic table, and to the building that was behind the table. The front of the building is packed. The volume increases with excitement and laughter as we walk through the clusters of people. Either everyone here has an IV of coffee, or life really *is* that good.

Similar to last night, it looks like all seating is outdoors, and most tables are taken. Flynn waves at people as we walk into the building. I brace myself for the cafeteria smells of stale vomit and freezer-burned food, but I'm consumed with an incredible aroma—more particularly, the scent of coffee has the hair on my arms rising.

I'm. So. Close.

"This is our communal dining area," Flynn says as we stop in a line.

He points toward an electronic menu on the wall. The menu is categorized into different types of breakfast foods from all over the world.

"Most foods are cooked on demand and can be customized, so choose whatever you like to eat. Any drinks will be determined after food."

Instead of overwhelming myself with the list of over a hundred breakfast options, I end up ordering an omelet with toast. I have three months to choose any type of breakfast I want.

"What's the weather like here?" I ask as we move up in line. There are some tables inside, but the majority are outside.

"In the Flatlands, it's moderate. We have a wet and dry season. We are currently in the dry season and the temperature usually is warm with a slight breeze. The wet season is cooler and damp. It's when most of our crops grow, and we take a break from the Otium Initiative. While it's crop season, it's also when a majority of the Flatlands rests. Some days, you can't go outside because of torrential downpours."

"So, what do people do for food?" Andrya has a kitchen, and my room has a fridge, but if food only costs a good deed, I wouldn't cook.

"We have markets for food. A lot of people here still cook—usually because they enjoy it. Though, in the wet season, a lot more people cook. When the weather is bad, everything shuts down."

Flynn places his order, walking me through the electronic ordering system. Once we order food, we choose our drinks. Flynn tells me that there are no specialty coffees available here as there is already a place for that, but we have options for juices, water, regular coffee, and smoothies.

When we have our entire breakfast on real plates and mugs, Flynn scans his hologram card again for the both of us. We find a two-person table outside and sit. Flynn got himself a coffee and some sort of egg and vegetable bowl, which looks incredible.

We eat in silence, and I consume the much-needed caffeine. While my drink of choice is a chai latte, black coffee does the trick too. Especially when it's made with this divine water.

"Is caffeinated Theodore activated?" Flynn asks as he scoops his last bite into his mouth. He's smirking when I look up at him.

I roll my eyes but offer him a smile. "Almost."

As I finish my coffee, he gives me a brief overview of the

day; a tour of Olive, collecting my schoolbooks, and getting a phone, where my points will be transferred to. Before we leave, there's a space inside the building where we load our dishes onto racks. There's a rack for each type of dish. Flynn explains that once the rack is full, it gets pulled into a machine that automatically washes everything. A large dishwasher of sorts.

"What happens if people don't clean up after themselves?" I ask.

"You lose a point per littered item." He shrugs as we walk away from the building.

This time, as we walk through the town center, Flynn names each storefront. There are about ten shops within the center and five that line the path to the dining area. There's a coffee shop, a fabric shop, a few different clothing stores, a wooden toy shop, electronics, a spa, and a food market.

It's amazing that each shop was voted in. It makes sense how they can be successful compared to some small shops in New York. Presumably, with the help of others, your wealth of points doesn't determine whether or not you can open a business.

We head down the straight route from the town on the dirt path toward a cluster of larger buildings. While they are all cob-styled buildings, these are more rectangular than the homes. The windows are nearly floor to ceiling on some too. Most of the buildings are straight ahead and to the left of the path. To our right, farmland begins and seems to travel for miles.

There's an art building with a wraparound porch, a stadium-sized building that Flynn says is the gym with a track circling it. There's a two-story building where therapy is located—apparently, I'll have individual therapy as well as group therapy. There is even a separate cluster of education buildings; these are all domed circular buildings. There is a ginormous playground behind the cluster of buildings with swings, slides, monkey bars, seesaws, and what looks like trampolines. Flynn said that I have my own room in one of the education buildings to do my schoolwork for two hours a day. Honestly, it's a win from actually attending school. But two different therapies, high school work, and training with Flynn on god knows what . . . this is definitely not a vacation. Beyond the education buildings, the path continues, but there isn't another structure for at least a mile or so.

"Where does that lead?" I ask as Flynn starts to turn around.

"If you follow this path, it leads to the next town in the Flatlands. Olive is the most populated and established town, but the Flatlands has two other towns. They are more so for people who like to be left alone, like a quieter life, or those who actually travel the planet to discover more and just need a place to call home. A lot of our farmers live in those towns. The towns have their own schools, shops, and dining, but they don't participate in the initiative. That isn't their focus."

That makes sense. Like those who move away from the city in New York to go live in the mountains.

"Let's go get your schedule. It will officially start tomorrow morning," Flynn says as we head back toward the center of town. "Your program is entirely customized to you. Ideally, we will interlace healing you alongside the Otium Initiative training, but our priority is you. Sometimes training can extend longer than three months, but it has never happened. Just a clause in the program. We'll be doing a lot of hands-on learning, which is usually covered in group settings, but it'll just be you and me. So I hope you're not sick of me yet." Flynn winks.

I hate the rush of energy that soars through me. The damn validation I need for my anxiety. I can have a person here if I choose to let him in . . . if I choose to risk getting hurt again.

"How will I meet people if I'm always with you?" I counter.

"Ouch, Theodore." He clenches his shirt. "Hit me where it hurts."

I smile a little. "I mean, part of the program is socializing and getting to know others, right?"

"We always have gatherings. We actually have one tonight. It's an Open Mic night, ranging from individual singers, poets, comedians, and bands. It's usually a wild turnout, and surrounding towns sometimes come out to watch. There will be events you can attend in other towns, too. We'll head to the community center, and I'll show you where you can find all this information—it's also where your phone will be."

I was only joking. There is definitely no need to find a gathering and introduce myself. Flynn seems like he'll consume a lot of my social output.

Our path takes us toward an octagon building in the center of this part of town.

"Now the phone you're about to get is more high-tech than what's on Earth, though I'm sure you've already noticed." Flynn waves his device—phone—in front of me. "We don't have social media like Earth. But this phone gives you the ability to talk, text, research on the internet, check your schedule, watch movies or television, order food ahead of time, and read books. You don't have a television in your room, but you have a clear wall across from your couch that you can project any of the apps from your phone. Or you have the ability to project a screen immediately in front of you with a solid background. Like how my mother did in her office. It can act as a computer screen."

Got the damn iPhone beat. I hide my grin as he speaks, itching to have the phone.

We arrive at the community center that is buzzing with energy. Since we left breakfast, this is the most movement we've seen. There isn't a blast of AC like in the United States when you enter a public building. Instead, it's relatively the same temperature as outside—lukewarm.

A woman behind the main desk greets us with a broad smile, and Flynn by name. Flynn waves as we take a sharp left. Directly in front of me is a giant chalkboard.

I take a few steps back, trying to decipher all the messy handwriting through the chalk dust. There are squares similar to a calendar marking 1-30. Above the squares is the number 8 and day 16 is circled. It's August 16th? On the 16th square in capital letters it says, "Open Mic in the Theatre."

"Where is the theater?" I ask. Out of all the buildings we've passed, Flynn hasn't pointed that out.

"It is next to the gym. It's an outdoor area where different events happen. Like the Open Mic will be there tonight, and in a couple days, there is a corn hole competition. These events aren't often scheduled in the wet season, but if they are, they are inside the gym."

I sure as hell am not walking into an open mic alone. So if I'm going, I'm going with him. That is if *he* isn't sick of me.

The calendar is filled with an array of different activities. There are classic knitting and sewing classes, singing and painting lessons, a book club, a movie club, and more. There is even a wide assortment of fitness classes.

"Alright, so this calendar is always updated, and you can find the digital version on your phone. While you likely won't have time in your schedule, you can host a class. The class options are chosen by the community. All you need is ten people that say they'd like to partake, and then you find building space."

"That's pretty cool," I admit. Whenever I tried to get a club started in middle or early high school, it would always be such a challenge. There was so much paperwork involved with the administration, and they'd always "lose it."

Flynn eventually drags me away from the calendar. Within minutes, I'm holding my own black rectangular device that is identical to Flynn's and smaller than my current iPhone. There are a ton of apps. There's an app for fitness, therapy, education, community, points, entertainment, calendar, and schedule. I'll have to check these all later. There are even numbers already added in the phone. I have Flynn's, Andrya's, Lana's, and Corie's. Next to Corie's name, it says "therapist."

"I can call your mom?" While my brows crease, my mind races. It might not be too complicated to get her to talk about my position here. I could just send her a quick text—

"Not necessarily."

My lungs deflate, and his lips turn into a smile.

"Is my mom that exciting?" He laughs.

I shake my head and search through the phone some more, ignoring him. If I want to investigate further into the potential fishiness of Otium, I need to hide my reactions better.

"My mom's number is really there, in case she needs to

contact you. This way, you'll know who is calling and can answer immediately. If my mom does call, it's important, so remove yourself from where you are to talk to her—except when you're in therapy. Your phone should be silent there."

My old self would be over the moon with the idea that a person in power may want to speak with me directly.

"It's also there in an emergency situation. Like how my mom has a light on, you can always give her a heads up that you need to speak with her. If you don't respect the boundaries of communicating with her, you will lose points."

Noted.

Flynn pulls out his own device. "I'm transferring your points now. You have more than enough to get you through the program. Having to figure out the point system is not the responsibility of the mentee. That said, you can still gain points, but more importantly, you can lose them. You are a guest on this planet, and we expect you to respect that. If you lose too many points, you will be dismissed from the program." Flynn tells me all this while he's typing away on his phone.

Suddenly, my device beeps with a notification of a point's transfer. I click on the app, and the hologram appears before me with my card I can scan. I have a balance of 200,000 points.

"The amount of points you have is way more than you need to survive. We know the sacrifice you are making, so we want you to be able to enjoy your time without worrying if you can afford it."

If tacos last night were only 5 points, this feels like a full-on luxury.

"Okay, your schedule is on your phone, but we will also print it out. Your school books are here too."

Flynn and I start walking to the back of the building. I wonder if they extracted my actual textbooks.

"After this, you'll meet your therapist and have your first session."

I halt my footsteps as my breathing accelerates. "I'm sorry, what? You said my schedule starts tomorrow. Couldn't you have told me this earlier?"

I know I have to go eventually, but surprises are not my thing.

Flynn turns around in front of me, a cheeky smile on his face. "Sure, I could have. But you've adamantly refused therapy in the past. This first session is short, to dip your toes in and meet Corie. Besides, we have to walk past the building to head back to the town center. You'll have your session, and then we'll have lunch at one of the restaurants."

The conversation ends the moment he spins on his foot and heads toward the back of the building, not checking to see if I follow.

I close my eyes, breathe in for four, hold, and breathe out for four. It wouldn't hurt him to *ask* me how I feel about it.

Soon, Flynn is standing right in front of me again, a stack of books—my torn, ratted textbooks—in his hands.

Wonderful. Is it too late to say, fuck you, I'm good?

Seventeen

Corie, my therapist, looks expectantly at me. We've gone through the "Hi, how are you" obligatory greeting. She seems sweet enough with her light brown eyes and dyed aqua blue-grayish, wavy long hair. She's younger than I anticipated. Maybe in her thirties. She sits cross-legged in her beige fabric sofa chair across from where I'm seated on a beige two-person couch.

Her informal attitude allows me to settle a little, but I don't know how therapy operates, and I don't know what to say to her. It's the first situation I've interacted with someone on Otium without Flynn. He said he'd be right outside the building waiting for me. I have to believe that in order to remain seated here.

"Theodore?"

I blink, refocusing my attention on Corie. Her head is slightly tilted, and her pink lips give way to a kind smile. She's hands down analyzing me and definitely knows I just escaped for a bit. *Fantastic.*

"Let's start with some happy memories. Tell me about

the good things in your life. This will help me get to know you better."

My mind instantly flashes to Alejandro . . . and then Jonah. They've been saviors this past year, but now? Now I'm not certain what is good. Does she want a happy memory of my parents? My friends? Myself? Am I supposed to talk about how wonderful volunteering is and how passionate I feel about doing better in the world? Or is it as simple as the little bit of joy I get when Alejandro surprises me with chai lattes? Or when my follower count grows because each person means a person supporting me, helping me, even if miles away. Or could it be the simple fact that I can breathe a little easier each day I don't have a chore list from my aunt?

"When I say happy, what is the first thing you think of?" Corie asks.

I glance out the large window that brightens up this room. The white sky is bright against vita's lights. I want to be out there, sitting under one of the oak trees, soaking in the rays.

I think about Alejandro and Jonah, my parents, my brothers, Sam and Ellie . . . each person right now has a gray cloud above them. Every memory is tainted, even if they are happy. I filter through Alejandro's excitement over a video idea we had and my first kiss with Jonah. The day my parents adopted my brothers comes to mind, but that's darkened by how they are growing up as despondent, rude individuals. The excitement I felt every time Sam and Ellie announced a pregnancy is now overshadowed by their disappearance. Though, the enthusiasm they both had with each new Marvel movie or show they introduced me to still brings a smile to my face.

"Why don't you tell me about a memory with your parents?"

I lock eyes with Corie, and she smiles with a nod. Her perfectly shaped brows and the slight outline of her eyelids brighten her eyes.

"When I was seven, my parents and I were supposed to go to a women's march. I remember them switching up the schedule last minute. We had a birthday party to attend for my best friend at the time. It felt like his party was sprung on me. I don't know if it wasn't planned well or if there was a rain date, but my parents canceled our plans so we could go to the birthday." I let out a laugh, remembering this being the first major tantrum I had. "I threw pancakes across the room and yelled about how important it was for us to be at the event. I really singled out my mother, spewing back her words from the week before about how this march was important to her as a woman. My parents were shocked, but looking back, I can see their amused smiles in my memory. Because why was their seven-year-old upset about going to a birthday party with cake, a pool, and unlimited sweets?"

Corie smiles, but it's calculated as she taps away on a tablet she has. *This* is one of the reasons I've rejected therapy. What the hell are they always writing about?

"Did you win? Did you go to the march?" she asks when I pause.

I shake my head. "Nope, I had to go to that stupid party for a person who isn't friends with me anymore. My parents told the story all the time, though. I was stubborn and refused to eat birthday cake and refused to swim. I kept telling the adults how my mom didn't care about herself as much as she cared about cake. I had to apologize to my friend, but he wasn't thrilled that I was the downer at his party. Soon, he stopped talking to me. He didn't want to be friends with the raging activist I was becoming."

"Why is this story important to you, Theodore?" Corie types a few more things before looking directly at me.

I lean back against the couch, twisting my fingers in my lap. I don't know why that memory came to mind or why I shared it. There are likely some deep-rooted issues I have because of that single memory.

"My parents always wanted their children to be involved in creating a better world. I don't really remember a time when that wasn't important."

"Are your brothers as active as you?"

I laugh out loud before covering my mouth. It's a fun thought to imagine them trying to be like me, with their sour faces and monotone voices.

"No. It's hard to believe my parents even raised them." I blame it on them not being blood-related. Activism seeps through the Montgomery bloodline. "My parents adopted my brothers when they were four. They were the brainchild of my parents' agency. Despite that, they are pretty clueless about what my parents did and the impact they had."

"Do you resent them for that?"

I feel the air escape from my lungs. I don't know the answer to that question. I was an only child until I was nine. I always volunteered with them and went to protests. I had every ounce of my parents' attention. When my brothers came into the picture, I doubled down on my volunteering to get that time with my parents. I had to be the better kid. I searched and found new events for us to attend. And while I learned that I liked making the difference myself, it did hurt that my brothers had the ability to say no to an event. To be driven to a friend's house if they didn't want to do something. And by doing so, they still had so much of my parents' attention.

"Theodore?" Her voice is gentle as my heart constricts.

"They have never once felt the weight of the world on their shoulders," I mumble. I watch as my left fingertips turn bright red as I twist my fingers tighter.

"Do you feel that weight? Have you had to choose between volunteering and relaxing? Shutting down?"

My quick answer is that no, I haven't had to choose between volunteering and relaxing. There is no choice in that. I can't relax if someone else is struggling. But that isn't true. I know deep down I can't save the world, but I always choose to put others before me.

Even before my parents died, Jonah and I fought about my lifestyle. It just got worse when my parents weren't around to mediate. Whether it be a friend's birthday, going to the movies, canceling a date because of watching a press conference, attending an online rally or protest, or even attending something in person. For the most part, events are planned in advance, but I was always really good at finding new things to get involved in. When my parents were around, they would have events that they'd tell me about at the last minute that I'd always jump onto. Since they had their own agency, there were so many work events they wouldn't think to invite me to, but I'd find out and invite myself.

It wasn't just Jonah, though. It was bailing on a few friends throughout middle and high school and then harping on them about their lifestyle. I'd scare them away with my "Don't drink out of plastic bottles," "Don't litter," "Turn off the lights," "Don't use the water when brushing your teeth." There were many times it was hard for me to turn off and just live. But that was also the problem. There were too many people "just living" to put in the care to change their routine slightly.

"Theodore, you've disappeared again."

My face warms, and I look out the window. I'm done. I don't want to do this anymore today. This was supposed to be a quick session, a meet and greet. Not an investigation into my life before the official day one.

"There is no choice," I say softly. "Someone has to fight for the greater good."

Corie nods and jots down a few more things. "Have you lost people because you chose volunteering over them?"

I nod. I refuse to look at her. Vita shifts and beams into the room. I stare at it, wondering how far away I really am from reality. The initiative exists to convert more people on Earth like me. It's proof that there aren't enough people like me at the moment, and those currently fighting can't do it all.

"Either you're working toward creating a better world for everyone, or you're actively working against it. I don't have time for the latter," I say.

My foot bounces, and I try to stifle it before her eyes catch the movement. I can't sit here and defend myself. My way of life shouldn't be up for investigation.

"So people who are kind, caring, and compassionate but don't attend events, protests, or consume their lives to make the world better, are they bad people?"

I believe so. But psychologically? She's paid good points to learn how to twist my words.

Jonah used to attend events with me when we first became friends, though that faded throughout the years. I know I say he's a bad person in arguments, but he isn't, is he? He wasn't wrong in the hospital. He has helped me so much and has been patient and usually kind. It just wasn't the help I was looking for.

"I—" I grip my knee, pressing my leg to a halt. "I don't know."

"Okay." Corie nods, tapping away. "That's a great start. Our time is up for today. I will see you at the same time tomorrow. Think about some more memories we can talk about."

She stands, and I follow suit slowly, forcing my legs to remain steady. My movements are hazy at her abrupt end.

Is Jonah a good person? Are these people good even though they don't help Earth?

Instead of clarity, my mind is in a deeper fog as I leave the room and head toward the stairs. I don't want to share any more memories with her if she is going to dissect them and make me question the validity of my beliefs and memories. Shouldn't we be discussing bad things that have happened? Can't we talk about how to get over my parents' deaths or work through my break-up with Jonah? She should be able to make my awful memories turn into ones I can cope with.

"How'd it go?" I jump as I hear Flynn's voice. He's sitting in a chair at the bottom of the stairs, reading one of my textbooks—for fun? "You know," he continues, "it's pretty awful that we still have to provide you with this biased history bullshit. This isn't what we learn or know to be true, and I think you know that, but to have it here because you're required to test on it back on Earth? It's a waste of time." Flynn slams my U.S. History book closed.

A smile tries to fight its way through my grimace. I don't answer him. Instead, I just open the door and walk outside. The vita is hot on my skin, and I lift my head toward the light, covering my eyes. I'll likely start sweating through this shirt soon, but the warmth is comforting, like a cozy blanket.

"So," Flynn's voice is joyful as he skips into step with me, effortlessly carrying my books. "I can't promise you tacos, but I can promise you the best veggie burger you've ever had." I can feel Flynn's grin as I try to ignore it.

I should offer to help because they are my books, but I can't find the decency. It's hard enough not commenting on the fact that these veggie burgers are probably *the only* veggie burgers he's ever had.

"Lead the way."

His strides are longer, with a pep in his step, as he walks a few paces ahead of me.

We arrive at the first restaurant I've seen here in Olive. It's quaint, with, again, all outdoor seating. This one doesn't have an inside building for the kitchen, though. Instead, there are massive grills lined up in the back of the restaurant. I breathe in, taking in the barbecue of seared burgers, sautéed vegetables, even french fries.

My father used to make the most incredible burgers. We usually ate turkey burgers as we preferred them, but for the most part, my family was vegetarian, and I still try to be.

"Flynn!" A girl around our age strides up to us, leaving her table. "Are you going to the Open Mic tonight? A few of us are planning on having a get-together beforehand and then walking over. Wanna join?" She rushes to finish her speech, eyeing me the entire time.

The blood drains from my face, heating up the back of my neck. I'm entirely caught off guard by a friend asking another friend about plans. *Of course, Flynn has a life here.* It's silly to assume that he wouldn't have a normal life on his *normal* planet. While my world got flipped upside down, today is just another day for him. I'm just his *job*.

The thought bubbles in my stomach. Flynn is not going to be around me 24/7. I will have a separate life here, not attached to him.

"Yeah, definitely. Meeting at your place?" Flynn grins.

Neither of them looks at me as if I'm invisible. This should be the part of the conversation where he introduces me and maybe even invites me.

I swallow hard, wishing I had water to distract myself with as reality settles. I'm just a paycheck to him.

Change the world, Theodore. They'll expect everything and give you nothing in return.

"Yes! Around 15:30. We've got the drinks. But if you want to bring some snacks, that'd be great."

"No problem." Flynn gives this girl a hug, angling my books away from her before she retreats back to her table with a wave.

Without an explanation or an introduction, Flynn continues to walk over to an empty table and gestures to the open seat.

A waitress comes over with menus as we settle. We both thank her before my eyes dart straight down. Flynn had mentioned the Open Mic to me, which I assumed meant we were attending together, considering it's my first official night in town. I'm not sure I'm ready to embrace this whole world yet; it's way too much for my brain to comprehend that this is a functioning society. I knew that—obviously. But we were in a bubble where only a few people existed, and my person was Flynn. Eventually, real life needs to integrate, but everything about this place is *abnormal*. How could there be no suffering? Or trying desperately to make things better? Are their days filled with numerous yoga and meditation sessions, journaling, and counseling?

Am I supposed to adopt this lifestyle? Forget that I have

another life on Earth? Do I embrace this and try to make friends that I have to leave behind? Or is my life at a stand-still? Do I go to these classes and courses and not make friends? Do I not try to connect with others who are techni-cally around *after* I've most definitely died?

"Theo-dore," Flynn sings, swaying his hand in front of my face.

I wipe away the tears that try to lubricate my eyes, but I still keep my eyes down.

"What's going on in that head of yours?" he asks.

There is no apology. No discussion of who that person was. In a world that should be better, you'd assume that they've mastered anxiety and how to make people comfort-able in all settings.

"Nothing. I'm fine." I pick up the glass of water just delivered, taking a few sips.

He shifts his focus to the menu. The silence is precisely what I want and exactly what I don't need.

"Shall I order my favorite burger, or would you like to choose?"

I can't even try to focus on the different food options at the moment.

"Order whatever is your favorite," I say, finally looking up at him.

He signals to the waitress that we are ready. He orders us two original veggie burgers, which their menu says are topped with their secret sauce, pickles, and spinach. I usually hate pickles, but I stay quiet. If my mind can't focus enough to look at a damn menu, I don't think it can focus long enough to know what I do and do not like. I think I'm more excited about the fact that these burgers come with curly fries. At least I can find comfort in the fact that pota-toes exist here.

"So, how is Corie? Do you think she will be the right fit for you?" Flynn takes a sip of water before fiddling with a reusable napkin in front of him.

I take a few gulps of water, giving myself some time. How does someone know if their therapist is the right fit?

"She's fine." I place the empty glass on the table.

"You're a man of many words today. What's going on?" He stops his fiddling, tilting his head just slightly.

I shrug and force a smile. I want to snap at him. Tell him I'm uncomfortable, that maybe I just want to be silent because I was uprooted from my entire life and asked to adjust immediately. That Corie never gave me answers and just has my mind spiraling more. But the words remain buried.

"Just taking it all in." For show, I gaze around the restaurant.

I'm on another planet . . . with human beings . . . originating from Earth. There is a society. An entire functioning planet. In a different solar system. In a different goddamn universe.

How the hell am I supposed to convince people of this on Earth? It's bad enough that there's a large group of people who don't believe in science. But for those who do believe, this is still a lot to comprehend. A part of me doesn't believe it's real.

"Of course." Flynn's eyes are soft, like he understands what I'm possibly going through. He will never understand the gravity of pressure and expectation slowly drowning me, all because his mother wanted to learn more about her family.

Eighteen

Not guilty. Pew. Pew. Theodore! Your father! Officer Manson, Officer Jans, and Officer Jeffers are not guilty. Pew. Pew. Pew. Me and Daddy are so proud of you. Not guilty. Not Guilty. Not. Guilty. Pew. Pew. Pew.

"Stop it, stop it, stop it!" I scream, bolting up and leaning forward in my bed. I press my palms against my ears and scream into the comforter, suffocating my face.

The gunshot radiates through my bloodstream, clogging my ear canals and restricting my lungs. Every time I try to go back to sleep, the nightmare manifests into a web of memories, twisting and slicing through my brain. The original nightmare of the memory was hard enough to come out of, but with the trial interlaced, my depression started to seep in, paralyzing me.

It's the anniversary of my parents' deaths, and I spent a good portion of the day distracted by this damn planet. I had a countdown to this day. I had already decided that I wouldn't go to school, Jonah and I would go to their graves, and that I would grieve according to the trial results. But none of that happened. Instead, my mind had the audacity to forget.

I lift my head from the bed when I breathe through a violent sob rippling through my chest. I don't remember the last nightmare I had where I woke up alone. Jonah always had a way of knowing when it'd be a rough night. He'd always wake me from them. But I just woke from four restless sleeps; each one with tears streaming down my face, gasping for air, as if the gunshots were hitting me instead.

My phone flashes, and with a click of the screen, it shows the time as 3:03 am. with a few missed notifications from Flynn. I wanted him to want me at the Open Mic until my first nap resulted in a nightmare, and the event became insignificant to my parents dying. I couldn't process the time of day between my nightmares or what could be happening outside these four walls. Throwing the phone toward the couch, I watch as it tumbles to the ground.

Andrya is the reason I missed this day.

I slide myself down from the bed, needing to refresh from my cold sweats. My limbs shake as my clammy fingertips grip across the hardwood floor, helping me crawl to the bathroom. I manage to lift myself over the lip of the shower. With a deep breath, I discard my t-shirt and boxers before I activate the shower system. I can adjust the temperature and pressure myself, but there are also a few different shower modes. One mode is stress, and I click that.

I'm greeted with lukewarm water cascading down my body. The water pressure is lighter than earlier, but the waterfall spout calms me with each even and gentle drop. While the temperature only rises a little, steam fills the shower from tiny spickets, carrying a lavender scent.

I breathe in, keeping my head drooped so I don't swallow water. On the rare occasion that Jonah couldn't be near me, Timothy would sit with me. He didn't know what was happening or how to talk me out of an attack, but he'd hold my hand. While I don't connect much with my brothers, Timothy can have an empathic side.

Now, no one knows me. No one knows what happens to my brain when I'm alone. Does my file even mention these nightmares? I'm not sure if I'd be okay with them having that sliver of information. For them to know, they'd have to have private footage of me.

After a couple minutes, I soothe myself long enough to use the wall to help me stand. I press it a few times and lather my body with the soap. My muscles slowly relax as I breathe in eucalyptus now. The vibration of the streams courses through my bloodstream, starting from the top of my head down to my feet.

I don't feel the tears until I choke on a sob, causing me to double over, heaving. I inhale water, spitting out spurts before I gasp, collapsing to the floor. Pulling my knees to my chest, I watch as the soapy water circles the drain before disappearing.

I see the slippery floor. Water cascades onto my scalp. Lavender and eucalyptus transform my body from irritation to relaxation. My boney knees protrude against my skin.

"I am okay." I force the words out, not believing it for one second. But I repeat the phrase over and over again until my head rests atop my knees.

The water suddenly stops. Jerking up, I see a message on the wall.

Thank you. Your allotted time is up.

My allotted time? The fuck is that supposed to mean?
I reach up and try to turn the shower back on.

A new message appears.

Please allow twenty minutes between showers.

This is actually bullshit. I force myself to stand. I wish there was a shower door that I could open and slam so hard behind me the glass would reverberate.

I grab a towel, wrapping it tightly around my body. I take advantage of the bathroom door, slamming it hard, so the plaques on my wall shake before I collapse onto bed.

I hate to admit that the towel feels like a hug, and it takes everything in me not to toss it. Instead, I allow the comfort to settle in, closing my eyes again.

"For someone so keen on saving the planet, you sure don't save water when you shower." Jonah laughed.

"What if I'm only this long when I'm with you?" I wrapped my arms around Jonah's soaked body.

My brothers were shopping with my parents, so Jonah and I finally had some alone time.

The morning had been spent doing yard work for my father. Cutting up wood and stacking it for the neighbors and our own wood stove for the winter. Except, it was the middle of the summer, so naturally, we were drenched with sweat.

Jonah nestled his head into my neck, nibbling the skin. My body moved toward him, desperate for more.

Our first of many showers, the day we both gave each other handjobs for the first time. We had jumped on the opportunity when my parents said we should clean ourselves up, and they'd be back later.

I ride out the wave as the memory continues. Following the motions, thrusting my hips and squinting my eyes shut as my back arches before collapsing and curling into a fetal position.

I wake up, panting and shivering, stark naked in bed. I should have stayed out of bed and gone for a walk or perused the television options. I know movement helps. Even if I just did some stretching. I'm grateful falling back to sleep didn't equate to another nightmare, though.

Light seeps through my curtains. As I push some of the fabric away, I can see movement outside. Another day has begun—my first day of the initiative.

Flynn's knock raps on the door before his voice comes through. "Theodore? Are you okay?"

I don't answer. I can't. I don't have the power to lift myself out of bed and put on a brave face.

"Theodore, please answer me."

My doorknob rattles before the door is shoved open, hitting the wall behind it. I scramble to cover my body in my comforter. The bath towel drops to the floor.

"Oh! Oh, I'm so sorry." Flynn hesitantly covers his eyes.

I tighten the grip on my comforter, bringing it up to my neck.

"What are you doing?" I try to remain calm. My voice wavers as my breathing accelerates and tears burn my eyes.

Flynn had confirmed that these doors had locks because most people in the initiative grew up with door locks, so it was an added comfort. He failed to inform me that he had a key.

"I'm s-sorry. I was worried . . . am worried. I, uh, well, didn't hear from you last night. I wanted to make sure you were okay . . . you are okay." Flynn stumbles backward.

It brings me great satisfaction to watch him fall into my door. Serves him right.

"Get out." My voice is low, but anything louder will cause it to tremble or scream.

"I—well, it's uh time to—"

"I said, GET OUT!" I shriek, curling myself further up on my bed, wrapping my arms around my knees.

I don't have the energy to go through this process. If anything should be my sanctuary here, it should be my fucking bedroom.

He nods, his hands shaking slightly as he shuffles out of the room, closing the door behind him. I may have been able to get out of bed and meet him outside to potentially start the day—a slow-paced day. But now, my unsettled anxiety creeps deeper into my system, starting me back at square one.

Voices throughout the day stir me from my anxiety-ridden sleep. Each time I wake, the tighter I cocoon myself in my comforter. I may be sweating again, but I'm not sure if it's because I'm too hot or I have cold sweats.

I can't show my face. There is no way I can eat something in that crowded communal dining or walk to the coffee shop and place an order. Otium makes it ten times harder to get me up and out again because it's all brand new. There is no place of familiar comfort.

If I was having a bad day on Earth, I would go to a familiar spot, like my favorite coffee shop. However, even that didn't solve things. Sometimes, it would be too crowded, so I'd drive home or drive thirty minutes out to another place. There's very little I need in these moments, and all of them are on Earth.

Another knock comes hours later. My phone went off a few times, vibrating obnoxiously against the floor. Even if I did want to check and see who it was, the motion to get out of bed is impossible.

"Theodore, it's Corie. May I come in?"

I don't know what time it is, but I'm confident I slept through my therapy session. I probably don't have control over this situation. I hear Flynn's voice outside my door, speaking with Corie. He'll likely just let her in as if he didn't learn from this morning.

"I'm going to come in," Corie announces. "Make sure you're decent."

I reposition my cocoon and face the door. By now, my hair is matted against my head—my pillow still damp from my wet locks and sweat. One strand tickles my eyebrow.

Corie walks in, dressed to perfection, with her aqua hair curled and a magenta sleeveless romper that rests at her ankles. Her eyes crinkle as she gives me a friendly smile, closing the door behind her.

Thankfully, Flynn stays outside.

"May we talk?" Her voice is smooth and soft like honey. She helps herself to my couch, keeping her distance.

I shrug my shoulders. I know I need to talk through this. I know I need interaction with the outside world to temporarily rid my thoughts and fool my body and mind into thinking I'm okay. *Fake it 'til you make it.* But that's obviously easier said than done. Trying to pull myself out of this before I fall asleep and start brand new tomorrow seems impossible and unnecessary.

Let me live. Let me grieve. Let me feel it all before I have to go fucking save the world that shouldn't be saved.

I watch Corie as she tries to speak with me. My mind fights my vocal cords. My anxiety tugs me back into my shell each time I try to reach out. She reminds me I have people in my corner and that I'm safe here. She lets me know that she's just a phone call away and on-call for me. But I'm just a frame of a being in front of her. I look directly at her, but I don't see her.

Flynn is disappointed in me. That much is clear from their muffled conversation on the other side of the door. Honestly, what do they expect from me when they kidnap a teenager who suffers from anxiety? Who has experienced trauma?

I let myself flow in and out of consciousness for the rest of the day. The most compelling parts of my day are watching the excitement from afar through my curtains. It's helpful, I think. To see the normalcy of this lifestyle before I'm thrust into it.

Families walk to the communal dining together, friends go in and out of the shops, laughing. They come out with fabric bags filled with things. Children roam on bikes without supervision. There's a group planting near some oak trees. Some people even read books, play guitar, knit, or look like they are studying under the trees.

It's a fully functioning society. The question is, how much do I get to partake in?

Nineteen

The sky is still dim when I walk outside, but boy, does fresh air smell glorious. It smells like fresh-cut grass and a warm spring day. The vita is peaking through the horizon, softening the deep blues and purples from the night sky. I'm greeted by welcomed silence. No birds chirping or rustling of trees. Everything is stagnant—not a single person in my path.

Honestly, Otium is pretty spectacular. Even while these paths have buildings off of them, there is so much space. The paths are at least five people wide. The buildings could sometimes fit two to four buildings between every property. Yesterday, when people-watching, while I only had a small corner of this town, no one seemed to fight for space or awkwardly sidestep each other. Even those who chose to watch the one person with the guitar kept their space.

I walk the path to the town center. Flynn had pointed out a coffee shop the other day that I hope can bring me comfort. When I checked the hours of operation on my phone, the app said most of the places had flexible hours but gave a base of 8:00 am to 3:00 pm for the coffee shop. The only place that had definite hours was the communal dining, which said 8:00 am to 12:00 am.

Despite it being two hours before the coffee shop claims it'll be open, I knew after forcing myself through some stretches this morning that I also had to force myself out of my room. Get more movement, and ideally, human interaction, even though it can be difficult to speak after an extended period of time.

I let out a breath, a smile involuntarily forming the moment I see a light on in the coffee shop. My footsteps halt when I open the door and see three people inside. A barista, a girl from the initiative, and Flynn—who looks exhausted.

"Morning!" The barista and the girl greet me.

Flynn lifts his mug in a greeting, offering a hesitant smile.

"Welcome to The Espresso Bar. I'm Mattis," the barista gives me a smile with his plump pink lips. His frizzy, shoulder-length blonde hair is pushed back with a thick gray headband. "Come on in. What can I get for you?"

The shop is quaint, no larger than my studio apartment. A single family-style table is positioned between me and the bar that takes up the width of the building. The table has just enough room for ten chairs and a pathway. Flynn and the girl are both sitting on stools at the bar. Mattis is behind the counter in front of the espresso machine. It's dimly lit in here with "The Espresso Bar" carved in wood on the back wall.

"He'll have a chai," I hear Flynn order me.

My immediate reaction is to be stubborn and order something different, but I silence my demons. *He's just trying to be helpful.*

"Oat or hemp milk?" Mattis questions, looking directly at me.

I clear my throat, "O-oat, please."

I take a few steps in, and the girl moves down a seat, offering a spot between her and Flynn. I have no choice now but to sit there. Part of me wanted to get a drink and bounce. Though I don't have a travel mug like Flynn let me use a few days ago, and I'm psyched to taste this chai again. The spices are more vibrant here, each one hitting a different taste bud instead of the spices coated with sugar like in the states.

"Hi, I'm Amalia," the girl greets, offering her hand when I take a seat. She's the quintessential French woman with her "effortless" bangs and long, straight, light brown hair. Her skin is pale and highlighted only with what looks like bronzer. "You're Theodore, right?"

"Theo, yeah." I shake her hand before focusing my fingers on the tiny piece of smoky blue paint that is chipping on the bar.

Flynn's eyes burn into the side of my face, but I don't know what to say to him.

"The American in the Otium Initiative, right?" Mattis asks, placing the chai in front of me.

I inhale the steam before looking up at him. "Yup."

"I'm his mentor," Flynn pipes up, taking a sip from his mug. There's a beat of silence, and I catch Mattis eyeing Flynn before Mattis looks back at me.

"That's awesome! Flynn is amazing; been friends with him forever. You'll have a great time here, Theo." Mattis grins.

Flynn 100% mentioned my disappearance to him. Let me go crawl under a rock now.

I wrap my hands around the mug, bringing it to my lips, and take a sip. I exhale the jitters that try to filter their way into me.

"How are you liking the Flatlands so far?" Amalia asks, handing her empty mug to Mattis. "I haven't seen you in classes. Are you doing something different?"

Mattis takes the mug and immediately starts working behind the counter.

"It's a shock," I say. I don't know what I can answer about my program. "How do you like it?"

"Love it!" She beams. "This initiative is an amazing concept. When I got the letter, accepting me into the program, and actually spelling out the details, it felt like my own Hogwarts letter."

I wonder if my parents got a Hogwarts-esque letter when Andrya tried to recruit them. I'm curious what it looks like and how much is actually spelled out about another planet. How does it seem real to accept? In a world of scam artists, I'm not certain I'd trust a letter.

"That it is," I say softly, taking another sip of my chai.

Mattis hands Amalia a cup of tea. "So it differs for each person," Mattis starts. "Depending on who you are, where you're from, and how Otium thinks they can best reach you."

"Theodore, I think we should—" Flynn interrupts Mattis, but I hold up my hand.

"It differs?" I look between Mattis and Amalia. I know there is an application process and a sense of recruitment, but how people are notified differs? I wonder if they started realizing that I wouldn't trust a piece of paper telling me about a new planet. That I wouldn't trust it until I was on the planet—and even now, it feels unreal.

"Yes." Amalia smiles, blowing the steam away from her mug. "So I had two weeks' notice, which is great. I was right in the middle of deciding whether I should sign a new lease or go somewhere new in Europe. This allowed me to tell my family and friends I was starting a new adventure. Some-where deep in an European town to work with a nonprofit where I wouldn't have service." Her smile doesn't falter. If anything, it grows more striking when she mentions her family and friends. "They are always sad to see me go, but are always thrilled for my activism. My family threw me a big party, and then the next day, I was transported here. Obviously, making it look like my suitcases and stuff disappeared."

Flynn places a hand on my shoulder. "Maybe we should—"

"That's really amazing," I force out.

"What about you?" Amalia asks.

I don't miss Mattis looking at Flynn again. If they are friends, I wonder if he knows about my situation.

I suppose I ended up sort of having a goodbye, but it would have been lovely to be sent off with a party. Not having my friends worry about me in grief counseling. Instead, have them be excited about a new venture of mine.

"I didn't have—"

"Theodore, let's go." Flynn's voice is low but stern. I ignore the way it irritates under my skin. He shouldn't mess with me post-spiral.

"I didn't get a warning," I repeat. "I was transported here during a panic attack."

Amalia and Mattis pause mid-movement. Mattis has his eyes on Flynn, and Amalia's eyebrows knot as she looks at me.

"Oh," she whispers. "That's—" she pauses.

"Theodore has a different program than everyone else here. You'll see him in group therapy, but other than that, his classes are different." Flynn stands up. "It's time to go." He stresses each word.

I finally glance at Flynn. His eyes are dull, and his hair has more volume than it usually does. I shake my head, and his hand running through his hair is an answer to if it was styled from frustration.

"I'd like to make my own decisions," I say, nursing my chai. "Plus, I can't leave this drink unfinished."

"Flynn, it's still early. There is nowhere we need to be," Mattis says, handing Flynn another mug of coffee. "Sit and relax. You need it."

I watch them exchange a silent conversation. A minute later, Mattis pours Flynn's coffee in a reusable mug and hands it to him before Flynn excuses himself. He said he needs to freshen up before the day begins and asked me to please meet him at 8:00 am.

About twenty minutes later, Flynn sends me a message apologizing for trying to stop me from sharing my story. He just wasn't sure how Amalia would react, but it is my life, he reminds me. He says he just needed to gather himself and that he looks forward to starting our day.

I try to focus on Amalia talking instead of allowing my mind to fester and create a situation that doesn't exist. Flynn was honest about his feelings, and I need to accept that as the truth. Not compare his apology tactics to Jonah's. For a little over an hour, Amalia tells me about her life in France, interjecting every so often to ask about me, but I find that if I ask the right question, she'll carry the conversation for quite some time.

In the mix, I learn I'll forever be a special case. Amalia is twenty-five, and the other candidates often range from twenty-one to twenty-six.

Twenty

Flynn and I enter a room significantly smaller than some of the other classrooms we just walked past. Some were filled with two to three people, but I couldn't tell if any looked like they were a part of the program. We're in the education building, a building that was right next door to where I just spent two hours pretending to do school work. If this planet is what it's cracked up to be, my school work is insignificant.

"Alright," Flynn starts, closing the door behind us.

There are two desks with two laptops in this room—one is slim, silver, and compact, similar to a MacBook Air, and the other is black, slightly thicker, and wider. Honestly, I'm disappointed with the lack of a new computer. I thought I might be operating on a phone that would project on the wall in front of me.

There are two small windows on the wall with the computers, neither shining in much light. For a place with outdoor seating everywhere, this is quite dismal.

"Choose a seat and turn the chair toward this open

wall." Flynn motions to the right of the classroom that has an open red wall.

I grab the chair in front of the confirmed MacBook Air and turn toward the red wall, hanging my backpack off of it.

Flynn grabs the other chair and drags it next to me. "Your program here is designed around you and your well-being. While each mentee does have an individual therapist and has to partake in group therapy, just like you, that is their only form of therapy. The rest of their lessons are designed around their activism back home. They get training on how to do what they love on a grander scale and how to fix anything we've noticed isn't working. Often, mentees of similar activism backgrounds are chosen at the same time so they can all work together on Otium and on Earth, despite their distance in location. While individual therapy is intensive and personal, group therapy will be a round-up of your entire day."

"How does group therapy work for me if I'm the odd one out?" I ask.

Flynn sighs and kicks his feet out in front of him, his ankles crossing. "We can't keep you from expressing how you feel. *I* don't want to keep you from doing that. You are here to get the most out of this program. If that means you need to discuss your entry here, then Andrya, and I guess I, will have to suffer the consequences."

Oh. I don't want to harm him.

"The truth is, Theodore, there are mistakes made when creating a new world." Flynn stares at the empty wall in front of us. "Andrya isn't an almighty leader, and she isn't always correct. Be as open and as honest as you want to be here, and I promise you that I will have your back as long as the truth is spoken."

He seems relaxed, leaning back in the chair with his

legs out and his arms resting on his thighs, shoulders slouched. But it doesn't feel like his mind is relaxed. I'm not sure I've heard any leader's child announce they had someone else's back before their parents'.

"Anyway." He shakes his head and looks over at me with a gentle smile. "For you, the two of us will work together more on a community level, which isn't entirely far-fetched from what you do with your parents' agency. This will allow you to start healing yourself while also progressing in the program. The two of us will do work on interpersonal relationships. We will dive into friendships, relationships, family, fears, goals, and more. Your program also has flexibility. If we decide that something needs to be explored further, we can change up the schedule. What you and I work on will often carry over or piggyback on what happens in individual therapy. It's the natural course, but I will remind you that your therapy sessions are entirely confidential. Corie and I do not have communication unless we fear you're in danger, like yesterday."

His eyebrow raises just slightly, but I doubt he'll ask. We didn't discuss yesterday at all during breakfast. Instead, we had small talk over our favorite foods.

"To begin," he continues, "we are going to watch a video that is a bit more in-depth than the welcome video. It will explain what happened on Earth, how we got to Otium, and how we developed the planet. If you need me to pause at any point in time, let me know."

I nod my head, and he pulls his phone out of his backpack. He projects the screen toward the back wall, and I watch as he searches through videos in his education app. My education app is filled with my schoolwork from home, but his looks like a compilation of his own mentor studies and then workshops for the mentees.

Flynn clicks on a video, and suddenly, the projection is a hologram, Otium rotating in space.

The video is created just like any ridiculous history or science video that I'd watch in my high school. It's the over-the-top enthusiasm, hoping that with their inflections and drama, they'll get the kids' attention. Though, I think I'm more disappointed that it isn't Neil deGrasse Tyson or Bill Nye narrating. I do have to say that this is more fascinating than most videos I've watched in school. Maybe it has to do with the fact that I'm literally living it. It isn't something in the past that I can pretend isn't important.

I learn that the divide between humans became greater than it is now. As the years pass, more and more people believe less in science and more in hate, discrimination, and misinformation. The United States actually divides, which results in happier people in specific locations, but shows decimation in many states. With these divides, other nations start to thrive or collapse. Either way, similar-minded people seek each other out in order to simply survive. Through all this, protecting Earth and sustaining for the future generations gets left to the wayside.

NASA, and other scientists throughout the world, work together to figure out a way to get to Otium. It was an exciting moment that they found the planet, but now they had to figure out how to travel to another universe without taking lifetimes. For the first time, space travel was discussed amongst the average person. If you believed in science and were dedicated to finding a new future, the door was open to help—all minds on deck.

It resulted in creating technology that allowed astronauts to travel only six months through space into another universe to check out Otium. The original astronauts that survived stayed on Otium and started using the resources

Otium had to create life and further expand what they originally carried on the space trip. They had sent things to Otium for nearly ten years before the first human stepped foot on the planet.

In record time, the next trip started, which resulted in three months of travel. Followed by one month of travel. By the time they made it to one month, Earth was becoming toxic, and they had to start flying those interested to Otium. In order to get on the plane, you had to pass a series of tests. Those who had dedicated their time to helping the scientists for years got priority. Followed by those who were helping others survive. They only had a few space planes, similar to the capacity of an airplane that traveled to and from hundreds of times over the next few years. By the time they couldn't travel to Earth anymore, they had transported nearly a million people, which feels like a lot, but just New York State has more than nineteen million people.

Once the scientists started working on Otium, that's when they started designing the technology to go back in time. If they figured out how to travel to another universe, there were now unlimited possibilities.

The video shows the different locations of Otium, completely bare, with then a video compilation of building each community up and everyone helping each other. As the years passed, Earth became warmer, storms became deathly, and those who remained on Earth continued to damage the land. About fifteen years into Otium's timeline, Earth gets hit by space matter, leaving a good portion destroyed. Otium isn't sure if there is still life on Earth as they haven't traveled to that timeline of Earth, but the disaster is what created the idea of the Otium Initiative. Time travel and the initiative took decades to implement, but now, five years ago, it a became reality.

Much of Otium is still undiscovered. Thousands of people each day are exploring the lands, figuring out what's habitable, and starting to build new communities in order to accommodate the ideal influx of humans from Earth.

Because we are in a parallel universe, they learned that no matter what happens on Earth in the past, the present of Otium remains. The only thing that messes up the timeline is what happens directly in Earth's timeline.

I didn't recognize how much tension that question was causing in my body until I slouch and fall back into my chair. Whatever family past Theodore may have brought to Otium—if I made it to Otium—that family will remain safe here. Therefore, I'm only messing up my current timeline, which has an unknown future.

The video ends a few minutes later.

"What happened to all the people that couldn't go to Otium?" I ask as the screen goes black. "Surely, there were more than one million good people throughout the entire world."

Flynn clicks off the projection and turns his body toward me. "There were. Millions even. But between storms getting worse, income depleted by the wealthy, natural resources disappearing, and a pandemic, many people ended up dying before the first space planes were created. Millions were still left behind to die. The scientists underestimated the amount of times they'd be able to make the trip back to Earth. Soon, it just became unsafe to land, and honestly, people on Otium feared bringing new people in who could bring sickness to our new population."

"Are the wealthy here?"

"Some." Flynn nods. "But they had more rigorous testing to do. What did they do with their money? How'd they help others? What did they do throughout their lifetime? Our goal now is to increase the number of people who make it here to genuinely let in those who deserve another chance. We've got the technology to support the transition now."

I can't help but wonder who in my life might not have made the cut. Now I'm even more afraid to know whether or not I originally did. Had I accomplished enough in my life to be one of one million? Did Jonah or Alejandro make the cut?

"How is the transition going to happen?"

"That's still being discussed," Flynn says.

My eyes bug out at his calm demeanor, as if that isn't the most important question here.

"And you aren't curious?" I ask.

"Of course, but it isn't my job to figure it out. I need to trust those who are in charge. My job is to make sure I do my absolute best at being a mentor."

So his mind doesn't spiral in a million different directions when he doesn't know how something works or when he doesn't have the answer to everything? *Cool. Noted.*

"Okay," Flynn says, standing up. "We are going to start with implicit bias training. We have a computer system to see where we specifically need to work with you. Everyone in the initiative takes these tests, and then they are split into groups based on their scores. Since your program is different, regardless of your score, you'll be with me. But I'll adjust the training to suit you and your personal goals." He carries his chair back over to the thicker computer. "Are you a Mac or a PC person?" Flynn asks.

"Mac," I respond, and Flynn walks over to the MacBook Air on the left desk.

Suddenly, he's clicking into a software called "The Otium Initiative."

"Bring your chair over, and you can work on this computer."

I do as he says, sitting in front of an "Implicit Bias" module.

"There are a few tests on race, gender, and sexual orientation. They should each only take a few minutes to complete. Make sure you follow and read the directions carefully. This computer is the MacBook Air from your time. While it was just built a few years ago on Otium, it is the same specs. In order to do this training, we have to use computers that our mentees know so they don't accidentally make a mistake."

I don't exactly know what he means, but the familiarity is comforting. My parents both had MacBook Airs. While I haven't used it since my dad last gave me permission, it still feels like a part of them is with me.

Flynn leaves me to my own devices, going to sit at the other desk. He opens the laptop and immediately gets to work on whatever he's doing. Flynn did mention that he still had to complete his mentoring degree, but I'm curious if mentoring me requires paperwork like a teacher would have to do on Earth.

I shake my head. *Focus, Theo.*

The quizzes are simple. They require me to press two letters on the keyboard, categorizing race, gender, and sexual orientation with different categories. For example, gender categorizes who is better suited for sciences or humanities, so the pictures shown are astronauts, immunologists, doctors, and then, there are pictures of teachers, librarians, receptionists. The complicated part of this is remembering what keys to press with what category. But maybe that's it. Perhaps the brain would latch onto the rules faster if it meant it was being categorized similarly. While not verbatim, we are taught that men are more deemed for sciences, and women are suited for humanities. So when the quiz starts categorizing men and humanities together and women and sciences, my brain fumbles on the keys.

In the end, the quizzes tell me that I am slightly biased. I like to believe that's common. No matter how decent a person I am, I recognize that I'm a white male. I may be gay, but I'm also a *white* gay male that still comes with a privilege that I know Alejandro doesn't have. Alejandro was born in America; his parents are immigrants, and he identifies as pansexual. He has the privilege of a loving, supportive family, but his race and sexual identity line him up for ridicule sometimes.

I'm not sure anyone from Earth can be completely unbiased—or maybe I should speak on account of only Americans. The society I've been born and raised into is so keen on gendering you from birth. So many people say that they won't do it for their own kids, but it's so easy to fall into it. Everyone wants to know the sex when someone is pregnant. And eavesdropping on conversations between Ellie and my mom, I understand the necessity of knowing if you're someone who likes to be prepared—and biologically, there are differences to note. Though sex reveals—better known as gender reveals—are so common these days that it has me wondering what the gut reaction is for each parent who sees the stereotypical blue or pink. Naturally, I think we all have a preference engrained by society. But excitement over a boy or girl leaves out all non-binary, gender fluid, and transgender people. Still celebrating one sex over the other only makes closing the gap on gender bias that much harder.

"You all set?" Flynn asks, breaking me from my concentration. "You okay? You've just kinda been staring into space."

"Y-yeah, all good." I smile over at him. "Just thinking about the train wreck that is America."

He lets out a belly laugh. Flynn hasn't let on if America is the brunt of many jokes—that is if joking is okay here. I keep getting the vibe that Otium has been designed to specifically not be America.

"If it makes you feel better, from the history I have learned, while America has had quite a terrible run, there are many countries that aren't great. While my family is 'American,'" he actually used the air quotes, "there are many people in this specific town who are not. A lot of the geographic locations here have a widespread group of people. A part of what works on Otium is that each person must know a good portion of their family history, what their country did right and wrong, and how to improve upon the mistakes made. Without knowing our past, we cannot create a better future. Unfortunately for Earth, it seems as if it was in a constant, vicious cycle of repeating history—America being one of those countries, but definitely not the only one."

Suddenly, I feel very small. Flynn is just a tad older than me, yet he's far beyond his years.

"How the hell have you learned all that already?" I ask, and Flynn chuckles. I know he's laughing *at* me, but the sound brings goosebumps to my skin. I'm responsible for this little sliver of happiness he is having.

"Education is very different here—or so I understand from what my mom, dad, other mentors, and mentees have all said. It's a compilation of how education works throughout Earth, and it also has to do with the age in which we learn things. My mom said that a lot of American education is repeating information over and over for years, likely because you can't comprehend it at the age you're originally taught. Also, all school isn't taught in a boring classroom."

I raise my brow as I glance around this empty room with one single light above us.

"Touché." Flynn grins. "Not all studies are taught here. A lot of our family history education happens at home with our parents. Since we are still a young society, our parents are learning more too. It helps that we have the ability to travel to and from Earth now, so if there is confusion on anything, we have someone investigate further. You said my mom had a fascination with learning about my great-grandparents' friends, and while I never heard about this for my education, the timeline adds up."

I'd love the revamped version of education now instead of the bullshit bias in my history book.

Flynn continues on for the rest of the hour, talking about my test scores and what they mean. He says they were great scores, but then, he quizzes me more. He asks about specific toys for kids; what I played with being an only child versus what my brothers played with. A lot of my toys were hand-me-downs my mom and dad saved from their childhood. There were dolls and barbies from my mom and matchbox cars and Pokémon from my dad. They tried to reduce their carbon footprint. My brothers played with cars a lot but were more destructive and played imaginary games too, but then they got into video games. It wasn't until first or second grade that I started questioning the toys I played with because I was hanging out with people who weren't my parents' friend's kids.

Naturally, as I got older and came out to my parents, some people started to talk—especially my aunt and uncle. Those people said that I was gay because I played with dolls. But that's not true because my sexuality isn't something I chose—it's something that I am, always was, and always will be.

As the hour progresses, we go over a general understanding of implicit bias and some of the world's biggest concerns. We don't dive into anything too deep, like this might be Implicit Bias 101. Flynn says that we'll touch further on bias each day, sometimes in the classroom, sometimes exploring the area. Seems like another form of therapy, honestly, but maybe that's the point.

If I can't see the implicit bias in my life, how can I expect to help others change and grow?

Twenty-One

I tried talking my way out of counseling with Corie. I told Flynn that there were a ton of other educational things we could be doing with my time. Instead, he just smirked and grabbed hold of my handlebars from the bike he gave me at the beginning of the day and pulled me as he pedaled, leading me to the therapy building.

Mainly, I don't want to discuss what happened yesterday when Corie came to try and get me out of my funk. I know what my issues are. I know how to handle them. I know when the attacks come and go. I don't want to dive back through and explain every single feeling. Despite my past, it should be a pretty common occurrence for people to have trouble with their anxiety the first few days on a NEW PLANET.

"Theodore," Corie's voice reminds me that I've been sitting in her office, silent, for a few minutes.

I lock eyes with her, and her face softens. She has her pad on the armrest of her chair. I already heard her finger tap a few things on it.

"I'd like to dive into yesterday if you don't mind," Corie

starts. Her words are casual, as if yesterday ended with a lovely conversation.

"I thought I was supposed to come back with a happy memory?" Not like I thought of a happy memory in the midst of nightmares and anxiety attacks, but I can find one.

Corie nods, giving me that sickening therapy smile. The one where she knows my life is hard, but it's not like she's experienced hardships.

"Yes, you're correct. We can afterward. Your situation is more sensitive than most. You've been uprooted in the blink of an eye. You're grieving. It's definitely going to bring up some feelings. I think we should discuss them."

I sigh and lean back onto the sofa. It's one of the reasons that I don't like therapy for myself. I want to make therapy work for me on how I feel that day. Not discuss something of the past.

T - 52 minutes before I'm free of her.

"Sometimes, I get anxiety and panic attacks, but I work through them. I can function on my own. I'm here now, aren't I? No help from anyone."

"You don't have to rely just on yourself, Theodore. We are all here to help. How long have you had these attacks?"

"One year and two days." I avoid her eyes. I don't want there to be any connection with her as she recognizes the date.

"In relation to—"

"In relation to my parents being shot in front of me. Yes. I think that deems it acceptable to have them!" I'm gripping the arm of the sofa until I catch Corie's eyes staring at my hand. I release the hold, moving to the edge of the couch, shaking my right leg.

She should already know all this. I don't see the point in hashing it all out.

"Let it out, Theodore. It's okay to feel it all."

I press down on my leg, silently begging it to stop shaking.

"Is there anything that triggered you into an anxiety attack the other day?"

I shoot up from my seat and pace. I want to storm out of this room. She has to be fucking joking.

"Aside from my parents dying?" It can't be normal for a therapist to be this dense. They have all my fucking information. Corie *and* Flynn should have been smarter than this yesterday.

I should have remembered.

She solemnly nods her head. "Yes, I do know that is more than enough to set off a panicked state."

My blood boils as I tighten my hands into fists.

"What I am trying to figure out is what happened between the afternoon I met you, on the anniversary of your parents' deaths, to the following day when I saw you in your room."

The guilt fizzles inside my stomach. I hated and still hate myself for forgetting. I went through half the day without even thinking about it. Even with being uprooted to this godforsaken planet that my parents knew about.

"I forgot. Is that what you wanted to hear?" I raise my voice. "That I forgot about their deaths? That I got so caught up in escaping that I escaped too much? That I had nightmare after nightmare of their deaths when my mind finally remembered?" I scream, gripping my hands into my curls and yanking tight. The skin pulls from my skull.

I take a breath, trying to lower my volume. "Or are you nosey about how my mind is processing everything? How I didn't just lose my parents that week, but my second set of parents. The ones who are responsible for Andrya's existence." Her false shocked face doesn't cut it. I know she knows about Sam and Ellie. Corie has to know everything Andrya does, even if Flynn doesn't. "The ones who abandoned me and then suddenly reappeared right before I left Earth. The ones who are apparently responsible for Andrya uprooting me without notice?" I walk over to the door. My heart pounds against my ribcage. I need a breather. "Yeah, I'd say I've been fucking triggered." I open the door and look back at her.

Her face is solemn; I get it. I understand it. Those pathetic looks of sympathy are ingrained in my head from every person who never knew my family.

"Theodore, we aren't done here yet."

"I am," I say, slamming the door behind me.

I run down the stairs and outside to where my bike is. I contemplate leaving. There isn't anything keeping me from climbing on the bike and riding back to my room or somewhere else. I have complete access to the planet now—point system included. But if they tracked me on Earth, I'm sure they can find me a hell of a lot faster here.

I grab the water bottle from the holder on my bike and drink a few sips. It's a beautiful day, less sweltering than the first day I had therapy. I'd rather be out here roaming than stuck inside. Even if I had to continue therapy, I'd rather be sitting in the vita. I take a few solid breaths in-between sips of water. Each breath out has my heart rate slowing.

Across from me, there's a small park filled with some benches and big oak trees. It feels crowded for mid-day with children, teens, and adults all scattered and present. In my line of sight, Flynn sits cross-legged on a bench. His head is down, reading a book. That must be where he'll wait for me to finish my sessions—only coming closer to the building when he knows my time is up.

Bringing my water with me, I close the distance between us. I stand in front of him, blocking some of his light before he glances up. Flynn's eyes dart to his watch and he looks at me, confused.

"Why aren't you with Corie?" Placing his finger on a page, he closes the book as I sit down next to him. He's reading something about psychology.

"I got overwhelmed. Needed some water." I shrug, holding my bottle up.

"And now?" He raises a brow.

"And now I'm talking to you." I give him a cheesy, awkward smile. Hopefully, it hides the storm brewing in my mind.

"Theodore," he exhales, turning toward me. "You have to go back in and finish your session. This isn't always going to be easy."

"None of this has been easy, Flynn," I admit. "When will I find it easy?"

My body feels lighter at the confession, my shoulders dropping just slightly. I'm curious how the others handle this. Does anyone else have a traumatic experience to work through? Or are their therapy sessions more light-weight? Like soul-searching to find their deeper purpose rather than heal two murders.

This routine of having so many therapy sessions, learning new lessons, and continuing my high school education sounds utterly exhausting and unsustainable. I'm only part way through day one. Lana said something about a siesta, and if that's true, it needs to get here as soon as possible.

"I have a plan for the second half of your day when it'll just be you and me again—aside from group therapy at the end of the day. We'll grab some lunch, and then we'll go explore a place I think you'll like. We will cover more lessons while we do so, but it'll all be outside. Though this can only happen if you go and finish your session."

"And if I don't?" I question—curious what the real punishment would be.

"You're doing a disservice to yourself." Flynn then opens his book and continues to read. Case closed.

I breathe in deep and exhale loudly before nodding. Forcing myself up and off the bench, I trudge back inside.

⁂

THE VOLUME OF THE COMMUNAL DINING ROOM IS deafening. The tables are packed with people of all ages. This planet may strive for perfection, but you'll never take the energy out of a cafeteria setting. Just like at school, children yell and scream, laugh, and play pranks with their friends.

Flynn decided we were going to get takeaway and head to the Forest to eat. The Forest sounds like music to my overstimulated brain.

We both order wraps that are handed to us in glass containers with real silverware. We fill up our reusable water bottles, and before I know it, we are back outside. My ears ache as silence overtakes them.

"To-go in glass?" I question, tilting my container slightly.

"It's an honor system. Everyone trusts you'll bring the containers back when you're finished, whether it be today or the next day. For the most part, everyone follows the system. They keep track if you don't return them. If you don't, you are either suspended from the dining room for a few days, or you lose points. Depends on how often you forget."

I nod, processing the information while Flynn takes both of our containers and puts them in his backpack. The system makes sense, but I didn't see a code on the container to indicate that I'm the one who took it.

We bike down the path, through the neighborhoods that I only saw that night walking to Andrya's house. The blocks are vast. It's confirmed that everyone has equal space—sans Andrya—but there are far more people living in Olive than I initially thought. The neighborhood expands well past the street Andrya lives on.

Soon, we are only a couple hundred feet away from the Forest. I halt my bike, taking in the view before me. The Forest greets the edge of the Flatlands with mile-high pine trees. From our distance, the trees seem as if they are on top of one another, invading each tree's space to grow.

"Wow, this is much more impressive than I thought it'd be." I sigh. My love language is nature, and this feels like it'll be *my* place to escape. I've always wanted to explore Oregon's state forests, and this forest is nearly identical to the pictures.

"It's pretty magnificent inside. There are some wild animals, none that'll bother you if you don't bother them, but more than we have in the Flatlands."

"Let's go!" I exclaim, my energy rejuvenating. There's a tingling beneath my skin, a yearning to get lost in the darkness.

I bike off before Flynn does, but like running, he's quick to catch my speed.

"Toss your bike!" he yells over to me. "We walk in."

I hop off the bike right at the entrance. The pine trees

barely allow a morsel of light into the forest. A cool air drifts toward us.

I cannot wait.

He's slowing his pace, and I dart into the forest without him. My foot catches a root, halting my steps as pockets of light trickle through the branches.

The cool air has my body letting out an internal shiver as I take in the sight before me. Birds are finally chirping, and rustling takes over as small animals scurry away. The temperature drops a good ten degrees just by the shade. I push my vitaglasses on top of my head.

Flynn's palm rests on my shoulder, and I glance toward him, smiling from ear to ear. The wave of stress filters through my arms, down my fingertips, and out of my body. I shake my hands just slightly before I continue—slower this time—walking along the path.

We need to go deeper, farther, and never, ever come out.

Flynn leads me to a fallen tree that's taken residency in the spot. Moss covers a good portion of the thick trunk. Bunny burrows are hidden underneath the trunk and near the roots. Flynn gestures to sit on the log, and a family of bunnies eye us from a nearby tree. We may be in their territory, invading their home as they ventured to eat. I place my index finger to my lips and nod toward them, hoping Flynn is silent with his backpack.

Flynn slowly opens the bag, taking out our containers, and hands me my order. "They are always here. They aren't afraid of us, just fascinated." His voice is only a tad softer than usual. "Happiness looks good on you," he comments.

A blush heats my cheeks; my guards down. I look over at the bunnies, and they are no longer concerned or threatened by either of us. It always feels magical to be trusted by skittish creatures. I only ever want to watch them in their natural habitat.

"So, tell me about your friends back home," Flynn says once we're both situated on the log. It's wide enough for me to sit cross-legged with my lunch container in my lap.

"Friends?" I look over at him while opening my container. "Don't you already know everything about my life?" I take a bite of the garden veggie wrap, and my god, will there be food here that doesn't taste incredible?

Flynn sits up straight, keeping his container lid on. "Okay," he sighs, turning to face me head-on. "So let me explain how things work for the mentors, and we can go from there, okay?"

I nod, taking another bite. Frustration doesn't look good on him.

"We get a file of all important information, like their birthday, deaths, special events, monumental moments, some trends that the person tends to go through. Sometimes, there is visual footage, but contrary to your beliefs, they aren't following you 24/7. Footage is basically from public events. Therefore, I do not know everything about you. In your case, and many other mentees here, the special events and monumental moments have to do with activism versus anything personal. Case-in-point, friendships and normal routine of life."

"I live in a room right now that is made from a replica of my childhood bedroom. You're saying that's a public place?"

He shakes his head. "No one has ever seen you inside your bedroom. Most volunteers tell us what makes their homes or rooms special, and we accommodate that. Those in your situation, though, I'm not sure how they replicated your room. Maybe your parents got far enough on the application, or maybe Sam and Ellie contributed somehow?"

"You think they know about Otium?" Flynn shrugs, but his hands slightly shake as he opens his container lid.

"I don't know. A part of me hopes they have no idea because that means I was kept from meeting them. For your sake, I hope they do know so they can help you when you're home."

I nod, processing the information. My fingertips carve into the wrap, the dressing oozing out of the small holes I just created. What are the odds that Sam and Ellie happened to be home the day that I left for Otium? It is possible they came just because of my hospitalization, but it's all a bit bizarre.

I want to be creeped out by all of this. Pissed off. Annoyed—especially because some logic doesn't make sense. On the outside, it's impressive what they've done in sixty years here. They created a new world, figured out time travel, and somehow were bored enough to track me for years.

"So, friends?" Flynn asks.

It's unclear if he's clarifying whether the two of us are friends or if he's itching for more questions.

"Friends," I confirm. "You really don't know anything about my friends?"

"Nope. Well, I know you had a boyfriend, but that's because you told me."

I furrow my brows. I don't remember telling him anything about Jonah. The only person who would have known him is Lana. I like to believe she isn't spilling my secrets—but she *is* spilling Andrya's.

"How do you know about Jonah?"

"Jonah? Was that your boyfriend's name?"

I nod. Had. Was. The past tense twists knives in my abdomen.

"You told me the night you came back. When you were frustrated about what you lost because of Otium."

Memories of me breaking down in front of him flash through my head. I barely remember what I said when I started yelling. Apparently, he remembers every damn thing.

I take another bite of my wrap, avoiding his eyes for a moment. That night feels like a lifetime ago.

Flynn finally takes a bite of food. "So, tell me about your life, whatever you'd like to share."

"And you'll tell me about yours?" I lift my brow, eyeing him.

His eyes crinkle as he laughs, mid-chewing. "Well, yes, Theodore. Friendship 101: we get to know each other."

"Oh." *Silly me to think we were going to study at this time or learn.* I let my body relax, allowing a smile to appear. I can get behind this afternoon. I wonder if this is part of the siesta. If so, I hope in the future I have the decision on whether I want to actually rest or explore.

"I'll start," he says. "I'm a twin. My sister is finishing up her studies to teach grade school. We're pretty close, but we both invest heavily in our careers. She'll be around a bit. I have four close friends. Mattis, whom you've met, Amy, from lunch the other day, Remy, my ex and friend, and Ryleigh, my sister."

"You're friends with your ex?" My voice cracks.

"Yeah. The four of us have been inseparable since we started school together. Just because feelings developed for Remy doesn't mean that negates them as friends, first and foremost. Does it take time and grieving? Sure. But most things take time."

He's not straight. My heart flutters at the thought.

I sit there, feeling my food bubble in my stomach.

"How long were you and Remy together?"

Flynn's eyes glaze over for a moment. "About a year. The longest relationship I've had. We ended things about six months ago." My eyes bug out.

I can understand getting over a relationship in that time frame, even moving on to someone new, but to be best friends again? That feels nearly impossible.

"And everything is already back to normal? You don't still have feelings for them?"

He chuckles, his head tilting back. "Okay, twenty questions. Yes. We are pretty much back to normal. Someone jealous?" He wiggles his brows.

My face warms as my stomach settles just slightly. Maybe I am a little jealous. Whether it's because he's so emotionally stable or if I'm jealous of the ex, I'm not sure.

"I'm grieving." I try to give him a straight face, but his brow lifts a little higher, and my lips twitch.

"You sure it isn't because you think I'm attractive?"

A laugh bubbles out of me, breaking my straight face. I was not expecting that.

"Someone is full of themselves." I chuckle, looking down at my almost empty container.

"Oh-kay," he draws out. "Keep convincing yourself your demeanor didn't change at the sound of ex. Just so you know, I won't be your rebound." He winks before replacing the lid on his empty container and hopping off the log. "Okay, tell me about your life. 1, 2, 3, GO!"

He's bouncing in front of me now as if we're in an 80s workout video. All I can think about is the food stuffed in my stomach with each bounce of his. Sam, his great-grand-father, does this often when he has too much energy coursing through his system. Ellie and I would always make fun of him because it was like the moment food entered his system, his energy reactivated.

"I have a best friend, Alejandro," I offer.

"Man of many words. No dice." Flynn grins. "Tell me more. When did you meet Alejandro? Is he your only friend? Is he friends with you and Jonah—ooh!" He continues his sashaying from one foot to another. "Is it going to be hard to go home because Alejandro and Jonah are close friends?"

"No, actually." I let out a breath at that thought. Alejandro and Jonah may have been communicating recently, but they aren't close, and it wouldn't be detrimental to either of them if they never saw one another again. "My friendship with Alejandro is separate from Jonah. Alejandro became close with me because of our activism. He volunteered a lot with my parents' agency and helped me a ton with my parents' trial."

Flynn stops his movement as I finish speaking. "And Jonah didn't do this?" His head tilts slightly as he takes a seat in the grass, looking up at me.

The bane of my existence. A wave of relief courses through my body at his recognition that Jonah should have been involved, though. A part of me feels like I have to defend Jonah. Jonah is right; he should have his own life, but there should have been a balance too.

"How do you know he didn't?" I blurt out instead of confirming.

Flynn holds his hands up in defense. "Wrong for me to assume. We try to teach you guys not to do that. I just thought that if Alejandro and Jonah weren't friends, it might mean they never hung out? Therefore, Jonah wasn't around much with your activism?"

Can't get anything past Flynn, it seems. Flynn's blue, wide eyes are gentle. There's a comfort in them. In the way he crosses his ankles, arms wrapping around his legs. He's listening to every word. Ready to respond, nod, question. To think of it, I haven't seen him on his phone at all today. That's a rarity on Earth; he didn't even distract himself when he was studying earlier.

"You're right," I reply. I turn to face Flynn, dropping my legs off the log. I take my shoes and socks off, allowing my feet to graze the grass. Just the simple act of touching nature has me sinking into my seat. Nature really does the trick for me.

"Jonah used to be better when we were younger, and then he lost interest, and I started to get frustrated. Then my parents died, and he barely lifted a finger to help."

"He never helped you through a panic or anxiety attack?" He squints his eyes, looking over at his bag briefly, like he wants to check his device.

Our eyes connect, and I remember the first night here on Otium. How Flynn knew exactly what to do. How to help. How to be . . . Jonah. Flynn just said that they didn't have videos of me in private places.

My brows knit and my eyes blur. Flynn was starting to become my place of comfort. *Did he lie to me?*

"Your parents' fundraising event last year. Just days after their deaths," he says, breaking the tension.

My blood runs cold. I know exactly what he is talking about. How I broke down in front of everyone there. Screamed and yelled before collapsing to the ground.

"There is a video in your file," he continues, "from that event when you had a panic attack, and Jonah helped you through it. It was there for me to learn what methods worked well in case I needed it."

The confirmation boils in my stomach, twisting the wrap I just had. I fist my hands by my sides, trying not to let them shake.

"I'm not saying it is the correct thing to do, but the video *was* taken from a public space." His voice remains calm, and I hate that my mind tries to latch onto it, connecting dots between him and his great-grandparents.

"Why couldn't it just be a note?" I swallow the waver in my voice. "Like hey, ask the crazy, panicked kid how best to handle his attacks."

Flynn frowns and pushes himself up off the ground. My heartbeat accelerates as he steps closer, standing mere centimeters from me.

"Theo," his voice is soft, tentative. "Can I call you Theo?"

My hands grip my thighs. His invasion of space has popped my bubble, sparks erupting at the faint idea of his touch. That is, until his hand rests on top of my own. His fingers are careful, so they don't actually graze my thigh.

I inhale, slow, steady breathing. He asked me a question —a sign of respect—even though I introduced myself to his friend this morning as Theo.

"Y-yeah," I breathe. "Theo."

A gentle squeeze of his hand has my frustration disappearing, even if my lungs can't tame themselves.

"Theo." I love the way my name floats off his tongue. Breathy and present. Not a hesitant address or any interlaced negative feelings. "You're not crazy or panicked. We also try to refrain from using the word 'crazy' here. Your anxiety doesn't define you. It's a part of you, but it isn't your identity."

Tears drip over my waterline. Drying out my cheeks. I shiver as the air meets my tears.

Flynn's sitting beside me now, leaning his arm against me. He tilts his head briefly to touch mine before straightening. His arm doesn't move, though, nor does his clammy hand.

I don't know what's right or wrong or good or bad. This is all so fucking exhausting. Otium has rules in place—public videos only—they didn't lie about that, yet. But it is invasive. It is private. I was vulnerable, scared, and overwhelmed. They used that as a teaching method.

"I'm not condoning the method of giving me a video, but I am expected to know the content in my file. However, if you would like to tell me another way that I can help you through anything, I'd love to know . . . from you."

I take a deep breath in, lifting my hands to run over my face. Flynn's palm drops on my thigh, and unfortunately, and fucking respectfully, his hand moves. I massage my eyes, trying to dry the tears, then I tangle them in my knotted curls. I could use that spa right about now. I don't have money for one at home, but I sure as hell have extra points here to use.

"Why do I feel comfortable around you?" I whisper.

I can't fight the insecurity of it all. He's proven he's only doing his job when things get wonky. He can't make changes or be aware of how certain things affect others if no one mentions it. Otium is all he knows.

When I allow myself to look at Flynn, he doesn't smile or grin. There is no confidence exuding. Instead, he lays his palm flat out, and I place mine on top. His fingertips curl around my hand, absorbing his calm demeanor.

"It could be a variety of reasons," he starts. "You can find safety in believing that I'm temporary, and if things go south, you can either choose a new mentor, or you leave at your time and never see me again."

Well, I don't like that reason. I don't want to be reminded that he is temporary. That no matter how great he may be or how good a friend he could become, it all ends. We aren't living in the same timeline.

"There's also a part of you that may want a friend, someone to lean on. You're tired of fighting and need someone to help carry the burden. And then, maybe, there's a possibility that this might be my calling, and I'm able to create that space for you."

I don't like the idea of his calm presence being a reason that I'm comfortable. A reason that any of his future mentees may be comfortable. I want it to be because he is becoming a friend . . . because these sparks and tingles I feel are igniting something more than friends. The idea that someone else could feel similar for him all while he's just trying to do his job.

. . . is he just doing his job, and my heart pounding in my chest is one-sided?

We sit silently. A slight breeze filters through the trees. My hand is still in his. I'm not sure who is applying more pressure, but it's a grip I fear losing—a comfort that doesn't compete with Jonah's. Something new, invigorating, hopeful.

"Theo?" His voice cracks with an audible gulp afterward. "Is it true that this initiative is the reason you and Jonah broke up?" His hesitant words cause my heart to flutter. I try to remember exactly what I shouted about Jonah the other night.

Is he jealous?

"The initiative solidified a breakup that should have happened months ago," I say softly. I lift my palm from his, allowing my fingertips to dance in his hand. I like the way his fingers curl in at the touch, and his soft shiver doesn't escape me. "Jonah and I got toxic. We might be able to become friends when I go back—that is, if you teach me your magical ways."

A breathy laugh escapes him, but he holds back a portion of it.

"If Jonah and I stayed together much longer, we likely would have ended in an explosion."

He interlocks his fingers with mine, and my breath catches. I've held Alejandro's hand before, but in my head, the interlace is the next step forward. Flynn's made a move.

"If you'd like to learn how to become healthy friends with Jonah, we can definitely focus time on that. Ultimately, it all ends up with you becoming healthier."

I nod. Jonah isn't my focus right now. It's the way Flynn's fingers fit perfectly between my own. No additional pressure, no blood loss circulation. His palm isn't wide or longer than my own. The pads of his fingers are warm as mine are always cool.

I'm sad about Jonah. It will hurt now and again when things remind me of him, but each and every "off" day, I think I slowly fell out of love with him. The last time we were intimate was the barbecue before the protest. Each embrace after that was solely him being a caretaker.

My head tilts toward Flynn, and he meets me in the middle. We may have some place to be, but here, in the middle of the Forest, is where I've felt the calmest.

The bunnies hop toward us after a few minutes of complete silence. They glance up at our stagnant bodies before hopping toward their burrow, a few feet away from us, underneath the tree.

Yeah, I'm good here.

Twenty-Two

Group counseling is the last thing on my schedule and when Flynn is done with his job for the day. It's a weird finality. It'll be six once the group is complete. There is still so much time left to fill. I could go to bed early, but then I may wake up four hours early.

Flynn and I did have a two-hour lunch before diving back into implicit biases. Thankfully, Flynn allowed us to stay in the Forest for that.

"My class will run over your group session," Flynn says, "so I won't be able to meet you after. But if you're up for it, we could grab dinner tonight? That is, if you still want to hang out," Flynn says as we near the therapy building.

"Okay." I nod. I don't want to walk back into the therapy building after finally feeling light, like I'm on a cloud. Leaving the darkness of the Forest and heading back toward Olive felt like our moment was over. Whatever happened in those confines was there to stay.

Thankfully, hopping on our bikes took away any potential awkwardness of holding hands. The moment popped, and it might not reappear. I don't think I'm ready to move on from Jonah, but I do like the giddy happiness that comes from having a crush.

"I'll text you when I finish class, but no obligation, okay?" Flynn says as he stops his bike in front of the bike rack.

I push my bike into a free place before turning back to him. I like that he says he'll message me instead of placing the obligation on me, which I'd likely chicken out and not message him at all. Now I just have to convince myself that if he forgets to message me, it doesn't mean hates me.

"Sounds great." I flash him a small smile before entering the building.

Group counseling terrifies me. It's the first time I'll see every person who is part of this current program again. Amalia waves and pats the seat next to her as soon as I walk through the door. She's overly enthusiastic, but I guess it's nice to feel like someone is in my corner. Instead of allowing myself to shut down, I try to feed off of her energy. If she's this excited to be in group counseling, maybe it won't be dreadful.

Except, it is. I don't speak aside from introducing myself. I'm nervous, and I clam up. The therapist says she'll give me a day to see how it all works—a literal out that has me shutting down. I don't feel comfortable here. This isn't Flynn's presence. This isn't talking to a friend. There are too many strangers.

Group counseling is different from the individual in the sense that this is about our activism. It seems the program is arranged, so we learn certain things about Earth and Otium, different biases, and how to relate them to our lives. Then, we have our individual counseling. Group is when we get together to digest our day. Depending on the lessons, some days will be harder for others, and some days will be more carefree.

It's mainly intimidating because my schedule is different from everyone else's, and I'm the youngest. Really sitting in a circle with everyone makes it more apparent that I'm just a teenager. I always thought I could pass as legal in America, but maybe it was all in my head. The group is welcoming and friendly, but they've experienced a hell of a lot more than me in their personal lives, careers, and activism.

"Theodore!" Amalia calls as I walk out of the counseling room. She's next to me in seconds. "Would you like to hang out? Zhang and I are going to hang out with Mattis. He mentioned something about a corn hole competition? Would you like to join?"

It hits me that I don't have any other responsibilities for the day. There is no job to attend, no event to plan, no hours of homework, or social media to post on. I don't even have to check in on my brothers to make sure they are fed or doing their homework—or unexpectedly babysitting them. My only responsibility here is to attend the schedule as noted, and then I'm free.

I hadn't thought about what I'd do while I waited for Flynn to message, and I gave even less thought to whether he'd ditch me. Not a single person is expecting anything of me. I have nowhere to be, and holy hell, what a liberating feeling that is.

A real, genuine smile graces my face. "Yeah," I say to Amalia. "That sounds fun. Where are we going?"

"Near the gym. Zhang!" Amalia yells. "This is Theodore."

Zhang joins us; her soft, almond eyes match her red smile. Zhang skips to interlock her arm with Amalia, and I watch in amazement as her perfectly constructed, pitch-black ballet bun doesn't move a millimeter.

"Nice to meet you, Theodore. Come join us!" Zhang greets.

I look between Amalia and Zhang to make sure they do actually want me to join them. I don't want to be a charity case as the young one or the one without notice here. It didn't get brought up in the group, but it will, and I can't be certain that Amalia didn't tell everyone what she found out this morning.

They grin as we begin to walk out of the building. Zhang interlocks her arm with mine, too, once we are all outside. Amalia and Zhang start discussing something from earlier in the day that I think I would have been jealous about if I didn't have my moment in the Forest. This morning, I would have been angry that my program is different. Instead, I'm grateful I don't have to carry any awkward conversations and can remain in my own memory of today.

The town is crowded now. It seems most are finished with their day. Children run around unattended with their friends. Some adults are holding books or bags while others carry only water or coffee. The closer we get to the gym, the more people we are joined by.

I try to convince myself the crowds will be fine. That I need to step out of my comfort zone, and if it doesn't go well, I stay until I have the excuse of Flynn to get me out of here. However, the crowds disperse closer to the gym. People split off in different directions. There are less than twenty people at the corn hole location when we get there. The demographic is mostly late teens to late twenties.

"Theo! Good to see you." Mattis waves when he finds us. He greets Amalia and Zhang with hugs. "Are you two going to compete?" Mattis asks, glancing between Zhang and me.

"Nope," I blurt. I'm about to apologize when Zhang laughs, seconding my response.

Amalia and Mattis leave to enter the competition, and Zhang leads us toward a small domed shack next to the gym. This must be the open theater area Flynn had mentioned.

"She's got a thing for Mattis," Zhang shares as we walk. "She's a little head over heels for him, but it's cute. I don't even know if she knows how to play corn hole, but he asked her when she got coffee at lunch, and she immediately said yes."

We stand in line at the shack, which seems to be a bar with some food. I don't know what I'm getting or if I'm just standing here because I followed Zhang. I'm not even sure how I'm supposed to respond to what she just said.

Zhang came off as a complete powerhouse in her discussion in group therapy today. She seems to have the most interesting back story. While she's traveled a lot, she's mainly known for her work in her fight against communism and her role in the Hong Kong protests. I didn't exactly get the vibe that she'd gossip about her new friend, but maybe that's a toxic idea? I want to be seen as someone apart from my activism. Maybe she just wants to connect with someone new.

"Have you tried their cider?" Zhang asks. I breathe out as Zhang changes the subject. She was just trying to have a conversation. "Amalia and I tried it yesterday before going on a walk, and it's to die for."

"Is it alcoholic?" I ask. I'm hoping not, as a cider sounds really refreshing in the heat.

Her eyes bug out for a moment before she collects

herself. "Right, right. You're not my age." Her smile is gentle as we move forward in line. "I think fifteen or sixteen you can drink here. The alcohol is not as toxic nor as strong here, but it gives you a solid buzz. There isn't much fear of destructive behavior, as they don't drive. They all seem more responsible here."

I can think of a million disastrous things teens can do without driving. But Zhang gets up to order, and she orders a cider and a pretzel. That sounds like a phenomenal combination.

"You want something?" she asks.

"Uh." I calculate the options quickly. I have had beer before—nothing I've really enjoyed, but I have tasted it once or twice. It's reduced my anxiety a little too. So is it so bad to have a drink or two?

"Sure," I agree. I take my phone out to pay. My first solo transaction without Flynn's supervision. "I'll have what she's having."

As we wait for our food, I assess the situation. There is a stage behind where the corn hole is set up. It seems for any event, the seating is general admission and bring your own. We don't have blankets, nor foldable chairs. I guess it'd be okay to just sit on the grass—my eyes hit the jackpot. A box of blankets and pillows to get before we find a location.

We grab blankets and pillows before setting up on Amalia's side of the competition. Zhang gives her a thumbs up, and I take my first sip of cider. It's not sweet. Definitely nothing the rare party I've attended would have. Those were always sweet wine coolers and the grossest, cheapest beer kegs.

"What do you think? Good, right?" Zhang looks over at me excitedly as I take the cider away from my lips.

There isn't an overly obnoxious alcohol taste or a burn

in my throat. The taste of apple sparkles on my tongue before becoming smooth to swallow.

"Not bad, and definitely very cool of Otium to allow my age to drink."

Zhang laughs. Her mouth opens to speak, but she pauses as a microphone screeches.

"Welcome everyone to this week's corn hole competition!" the host greets. "We have a stack of competitors today; it looks like it's going to be a great event! Make sure to get some food and drinks at the bar, and let's settle in with our first competition."

Zhang cheers Amalia's name as it's announced, and our conversation ends. The competition takes over. It's entertaining to watch the contestants get competitive but also apologize to one another. The stakes are high; each winner gets one-hundred points, but when the language becomes aggressive, the host reminds the competitors that even if they win, they will be docked for foul play if necessary. It's nice that there are repercussions for people's negative actions. Between the game, the cider, and my pretzel, I don't even have to worry about social cues with Zhang or how to carry on a conversation. It's nice to just be in the presence of someone friendly.

"Well, well, well, what do we have here?" I hear his voice before I see him. Chills run down my spine. "I left you alone for an hour, and you've already found the alcohol?"

My head spins toward Flynn. I feel the blood drain from my face. Did I break the law? Was Zhang lying to me?

"I—" I place my drink on the grass. It's half-empty. I barely even feel a buzz. "I thought . . . "

Flynn laughs loudly, but it's kind. He isn't making fun of me, or at least, it doesn't feel that way. He sits on the small edge of the blanket that's free. His thigh is millimeters from my own. There's a pull deep within me to close that distance.

"Legal age is sixteen to drink here. You're not a rebel. Just making fun." He taps my shoulder with his, winking, and I relax.

I pick my cup back up and take another sip. Whether it's out of defiance or relaxation, I'm not sure.

"I didn't expect you to be here," he says, changing the subject. His eyes watch the game as he speaks. Mattis just scored three points, getting the bean bag right in the hole. Flynn cheers, and I cover my ears from his proximity.

"Well, I expected you to text me when your class finished," I counter when he stops cheering. It may be the alcohol in my system calling him out for breaking his promise. Though, I take my phone out just to double-check that I'm not wrong.

"You're correct." Flynn waves his phone in front of me. "Mattis texted me that he was competing, and I was mid-text to you. I thought I'd come see the competition while I figured out what to say to you."

"What to say?" Goosebumps rise on my neck. Maybe I make him nervous too.

Flynn hands me his phone, and he's right; he was mid-text to me. The message says, "Hi Theo, I was wondering," and then stops.

"What were you wondering?" I raise my brow and sit up straight. My knee touches his, but neither of us moves for space.

"Would you want to watch a Marvel movie tonight?"

My hands clench the cider glass. I'm grateful the cup isn't plastic; otherwise, it would have cracked. *Marvel? Just the two of us? In a comfortable location?*

"Y-yes." I clear my throat. "Yeah, definitely. As in, you

want to watch one Marvel movie, or do you plan to see them all? If so, we have to watch them from the beginning because there's an entire timeline, and we need to watch in order because—"

His hand rests on my knee, and my nerves tingle beneath his palm. The butterflies make me feel woozy, or maybe it's the cider.

Flynn's eyes are bright, slightly crinkled, and squinting. "You're cute when you're excited."

Jonah's face flashes through my mind as my pits start to sweat. I take a deep breath and try to rid him from my mind. There is no harm in getting excited over someone new. Emotionally, we've been done for a long time.

Cheers erupt, breaking me from the beginning of a potential downward spiral. Amalia and Mattis run to hug each other. They won this round.

Flynn leans in; his breath tickles my ear. "I want to watch all the movies. I expect you to know the order and can introduce me to them as such."

Blinking a few times, I swallow the rest of my cider before looking at Flynn. The fizz vibrates down my throat, giving me some extra liquid courage to be in this moment.

"Of course. Definitely. For sure." I grin.

Twenty-Three

After the competition, I excuse myself to go back to my room for a little bit. Flynn suggested getting take-away for dinner and watching Marvel in his apartment. He said the entire collection was in the entertainment app.

Despite how thrilled I am to be alone in his apartment, I also have to slow my roll and take some space. I haven't had a moment alone since six this morning. Today is the most I've had on my schedule in nearly a week. I need a few moments to shut my eyes and recharge.

It's fascinating, really. While I am tired, for the first time in a long time, I'm excited to go back out and socialize. I don't fear taking a nap and getting too anxious to leave my room again. I know I will see Flynn tonight, and I know I will have a great time. The thought lulls me into a peaceful cat nap.

I wake up to a text from Flynn that says his apartment number. The original plan was to meet outside to head to the communal dining.

The moment I'm on the second floor of my building, it's obvious it's just for mentors. While they have a notification wall like my floor does, this one has updates to the program and tips on handling specific situations with your mentee. My notification wall is the exact opposite. It's tips on situations with your mentor, tips on life in Olive, and it's updated with weekly events. The doors on this floor are farther apart. I reckon that Flynn has at least a one-bedroom apartment versus the studio I have.

When I get to his door, I knock, and within a second, he's greeting me with the widest grin.

I walk into a small, olive green living room with a similar wood-carved coffee table like his mother's, a gray two-person sofa, and two wooden side tables. It's immaculate and simplistic. There's no vibe of who he is, aside from the loafers he's always wearing by the front door. To the left of the living room, there's a dining room table with a candle in the middle and what looks like salt and pepper on either side. A kitchenette with an island countertop overlooks the living room. The island only has a reusable bag on it and a lit candle. The room hints of vanilla. A small hallway in front of me likely leads to the bathroom and a bedroom. It's quaint for sure, but perfect for one person.

"This is great," I say, taking my shoes off right next to his. I wish I had this space, but honestly, the room they set up for me has more character. It's also a hell of a lot nicer than my bedroom back home.

"Can I be honest?" he says as he walks over to the island.

"Have you asked before?" I grin.

"Touché." He chuckles. "I'm grateful for this space, and I don't need anything bigger. But I can't wait until I have a separate location, something with my own yard and entryway."

It's something I've thought a little about when my aunt

and uncle get on my nerves. About where I'd want to live with what I can actually afford in New York. It seems far more attainable to build a house on Otium. I wish I could build up good points to have a home. I'd thrive here. Instead of starving in the shoebox apartment, I may be able to afford in New York.

"Are you able to get your own space? Or, as a mentor, do you have to stay here?"

It seems like a silly requirement.

"I'm not entirely sure. The program is only a few years old, and everyone still stays in the apartments. Plus, I'm very young. I don't know what I want my house to look like. But I've always been active with growing plants and enjoying my own space, so the apartment feels stifling sometimes. It's lovely to know so many people around here, but it can be difficult when you want your alone time, you know?"

I know exactly what he means, but I haven't crossed paths with another person in this building. There are enough exits and not enough people to feel clustered. But it's wildly comforting to know he needs his alone time, too.

"Anyway." He shakes his head. "We aren't here to talk about that. We're here to talk Marvel!" He claps his hands like it's the end of the conversation. If Marvel wasn't on the table, I'd grill him to know more.

Flynn opens the reusable bag on the counter, taking out the food containers. All the food is still steaming as he lifts the lids. When he hands me one, I see it's a rice dish with roasted vegetables and soy sauce. It looks phenomenal.

"So tell me what movie is first." He hands me some silverware before leading me to the sofa.

I dive in as he gestures for me to sit. I tell him about the main Avengers: Iron Man, Thor, Captain America, Hulk, and Black Widow. I give him a brief synopsis of each superhero before telling him we start with *Captain America: The First Avenger*, because obviously. His amusement is evident, but he refrains from saying anything until my shoulders relax and I'm comfortable on the sofa. His sofa is just as comfortable as mine—not anywhere close to the heavenly sofa at his mom's.

"No talking unless I ask a question," Flynn says, and I love that he has movie boundaries.

"No asking questions unless you pause the film," I counter.

"Well, of course, we can't go missing a minute of Marvel!" He chuckles, and my chest thumps at his excitement. Jonah loves Marvel, but Flynn's anticipation of this moment, his thrill, the shaking of his legs as he searches the entertainment app on his phone to find the movie. It's intoxicating.

Suddenly, the movie projects on the screen, taking up a good portion of his wall. One of those obnoxious screens that movie lovers want to feel like a proper theater. My fears of quality are answered as the main menu for the movie pops up. The image is crystal clear despite the movie being almost one-hundred years old.

Holy hell, the Marvel Cinematic Universe is really old here.

"Are all movies from Earth on this app?" I ask before he hits play.

"A lot are. Some things were left behind, but really well-made movies and big franchises were brought here. We are starting to have our own films come out, but nothing big in production like this yet."

I hope I get the opportunity to see Otium years from now to learn if they upheld this idea of happiness and freedom.

He clicks on the movie and dims the light in the living room, all with his phone. As soon as the film begins, I sink into the cushions and fall into the chaotic mess of Steve Rogers. It's like I never even left home.

"Wow. Wow. Wow!" Flynn exclaims as the credits roll.

Our empty dishes are on the coffee table. We've sunk into the sofa, so our shoulders touch. I barely remember the reactions Jonah had the first time watching Captain America; it feels like a lifetime ago in our relationship. But seeing Flynn enjoy the excitement, heartbreak, and frustration was amazing.

"I mean, we have to watch the next movie," Flynn continues. "Holy shit, why have I waited so long?"

I shrug, but I'm smiling from ear to ear, and fuck, do my cheeks ache. These muscles have barely been used in months.

"Sometimes, it's hard to introduce yourself to these movies alone. But now you're hooked, and I refuse to let you watch them alone."

"Is that a promise?" He turns his head to look directly at me, only centimeters from my own.

"Yeah," I breathe.

His hand cups my knee. My nerves vibrate throughout my entire body. With a quick clap on my knee, he is standing. The rush of air cools me, and I have to remind myself to swallow, but my eyes follow his every movement.

"Okay, we need snacks," he decides with a nod. "And then, you need to tell me which movie is next."

Twenty-Four

I'm on a high most of the morning. Flynn and I watched two more Marvel films, *Captain Marvel* and *Iron Man,* before we reluctantly decided we needed to sleep. Once back in my room, I stayed awake, replaying the entire night; Flynn's smiles, gasps, anger, frustration, excitement. There are arguments to be made about it being my favorite way to watch a Marvel movie.

Despite only getting a couple hours of sleep, I find myself at The Espresso Bar again at 6:00 am. A sleep schedule like this won't last long, but it's almost hard to believe that yesterday was just my first day through this. The day flew by, but also felt like a lifetime.

I catch up with Amalia and Mattis, who seem closer than they were just yesterday morning. I congratulated them on their win, and they informed me they won the entire competition, which I hadn't seen. It almost feels intrusive to be a part of their morning hangout. Every other sentence is them confessing their feelings. Luckily, Flynn interrupts an hour later, as if he strides in here at this time every day. For all I know, he does.

I'm calmer and more at ease with him after last night. Our conversations are light during coffee and breakfast. I learn more about his favorite colors, turquoise and mauve, and favorite activities as a kid. Apparently, he and his sister would create stories in the Forest and get lost for hours. There's even a treehouse he may show me one day—if I'm lucky. I swear I didn't miss a wink, but there isn't time to focus on any of that before we dive into the day.

My energy remains throughout the two hours of homework for my high school. I'm eager to be in Flynn's presence again, that is, until Flynn speaks inside the dark, dank classroom of our first lesson of the day.

"Today, we are going to discuss our fears."

My world stops. The clouds aren't light and fluffy anymore; instead, they've frozen in place. Even my inhale feels like straight methanol invading my lungs.

I glance around the classroom. Yesterday this was fine. I was looking at a computer to take tests. But now it's suffocating—the air is stale and moist. This building, where a majority of the more intense classes for the Otium Initiative occur, is the only building without gigantic windows. They all have regular-sized windows. I should appreciate the privacy, but knowing what is right outside makes it difficult to concentrate. I didn't come to a new planet to remain indoors.

A light in the middle of the room flickers a tiny bit; a buzz comes from the electricity. My skin is on high alert, the hair on my arms rising with each buzz.

"I know this isn't an easy topic for most people," Flynn continues, but it's hard to hear through the thickness clogging my ears. "I believe you are a little more comfortable with me now, so this may be easier. Are my assumptions correct?"

I nod. He isn't wrong, but in this immediate moment, I grip my seat, trying to steady my legs. They want to bounce, squirm, find any relief in this claustrophobic place.

I would have spilled my entire life story to him last night. He could have asked all of these hard-hitting questions he'll have in the coming weeks. In his apartment or in the Forest, it doesn't feel like a prison. This does.

"Can we do this outside?"

Flynn blinks and glances around. The walls are the plain reddish clay that is identical to the outside. While I guess it's better to have some color than the brown dirt back home, it would be nice to break it up. Like Andrya had pink walls, and Flynn had olive green walls. Instead, every wall is the same.

"Yeah, I suppose that's fine. Would that make you more comfortable?"

I nod again, losing my grip on the chair. I wipe my clammy hands on my pants as soon as Flynn stands.

He gently smiles, leading us out of the building. We haven't touched this morning. No grazing of fingertips or feet while having coffee or breakfast. If we walked most places, I'd anticipate some finger bumping, but that's hard to do on bikes.

We head toward the Forest again. Flynn's in the lead on his bike, calling back that he knows a place. Despite my lungs growing tired from the physical activity, I feel them expand with clean air, space, and the smell of fresh, vibrant grass strands.

It's warm today, warmer than yesterday. I'm sweating through my shirt before we make it to the Flatland's edge. We drop our bikes when we reach the Forest, and this time, we venture off the route we took yesterday, stepping over tree roots and overgrown plants. We don't speak—allowing the birds to talk for us and the bunnies to rustle alongside our path.

My face is dripping with sweat by the time I've tripped over small and large roots and have pushed my way through branches that scrape my arms. When we arrive, we're on a small cliff. The elevation is nothing like back home—nor the mountains in the Valley here, but it's enough to see the entire town of Olive as well as one of the other towns in the Flatlands. Olive is the largest, which I knew, but seeing it all, taking in the minuscule buildings, homes, and shops, it puts into perspective how little the population is here. The largest portion of the Flatlands is the farmland that extends out past the education buildings. It looks like it may create a border around the three towns.

Flynn had mentioned that the Flatlands farmed for the entire planet, and it makes sense. The farmland could be an entirely separate location. Some of the farms were brown, and others were clearly in use with full-grown plants ready to be harvested. I'd love to see the land up close. The closest I've come is through the fence line at my education building.

I scooch to the edge of the cliff, dangling my feet. My walls are coming down, the stress evaporates from my bloodstream with each deep breath in.

"Well, I definitely don't fear you." I laugh. I know he's about to bring up our lesson again. A hike is enough of a distraction from his job.

"Nor do you fear heights." He nods toward my legs, dangling off the edge.

I've never done this before. I would never in a million years dangle my legs off a cliff in New York, but this feels natural. Safe as if the drop wouldn't kill me. Though, I'd likely be severely mangled.

"This is better. Thank you. That classroom—" I start. The panic rises in me at the thought of the small room. I don't understand it. I've never been given the option of educating myself outside of a classroom on Earth. But this sense of freedom and control over my being is helpful.

"—isn't conducive for shedding your deepest secrets," Flynn finishes. "I get it. It's not ideal."

I try to think about my fears. I know the question is about to come again. Whenever my fears present themselves, I push them away, quick to change the subject or change the activity to avoid thinking about them.

"Sometimes, fears can be painful," Flynn says, his mentor-voice activated. More smooth, an octave lower. "No matter the fear, how someone feels about it is subjective. No one should be able to tell another person that they shouldn't be afraid of something. Unfortunately, that isn't always the reality. Particularly on Earth. Here, we try our best to take everyone's fears seriously. We all have fears for one reason or another, but when we acknowledge them and sit with them, we can soak up the pain and transform it."

I nod, removing myself from the edge of the cliff. If this conversation goes south, I can't risk getting shaky or woozy on a ledge. I find a stump on the landing and sit back up against it.

Flynn is across from me. His eye contact is skittish, flashing to me and then toward a leaf, twirling it between his fingertips. The best part of me wants to believe he's nervous about my presence, about making another move. The worst part of me thinks he's nervous to hear my fear because what if it changes the way he thinks about me?

"I'll go first," he says.

I offer a small smile, resting my hands against my thighs, knees raised to my chest. I hope these lessons are always back and forth. They'll make me more comfortable about shedding my demons, and I'll learn about Flynn simultaneously.

"Sometimes, I wonder what the point of this initiative is. I fear that all the work we are doing won't make a difference, that I will do my best, and we'll be massively disappointed in our efforts. All I want is to make a difference and help others. But I wonder if it would be better for our efforts to be spent on all of us working toward a better Otium. Instead of half of us living in the past."

I inhale at his confession. I'd be lying if I said this hadn't crossed my mind—for their sake and mine. But I can't get over the video he showed me. Hundreds of millions of people never made it. I'm not sure I'll ever know how many of them wanted to make the journey.

His eyes meet mine, and they stick. He isn't shying from it or apologizing for his fears about the very program he's trying to teach me. He owns it. Flynn nods his head toward me, telling me it's my turn.

"I don't . . . " *Okay, Theo. It's okay. You know your fear. Just admit it. He won't laugh.* "I don't know who I am without my parents." The words shock me as they leave my lips.

Instead of feeling relaxed or like a weight has been lifted, I feel immense pressure. My throat constricts as oxygen expands my lungs, but I can't let out the carbon dioxide. It's lodged in my esophagus.

I never had a plan for after the trial and after the fundraiser. Each event at Majestic Park kept me moving forward, but with the trial going south, the factory will probably get built, and those weekend events will vanish, too.

Did my social media platform grow solely based on my

parents' deaths, or is there validity to continue it with my future activism?

I notice my tears when moisture drops to my hands. My parents were my entire identity. I built a life around pleasing them and wanting to be just like them.

Flynn is next to me. His shoulder presses against mine, his hand on my kneecap. The warmth rushes through me, igniting some confidence.

"I never had a chance to navigate my way into the world because my parents were taken in a moment," I continue. "Up until that time, I thought I still had a few years before I figured out my own path. Like when I went to college or took a year off."

"What do you think your parents would say to you right now at this very moment?" His voice is soft, directed just for my ear.

A rush of air escapes my lungs. They knew about Otium. Though, I don't think they knew the extent of this program. They didn't know Flynn. Nor that I'd be navigating it alone. Or maybe they do. Maybe wherever they are, they are watching me at this very moment. Giving me the courage to open up to Flynn.

I think back on the happier times with my parents when we'd discuss my future. My answer was always to work for them at With Love. I didn't have a specific department, but I knew I'd end up there. That I'd take the agency over when the time came. Whenever I would stress about grades and what school would help me with growing the organization, my parents would always say the same thing:

"Enjoy the journey and remain present. Don't worry about what is to come or where you'll go from here. Take the opportunity for what it is. If you find peace in the journey, the universe will provide the path." I repeat verbatim for Flynn, hearing my mother's voice in my head with every single word.

It hits harder this time—a time when the message couldn't be more accurate. I gasp, swallowing a sob that tries to erupt from me. Seeing her smile for the last time. Holding her head in my arms as she told me she loved me.

"M-my m-mom said I'd d-do great t-things in the w-world." I look over to Flynn, and his own eyes swell with tears. I squint mine shut and lean into his touch, resting my head on his shoulder. I hope they are watching over me, wherever they may be.

"You will, Theo. From what I know, your parents were quite magnificent."

I grunt an agreement, and he squeezes my knee.

"Sometimes, our anxieties get the best of us. They convince us that it's worth worrying when a lot of the time, the anxieties have no proof. They overtake our present state. Even if we are participating in the present, that doesn't mean we are taking in the present. We fear the unknown. Hell, I just told you my biggest fear of the unknown. How do I combat that? I take pride in the fact that I enjoy what I am doing, that I enjoy getting better each day, and that this present makes me happy and satisfied. If this entire experience doesn't work, if we do end up failing, at least I can live in peace knowing I did my small part of the puzzle well."

He's right, and I know my parents are, too. It's one thing to think that now, it's hard to work through when you're amid that anxiety.

"There won't be solutions overnight, Theo. This will be an uphill battle, and you will stumble a little. That's to be expected. But you were brought here to heal yourself before looking after the planet. I hope you can find comfort in the fact that you have resources at your disposal and time to try and figure out who you are and the path you want to take. We do believe your path is still helping the planet. However, if you want to walk away after this program finishes and live a quiet life, no one will fault you."

"But that will help your program fail, won't it?"

Flynn turns slightly, lifting my chin with his fingertips. He searches my eyes before he shakes his head, offering me a smile.

"On the contrary. No matter how you go back to Earth, you'll go back kinder, happier, free-spirited, and more at peace with yourself. That energy will spread amongst those you let back into your life. It'll still be a butterfly effect, Theo. Just because you aren't holding a sign and chanting doesn't mean you aren't making a significant impact."

Jonah flashes through my head. *Of course.* Jonah spreads his positivity and energy wherever he can, usually. He's incredibly helpful in so many aspects of his life. Just not in the parts I expected from him. But that doesn't mean he isn't making small butterfly effect changes. Each conversation about therapy has led me to this point of acceptance, and I'm only one person in the many lives he touches.

Twenty-Five

I've been sitting in therapy for what feels like forever. Really, it's only been five minutes. When I first walked in, my therapist asked me something, but I can't recall whether or not I answered her or even what the question was.

"Theodore," Corie prompts. "This question may be difficult, and I want you to take a moment before answering."

I hold in an audible sigh. My battery is low. I can feel the inner workings of my mind trying to remain in check. Reminding my demons not to snap. I have never dug so deep within myself as I have this week. It's Friday, but the day still has so many hours in it. All I want is to lie horizontal. Maybe take a nap. If anything, just stare off into space until my eyes glaze over and the world disappears.

I'm also not thrilled with my therapist prefacing her question with "difficult."

Will there be an "easy" here?

"Can you tell me who you were before your parents' deaths?" Corie asks.

My eyes shoot up. I hate the comfort they bring. Her round, kind eyes are so similar to my mother's, even the slope of her nose pointing up is the same. If she had short, brown hair instead of her aqua waves, Corie could play the role of my mother in her younger years.

What I'd do to fall into my mother's arms. For her to kiss the center of my scalp, matting down my curls with her palms. She only topped my height by an inch, but I'd shrink myself, and she'd be on her tippy-toes to continue the tradition.

My knuckles knead the tension above my brows before moving to my temples. Flynn and I had another session in the Forest today. We discussed different fears that ultimately led back to figuring out who I am, which resulted in spending most of the lesson in a puddle of my own tears.

Between the start of the fear conversation yesterday to this moment, all my brain can sift through is trying to figure out who I am. But I can't answer that question; I don't know who I am. My entire being was formed and molded toward being the perfect child. I don't think I can even consider myself a child anymore. By a single action, I was forced to grow up.

Who was I before my parents passed? Before I ran myself dry, digging deeper and deeper into finding an ounce of justice? Peace? Acceptance?

"I was one of the youngest activists in New York State. I was the favorite child. I had my life on track to work at my parents' agency. To one day take it over." My voice is low, borderline monotone.

I don't think I have it in me to overexert myself. I'm dehydrated; I had to race the clock to make it here on time. We were too deep in the Forest.

Corie nods, and I wait for her to tap on her pad some psychoanalytical thing about my response, but she doesn't.

"Who are you today?" Corie asks.

"I'm a time traveler." I give her a cheesy fake grin, punching up in the air with my fist.

Thankfully, she chuckles. It settles the frustration building in me. Though it's a reminder of how hollow I am. There is no way it's a coincidence that I'm having the exact conversation with Corie as I had with Flynn. My sessions are supposed to be confidential.

Corie waits patiently. I didn't give her the answer she was looking for. It's easy with Flynn. I don't agree with his theory that I'm comfortable around him because I won't have to see him after this. If that were the case, I'd be just as comfortable with my therapist. Just because Corie is open about analyzing everything I say, I'm confident Flynn analyzes everything too. I think my comfort with Flynn comes from his family ties.

Who I am today is a difficult question to answer. My planner sitting on a desk in some random education building on some bizarre planet tells me that my Earth events end this weekend. The last thing I threw myself into. And now I have to just trust that it's all okay. Trust that it's in the right hands, and there will be another event to plan next year. But what happens between now and then? I may be chasing another trial of my parents, fighting harder and dirtier, or I may lose everything I built with these three months away.

Trust the process, Theo.

"I don't know," I whisper.

"You're allowed to be whomever you choose to be, Theodore."

I refrain from rolling my eyes. As if it's ever that simple.

"Why do you think you were the favorite child?" Corie asks. "Or why did you need your parents to have a favorite?"

My immediate answer is my brothers. They were treated differently because they were adopted, and everyone wanted them to feel welcomed, and because they were twins. *Everyone loves twins.* I internally roll my eyes.

"I was the favorite because I was a mini-version of my parents. Isn't that what all parents want?"

"You mean a mini-version as in you volunteered and went to events?"

"Yes."

Corie pauses, scrolling through her tablet on her lap. It's unsettling to see the white screen scroll through so many pages. It's only been a week.

"Is activism the only thing that defines your parents?" she asks, looking up.

I twist my fingers together. I don't think I like where this is going. "No. They were parents, friends, and business owners."

"And what did they do for fun?"

They were *always* having fun. Whether it be birthday parties with my brothers' friends or hosting their own get-togethers, the house was always busy.

"They hung out with their friends a lot. Hosted barbe-cues," I say.

"Is activism the only thing that defines you?"

My heart skips a beat at the transition. My immediate answer is "yes." It is what I created my entire world around. Activism *should* define me.

"Would you consider yourself a friend? A brother? Son? Maybe a partner? A good student? A content creator?"

I lock eyes with Corie, and she squints a little. My

silence says something. My words say another; either way, I'm under scrutiny.

Time is moving so slow.

"Why do you think you consider activism as your only defining characteristic?"

I shrug, twisting my fingers to lose circulation as I breathe in. "That's all I know," I whisper, exhaling and sinking into the couch. "My parents did only define themselves as activists. There are pictures of me wrapped up on my mom's chest, only a few months old, volunteering for the community. They never took me to a march or protest until I was a few years old, but my parents barely took a moment to breathe when I was born. I was raised in soup kitchens, homeless shelters, working with local charities. You name it, and I was likely there, being passed from person to person." A weight lifts as I spew my words.

"I think the only reason the board of With Love gave me permission to run my parents' fundraiser was because a lot of the community adored me. I was the baby of the community that everyone had a hand in raising."

I'm banking on the fact that she knows everything. Really, I'm ready to ramble all to avoid the dark, spiraling cloud nearing me. The one holding the sentence I don't want to admit.

"When do you think your parents started defining themselves differently?"

The vacant glances my brothers gave me the last time I saw them say it all. It wasn't just the three of us anymore.

"My brothers were adopted."

Corie nods. "Right. You said that your brothers had the opportunity to say no to events, but you didn't. Do you think that's true?"

"100%." I could never say no to an event.

"This could be wrong," Corie starts. I hold my breath. "But is it possible that bringing three kids to events was a lot for your parents to handle? Your brothers had been uprooted. Your parents likely wanted stability for them. Your brothers were just entering school, where maybe they were making friends? At this timeline, Theodore, you mentioned having lost some friends because of going to these—"

"—I had friends." I huff, crossing my arms and looking out the window. I miss the cool air on my face and the bunnies trusting my presence.

"I'm not saying you didn't. I'm speculating. A part of my job is to question things you may not have thought of. This will allow us to dig deeper. Now hear me out, and then it'll be your turn, okay?"

I nod as I tense my arms. I don't like the chaos her questions bring. The perfectly filed cabinets in my brain are being yanked open; thoughts and memories, and photographic evidence are all scattered.

"As a child and now a teenager, you might not have known all your parents' motives, concerns, struggles, fears. These are often things parents hide. As a parent, it's their job to protect their child, make sure their child is loved and happy. It isn't their job to explain what's going on with them. Going from one kid to three is a massive transition. They could have thought that they made mistakes by starting you too young into all this. Maybe going to these events just didn't have the same impact on them because they had to worry about three kids? Maybe it's as simple as your brothers started defining themselves differently, and your parents allowed that. It's likely they had more flexibility to get away with things because your parents wanted your brothers to trust and love them. But you also have to remember, your brothers weren't at these events from a few months old.

"Now, with all this information, you say your parents defined themselves differently. Do you think this actually stems back to the birthday party incident? That was a couple years before your brothers were in the picture."

I shoot my eyes back toward her. The tornado of files in my head pauses for a moment. "What do you mean?"

"You were seven at the birthday party. You were nine when your brothers came into the picture."

Oh. I lift my feet onto the couch, scrunching myself into a ball as I rest my chin on my knees. I close my eyes, trying to sort through the memories. That was the first tantrum I had that I remember, but it definitely wasn't the last.

"Do you think your parents started changing their lifestyle around then, too? When children are young, it's easier to be more flexible. But now you were getting invited to birthday parties, likely had school events, maybe your parents became friends with your friends' parents? They had much more on their schedule than helping others. They now had to make a difference in their family."

"Why is this important?" I ask, clenching my eyes shut.

I lost all my friends by the age of eleven because I hated birthday parties. I always wanted to be volunteering. Even if there wasn't a big march or protest, I'd spend my weekends at the soup kitchen or helping sort through clothes for the homeless in the region.

"How did you feel when these changes started happening? It doesn't matter exactly when you remember them happening. But you felt a shift. You were acting out because of it."

"I felt like they were giving up. They had friends, things

with my brothers. We threw our own parties that I hated, that I hated to be a part of."

"And why did you hate those parties? Were they bad?" Her head tilts just the slightest.

I shrug because I don't know. The only constant friends who had been in my parents' life before this shift were Sam and Ellie. And when the parties started happening, it was always Ellie who weaseled me out of my bedroom or Sam who'd curl up in my bed and start watching Marvel with me. Sometimes both of them would escape to my room if I really was stubborn. Those were my favorite days, but they have a gray cloud over the memory because it wasn't just a normal day. It was a day of hiding, being stubborn, being angry that I wasn't allowed to volunteer. They forced me to stay home, and they were distracted when I did.

"My parents were forgetting me," I whisper, shoving the palms of my hands over my eyelids. I breathe through the tears escaping.

"Were they forgetting about you, or were you just not hanging out with them?"

"They didn't want to hang out with me!" I yell, throwing my hands into the air.

I catch Corie's jump when I open my blurry eyes. The only people who never forced me to speak until I lost my patience were Sam and Ellie. They allowed me to be in silence.

On the rare occasion I made it down to hang out with everyone, my parents barely acknowledged me. They'd be pouring wine, grilling, and laughing with friends. My brothers sometimes had their own friends over. I was alone on the porch swing up until the day Jonah came into the picture. The parties got easier when Jonah was around because I wanted to spend time with him. I started defining myself as more than just an activist. Though, in the beginning, Jonah would spend some weekends at the soup kitchens with me, or we'd clean up the rivers and highways. He didn't care because he was with me. I thought I had the best of both worlds with him.

"Do you feel you only got love when you were Theodore the Activist?"

She pushed away the impending dark cloud. She spoke the unspeakable sentence. It can never be taken back.

Corie leans over and hands me a box of tissues. My shaky hands grab them, crumbling a tissue to wipe my tears. My breath trembles with every inhale and exhale. I have to remind the wires in my head to breathe as everything is askew.

"Do you have any proof that this is true? Or proof that you are worthy of love if you aren't helping the world?" Corie presses.

Jonah fell in love with me as I was, and I lost him as I was. The only other friend I had was Alejandro, who became my best friend because of activism. I have nearly five million followers watching my every move. Hundreds of thousands of them showed their love and affection for what I did every single day.

Corie tries to hide the pity on her face when I don't answer. She knows the answer; she knew before she asked it.

"Theodore, I have homework for you."

And the weight is right back on my shoulders as if it never left. Flynn told me weekends on Otium were for fun and relaxing. That we got to take a break from the initiative. The last thing I need right now is homework.

"I want you to find some joy," Corie says. "I want you to think about what makes you happy. Find some hobbies that you may be able to take back home. This doesn't all have to be done this weekend, but go have fun. I imagine this will be the first two days you've truly had off in a long while. Give your mind a vacation, too."

How the hell is my mind supposed to take a vacation when Corie has torn apart my filing cabinets? What was status quo is now complicated by a ton of questions that I'll never get the answer to. I can't even ask my parents what it was like for them to raise three kids or why they had a life other than activism. It'll forever be a secret unless I can travel back in time, but I can't. Having the hindsight to question my parents on these things would *definitely* affect the timeline.

"Theo! Theo, wait!" Flynn shouts.

I come to a halt, blinking as I realize I'm outside the therapy building and down the path toward the apartment building, disregarding Flynn and my bike.

"Are you okay?" he asks once he's standing in front of me. Despite running to catch up, Flynn isn't panting.

Am I okay? Is it possible to be okay? I can't really think that my parents only loved me because I shared their activism. That they never showed love in any other aspect of my life. That can't be true. But I can't fight the nagging feeling that it is. I was never good enough if I wasn't helping someone else. They praised me so much as a kid for being so loving, kind, and selfless. For having so many incredible ideas, and always giving up my last portion of anything. I was a phenomenal sharer because I knew what it looked like to not have something. But when the hell did caring about someone else start to mean I wasn't good enough in any other aspect?

When did Jonah's love for me switch? When did my parents' love for me go from them bringing me to all these events to begging me to not attend some? For them to send me away to summer camp just so I would chill.

Is that what they did? The thought twists my insides. *Were they trying to help me by taking the weight off my shoulders, or were they trying to get rid of me? Take a weight off their shoulders?*

"Theo, you're really pale. What's going on?" Flynn's hands rest on my shoulders, holding me steady.

I look up at his concerned eyes. The right side of his lip tilts upward.

"I think my entire existence is a fraud," I whisper. The tornado in my head speeds up. The dark clouds hover closer as a fog creeps in.

"I'm going to need you to explain further." Flynn's voice is distant.

I narrow my eyes to remain focused. Two wrinkles rest between his eyebrows with his sentence. I can't explain anything further. My muscles are becoming dead weight; my jaw tightens.

"Did you tell Corie my fear?"

His eyes widen, his grip stiffens on my shoulders. "Never, Theo. The only time I contacted her was the day you stayed in your room. Your sessions are confidential unless you give permission."

I nod, flexing my fingers to try and stretch any part of my body. I'm so close to being paralyzed into position. I have to claw away at the fog, walk through it. Break through the cycle instead of being swept into it.

"I need a break," I whisper. The tornado slows at my words. "I . . . need—"

Flynn's eyes search mine before he pulls me into a hug. My temple rests comfortably in the crevice of his shoulder and collarbone. His head tilts on top of my own, and he tightens his arms, giving a squeeze. I fit like a glove in his arms. Warmth radiates from his chest, and I listen to his breathing, following the rhythm with my own lungs. My frame loosens and collapses into his embrace. He adjusts his arms to hold me closer.

The tornado stops. While the dark cloud hovers, vita's rays wash over me, filling up some of my hollow shell.

"I can't get you out of group therapy, but we can postpone the rest of your lessons today and take a longer break. Then you'll only have an hour of group before you're free for a whole weekend. Does that sound like a deal?"

I nod against his chest, blinking away tears. His presence, the way his arms envelop me and the sound of his voice creates a tranquility I forgot I needed.

His hands rest on my shoulders and he takes a step back, looking down at me. His thumb brushes away a tear rolling down my cheek as my stomach plummets at the slight separation.

"Shall we get some lunch and escape into a Marvel movie?" Flynn suggests. "We can play hooky and allow your mind to relax?"

A small smile appears on my face. It takes every ounce of energy I have to say, "Yeah, I'd like that."

I don't remember heading to the communal dining or what we got for lunch. I was too distracted by the pit in my stomach the moment I had to hold myself up and what it might mean.

The moment we're in Flynn's apartment, we sit on the couch, and our feet connect. I'm desperate to know if the immediate touch fills a hole in him, too, or if it's just my shattered frame trying to rebuild itself. But between his comfort, the crusted, gooey macaroni and cheese, and *Iron Man 2*, I'm drawn into a fantasy world that isn't mine to fix.

Twenty-Six

I made a mistake yesterday. I spoke too much. Offered information that has me lugging a kayak over my head while balancing my weight on loose rocks.

I rambled in group therapy. Marvel had rejuvenated me enough to surround myself with people for an hour. Since it was my first time speaking, the therapist allowed me to continue until my words stopped. In that blurting, I mentioned how my homework over the weekend was to find joy. Zhang and Amalia didn't hide their wide grins when they glanced at one another.

I don't know what I intended my joy to be, but I didn't expect it to be with the six mentees, Mattis, Flynn, and another mentor.

I also didn't know everyone was in on it until Amalia knocked on my door with a chai latte and asked me to meet her outside dressed in my bathing suit.

Nothing like my first day off instantly being riddled with anxiety. I searched through all the dresser drawers until I found swim trunks. I made a note to see if I could go shopping this weekend for my own clothes.

When I finally walked outside, Amalia, Mattis, Zhang, and Flynn were waiting for me. The rest of the crew had already headed to the Valley.

"Are we almost there?" I grumble. I've tripped on numerous rocks, hit my kayak into Flynn's a few times trying to regain my balance, and my arms are sore. I've never kayaked. And kayaks are fucking heavy.

"Yeah, look ahead." Flynn nods forward. His muscles bulge as he hoists the kayak further above his head.

I feel scrawny as I study him. His tank top is thin, giving way to his shoulders, and the cut of the fabric under his arms is low enough to get a peek of his pecs when he moves a certain way. He's been in proper button-up short-sleeve shirts since I've known him. Flutters erupt in my stomach at the idea that I may get to know another side of him this weekend.

I do look ahead, though. I see the land's edge and the other mentees putting their kayaks in the water. *Thank goodness.*

Flynn and I are the last ones left to get into the kayaks. Apparently, I'm the only person who has never been in one. No one made me feel bad about it; they told me it'd be great. Flynn even said we could head back if I didn't like it. But I feel silly. I've lived in such a prime location my entire life, and I've never done anything on the water except for cleaning the surrounding area.

"Okay," Flynn says. His kayak sits on the rocky grass while he grabs mine. "This is the easiest way to get into a kayak. You do have to walk into the water a little." Flynn puts my kayak in the water and walks it out, so he's a little more than ankle-deep. "Caution, it's slightly cold. I'm going to hold it steady, and you're going to climb in. It isn't as rocky at this level." Flynn holds the kayak into position, and the flex of his muscles give me a little comfort. He genuinely is holding it steady.

Flynn isn't wrong. The water is cold; goosebumps cover my skin. I don't want to fall into this.

I do as he says and step into the kayak. It rocks a little, and one of Flynn's hands comes to balance me instead of the kayak, but I'm seated before I know it with a little water resting at my feet. Thankfully, my room had a pair of hiking sandals. It seems everyone has them as we all wore them today.

"Now what?" I ask as Flynn's hand rests on my shoulder still.

Our crew has already kayaked away. We can still see them, but I have no intention to try and catch up. My idea of relaxing is not spent with eight people I don't really know.

"Now I push you into the water, and I follow behind."

He didn't give me a moment to react. My body jerks forward as I'm shoved toward the deeper water. My kayak wobbles a little before it steadies. I want to turn around and watch how he gets into his kayak, but I'm forced in a forward direction, and I'm afraid of twisting my head.

"Okay," I hear Flynn's voice next to me. "Let's paddle. The inner curve turns away from you when you put it in the water. Think about it as scooping the water to help push you forward. You scoop water on one side, and then you move to the next."

What the hell.

He shows me what he means, a few trickles of water hitting the outside and inside of the kayak. But he's moving forward and leaving me behind with his motions.

I do as he says, scooping the water behind me on each side. This takes work. My arms burn by the time I reach him, and my bathing suit and tank top are wet because I've flung water in every direction.

"You're doing great." Flynn beams. His eyes sparkle as he watches me. "I'm proud of you."

Shivers run down my spine as I blush. I don't remember the last time Jonah looked at me the way Flynn is. Like for this moment in time, I'm the center of his world. He doesn't care that we are far behind the group or that he's stuck with the inexperienced. He doesn't even seem to care that his best friend is up ahead, and he's trapped with his job.

"You ready to tackle some more? There's a small beachy area up a ways that I was thinking we could stop and eat?" He grins.

Maybe "trapped" is a strong word.

His smile is infectious. "I'm starving!" I exclaim.

"Great!" Flynn chuckles. "I brought breakfast." He taps the backpack in between his legs.

"Oh, thank goodness," I sigh. I didn't want to mention it to anyone because I didn't want to be a burden, and I didn't want to make it seem like I wasn't interested in their plan.

Flynn paddles closer to me, unzips his backpack, and hands me a water bottle. No one told me to pack a bag. I was just told to wear a bathing suit. But of course, Flynn thought of everything.

"Have some water to hold you over. We can be there in a couple minutes if we keep paddling."

And we do. After some water, I motivate myself to get this down to a rhythm, so I eat. I'm decent at paddling if I don't mind my clothes getting dripped on. My main objective is consistency.

The group disappeared around a bend in the river, but before long, we reach them. They stopped at the area, too. It's an insanely small pull-off with sand mixed between the grass. Definitely a stretch to call it a beach, but I know back home, it'd be called that too. We have a lot of beachy-grass portions throughout our river. Because we're far from the actual beach, any type of sand is welcomed.

The vita is warming the air as it gets later in the morning. I think after we eat, the water I drip on myself will be necessary.

The group is loud when we paddle up behind them. Laughing and carrying on different conversations. It's hard to follow with all the accents and overstimulation from the pure silence we had just a few moments ago.

I'm a bit disappointed that it isn't just Flynn and me eating here. It looks like a few people have food in their backpacks as well. An unsettling feeling nestles within me, upsetting my gut. I don't feel welcome here.

"Why am I never included in plans?" I ask. I don't mean to say it out loud to Flynn, but it's frustrating nonetheless. Everyone here knew what was happening. I despise being in the unknown, and it's becoming a thing here.

"What do you mean? You're here?" Flynn's brows crease. He holds my kayak with one hand and paddles us forward with the other.

"Yes, I was invited. But when this was all planned, why wasn't I asked about it? Why didn't I know to pack breakfast? Or know the night before that I had to be ready at a certain time?" I raise my voice and it wavers. I fucking hate how my anxiety overtakes my confrontations. Making my words seem less valid with each quiver. "Or even what the hell we were doing until a kayak was shoved into my hands?" I breathe in deep, letting out a frustrated groan.

Flynn pauses the paddling right before we reach the shallow water. Everyone is starting to eat, all their kayaks are pulled out of the water. I don't want to be around anyone, but I don't want to be left out.

"Amalia organized the entire thing. You're right. You should have been told. I didn't know until this morning that you weren't messaged last night. When Amalia told me when we all met up, I asked her to get you out of bed because I didn't think you'd listen to me. When she went to talk to you, I grabbed us both breakfast and made sure to get water and a towel for you, too. I made a mistake by not picking you up myself. I just assumed because you came, you were okay with it all. I'm sorry."

I watch as his face goes through a series of emotions. Serious, to ashamed to admit that he knows my habits about saying no to events I don't know about, to a semi-smile asking for forgiveness.

I just want to be included in the plan-making. Why is it so hard for people to understand? I wanted to be told about Otium. I wanted to choose my exit from Earth. I want to know everything about why I'm here. I want these people to include me as a friend if they want to be my friend.

"All Amalia said is that you are supposed to find joy this weekend, and she wanted to try to help with that," he says gently.

I look down at my feet as tears burn my eyes. I know I blurted my frustrations out yesterday in group therapy, and that includes six people here, but therapy is confidential. What I say shouldn't be discussed outside of the group with other people. If someone wants to talk about what I said, they should talk to me and only me.

"You were telling that to Amalia, right?" Flynn asks.

I shake my head.

I didn't discuss my assignment with Flynn yesterday. I wasn't ready to dissect my joy and wanted to just *be* with him. We went to dinner, but afterward, I excused myself to go to bed. I didn't really fall asleep, but I decided to project the entertainment app on my wall and watch *The Good Place*, a show my parents were always watching. They asked me time and again if I wanted to watch it with them, but there was always something going on that was more important.

"Was this discussed in group therapy?" he asks.

I only give him a glance before I position my paddle to try and turn around. "I'd like to go." I was good with paddling straight, but now I'm cornered.

Flynn sighs. "Let me talk to—"

"I'd like to go," I repeat, looking down at his hand that is still holding my kayak.

He lets go and helps turn my kayak a little with a push to the side. "Focus your paddle on the right side. It'll help you turn. Can I go with you, or do you want to be alone?"

I don't know how to get out of a kayak, but I can likely make it back to the rental shop if I follow the path I took. But there are a lot of steps I need to take in order to get back to Olive.

"You can come if you want," I say softly. I don't give him a chance to respond. Instead, I shove the paddle into the water on my right side and give enough of a push that I nearly 180 into his kayak.

I powerhouse left and right, splashing more water than before on myself. My tank top is uncomfortably sticking to my stomach, but I don't want to stop paddling to take it off, even if I am now breaking a sweat. My stomach is ravenous; I need to eat pronto.

"I'm here to help!" Flynn calls out when I near the wooded opening we came from.

I appreciate that he kept his distance. I couldn't hear

him behind me with all the water sloshing. But I also don't need him.

I paddle until my kayak thumps to a stop in the mud. When I step out, Flynn is close enough to hit my kayak.

"That was smart," he says, thumping his own kayak. "Now, just yank it out."

I do as he says. The last thing I want to do is lift the kayak above my head, but once I do, it's one step closer to being done with this activity. Which is kind of a shame because I think I might enjoy it, especially if I work up stamina. I just want a proper invite.

The two of us walk in silence through the scattered trees toward the rental shop. Flynn lets me lead, and he stays a few feet behind at all times. Only once did I almost go the wrong way, and he piped up.

I'm a little lightheaded by the time we reach the shop. Behind it, there's a small dock in the distance. I could go back to Olive and do my own thing, which may be holed up in my room, or I can choose to be with Flynn, which is how I originally wanted my "joy" weekend to go. Either way, I need to eat. Physical activity and no breakfast are not a good combination for me.

"Let's go eat at the dock," I say as Flynn finalizes the transaction.

When we get to the dock, I sit on the right-hand side and unstrap my sandals, dipping my feet in the water. The cool temperature is now welcome as the UV seeps into our skin, searing our backs. I place my vitaglasses on my head, looking up the river. The water is a deeper purple the further away I look, complimenting the violet sky above. We're at a narrow end where we can see both sides of the river, but as it expands, the river bends with the tree line, widening the gap.

"The sky looks beautiful today," I comment, leaning back on my palms. "Wait," I pause, sitting up straight. I look between the sky and Flynn. If possible, his eyes are more vibrant. "I can see violet!"

Holy shit, this is incredible.

"Welcome to Otium, Theo." Flynn's eyes are intent on me as I gaze around at my surroundings.

While the grass was always green, it's taken on a shamrock hue. The wildflowers blooming between the trees are nearly neon colors of yellows, pinks, purples, and blues. It almost feels like they might shine through the woods when it gets dark. The river is, in fact, a dark purple as it gets deeper. Instead of crystal clear in the shallow waters, there's a soft violet hue taking the place of the Caribbean-esque water back home.

"We have to go to the beach." I look over at him, grinning, feeling like I have a superpower.

"We will soon." He laughs. "But yes, the ocean is just as majestic as you imagine."

I lay back on the dock, looking up at the sky. He said I shouldn't have to wear the vitaglasses when my eyes transition. I look toward vita.

"Fuck! Ouch, okay, that hurts." I shoot up.

A rumbling laugh comes from Flynn. "What the hell was that?" he asks between laughs. "We don't look at the vita."

I rub my eyes, trying to get the black spots to disappear from my vision. "But you said—"

"I said you may be able to avoid vitaglasses. I didn't say to look right up at the light. Do you look right up at your star?"

We make eye contact. He's trying his hardest to hold in

his laughter, and I can only take in bits and pieces of his face. We both burst out laughing.

The laughter helps dissipate the uneasiness from this morning. I love seeing him hold his belly as he chuckles, and the sound is music to my ears as he wipes away a few tears. Somewhere in the midst of laughing, his eyes hold mine, but they aren't smiling. His fingertips reach out, brushing across my temple. I inhale, taking note of every single goosebump that appears beneath his fingertips.

"Joy looks good on you, Theo."

An internal shiver rushes through me, and all I can offer is a smile. It feels pathetic, but he makes my thoughts stop at a moment's notice, and I don't know how to return the favor.

"Breakfast?" he whispers. His fingers disappear from my skin. He unpacks his backpack, handing me a circular glass dish.

I blink a few moments, wanting to shake off the moment. I open the lid, disappointed by the smoothie bowl staring back at me. I'm sure it's delicious, but I'm far too ravenous for this to satisfy my hunger. He then hands me another container. This one includes a croissant.

"You like your starch," he says when an involuntary grin crosses my face.

He's not wrong. I like my egg sandwiches or toast with eggs or burger with the bun or garlic bread. It's an added comfort for me.

"Thank you," I say softly, taking a bite of the croissant before anything else. It's not warm like I prefer, but it's still flaky, and the buttery taste calms me.

I like joy in smaller quantities—and Flynn.

"I'm sorry about Amalia," he says. "I wish I had understood the situation better. She seems like she enjoys surprising people, but I will talk to her about how it isn't always okay if she isn't confident that the person she is surprising likes surprises."

"I don't want to be a nuisance," I say. It actually sounds like an awful idea to have someone speak on my behalf.

"It isn't a nuisance to have preferences and boundaries."

I look over at him as he offers me a gentle smile. It's a nice reminder.

"I will also remind her that all therapy sessions are confidential. I'm sorry that she told us about your assignment this weekend."

"I'd really like it if my 'finding joy' wasn't spoken about in terms of an assignment or a chore. It makes me sound and feel pathetic. Broken even. How lame is it that a seventeen-year-old doesn't know what happiness is?"

"I think you know joy. I just think you've forgotten what it feels like. There is no shame in that. You've gone through a traumatic experience. It's normal to have to search your way through it to find the person you were before."

"And if I'm not sure I want to be the person I was before?" I ask, looking down at the pink smoothie with blue and black speckled dots.

Flynn's fingers gently graze my chin. I glance over at him, and his fingers turn into more of a caress, with his palm on my jawline.

"If you don't like who you were before, then you've got the opportunity to reinvent yourself. The beauty of your time here, Theo, is that we are helping to heal *you*, not Earth. You have control over how much you want to partake in this program. You can either work with us or against us. But if you work with us, our goal is to push you to break through the barriers you've created. We are going to work through the nitty-gritty, and you will be tired, and angry, and frustrated. But you also will have opportunities to relax, try new hobbies, figure out who you are in all of this. The added benefit? You don't have those at home who have a clear identity of you hindering your growth."

We sit in silence, eating our breakfast as I sort through his words. Jonah hindered my growth. My aunt and uncle don't know what growth is. Alejandro is good with growth, but he's helped me create such a platform that I don't know he'd be keen on me stepping away.

I don't know who I want to be or where I see myself. Even if I may have been hindered at home, it's not like I tried to break out of the mold. I never had time.

"Have you ever had a massage?" Flynn breaks the silence.

I look over, and he's done with his breakfast. I still have a few more bites. I'm shocked that I'm actually more full than I anticipated.

"No, but I've been interested. I just can't afford them."

Flynn lights up and searches through his backpack, pulling out his phone. "Great, let's start with a massage. I'm thinking we can get your mind and body relaxed and then go from there?"

Suddenly, the next few minutes are consumed by Flynn scheduling an entire spa day. We are getting massages, followed by a gentle yoga session, then a facial, and afterward, at my request, he schedules me for a hair appointment too. If my body is going to be rejuvenated, I want my curls to be as well. The one thing I really miss about old Theo is that he had really nice curls and always made time for them.

Total and pure bliss relaxation is joy, I've decided. Not sustainable on Earth for me, of course. It's natural I'd find my joys in something that costs a fortune to maintain. But I can definitely get more used to weekends here like this. My body is loose, and my mind is dazed and happy. The relaxation even has me roaming the shops on my own, as Flynn had other plans after our facials. With a gap in my schedule between the spa and my hair appointment, I take the time to gather some clothing that makes me feel more *me*. Instead of the plain t-shirts that are in my drawers, I find more short-sleeve button-ups, and I even find a pair of dark blue jeans similar to what I have at home.

Flynn and I mentioned grabbing dinner together, and by the time I'm walking out of my hair appointment, I'm feeling confident enough that I want to ask him out to dinner.

The hairstylist was amazing and thorough, going through everything with me. A nice shampoo and condition, and a shorter shave on my sides, letting my curls bounce and poof on top. She even walked me through the proper technique of shaping my curls, a technique I've never used before. My jaw aches from the goofy smiles I've had on and off all day—especially when I catch sight of myself. There is really something to be said about feeling and looking your best.

When Flynn messages me to let me know he's home, like I had asked him to, I'm finalizing my outfit in the mirror. I may be jumping the gun. I may be feeling something that isn't there. But if I'm supposed to take chances and discover joy this weekend, I'm on a roll that I don't want to stop. I can't remember the last time I felt this bubbly. Just the thought nearly makes me cringe. Theodore the Activist is not carefree.

With a sage green button-up and my new dark blue jeans, I give myself one last smile in my mirror and jog up to the second floor. My hands are clammy as I get closer to Flynn's door. I do my best to physically shake off the feeling. Worst-case scenario, Flynn tells me no, and I spend the rest of the weekend without him, trying to recover from embarrassment.

Honestly, it sounds like a pretty awful worst-case scenario.

"Theo," Flynn breathes the moment he opens the door. A gentle smile eases across his face as he looks me up and down. His eyes light up when he reaches my curls. "You look amazing. How are you feeling? Is that a new shirt?"

My heart swells. I force myself to stay focused. "Flynn, will you go to dinner with me?" I rush out. I attempt to keep from bouncing back and forth on my feet. Seeing him here, right in front of me, has me second-guessing everything.

"Yeah, of course. That was the plan, right?" He steps away from the door, gesturing me in. He still needs a pair of shoes.

"No," I say, trying to keep my voice steady. Flynn glances over at me before he slips on his shoes, his eyes narrow. "No, I mean, yes, that was the plan."

"Good." He grins. He looks amazing too. He changed from earlier; now in coral chinos and a dark gray short-sleeve button-up. I wonder how often he treats himself to a spa day—his skin is glowing.

I shake my head, focusing. He isn't getting the point.

"I mean," I start again, and Flynn walks back over to me, holding my eye contact. "Will you go out to dinner with me?"

The way his brows furrow has my stomach twisting. I

definitely read the signs wrong. Maybe he's just a touchy-feely person. Maybe that's his love language and comfort.

His brows relax as his eyes widen. "Are you asking me on a date?"

I want to say no. Take it back. Run out of the room and just grab something from the communal dining. I can spend the night in my room with a movie by myself. It'll be fine.

Flynn's hand rests on my shoulder as my eyes dart around his face. I don't want to chicken out, but now I'm not sure I can handle a no.

"If so, then yes, Theo. You can take me on a date." Flutters erupt in my belly, replacing the tension. Flynn pulls me into a hug, and my body relaxes against his frame. His heartbeat increases with my own. "Thank you for not running." He pulls away after he speaks.

I like that he knows me. Even if so much of me is in a file, he's at least memorized it. It's nice to be around someone who can anticipate my moves. Acknowledge when I work above them. Calm me before I panic. All the while being patient.

Jonah was always more forward in our relationship. We never specifically went on dates after my parents passed. It was more so getting together at his home. Before, though, he'd plan things. We were adventurous, and I loved it. It just wasn't my forte to think about dates, but he thrived on it.

Now, I felt like I was flying by the seat of my pants. I didn't actually think about what would happen after Flynn said yes. I focused too much on not worrying that I never planned anything. I also don't know much around here, so I can't take him to some place he's never been. Or somewhere that's brand new to him.

Thankfully, Flynn carries the conversation as we ride

our bikes to the train station, get on the train, and head back to the Mexican restaurant in the town of Laurel. I hate that I ruined our first night, and I want to replace that memory.

Flynn said he wanted to be surprised by the plan before we left, so I use my memory to retrace our steps back to the restaurant. I'm certain he knows where we are going, but he doesn't let on. Instead, we talk about simple things like our favorite foods and foods we hate.

Similar to before, Flynn talks and greets everyone when we enter the town. For music tonight, there are two people playing the violin and one person on the cello up the road. The energy is slightly dimmer without the mariachi band, but I'm grateful to have more opportunities to talk at a normal volume.

Flynn interlaces our hands when I turn to enter the restaurant. He gives my hand a squeeze as we are led to another two-person table. A waitress is here tonight. The guy from the other night isn't around.

Flynn lets go of my hand, and I want to help Flynn into his seat, but I'm awkward, and I think about it too late, and then I'd have to backtrack, and Flynn is sitting all before I can think to sit.

I blush when I settle and look over at his amusement.

"You're doing great," Flynn says. "And I was craving this, so thank you."

I take a few deep breaths, walking myself through the proofs of what he's given me. There isn't any need to be nervous. Flynn is the same person he was earlier today. He knows this is a date. He said yes. He knows I'm awkward and anxious, and he's still here with me.

"You should try one of their fancy drinks tonight," Flynn says, handing me a menu I didn't see before.

"Like alcohol?" I ask. I know I've had it here, but I don't

think it's smart starting off a first date with alcohol. I don't have a tolerance, and I can't get used to that. Going home, I'll be upset for the next four years before I can have another drink.

"No, no. Well, I mean you could. It's legal. But they have mocktails here, and they are delicious." He points to where it reads, "cócteles sin alcohol."

I've never had a margarita, nor a non-alcoholic one, but they are always so popular with tacos back home. We place our orders. Both of us getting the street tacos like last time but with the addition of non-alcoholic margaritas.

"So uh, what was it like growing up on Otium?" I ask after the waitress leaves with our orders. I feel like we've covered some pretty intense conversations already, but it feels different now that the word "date" is involved. I kind of hate the additional pressure it places on us hanging out.

Am I even allowed to be doing this? We're essentially the same age, but he is in charge.

His smirk stops my thoughts. I cross my ankles under my chair, shoving my hands between my thighs, trying to keep the anxious shakes from starting.

"What was it like growing up on Earth?" He laughs.

"Touché." I laugh, breathing out as I try to settle back in my seat.

"It's a common question as a mentor. I get it. I think people in the initiative see Otium as this mythical place, especially at first. It's a hard question to answer because this is my reality—this is all I've ever known."

He makes a fair point. I can't truthfully answer what life is like on Earth, even with experiencing both. Flynn only knows Earth from books and artifacts.

"If your question is, did I have a good childhood and do

I like my location versus the other locations on Otium? Then the answer is yes to both," Flynn says.

It's hard to imagine that he likes Olive better than the town of Laurel. Even with my limited time here, I thrive with the surrounding trees, mountains, and river.

"My parents," Flynn continues, "were and still are an active part in mine and my sister's lives. I had and have a great set of friends. My mom was and is very busy, but she's good at multitasking, and support is given whenever we want or need. One thing we've improved here is quality time versus work production. So while my mom is the leader of the Flatlands, she is a mother first and foremost."

"What if there is a crisis or an emergency?"

"Honestly, it's limited. When I was younger, and my mom was working toward being the leader, there were more situations where she'd be away. She had to prove her place still. My father sheltered my sister and me well, though, and if my mom was ever away for a while, we'd have sleepovers with my cousins on my dad's side. We are a very young society. There were a lot of issues to sort, and there will always be new ones. But Otium is a compilation of really amazing people from Earth. Everyone who came here was so desperate for a change and to do better. It has made conflict resolution easier."

The waitress brings us our mocktails, and we thank her before I quickly grab mine. It's a pale to bright orangish color. Flynn lifts his, tilting slightly to me.

"Cheers, Theo. To new beginnings."

I pause mid-lift, processing his words. I'm not unsettled by them, but I feel I should be. Everyone at home thinks I'm in grief counseling, and here I am, having a mocktail with a cute guy who happens to be my mentor. This isn't healing. This can't be.

"What are you thinking about?" Flynn's words are soft as he takes a sip from his glass before placing it on the table.

I open my mouth, but I don't know what to say. Where is the line between mentoring and dating? Maybe they have to mesh for both to succeed.

"Today was the fundraising event," I breathe out, putting my glass down, so I don't drop it.

"It was. How are you feeling?"

I search his crystal blue eyes that crinkle a little, but I don't see the smile. His hand tenderly grabs mine across the table.

"It's okay to feel however you feel."

"I'm happy," I admit, slouching my shoulders with the pressure that slides off. "I don't think I deserve to be." I look down at our hands, watching as Flynn squeezes mine. His hand fits more comfortably in mine than Jonah's ever did.

"Why not?"

"I feel guilty. Here I am getting free therapy, essentially getting free food and massages and facials—free clothes. I'm able to kayak and hang out with people and spend time with you. None of it feels okay. Not after all the stress I've put Jonah under, or even Alejandro."

I take my hand back, shoving it in my lap as I interlace my fingers. Twisting them. It feels lovely to hold his hand, but that adds additional guilt.

"You're not on vacation, Theo. You've already started some grueling therapy, and it's only going to get harder. Honestly, it's good that you recognize the positive. We will work on the guilt because that's counter-productive, but I think you're finding joy, Theo."

I hate, but secretly love, the smug smile on his face. My face heats up, and I'd love to curl into myself—or rather, him.

"Try not thinking about this in terms of Jonah and Alejandro. If they are as good of people as you say, they will be there for you. Likely, though, they are treating themselves to some joy as well. Try thinking about this in terms of how much you have given to others. How much you have helped out your town and state? You do deserve a break. You deserve to learn these little and big joys because you'll need them when you get home. In order to sustain a similar lifestyle as you had—if you want to—then you have to learn the balance of activism and self-care."

Tears prick my eyes. I hate that he's right. I know that Jonah and Alejandro also are home with supportive families who can help them right now.

"Thank you," I whisper. I can focus on my past, focus on what I can't control, or I can be here in the present with Flynn.

I lift my glass up and tilt toward Flynn. A smile breaks out on his face, and he lifts his glass again.

"To new beginnings!" I cheer.

"So, what movie are we on tonight?" Flynn asks as he opens his apartment door.

After dinner and some churros, we hopped right back on the train and beelined it to the apartment. We have some serious Marvel damage to do.

"*Thor*, and then the *Incredible Hulk*, though it isn't highly rated, and it isn't the same Hulk."

"You're not really selling tonight." Flynn laughs and kicks off his shoes.

I follow suit and head for the couch. Flynn walks down his hallway as I curl into the couch.

"I know, I know. But after Hulk, we get to our first Avenger movie," I call out.

"And what's the Avengers about?"

My mouth drops for one of two reasons. First, I've done a terrible job with Marvel so far. Second, he's now standing in front of me in gray sweatpants and a white t-shirt. He hands me clothes too.

"If you want to be comfy, those are some sweats."

"I can just . . . " I stumble as I grip his clothing. My room is literally right downstairs. I can grab my own comfort.

"Nonsense." His eyes sparkle as he speaks, so I jump up and head to the bathroom to change.

His smell consumes me, vanilla with a hint of citrus, when I pull his clothes on. They are slightly too big, and I have to roll the waistband and cuff the pant legs, but I love the fabric touching me. Inhaling him.

Jonah and I rarely shared clothing, likely because I was always overly prepared for everything.

When I step out of the bathroom, he already has *Thor* waiting to be played. I sit down on the free cushion next to him, and he opens his arms.

"Do you want to cuddle?"

I nod and cross over the cushion, leaning into his side. He interlaces our hands, setting them on my thigh. It's not as comfortable as being able to kick my feet out on Jonah's bed. But being in Flynn's room isn't appropriate right now, and this feels right. *Safe.*

"So now what is the Avengers movie about?" he asks, as if every single part of him isn't tingling from our hands and shoulders and feet touching. As if I'm not wearing his clothing and falling so deep down a hole I can't see the end of.

He watches me intently as I explain who the Avengers are *again* and how the timeline works with Avenger movies interlaced. When my rambles come to an end, his fingers are on my chin. His gaze causes my breathing to accelerate. I'm not certain much registered in his mind; his eyes glaze over when he leans in closer.

Holy shit. Holy shit. Holy shit.

"I love when you get excited about something you love," he whispers.

I can feel his breath on my lips. The sweetness of the churros and sourness of the margarita greet me. I squeeze his hand.

"Can I kiss you?" If he were any closer, his lips would have touched mine.

Instead of answering, my free hand cups his left cheek, and I press my lips against his. They are so soft and plump. A gentle embrace for my lips to fall into. A twinge of excitement courses through my bloodstream, and I lean in more, captivated by his taste.

This is joy. Unfiltered. Walls down. A warm embrace and somewhere safe.

Twenty-Seven

To say I'm on Cloud 9 would be a vast understatement. I dreamed about Flynn's lips the entire night and our cuddles and the way his laughs rumbled his body, and my own, when I leaned against him. We made it through the end of the first Avengers movie, though both of us could barely keep our eyes open at that point. Flynn walked me down to my room, kissed my lips, and left me floating to my bed.

He invited me to his sister's graduation party, which I said yes to on a whim because that meant it was guaranteed that I got to see him, and I've been curious about this mysterious twin of his. But now, as Flynn and I walk closer to his parents' house, I'm questioning whether or not it's really a good idea.

"I don't think we should say anything to anyone yet. About us," Flynn says as we turn onto the path his parents live on.

We were discussing the movies last night when he interrupted with the bombshell. Not that I necessarily want to have a conversation with anyone today, but my muscles tense.

"I don't want to hide you, Theo. I just—" he pauses and turns toward me, interlacing our hands. "I don't want to overshadow my sister on her day."

It makes sense. It's logical. I shouldn't overthink it. Nor should I overthink the way his eyes glance around the area before he pecks my lips quickly.

"I like you, Theo," Flynn says as we start walking together side-by-side.

"I like you too, Flynn."

And I do. More than I feel I should. I was fine a few minutes ago. Now my mind starts to spiral, overthinking everything he's saying. We didn't clarify whether we could be in a relationship or even if we were in one. This could be all just fun for him. So why would we be telling his parents? Would we even mention anything for a few days if there wasn't a party happening right now?

I nearly stop walking at the realization that I'll be seeing Andrya for the first time since the first night on Otium. I have yet to run into her. I haven't been able to talk to her about Sam and Ellie. Not that I know exactly what to say. I guess I just want her to confirm what Lana said.

Flynn leads us around the side of his parents' home to a gate door that opens up to the backyard. His hand gives me one final squeeze, and I take a deep breath in before he announces our arrival.

It's a quaint backyard, nothing too different from what the surrounding houses have. There's just enough space to have a barbecue for a small party. They have some picnic tables with a patio—a fire pit in one corner of the yard and an enormous garden in the other corner.

"Flynn!" a girl exclaims, running toward us.

The photograph in Andrya's home doesn't give his twin

justice. She's stunning. Her previously long auburn hair is now cut just below her shoulders, properly curled, and a mixture of blonde and red highlights.

"Rys!" Flynn hugs his sister tight before pulling away and placing his hand on my lower back. If he doesn't want anyone to know, he's already off to a bad start. "This is Theo, my friend."

Her smile is so enthusiastic, I'm nervous she's going to pop her jaw. "May I give you a hug?"

I shrug, and she nearly suffocates me in an embrace. "It's nice to meet you. Flynn's told me so much about you." Her voice is angelic. I don't remember what grade she got certified to teach, but she sounds like she'd be perfect for children.

"Theo, this is Ryleigh, my sister," Flynn continues the introduction as my eyes dart over to his awkward grin.

"Thank you for coming," Ryleigh says as she pulls away. Her name gets called in the distance, and she tilts her head toward it. "Let's go back to the party!" She skips to the backyard ahead of us.

"Ryleigh knows about you as a friend. I have not said anything about our date last night," Flynn whispers.

I nod, but I'm feeling out of my comfort zone now. I can hear the laughter and voices just around the corner. I'm the random mentee at a party with all close friends. I don't belong here. I'm not even a random mentee, but someone Andrya wanted here so badly. I'm not sure I even want to know what Flynn's family knows about me.

The icing on the cake is Flynn's hand disappearing from my back the moment we turn the corner.

"Theo!" Mattis greets, jogging toward us and clapping a hand on my shoulder. "I didn't know you were coming."

I let out a breath that I know at least one more person.

Flynn's dad is at the grill, and I can't find his mom, but there's a handsome person around our age as well as some other girls who are clustered together.

"Last minute plans." I shrug again, feeling slightly awkward. It's one thing for Flynn to hang out with his mentee on his time; it's another for me to attend a family event.

"Figured it may be nice," Flynn says with a smile before hugging Mattis.

"Definitely." Mattis grins my way.

We head toward the rest of the crowd hovering around. I'm introduced in a quick, "Hey, this is Theo," and people dart off their names I'll likely never remember. Flynn's dad hands me an iced tea, and the conversations continue like we didn't just interrupt them. My presence here really isn't important to everyone else.

Everyone around me talks about memories like they would on Earth, except I don't know these people, and I don't know Otium. I'd love to ask questions, but questions would result in the conversation switching to the kid from Earth, and I don't want that. All I can do is clasp my drink and try not to drink too much, so I don't have to pee, and listen.

"Hey," Flynn whispers, leaning down to my ear.

Goosebumps rise along my skin. It feels intimate now, even though he did this the first night we met. My eyes scan the group of bubbly, animated faces, but no one is looking.

"I'm going to find my mom and see if she needs any help," Flynn continues. "You okay here for a few minutes?"

"Y-yeah, definitely." I smile, trying to hide my "please don't leave me alone face." I *know* I'll be fine. No one is going to hurt me, but I'd be cool to hide in a corner for a bit.

Flynn jogs off, and Mattis tries to include me in the

conversation every so often. But this is still a party for his friend, and it's normal to forget the random person at the party. It's all so real being here. These people have lives, jobs, hobbies, joys. They are living in a functioning society. On a new planet. In my lifetime, they really managed to figure this all out. It's so cool when it's not so hard.

I watch Ryleigh, mesmerized by her being a spitting image of Flynn—even down to her blue eyes. They are as identical as fraternal twins can be. If possible, she's more outgoing than Flynn. Everyone is captivated by her when she speaks. She has an inflection that soothes my often-over-stimulated ears. When she speaks, she catches my eye each time, as if I know exactly what she's talking about. It's nice. My presence exists to her.

Remy, Flynn's ex, on the other hand, is someone I feel I'm in direct competition with. I heard them introduce themselves earlier, but as everyone talks, it's easier to focus on their flawless, brown skin tone. Not a blemish or a wrinkle on their skin. Remy wears thin golden-framed glasses that highlight their chocolate eyes. I understand the attraction wholeheartedly. Even when they laugh, I get butterflies in my stomach, and the way they speak, the right side of their lip turns up into an involuntary smirk. Remy even has an endearing lisp.

Whereas I'm some kid who had wildly dry skin from the climate and atmosphere change up until my facial yesterday, and I didn't even style my hair. Although, waking up this morning to only having to fix a few curls and liking who I saw in the mirror has been a nice change. But I'm nothing comparable to Remy and their curly, silk black hair. If anything, I'm just a charity case.

I don't see Flynn come back outside, but suddenly, he's across my path, standing next to Remy. They embrace each other, and a wave of nausea courses through me. Remy has Flynn laughing that deep belly laugh that I cherished just hours before. The laugh played on repeat throughout my dreams last night, solidifying it as *my* laugh. But it isn't because that doesn't even make sense. I can't gatekeep a laugh.

"You're staring," Mattis says softly, bumping his shoulder into mine.

I jump at his words, a few droplets of tea spilling out of my cup.

"They are long done for," he clarifies.

I clear my throat. Mattis cannot possibly know I have feelings for Flynn.

"Okay." I let out a light laugh, trying to avoid his gaze. "It doesn't matter if they weren't."

Mattis steps in front of me. He is only a couple inches taller, but as he peers down at me, my pits grow sweaty. I can't let the secret out.

"I'm just saying," Mattis continues, "that there is no reason to be jealous. Believe me, Flynn's eyes are on you."

I lean around Mattis to look at Flynn, and his eyes actually are on me, and he winks. I can't hear what Remy is saying, but the wink has them looking at me, too. Remy waves before continuing their conversation with Flynn.

Whether or not Mattis is correct, it still feels shitty to hover around a party alone. Mattis moves away and jumps into the conversation. I catch sight of Flynn's father going into the house, and I excuse myself, saying I'm using the restroom.

I just need a moment. A moment to either find Andrya and ask my questions, or actually hide in the bathroom.

I open the back door, watching as Jay and Andrya pull out empty plates and clean silverware from the cabinets and drawers. The walls of the kitchen are painted white, accented with purple appliances and yellow curtains. The counters are all built from the walls; even the kitchen table only has three sides for chairs and then a framed out bench from the wall.

"Oh, Theodore, hello," Andrya says, clasping her necklace. "Flynn said you were here. How are you?"

"Hi, Andrya, I'm good," I greet, and suddenly, I feel foolish. I don't know what I'm doing inside. I don't actually have to use the restroom, so now when I have to later, it'll look like I pee way too often. I don't even know why I felt like I'd have more room to breathe in a closed home versus the nature outside. This isn't the time and place to talk with her.

"Is there something we can get for you?" she asks.

"Uh, I actually want to speak with you about one of the reasons I'm here." I place my drink on the countertop before twisting my fingers together at my waist. "Can we maybe talk?"

"Is 'here' my home or this planet?" she asks and glances over at Jay. He places all the silverware on the plates and then takes everything outside.

"Uh, oh, um, this planet," I say when the door closes.

Andrya nods, and my heart begins to race.

"Now isn't the best time, but we can schedule a meeting for tomorrow."

"Oh, um." I tighten the grip on my fingers, and all my knuckles crack in one go. "Y-yeah, of course. I just, uh, wanted to make sure I talked to you."

She places her hand on my shoulder, and I try to stand up as straight as I can. "Of course. I'll send you a message first thing in the morning with an appointment time. I'm sorry if you were hoping for something more urgent, but I like to keep my personal and work life separate. Let's go back outside, and today, you're Flynn's friend and not his mentee." Andrya releases her hand from my shoulder and walks over to the fridge.

"Yeah, okay. Thank you. Uh, may I use your restroom first?"

"Third door down the hall." She points toward another door that doesn't lead to the front of the house.

I slip past her at the fridge and head down the narrow hall. At the third door, I walk into the bathroom, closing the door behind me. It's a small half-bath, so I lower the toilet seat and sit on top of it, laying my head in my hands.

I shouldn't be here. I shouldn't have crossed a boundary with Andrya. I shouldn't be at a family party for a family that isn't mine. I'm not great at parties, anyway. I'm awkward and weird, and there's always something more important I'd rather be doing. Even if that's being alone. This isn't even Flynn's party. I'm just the mentee crashing his sister's graduation. I'll be gone in a few weeks, just a speck of dust in their memory.

Maybe I can follow the rest of this hallway down and it'll circle through to the front door. No one will even see me leave. I can then take the day for myself, explore somewhere new, or get lost in the Forest. I only placed myself in this awkward situation because Flynn asked. I only did so because he likes me. If I'm honest, I just want to make sure he keeps liking me.

A tap on the door has me bolting up.

"Theo, are you actually using the restroom, or are you hiding?"

I take a deep breath before exhaling everything inside my lungs. I open the door slowly.

Flynn walks in and closes the door behind him. "You

okay? I know this is a lot, and I haven't been by your side. I'm sorry." He steps close enough to me, so our feet are touching. His fingers grab mine, giving them a squeeze.

"Honestly? I'm trying to think of an exit strategy. It's difficult to come up with a lie on a planet that is all about doing the right thing."

Flynn cups my cheeks. His thumbs brush right beneath my cheekbones.

"It may not be a valid excuse on Earth, but you are allowed to say that you don't want to be here and can leave." My eyebrows raise, and he laughs. "I know, I know. You aren't going to say that. I'm just saying it isn't offensive here unless you're rude about it. You're allowed to live your life the way it makes you happy. With that said, we'll likely be here for a few hours. So if you want an out, now is a less awkward time."

The issue is, leaving means not seeing Flynn for at least a few more hours. My fingers are throbbing before I realize they have interlaced again. Flynn looks down and takes my hands in his, unraveling my fingers. He doesn't let them go. Instead, he massages my fingers with his thumbs.

"Let's get together tonight for some late dinner or dessert and watch another movie. Sound good?"

I look over at him and swallow the lump forming in my throat. It's not the perfect situation. If I leave early, I have the guilt of not staying for the duration of the party. If I stay, I'm anxious the entire time.

"Okay, I like that idea."

Flynn pulls me into a hug, breathing in, and my body naturally follows his course. As my shoulders drop, he lets go. He leans forward, connecting our lips for a brief moment before stepping backward.

"Continue down the hallway, and to the right will lead

you to the foyer. You can leave through the front door. I'll tell everyone you aren't feeling well. No harm done."

"That's lying." But my anxiety latches onto the idea and starts to fade.

"That's protecting a friend. Now go have fun. Don't feel guilty. I'll text you when I'm done. You need to promise me something, though, okay?"

I nod, trying to hold back a smile.

"At eight o'clock, if you haven't heard from me yet, my sister has held me hostage. You must call and rescue me. Deal? There are no thoughts of 'Oh, he is having a great time. I'm not going to bother him' or 'He wasn't serious, it's okay.' Screw those thoughts. I have plans with you tonight. No exceptions."

I laugh at Flynn's spot-on impersonation of me. I close the space between us, giving him a tight hug. He did my voice and everything. If anyone else impersonated me like that, especially Jonah, I would have walked out of the party and been furious. I wouldn't have recognized it as my down-fall, of me keeping myself from things that I want because the anxiety festers. But Flynn is learning to be a step ahead of my anxiety, reminding me of my place and its importance in his life. I think I can get used to this.

Twenty-Eight

"Good morning, Theodore." Andrya smiles as she opens the door to her office.

Lana had welcomed me into the home and led me down the hall. It's a little strange being here alone. It's quiet now. No laughter or music playing in the backyard. Despite having an appointment, I almost feel like I'm intruding.

Andrya had sent a message before breakfast asking to meet at 9:00 am. It coincides with my schoolwork schedule, but there are far more pressing matters. Flynn was ominous this morning, too. He knocked on my door earlier, rambling on about how he was stressed and needed to study this morning, but would show up on time for our 11:00 am session. I barely understood what he was saying as I was half-asleep.

I kind of assumed that part of Otium was living stress free. Nonetheless, it let me off the hook on whether I should tell Flynn about my meeting with his mom. It's not that I wanted to keep him from it. I just didn't want to be talked out of it.

"Let's sit." Andrya interrupts my thoughts, pointing

over to the two sofa chairs she has in the corner. She takes a seat in the furthest one from the door, and I sit next to her, placing my backpack on the ground. The phone in her hand gets placed on the table between our chairs. She shouldn't trust me to not steal her holy grail. "Thank you for being patient with my time, Theodore. Now, what would you like to discuss?"

I smile, sitting back in the seat. *Straight forward. This is good.* She's relaxed, hands in her lap, ankles crossed.

"Sam and Ellie," I say, interlacing my hands.

A smile graces her face as she centers the necklace on her chest. "I was wondering if you had figured out who Lana was speaking of. What would you like to know?"

I let out a small breath. There are no secrets between Lana and Andrya.

"I know they are your grandparents. I just feel like there is some secrecy around them? I want to know the role they play in my life going back to Earth, why they were in the hospital, and why Flynn didn't know that I knew them?"

Andrya smiles and stands up, walking over to her filing cabinet. "I guess I shouldn't be surprised you told Flynn about Sam and Ellie. You two have become quite close."

She's not staring me down as she says that, instead her head is searching for a file in the cabinet. I definitely don't want to be in a position where she might know that I've kissed her son.

Is it okay that I've kissed her son?

"I am not able to tell you about your future, Theodore. How you choose to live your life going forward must be up to you."

My heart sinks. Logically, it makes sense. My future on Earth is affected. Just being transported to another planet disrupted my timeline.

They say my purpose here is to choose the path I now want to live. Though, sometimes I think I'd rather just follow.

Andrya has an envelope in her hands when she closes the filing cabinet, turning back to me. "Sam and Ellie are living near you, in Creston."

That's not my hometown, but it's a hell of a lot closer than Colorado.

"Do you know why they are back? I don't understand why they left and how they happened to be at the hospital. How did they know?"

The envelope in her hands has my name written in script, but she keeps it on her lap.

"They came back earlier that week. They went to your last protest, and they were at the verdict. They alerted the ambulance on sight."

I blink, twisting my fingers and stretching my arms out in front of me. I don't know what to do with this information. I know they were watching everything, but it doesn't make sense why they wouldn't let me know they were in town.

"In the hospital . . . they told me they hadn't moved back yet."

My eyes blur as her head tilts. Her left arm reaches out, gently caressing my shoulder.

"We decided that it would be best if you didn't know they were already home. I feared that if you knew, you might not be as eager to come here."

I shake off her arm, scooting as far away from her touch as I can. *More fucking lies. When do they stop?* I blink through the tears, watching my fingertips grow more pink the harder I squeeze. I want to be wrapped up in my comforter on my bed, surrounded by things that feel like home. My room here is slowly becoming more of a home than the one I grew up in.

My gut twists and I pull my knees up, feet resting on the edge of the chair. I squeeze my legs in close, resting my chin on my knees.

"W-we? What? W-what is going on?"

Andrya sighs before she hands me the envelope. My shaking hands take it, and I outline the script against my thighs. It's Ellie's handwriting. She used to write me notes all the time. Letters to open at school to brighten my day. She always wrote them in cursive.

"That is from Sam and Ellie. I don't want you to open and read it now because we have some things to discuss. But they wrote that for you and asked me to give it to you when I thought the time was right."

I grip the envelope tighter, trying to stop my shaking hands as my eyes dart up to Andrya's. I can barely see through the tears blurring my vision. My heart starts to race and my mind freezes. Sam and Ellie do know about Otium.

"What is . . . how d-did y-you . . . "

"Last year, I met Sam and Ellie for the first time. I took some time away from Otium and stayed on Earth for a little while."

I can't control the tears. I'm not even sure why I'm crying or what I feel or how I should fucking feel. I don't even know what's true between the lies and the information held from me.

"They know about here?" I ask, letting the envelope lay on my lap as I swipe the tears with my fingertips.

"Yes. Well. They knew about the initiative around the same time as your parents. They just didn't know who I was. I originally tried to recruit them with your parents."

"Why didn't they go?"

She smiles again, soft crinkles in her eyes. When I really look at her, separating the fact that she is a leader, she seems like she could have similar mannerisms to Ellie. She can be kind, but she's a go-getter.

"My grandparents loved your parents too much. They wanted to go with your parents—as we wanted them all together. But your parents' agency was too new for them all to leave. It hindered my plans, but I respect it, and I'm proud of them."

I shove my fisted hands between my legs.

"So why now? Why, when I need Sam and Ellie the most, do they disappear? Do you happen to show up?"

"The summer before your parents passed, they contacted us. They were ready to check out the initiative again but also wanted you to join. They wanted you to be a part of something grand before your senior year."

I try to think back to any conversations that could have led to this. I understand this conversation going above my head when I was only twelve when they first got the information. But at sixteen? How could I have missed the ultimate way to help the world?

The summer before they died, I kept telling them that my goal was to take over the agency. That they couldn't talk to me about doing anything else with my life. So I volunteered with the agency and got my hands into as much as I could to learn the ropes. I knew I'd still need college, but I didn't want to give the board any reason to not hire me when the time came. I was at the agency more than my parents that summer. There were plenty of moments when they had time to discuss things without me.

"Their deaths hindered our plans significantly. Sam and Ellie finally getting pregnant delayed everything, too. Obviously, we knew that my mom was born sometime soon, but I was so distracted by finally getting everyone to Otium that I didn't take into account what year it actually was. With the pregnancy and your parents gone, I had to go back to square one, which had me traveling to Colorado to meet them instead of them coming to me."

I blink, trying to process all this information. But instead of anything filing correctly, words are swirling through my mind like a tornado.

"So they already decided to move to Colorado before you showed up?"

"Yes," she says, "but that isn't my story to tell." Andrya nods to the envelope.

I want to rip it open. See what plausible excuse they had to abandon me. Instead, my right index finger and thumb bend the right-hand corner of the envelope back and forth.

"I stayed with them for a few weeks. Met my great-grandmother, who nearly had a heart attack at who I was. Eventually, we arranged that once their baby—my mom—was born, they would come to the Otium Initiative. After all the changes in your life, I wanted to make sure that you had someone to discuss this with when you went back."

"So why didn't I go with Sam and Ellie? They seemed to get fair notice. Why didn't I?" Anger brews within me. Yes, this information is helpful, but it's another knife in my stomach, twisting and carving in me. A reminder that I still haven't gotten the decency of notice like everyone else.

"Collectively, after I told them the plan to use the initiative as grief counseling for you, we decided it would be best for you to experience Otium on your own when you were eighteen. Sam and Ellie completed the initiative and were back on Earth a week before the trial. The plan was to explain everything after your parents' fundraiser when your schedule settled down, but then you ended up in the hospital."

"And you panicked?!" My volume is louder than I expected. My legs shake. Between my clammy hands and tears, the envelope is growing damp.

Sam and Ellie know how I am in these situations; they'd know it wasn't best to uproot me immediately.

"And I panicked. I reacted before Sam and Ellie knew."

Bingo. Sam and Ellie wouldn't have approved. Andrya could have avoided this entire mess. If she had the ability to extract, she could have extracted all of us—my parents included—at any point in time. In a split second decision, she could have changed my entire life.

"I had made it my responsibility to protect you—"

"But you didn't protect them!" I yell. I stand, shoving the envelope in my back pocket before I pace. "You're living in the fucking future. How did you not know my parents were going to die? Why didn't you extract us before they died? They could still be here, alive and well. We could have all been in the initiative, and I wouldn't be in this stupid grief counseling! You fucking knew about the protest, and you still let us go!"

"Theodore, please sit."

"No!" I scream. A few spit droplets escape as I turn toward her. I can't control the tears or the snot escaping. "If you had no issue extracting me without notice, you could have done so with my entire family. You're the reason they are dead. You had the ability to change the future, and you didn't."

The words sit heavy on my chest as I stop walking in front of the door. If they have the power to go back in time, we shouldn't even be having this conversation.

"That's not how this—"

"Fuck you." I swing open the door. "Fuck this entire place." I slam the door behind me.

I jog down the hallway and out the front door, grabbing my bike and pedaling down the path. I take the sharp right that leads me to the Forest, pedaling like my life depends on it.

How can someone live in the future and be so ignorant of the past? She's not any better. She's not looking at all sides of things. Being proactive. It's been years of her trying to recruit everyone. How could my parents' deaths, something already written in the timeline, be missed?

I drop my bike, darting into the Forest. I trip on a root, blinking a few times, trying to adjust to the darkness. I continue into the Forest when I can see clearly.

How is every action here disrupting the original timeline? Before my parents knew of the Otium Initiative, was death always in their cards? Is it possible that Andrya didn't catch it because originally, my parents were going to live? If she wanted them so badly, that has to mean that my parents had a future. Otherwise, it would have been a waste of time and resources for her to focus efforts on them.

Every single action has a chain reaction. Every mentee who has stepped foot on Otium has gone back to Earth to start making changes. That has to mean that the future timeline on Earth is never set in stone. Yet, everything here is permanent. With Sam and Ellie having their daughter, they now know about the future. They know of Otium, and that their parenting results in a leader down the line. What changes will they make in their future that are different from the original path?

Knowing all of this, working with Sam and Ellie in the future, being with Flynn, likely wanting to be with him when I leave, how does all of this affect my original timeline?

I pause for a moment. *That's the point, though.* We were uneducated. Going into the unknown. Now my future has hope. I can be responsible for continuing that hope, altering the timeline in my own way. Instead of millions dying on Earth, the idea is that the timeline changes, so millions now live.

But how? When? Is the plan to wait thirty years, live through all the disastrous pollution, warfare, and hate? Or does the transition happen sooner?

I make my way to the log that Flynn and I originally had lunch on. It feels like a lifetime ago. The bunnies are hovering in the grass nearby. They glance at me for a few seconds before they carry on with their routine.

Taking a seat, I pull my bag off my back and find my water. I drink a few sips, trying my best to regulate my breathing. From biking with my anxiety, the last thing I need is to have an attack in the middle of a forest when no one knows where I am. I still have an hour or so before I need to meet Flynn. Before anyone realizes I'm missing.

I need to talk more with Andrya. Just the thought of her at the moment boils my blood. I can't see past her worst mistake. I can't forgive her for not extracting my parents. For not having them cheat death. Her panic about me was no doubt fear that I might die before she had a chance to bring me here. So why couldn't she use that same fucked enthusiasm with my parents?

I situate myself comfortably on the rock and feel the crinkle of the envelope in my pocket. I pull it out, tracing my name once more. This letter could be written at any point in time throughout the past year. Maybe before they met Andrya, maybe after they did, after the baby was born? They could have written it while here, on Otium.

I wonder if they stayed in the apartment building. If so, which one? They would have been in the previous program. But if they were here, Flynn would have seen them. He knows what they look like. He even said if they were here, he'd be disappointed that it was kept from him.

Everything is interlaced with lies.

I gently rip open the envelope and pull out the two-sided letter, all in Ellie's handwriting. She writes to the very end of the second side. "Ellie and Sam" are barely legible next to the heart at the bottom of the page. I flip it over to see "Theodore" written at the top as its own line.

"If you're reading this, Andrya must have thought it was time." The letter starts.

I want to fold it back up. I don't know if it is time. This just confirmed it was written after they met Andrya. The contents of this letter could be so vast I can't even prepare for worst-case scenarios.

A crunching of sticks has me sitting up straight, folding the letter. It sounds like footsteps near the entrance. While this is the perfect place to hike, Flynn and I have never passed another person on this path.

Flynn walks through the clearing. I shove the envelope in my backpack, zipping it up before he finds me, and I stand up.

I don't know how he found me. Pressure increases on my chest just at the sight of him. He's supposed to be stressed about studying or something and ditching the routine *he* created for me. He told me communication was key here, yet he hasn't been the best model for that. Nor has Andrya.

"What are you doing here?" he asks before I can do the same for him. He projects his voice as he continues to march toward me. "Why is my mom calling me, telling me that you ran away from her? Why is she questioning me about not knowing your original whereabouts? Why are you with my mom to begin with?" He spews question after question until he's standing a few feet in front of me, hands on his waist, taking deep breaths.

He's wearing the gray sweat shorts and a gray t-shirt he had on this morning. Some sweat drips down his face and onto his shirt that already has pit stains. It's the warmest day here so far, but I assumed he was immune to sweating.

His hand brushes his hair back, the moisture matting it down. "Theo, what is going on?" he asks.

His impatient tone has me stepping back. This isn't the caring Flynn who genuinely wants to know what's happening. He's frustrated and maybe even spiraling.

"I'm a little stressed at the moment," he reminds me. "I have a lot to do this morning, and that got interrupted. So, can you please fill me in on why I rushed here?" His breathing starts to regulate.

I reach into my backpack and hand him my water, which he takes a few sips of.

"How did you find me?" I manage to ask, sitting back down on the log after he hands me my water back.

"Every mentee has a tracker on their phone. We are only supposed to use it if we lose you." He narrows his eyes as I open my mouth. "It's a safety feature before you bug out."

Bug out? Being concerned over a tracking device isn't insane.

"I'm not lost. You can carry on with whatever is stressing you out," I say nonchalantly as I look down at the log, picking at the bark. I try to play it cool despite my insides scrambling.

"Why are you keeping information from me?" he asks, crossing his arms.

"Why are you?" I retort back, and he squints his eyes. "What are you so stressed about that you came to me in a panic? Why did you ditch me this morning? I'm only keeping info from you because you didn't have room for me this morning."

"I don't get paid to eat breakfast with you!" he yells.

I flinch at his volume, and he immediately turns around. *And there it is. Exactly like I feared. I'm only a job.*

His palms cover his face as he takes a few deep breaths. The gray shirt sticks to his skin more and more with each inhale. He exhales loudly before he walks over to the log, taking a seat, leaving a few extra spaces between us.

"I'm sorry," he whispers. "My life got uprooted, too. It's not an excuse to treat you like shit, and I will lose points for my behavior."

I roll my eyes. I don't care about the stupid money system.

"Do you remember when I told you most mentors finish their studies at twenty?" I nod, and he continues. "My degree was always going to be fast-tracked, but the plan for you to arrive was at least six months out. The decision hadn't been made on if you'd start with the first program of next year or the second program. Either way, I would have finished my studies. I technically don't graduate for another five months, then I have a few weeks of mandatory training that every mentor has before the new year programs."

I let out a breath. Andrya clearly hasn't thought about anyone but herself here.

"I only have one class to attend, which is during your

group therapy, but I have loads of additional work to do on my own time. As you can tell, I haven't done much work because I've spent the majority of time with you. Being your mentor is also different from how I've been trained, in almost every single way. It all caught up to me, and I panicked. We make mistakes and panic here, too," Flynn says. "We aren't perfect."

A laugh bubbles out of me. "You can say that again."

Flynn furrows his brows, crossing his arms again. "Theo, I'm trying to open up to you. Why are you laughing?"

"Because everything is a big mistake." I flick off loose specks of bark, watching as they disappear between the blades of grass.

He straddles the log as best he can, but I keep my eyes focused on the log.

"What are you talking about?" he asks. His voice is calmer, but it doesn't settle the vibrations in me; the questions, the confusions, the assumptions fueled with anger.

"It doesn't matter." I can't tell Flynn that I'm pissed at his mom. That I think his mom could have done better. That I think she could have prevented my parents' deaths. That she could have at least cared a little about her son's stress levels to not panic-extract me.

"It does matter. Because I have no idea what you're talking about. Why did you even schedule a meeting with my mom? Why did you really keep that from me?" I don't answer him when he pauses. "Are you unhappy with me? Unhappy with my mentoring?" He inhales sharply. "Oh no, you didn't tell her about us, did you?"

I spin toward him. "No, I didn't tell your mom about us," I spat. "But why are you freaking out? Are you trying to hide us?"

Flynn drops his jaw. His hand reaches out before he pulls it back and grips his thigh. "I'm not hiding you, Theo." He sighs. "There's just a time and place, and I'd like to be included in the decision to tell anyone. Frankly, I like having a private life, and I don't think that everyone needs to know who I like the moment that I tell that person. I'm 'freaking out' because if you told my mom about us, maybe you did so because you were uncomfortable, and the last thing I want is for you to feel uncomfortable with me. With that said, just because I'm your mentor, you're allowed to end things. There is no power dynamic here."

"I don't want to end what we're doing. But what are we doing?" I ask softly. "I don't know how to do this. How do I have feelings about your mom and what she is doing, and work through my anger and frustration when I should be able to talk with my mentor about it all, but my mentor also happens to be the leader's son, and he also happens to be someone I really like. How the hell do I balance it all without insulting you or pushing you away and staying sane myself? And on top of that, how am I supposed to react when the person I like, the one who I'm supposed to be completely honest with, all of a sudden panics on me this morning, canceling the everyday schedule they created, leaving me with no idea of what they're even panicking about because they haven't been honest with me!" I end with a yell, gasping for air as I finish.

Flynn nods, looking down while he does so. His fingers clench and unclench on his thighs. "We start with communication that goes both ways because it seems while I can harp on you to grow, I'm pretty shit at it myself."

I sigh. "You're not sh—"

"I am." He reaches his hand out, and I scooch down the log toward him, taking it. "In the chaos of getting you here, I was asked if I wanted to back out. My mother did explain that it would be complicated to balance my schedule with yours, but she asked me to be flexible and sacrifice some of my personal time to make sure you were comfortable."

"I didn't ask you—"

Flynn squeezes my hand. "Hold on, please. Let me speak." I nod while he interlaces our fingers. "I agreed to it. This is what I was working toward. I wasn't going to walk away from a candidate that my mom was trusting me with. It felt like the highest honor. I had the opportunity to say no. I could have finished my studies while goofing off with my friends during this time. Instead, I chose the challenge. I assumed that I'd have plenty of time. I mean, we have four more hours than Earth, right?" He lets out a breathy laugh, but I can only offer him a sad smile.

We really are so similar. Different planets, different timelines, different upbringings, and he's here, trying to do everything in his power to make a difference, even if that means stressing himself out.

"Technically, I have plenty of time to balance both. I just never intended on falling for you. That wasn't in my scheduled plan." Flynn raises our hands, and he kisses the top of mine. "From the moment you came back to Otium, all the extra time I spent with you was because I wanted to. Not because of my mom asking me to be your friend, not because I thought you might need more training, not because I felt bad for you, not because I was trying to do a good deed for extra points, but because I genuinely enjoy spending my time with you."

"How many hours are you actually supposed to spend with me?"

"Our three hours of training a day, plus I have an hour every day to write up how you're doing. This gets submitted to the head of the program. At the end of the week, I have an extra hour to sum up the week and submit a plan for the following week based on how you did the previous. This past week, the hour took me a little longer each day because you aren't following the regular protocol; therefore, everything is new. Technically, our day together doesn't start until eleven."

Oh.

"And my schedule doesn't include spending siesta with you."

Right. I'm teetering on the edge of a downward slope about to lose it all.

"What are you doing when I'm doing schoolwork?" I ask. "Shouldn't that be a good amount of time for your stuff, too?"

"It is for mentoring. But not for my studies. This past week I used that time to write my notes about you from the day prior. I got overwhelmed this morning because I didn't know how to stop the cycle, especially now that we kissed." He keeps my hand close to him, as my body wants to jerk it away. "I want to kiss you. I want to enjoy whatever this might be, but I also know that it solidified in my head that our time together wasn't going to decrease unless I changed something. My other work was piling up, and each day we got closer, it became harder to make boundaries. There is more than enough time for everything; I just didn't communicate."

"So we adjust our schedule." I shrug, but I don't feel good about it. I like spending all my time with him when I can. It's strange because I used to need my alone time. Despite whatever activism I was doing, I still needed a recharge time. This past year, I filled every portion of my day, so much so I would send myself in a spiral just to recharge. On Otium, I haven't taken that space either.

"You're right. We can figure it out because you're my friend, and I'm also allowed to come to you like you come to me," Flynn says with a nod, as if confirming for himself.

I take in his smile. I hate that he keeps saying "friend" even though we haven't solidified more than that. There's no term for the in-between of having a crush to having a relationship. We aren't friends with benefits.

I lean in, and he meets me halfway, pecking my lips. He reaches for my hips, tugging me forward. I situate myself, so I'm facing him, sitting cross-legged.

"Okay, it's your turn communicating," he says. "What has you running into the Forest?"

I was kind of hoping we were past this conversation. That he got distracted by his problem, and then maybe my lips were good enough to just continue kissing. I try leaning forward and pressing my lips against his again.

He smiles into the kiss and pulls away. "Stop distracting."

I grin, but I don't offer him anything else.

"Next time you'd like to talk to my mom, can you please give me a heads up?" My grin disappears. "If anything, because you're my friend? She's pretty annoyed I didn't know your whereabouts this morning."

"That's not your fault. You don't need to know my every move." I lean back on my hands, creating distance between us.

"On the contrary, if I lose you, I also lose my job."

His words gut me. Not because he could lose his job, but because even if I want to run away, have a single moment of peace, it's not even granted on the almighty planet.

They stalked me unknowingly for five years. They lost tabs of my parents in their stalking. I wish they'd lose tabs on me, too. The anger starts to rise within me again. I've been on their radar for so fucking long. How could they make such a big mistake?

I swivel on the log before hopping off and grabbing my backpack.

"Where are you going?"

"Why don't you use your tracker to find out," I say before I jog toward the opening of the Forest.

Twenty-Nine

When I walked away from Flynn, all I did was go to the education building and do my schoolwork until therapy. I disregarded my session with Flynn completely. I figured if he was desperate to do our lesson before my session with Corie, then he'd find me. But he never did.

I had to tell Corie how pathetic I was with her assignment. Not only was I presented with the joy of kayaking and I ran from it, but I also already fucked things up with Flynn. Though I did find joy in the peace and relaxation of the spa.

"Why do you think people reject change?" Corie asks. She really didn't comment much on my weekend, which irritates the hell out of me because if she's going to assign something, the least she can do is give me a grade. And now she's changing the freaking subject *again*.

I keep myself from rolling my eyes, but the frustration stumbles out of my mouth. "We fear what we don't know," I grunt. A phrase I've muttered, stated, written, and chanted for years. It's ingrained in my mind.

"Sure. That's definitely a part of it. For those of us who know this, like you and me, why do you think we still reject change? Even in times when we know we have to break out of the cycle? We need change, and we still don't go in that direction?"

There's some deep psychological bullshit she's trying to pull here. And I'm not certain if I want her to succeed. Right now, I'd rather just be frustrated and petty.

"We get comfortable."

"Good, yes." She nods. "And when we are comfortable, do we sometimes question if we are worthy of the change?"

"I guess so," I mutter. I pick at my pant leg. There's a dry hard spot of oat milk that I spilled on myself this morning. This day was doomed from the beginning.

"Our perceptions change based on how we feel and believe others perceive us. Sometimes even proof can hinder us from making a change. Do you like the way reality is for you right now?"

Well, that's one hell of a loaded question.

"Which reality? Earth or Otium?"

"Your present is your reality."

The weight of her words hit me. There is no dual timeline. There is me, here and now. No Theodore is present on Earth. No one can contact him. No one can see him until I travel back through time.

Therefore, the timeline has changed. This I knew. The moment I left, it had to have, but maybe Corie can provide information.

What is everyone else doing? What is Jonah's reality? Is he working on his art portfolio? Is it ready to submit? Is he heartbroken over us or moving on with his life? Is me in grief counseling really positive for him or actually detrimental? Or my brothers? Have they started their grief counseling yet? Have my aunt and uncle even attempted to get in contact with the therapist? Or Alejandro? Did he cover the fundraising event? Is he viral with his challenge videos? Is he upholding my social media, or has that all crumbled with my disappearance?

Time hasn't stopped. When I go home, I will be entering a reality where they all continued living the life I got to leave. I'll have to learn what everyone was up to. I'll have to somehow lie about my time here until the time is right. I'll have to integrate my potential new self into the mold they have of me. I have to keep myself from falling back into the shell of the person I was.

"My reality is messy, real, unrealistic, and a lie."

"Okay. Now, how would you like your reality to look?"

"Peaceful. Truthful. Optimistic."

"Those are good. Now, what changes do you think you may have to make in order to achieve that reality?"

"I need information and better communication."

"What do you mean by that?" she asks, tapping away on her pad. She was pretty consistent about listening to me, but now she's writing everything down.

"Does what I say leave this room?" I ask, and her fingers pause their tapping. I need to make sure nothing gets back to Andrya or Flynn.

"Never. Unless there is an emergency, like if you wanted to harm yourself."

I nod, twisting my fingers together and shoving them between my legs. "You know my communication about my purpose here has been shit. But I need to know more about time travel. What effect this program has on Earth's future, what me being here changes for my future. I think Andrya could have prevented my parents from dying, and I need to know for sure."

Corie's pad falls off of the arm of her chair. It tumbles face down, and she's frozen for a few seconds before she leans over to grab it. Brushing her aqua curls out of her face, she takes a deep breath.

"That is a strong accusation, Theodore."

"That's how I feel."

She nods, situating herself to sit up straight, the pad on her lap. The screen is off, thankfully.

"Okay, you know that everything you do has a butterfly effect." I nod. "So yes, us going back in time to take people from Earth and train them in the Otium Initiative does affect the timeline. Every single moment since it started. When we learn about history before Otium, we learn about events that are set in stone. Everything prior to forty years before Otium existed in Earth's timeline. So you're seventeen?" I nod. "When you were seven, that is the last concrete thing we have in history. We do have Earth's current history that we learn and have to keep up with, though. This history gets updated periodically with any drastic changes that may have happened because of us going back in time."

Corie pauses, and I stare at the blank wall right behind her as I try to process the information.

"Why forty years ago?" I ask. That seems so random.

"In your timeline, it's nearly ten years before Otium is discovered. However, we only started the program going back to thirty-five years before Otium. There were kinks that needed to be sorted once a definitive timeline started. Not a single candidate in the initiative has their Otium self still alive. No candidate can be in the initiative in a location where their family might be living on Otium. We are trying our hardest to make unnecessary changes as small as possible. So, for you, your family came to Otium and started life in the Valley. You passed away in the Valley a few years ago. Now, that doesn't mean you can't visit that location. But when you're in the program, the people who live in that area know you're in the program. We don't want our current candidates intermingling with their future families."

I'm dead. The idea almost makes me want to laugh.

"I'm confused." I'm sure as hell not about to tell her that I plan to track my family down because that seems really freaking cool, even if seeing them from a distance. "If big changes happen on Earth, does it affect those living on Otium? Like if a change causes someone to not have a kid or a big change resulted in someone dying early, and they didn't make it to Otium?"

"We traveled to a parallel universe, so everyone who made it to Otium has entered this timeline. They are concrete. We don't want mentees intermingling with their families here because it could distract you from your mission on Earth. It could cause unnecessary changes because we've never been able to see our future before. I don't know where I end up, and you don't know where you end up. That's something that has always been a given, and we want to keep it that way. Whatever decisions you choose to make on Earth are up to you. But you can live in peace knowing that the people you've met here are not affected by any single action you make. We may only benefit from the overall outcome."

I'll be a fool if I don't find out my future when the opportunity surrounds me.

"When do I come back to Otium? Am I coming back to a fully established planet? Will I be able to see Flynn again? Will I be able to see you? Or am I in a new timeline? Could that be why no one here is affected? Like Dr. Strange says with the infinity stones. If you alter the timelines, another one branches off. Will I be going to an Otium that isn't this one?"

Her eyes dart back and forth and to her pad before her finger starts tapping different buttons on the pad.

"Theodore, what does this have to do with your parents dying? What do you think Andrya could have done differently?"

She might not know, but how is everyone here willing to be so ignorant to the massive changes that may occur in thirty years or less?

"Has anyone questioned the leaders of Otium about it? This is pretty important."

"We are done with this conversation. Would you like to tell me why you're accusing Andrya, or would you like to move on?"

She challenges my eye contact, and I let out a sigh.

"You say that we don't know our futures, but the leaders of Otium know my planet's future," I start. "They know the future of those they are interested in. If they had conversations with my parents, if they saw that my parents were going to be murdered, why wouldn't they have forced them to come to the initiative like they forced me?"

"I think you have to set up a meeting with Andrya. She's better suited to give you this information."

"I already did." I cross my arms, pressing back into the sofa.

Her eyebrows raise at that. "Oh." A soft smile crosses her face as she takes a moment. "And did you ask Andrya?"

I grip my pants, twisting the fabric on my thigh.

"Theodore." Corie's voice is stern. She already knows what happened. I'm a predictable catastrophe.

"I don't know. I ran out."

I can see her nod from my peripheral vision. "The only information I can give you is what we've already talked about. Every moment since you were seven is no longer set in stone. In a way, Otium may be responsible because of that. But, like I said, we don't study concrete information from that future because it is constantly changing. When Andrya first contacted your parents, it's possible their deaths weren't in the timeline. But any small butterfly effect up until the minute your parents died could have altered the timeline. That doesn't mean it was Andrya. It might not have been a specific action by a mentee, either. We will never know, and it's part of the consequence when messing with time."

"Is it possible that Andrya knows what their future did hold? Like when she first contacted them?" I ask, letting go of my pants and looking up at her.

Corie's eyes are glossy as she sits back in her seat. It's not fair to put her in a position that isn't hers. But Andrya should also know enough that when I want things done, I get them done.

"Do you really want to know?" Corie asks. "Would that information be helpful for your grieving? Or would that make you angrier? Too angry at the initiative that it could mess up your opportunity to do more good in the world?"

"If Andrya knows, I need to know," I say without hesitation.

Corie picks up her phone and asks me for permission to call Andrya. Lana picks up, and Corie sits on hold for nearly ten minutes. Honestly, I'm shocked she called. I expected some bullshit answer explaining to me how it wasn't a good idea. That without Otium, I wouldn't know the answer, anyway. That I'd need to heal without it.

But as Corie rushes to get Andrya up to speed on our

conversation, I grip the couch, digging my fingernails into the fabric. I'm actually not sure if I want this information.

Corie confirms numerous times with Andrya that I need to know to further my growth, and no matter the answer, she'll help me through it. The moment Corie closes her eyes, dropping her shoulders, I know the answer.

I push off the couch and get my hand on the doorknob by the time Corie ends the phone call.

"Where are you going?" she asks.

"What'd Andrya say?" My back's rigid as I glare into the clay-framed door.

"Our session isn't complete, Theodore."

"Corie," I groan. I lean my forehead against the door to steady myself.

"When Andrya contacted your parents five years ago, they had a long life ahead of them. They did a lot of good in your state and helped with vetting who could go to Otium. They passed away before the final transport. Though, because of their age, they wouldn't have been eligible for the trip."

I swing open the therapy door and slam it behind me, running through the hall, down the stairs, and shoving the main door of the building open. I skid to a stop as Flynn stumbles backward, dropping drinks out of his hands. The reusable mugs crash to the ground, leaking liquid in the grass.

"My god!" I yell at Flynn. "Get out of my way!"

"I came to talk," he says as he squats down to pick up the drinks.

"I don't want to talk." I grab my bike from its rack.

"Theo, please," he pleads.

I hop on my bike, tighten the straps of my backpack, and pedal as fast as I can. This time, I'm headed to the cavern.

It's lunchtime, and I need to hole away in the darkness—one that will eventually force me to leave, unlike my bedroom. I can scream at the top of my lungs and listen to it echo in the cave.

Flynn is alongside me, peddling in pace, sweat framing his forehead.

"Level 1-10, how pissed off are you?"

"10!" I yell. Even as I start to pant, the volume seems to lessen the pain.

"Bike to the cavern. Blow off some steam. I'll be right here with you."

I don't want him to be. I want to be alone. I race off past him, pushing through the exhaustion. The fire in my legs screams at me to stop, but I can't. I reach the train station, and there is nothing more I want to do than hop on the train, but Flynn shouts from behind me to keep going. I won't fail in front of him. I refuse to.

"Fuckkkkk!" I scream as loud as I can.

At home, when I'd get angry and scream at the top of my lungs, swarms of birds would burst from the trees. In the middle of the Flatlands, it's just my voice and heavy panting.

At the cavern, I'm pouring with sweat. My button-up shirt is soaked against my skin. I can already predict the rashes that'll appear from my underwear if I don't let them dry before moving again. My pants already chafed my thighs. Every single muscle burns as I climb off the bike.

Flynn isn't too far behind. He looks like he's been casually biking behind me as I just biked to my death.

Leaning forward, I rest my forearms on my thighs, gasping for breath. I don't necessarily want him here, but this is his spot, and it'd be rude to keep him from it.

"How'd that feel?" he asks, only a soft pant in his voice.

I barely lift myself up to make eye contact with him. His bike flops next to mine before his hands are on my shoulders, lifting me up to stand.

"C'mon, let's get you inside. You can scream it out if you have any energy left."

I hate him.

He's sweating, and the outfit he changed into now has sweat stains too. But he isn't gasping for breath like me. It's more like the heat of the day got to him versus the actual physical activity. I want to smack him.

Flynn walks me over the rocks. My breathing is sharp with each step. The only motivation I have is knowing how the rock will feel on my warm skin.

When we finally get inside, I collapse next to the rock slab that he likes to sit on. I unbutton my shirt and strip off my jeans. I toss the soaked clothing underneath my head as a pillow and lay down. Of course, the stupid rock only feels like room temperature against my burning skin.

Flynn is rummaging for something as I try to regulate my breathing. My lungs are on fire.

A cool bottle rests against my skin. Flynn helps me sit up a little, and I take a few gulps of water; wincing as the water coats my esophagus. I look down and realize that I'm just sitting next to him in my boxers—my sweaty boxers. In my overheated state, I needed as much off of me as I could get. Thankfully, it's nearly pitch-black in here.

I lower the bottle from my lip and place it next to me. There's no way I can put the soaked clothing back on right now without it irritating my mind. All I can do is lay back, let the slab cool me, and pretend it's no big deal that I'm nearly naked.

Flynn lays down beside me, his hands underneath his

head. "I'm here if you want to talk. If not, we can sit in silence."

He's not your enemy. I have to remind myself over and over. I'm not angry with him. There have been numerous times that I've panicked and ditched someone. Over and over again. I've been pretty good at it this past year. I'm frustrated by the day. By all the new information. By the lack of preparation for the fucking future.

"I never asked for this," I start. "I know I came back, but I didn't understand fully."

He's silent, aside from his breathing in and out. The only reason I know he isn't sleeping is because he interlaces our fingers.

"If my timeline changes, the timeline of those I love changes, too."

"Do you want what I think or do you need to vent?" he asks after a few beats of silence.

"What are you thinking?" I whisper.

"I'm confused. You watch all these Marvel movies and you tell me about future movies with multiverses. Of course, your timeline is going to be altered. We want it to be. Hell, that's why we have the initiative for more positive changes to be made in our history."

"When your mom originally tried to recruit my parents, they lived to watch people travel to Otium. They helped with the process of starting this planet. But then something changed the timeline, and they died. Your mom just doesn't know what changed. I assume that's what she panicked about because, obviously, in the real, original timeline, I didn't end up hospitalized from a panic attack because of my parents' deaths."

"Fuck," he breathes. Flynn sits up and turns to face me.

His hand rests on my bare side. Even his fingertips aren't cool. "Do you think it's the initiative's fault?"

I shrug, looking up at the ceiling. I can barely see any of the texture in the darkness. "They don't know for sure, but nothing is set in stone in my timeline."

"How do you feel about it all?"

I wish he could see my glare. "Like I want to steal your watch and transport myself back five years, extract my parents, and keep them safe here."

He sighs, trailing his fingers along my skin. "You know you can't do that."

"But why?" I pause for a moment. Water drips from the stone around us. "Honestly, Flynn, why can't I?" I whisper.

He's silent still, and I shove myself up from the floor. They have a plan. A system. *Variables* that need to be controlled. Going back in time further than the plan would alter the timeline even more.

I *know* that. I *understand* that. But I'm still livid.

Swallowing the thick saliva in my mouth, I trudge forward, feeling the burn of my muscles. Once in the center of the room, I take a massive breath and scream at the top of my lungs until I'm kneeling and then in child's pose, resting my forehead on the rock's surface, sobbing.

Flynn's next to me in seconds—his fingertips trace my bare spine, causing goosebumps yet easing my tears. I don't move when I regain my breath. I remain in child's pose, sinking into the movement.

I'm so utterly exhausted. I hate knowing that the technology is right in front of me to bring them back. I hate timelines and loops and parallel universes. I hate rules and regulations and bullshit that's manipulated for someone else's plan.

"I just want my parents back," I whisper, my voice

muffled by the ground. The tears pool in front of me on the rock as I close my eyes, allowing myself to lull with Flynn's fingertips.

We sit in silence, listening to the dripping stone. Eventually, as my breathing levels, Flynn tells me he is going to grab us tacos for lunch. Frankly, I wanted to ask him about a margarita with real alcohol, but the last thing I need is more confusion with a foggy mind.

When he leaves, I push myself up and grab my shirt and jeans. The jeans are fine, but I keep them off as my legs still feel too warm, and I don't want them to chafe more. I lay my shirt out on the rocks outside the cave, hoping the warmth from the vita will help dry it a little. I open my backpack and search for my phone. I feel the crushed envelope from Sam and Ellie at the bottom of my bag. Ignoring it, I grab my phone. I don't need any other bombshells today. Instead, I sit up against the slab, turning my body just slightly so I can project *The Good Place* TV show up against the wall. The show is a little grainy and slick from the wall it projects from, but it'll do the trick for now. Right now, I need my parents and something silly. This is the closest I have.

When Flynn comes back, he's shirtless. Just in maroon chino shorts. My eyes have adjusted enough to the darkness to catch his wink when he walks in. He has the biggest smile on his face. So big that I have to fight the tiny one that wants to erupt from me.

"Your shirt idea is great. Hope you don't mind." He does a little dance, shimmying his chest at me. His backpack is in his hand, and drinks are in glass bottles in both side pockets.

"Definitely don't mind," I say, letting out a breathy laugh. The only thing I mind is that he's only glowing from the projection. I'd rather see him in the vitalight.

"Great." He grins and sits beside me, our bare shoulders touching. It feels like it's been days since my body has reacted to him. Since I've been allowed to process something simple, like the rush of shivers from our bare skin meeting or the flutter in my belly from his closeness.

I laugh at the thought as Flynn opens his backpack.

"What are you laughing at? Hopefully, you're not making fun of me?" He pouts before giving me a smirk when my laugh stops.

Flynn hands me a container, and my stomach growls. I'm so excited to eat.

"I just had the thought that liking you is the simple part of my life here. When liking someone back home can be so complicated."

Flynn pauses, opening his container as he looks at me. I catch the furrow of his brows before he looks down at his food.

"What? We said we'd communicate," I say, nudging his shoulder with my own. I kind of love being shirtless next to him. Hidden away from the outside world.

He sighs, and when he looks up, his blue eyes seem conflicted. "Us liking each other is far more complicated than either of us have spoken about."

I immediately put my hands up in an "X." "Nope. Your communication is shut off."

He chuckles as I try to keep a straight face. I think I'm falling into my loopy, mental exhaustion state.

"I do not claim that energy." It's a phrase I used to see in so many videos back home. I don't think Flynn understands it, but he continues to laugh, shaking my body with his.

"Me either." He leans forward, connecting our lips. I sink into his touch, gripping his forearms, so I don't fall into him.

I hover near his lips when he ends the kiss. "Can we pretend this is simple? We let this flow however it does, not worrying about the disaster fire at the end?"

Flynn's hands cup my cheeks, and he tilts my head, searching my eyes.

I clasp my hands over his. "Please, Flynn." I don't want to handle any more conversations. Our romance can only last here and will likely end in a devastating heartbreak that I'll somehow have to explain when I get home. But I don't need to worry about that now.

"Okay," he whispers, pecking my lips quickly before turning toward the TV. He lifts up my device and clicks a few buttons, setting up a solid background for the TV show instead of us using the rock. "Perfect. Now, let's eat and relax."

I lean my head on his shoulder while he's situated, and we fall into the world of *The Good Place*.

Thirty

Despite a breakdown in the cave, anger and anxiety still course through my body. A week and a half passed, and I'm no closer to answers on what happens when Earth and Otium connect. Nor am I any closer to forgiving Andrya for not rescuing my parents.

Flynn decided that before we tried to get any answers about Otium's future, we first needed to be at our best. We needed to get a schedule that worked for both of us, and I needed to be more in tune with myself. I didn't want to agree because I wanted to know everything immediately, but he pointed out that I had a lot of anger and chaotic energy that demanded my attention. He reminded me that my goal here was not saving Earth. It was saving myself first. While I can stress about what happens thirty years in the future, I need to focus on my present as well . . . so I have a thirty years to stress about.

When he said that, it helped settle me . . . just a little.

Therefore, we started with getting a schedule down and helping me find little joys, and for him, some sanity. We eat breakfast together and then go our separate ways until eleven, when it's time for my lesson with him. We spend siesta together, but after we eat lunch, I'll read a book while he studies. Sometimes our lessons happen in his living room if we run over our siesta. Other times, we head back to the Forest. The cave is nice, but the Forest has become my place of center.

Flynn always gets out of his class a half-hour after my group therapy finishes, so I spend that time with Amalia, Zhang, and Mattis. Amalia and Mattis are seeing each other now, too. Zhang jokes about being the fifth wheel but likes to shove it in our face that she's really the lucky one. She won't have a broken heart going home. She says it as a joke, but each time, it breaks my heart a little more. I don't want to think about the inevitable. When Flynn gets out of class, we all eat dinner together and sometimes check out a community event before Flynn and I head back to his apartment to relax well into the night.

I'm falling for him. Hard. I loved Jonah, but the connection I'm building with Flynn is more intense than that. I don't know if it's because there's nothing to lose. There's not a single way our relationship can last past this program. So maybe it's the thrill of the short-lived. Maybe we can be honest and open and vulnerable because there is no future? We don't have to worry about plans or life after a few weeks. If it's not that, though, and this relationship is as real and intense as it feels, I'm not sure how I'll survive going back home. The way I feel, feels more mature, adult, powerful, even. Like our relationship could stand the tests life's chaos brings our way. After the one mini-fight we had when he panicked about stress, we haven't had another disagreement. It's hard to believe that I stayed with Jonah for as long as I did. That I still felt love after every fight. But it's a different love, I think. A love of familiarity. Comfort. Like

Corie had said about people fearing change. Some change isn't that bad.

Today, though, there is something off. I woke up in a panic. I don't remember my dream. It wasn't my parents' murders. It was something new, something without answers. Angering but blurry. More like all the happiness and normalcy surrounding me finally came to a head.

I am happy more often than not now, and it's terrifying.

Flynn's wild excitement this morning about something he's doing in class later keeps me from venting my mood. I plaster on a fake smile. It works throughout our session about healthy friendships, but in therapy, Corie asks me how I am processing the information of my parents. How I feel about the timelines. If I have finally read the letter from Sam and Ellie. The answer is no. I have not touched the envelope that is buried deep in my backpack. I haven't determined when my time is right yet. I've just been enjoying the blissful bubble Flynn and I created.

But therapy brings up all the pent-up anger I shoved down. That I covered with tiny joys and kisses from Flynn and happiness with a group of new friends. All essentially superficial things I won't have back on Earth, but I will have the anger.

After a tense, stubborn lunch on my end, Flynn decides he is throwing away the rest of the lesson plans he created and we are going to finally tackle my anger. He demands that we go to the open field right before the Forest. This gives me an escape to my place if the lesson becomes too much, but it also won't tarnish my favorite place by doing the lesson in the Forest.

So that's how we randomly got to standing across from each other in an open field. Cottages are in the distance to my left and the Forest closer to my right. Thankfully, no one should be able to see us.

"I think it might be helpful to role-play," Flynn says.

"I'm sorry, what?" I laugh. I may have created content for social media, but I don't act. I don't know how to do that.

"We are going to take situations in your life that cause you anger. I'm going to be the person you have anger toward. I want you to get out everything you need to say to the person I'm acting like. These are likely conversations that you can't have with that person. From what I know about you, these are conversations or arguments you have spiraling in your head. My hope is that you'll be able to release the anger and words out into the world, and we can start to heal that part of you. I have a few people and situations that I know we will do, but if you have anything else you'd like to add, we will."

I just blink at him. It's honestly brilliant. And I have things I'd love to yell at the police and my aunt and uncle, even Sam and Ellie. It all spirals in the depths of my mind. I just don't know if I can take it seriously.

"I think, and correct me if I'm wrong, that our relationship is solid enough that you won't mistake my actual feelings for you by this lesson." Flynn raises his brow, questioning me.

That's hard to answer because I am sensitive. Most of the time, when Jonah was angry, it'd filter through to me being angry too, even if it wasn't how I actually felt.

"I don't know," I say.

Flynn closes the distance between us, cupping my cheeks with his hands. Our foreheads connect, and our breathing syncs. It's one of my favorite things he does. Whether to calm me instantly or to stop me out of the blue.

It's like our energies radiate between us, growing with the silence.

I lean up, connecting our lips, wrapping my arms around his neck. He inhales, and I sink toward him as we become one.

"Let's make rules," Flynn starts, his breath tickling my wet lips. "You can cut the scene at any time. If I don't think you pushed hard enough, I'll let you know. If you need a moment between role plays or if you need me as your partner and not your mentor, I need you to tell me that. Ask me for what you need. If you need space from me before I can be your partner again, that is okay. Ask for that. But I like you, with all my heart, Theo. I wouldn't do this if it hasn't proven to work with others, and if I didn't think this would benefit you."

I take a step back, searching his eyes that crinkle in the corners when he finds me. *Sees* me. I'm anxious. The bubbling in the pit of my stomach and the sweat in my pits tell me as much. But I do believe him when he says this will work.

"I like you. With all my heart," I whisper.

He seals the sentiment with one last kiss.

"Okay, so we know you have choice words with the police officers who killed your parents. Likely the police officer you don't remember attacking? Or maybe the jury? I'm sure you have some words in there for my mom?"

I look down at that suggestion. I can't ask him to play his mother so I can yell at her. That feels like crossing a line.

"My uncle. Sam and Ellie. Jonah?" I tack on. "I'm starting to feel like I have an anger issue," I say with a sigh, sitting down on the grass.

Flynn sits in front of me, setting his palms on my knees. "I think you had a tragic thing happen and weren't given the support you needed. Now the anger has manifested so much that it's a part of you."

I don't like that thought even if I agree. I would love to experience more of the carefree feeling I had most of this week—just without the underlying anger and frustration.

"Who do you want to start with?"

"How are you going to role-play these people you don't know?" I ask.

"It'll be rough and not clear-cut situations you've had but I'm pretty good at improv if you start the argument."

"Let's start with Sam and Ellie."

I had already filled Flynn in on what his mom said about Sam and Ellie being here in the initiative. Likely in a different location. I told him that his mom traveled to Earth too. He confirmed that his mom and dad did go away for a few weeks last year, but they said they went to the beach for vacation. I don't think he's followed up with his mom—he was pretty angry about the situation, too. Flynn doesn't know about the letter, though.

I turn away from Flynn, looking toward the Forest. If he is going to act like someone else, I can't watch him. At least at first.

"Why did you abandon me?" I start.

"We didn't think that's what we were doing." His words are soft. I want to glare at him because he's said that before, and I think they know damn well that they did.

"How come? You literally up and left me when I needed you the most."

"Theo," he sighs.

I look over at Flynn, and he gestures to me to turn back. *Well, this is confusing.* I thought he was trying to get my attention.

"We didn't know what to do. We lost our best friends.

We were pregnant. We panicked, and we needed our parents."

His words puncture my heart. I never thought about them wanting to run back to Ellie's mom and dad. That Ellie might need their love and comfort. That she may have been scared.

"I needed my parents too," I whisper.

"We know that. We knew that. We just didn't know the role we played."

"You were my second parents."

"We know."

"You said you'd never leave." My vision blurs as all their promises run through my mind.

"We know."

My heart pounds in my chest, making it hard to breathe. "No, you don't!" I scream, pushing myself up from the ground. "You don't fucking know. You said you'd never leave. You said you'd always be there. That I was the son, you both always wanted. That you'd do anything in the world for me, and then you left. Like I meant nothing. Vanished and barely even said goodbye."

"We said goodbye."

I spin toward Flynn but my eyes are so blurry now it's easy to believe something different. "When I was in a state of continuous panic! I was awake for maybe five minutes after having just slept off a panic attack, and you both left. Jonah had to pick up the pieces. All the fucking pieces. Maybe it's both of your faults that our relationship fell apart. He is only a teen. He doesn't know what he's doing. But he was there day in and day out, and you two never were." I heave through a sob as the weight of Jonah's responsibilities crushes me.

"We're sorry."

"Are you?!" I scream. "I don't even want to read your goddamn letter. I don't even think you are sorry. That you guys know what you've possibly done."

"Theo, we need you to relax." I glare over at Flynn, swiping my eyes with tears. I'm not ready to relax. "We didn't have a plan. We didn't have a letter from your parents explaining anything. We weren't even parents ourselves. We made the biggest mistake of our lives. But we're back now."

I pause as the words hit me. The words I so desperately want to be said to me—that leaving was the biggest mistake. But knowing what I know, how they met Andrya, came to this planet? Had a baby? Leaving was likely one of the best things they did.

"You don't know they'd say that," I whisper to Flynn. "It might not have been a mistake. They may not regret it. They may think I'm the world's most needy teen. Don't put that hope in my head," I say as my vision blurs.

"I'm sorry!" Flynn rushes toward me, rubbing his hands on my arms. I tense. I don't like the feeling. It's weird. This is weird. "I'm sorry. I won't give you hope. But a letter? You never told me about a letter."

I shrug. "It's in my bag. I'm not ready to read it. Your mom gave it to me. They gave it to your mom to give to me when she thought I was ready to read it."

"Whoa," he breathes out.

"Yeah." I look down at the ground, and his hands stop rubbing.

"Do you want to keep yelling at them, or would you like to move on?"

I let out a sigh, and his hands drop to my own, squeezing them.

"How do these end if you wanted to give me hope but can't?"

"I think it ends in pure exhaustion. I think if we end with the police, you'll just be getting all your anger out, and I won't have to do much. I think you'll know when you're done."

I nod. That sounds pretty terrible.

"Let's do Jonah," Flynn suggests. "Piggyback off what you were saying. You praised Jonah here. Where does his anger come in?"

I step away from Flynn and turn my back. I really don't like the idea of screaming at my partner about my ex. But here we are.

"I never asked you to take care of me," I say.

"Someone had to."

My god, with the gut punch. Sometimes it sucks when Flynn listens.

"I can take care of myself."

"You weren't eating or drinking or showering. You were a shell of a human, Theo. You needed someone."

Fuck talking to him about my grief. Flynn never said it'd be used against me.

"Well, I don't anymore. I need you to give me space," I say.

"I need you to be my boyfriend."

"I can't be if you're my caretaker!" I yell. "You can't be both. You're hovering. You're always around. Always checking in. Always telling me what or how to do things. Feeding me goddamn breakfast because my guardians are incompetent. I only want a fucking boyfriend."

"I'm sorry for loving you. For trying to be the best I could be."

Well, what a way to make me feel like the shittiest person in the world.

"This is on you," I say. "You wanted to take care of me. You decided you'd go above and beyond. You decided that you hated volunteering all of a sudden after starting the relationship, seeming like you cared about all the same things." My voice raises. My anger is boiling, and my fists begin to shake. "You were the one who decided you were annoyed and frustrated by my activism. I'm never good enough for you."

"And I'm not good enough for you!" Flynn screams, and I jump before collapsing to my knees.

I can't turn around and look at him, but his scream frightens me. It's so similar to the screaming matches Jonah and I have had in the past. I double over, allowing the rippling wave of emotions to overcome me. I try gasping in air. We were so close to this moment in person, and as awful and painful as it would have been to complete this, I wish I could have said what I needed in person instead of the text I sent before I left Earth.

"Maybe we've both changed," I say softly.

We were so young when we became friends and when we started dating. We've gone through the transitions that any normal kid our age ebbs and flows through. Relationships, friends, things they like and don't like. But we added love and dead parents. How were we supposed to survive that?

"Maybe we have," he whispers. "But that doesn't mean we have to hate each other. I don't hate you, Theo."

I turn around. Again with hope. Flynn doesn't know that.

"If Jonah is anything like the good person you've described him as, he doesn't hate you," Flynn says softly.

"He probably wants what's best for you. If you go home and tell him—and mean it—that you want what's best for him too, you'll get somewhere."

"I don't know if this is working." I sigh, taking a seat. I don't want his positive, happy endings. I want to scream and yell and kick and scream some more. I need to be realistic because what if everyone has had peace since I've disappeared? What if they don't want to include me back in their life?

"Okay, how about you just yell about whatever's on your mind, or maybe we go to the gym, and you can use a punching bag? If you wanna yell, I can add fuel when it's needed, but you can do your own improv."

"You won't interject with happiness? I don't want happiness."

Flynn sits next to me, bumping his shoulder against mine. "Only anger. Zero happiness," he says in a deep voice, similar to Darth Vader.

I know I should laugh or *want* to laugh, but it's buried so deep within me like I used up all my happiness for the year this past week.

"I hate my aunt and uncle. And the police who used teargas and the one that shot my mom and the one that shot my dad, and the very smug faces they had on national television at the beginning and end of the trial. I hate the person that read the verdict. The way his voice sounded. The way he spoke like nothing was bad in his world. Like he was casually announcing that someone just made a mistake. Instead of killing someone. Wrongfully shooting someone."

I shove myself up and away from Flynn. I feel like I'm infecting his happy brain with tragedy.

"I hate my aunt and uncle. I hate their backward beliefs.

I hate that they hate me. They don't support me. They are racist and homophobic, and they hate kids. They never wanted this. They don't like my family. This ruined their life, so they've chosen to ruin mine."

I pace back and forth. Moving further from Flynn each time I turn.

"I hate their chore lists and them locking me out. I hate their demands. I hate that my brothers aren't like me and that my parents raised me differently, and that the goddamn world always feels like it's on my shoulders. I don't want to save people all the time. I don't want to educate people. I don't want to help awful fucking humans that don't give a shit about anyone but themselves. I don't even think they care about themselves. That'd be too much decency. I hate the leadership, corruption, and poverty. I hate that there are children without parents because their parents made dumb decisions. I hate that there are other kids like me without parents, because of murders, because of guns, because America doesn't care about a single one of us.

"I hate how much power people sometimes have. The police. It was a goddamn peaceful protest. No one had weapons but them. No one was screaming in their faces. No one was violent until they were fighting for their life. I hate the memory and nightmares of watching my mother die. Of seeing my father run off to his death. They had a chance to be here! A chance to help save our planet with me. Alongside them. Like the old times. Your mom messed with that. I choose to believe she messed with the timeline, and because of that, they died. Because we don't know what's happening. We don't know what our actions are doing. I don't know if it's worse to make new tragic mistakes or repeat history like Earth likes to."

I'm nearly running back and forth in my paces. My

arms are swaying left and right, and sweat mixes with my tears. It's not enough. There's more. It's beating against my rib cage, slicing through my esophagus. There's so much inside of me that needs to get out.

"I hate that no matter what I do here, I still have a fight at home. A fight with my friends and my family. A fight with my town. A fight with my state and country. I go back to tragedy. I go back to chaos. No matter how much happiness I have here, it'll be swept away as soon as I enter Earth.

"God!" I scream, kneeling on the ground. "Goddamnit!" I hit the ground with the sides of my closed fists. "Goddamnit!" I hit the ground over and over and over again. The sound grass smushes against my fists, and I hate it even more.

"I hate that I'm falling for you, Flynn, and I won't ever be able to be with you. Why! Why me? Why did I get chosen to live this life? Where is my choice? I want a refund. I want to stop and escape and give up. I can't do this anymore."

I look up at the stupid violet sky with the stupid light from the vita and scream at the top of my lungs. As my lungs empty, I hunch forward. And the gravity of reality hits me.

I place my palms flat on the ground. Trying to take a deep breath, but it gets stuck as my words surface.

"They'll never come back. Forever. If Sam and Ellie really needed their parents after my parents passed, who the hell do I turn to? Never again, in my entire life, will I ever be able to run to my mom or dad because I'm scared or frightened or nervous. If I become a parent, I can't run off to my own parents. If I get hurt, I can't curl into my mom's arms and have her kiss my head. I'll never feel their arms around me again.

"They are gone! Dead. Cremated. Fucking dust. Who decided I could handle this? That it'd be cool if Theo didn't have parents. 'It's fine; he can survive.' I don't want to fucking survive! I want to live.

"God, I want to live so bad, but they'll never have the chance to. They won't see me graduate. They won't see me get married. They won't see how incredible their agency is. They can't ever have grandkids or granddogs.

"They lost everything. All their future. How am I supposed to live with them gone? How do I carry on? How do I have happiness? It's a fucking joke. That's what those officers don't understand. The jury. The judge. They don't understand that those officers took my entire life and demolished it. In a single second. Why does their fear surpass my life? My parents' lives? My brothers' lives? Why can they even claim fear in a peaceful protest? They took everything from me. Everything I've ever known has been touched and broken and shattered."

My chest is tight as my lungs expand, gasping, desperate for any sort of breath.

"I need . . . I need . . . " I lean forward, my head to the ground, crushing my ribs against my thighs. Suffocating my lungs. "Mom and Dad, I need you." My words muffle in the grass. I spit the grass out with my inhale. One last deep breath, I lift myself just a little and yell into the fields, "Can you hear me? I said, I need you!"

A sob ripples through my chest. I fall to my side, wrapping my arms around my legs in a fetal position as I ride the wave. I don't have any words left in me.

They are gone.

They. Are. Gone.

I don't have parents.

I don't have a mom.

I don't have a dad.

I don't have anyone.

Arms wrap around me from behind. Flynn spoons me, shaping his body around the curve of my spine. His deep breaths try to create a rhythm with my scattered, gasping, heaving breaths. I try to think. Try to focus on anything else I need to say or scream, but my mind is blank. There's darkness and exhaustion. An ache behind my eyeballs.

Flynn tightens his arms around me and rests his chin on the top of my head. The breathing helps. He's steady. My sobs have something to leech onto. Something safe. And warm.

My eyes grow heavy.

Thirty-One

"Are you doing okay?" Flynn squeezes my hand as he leads me through the Forest.

We've gone past our usual spot and turned away from the path that leads to the hikes we've done. Instead, we're taking the Forest head-on. Flynn said that he wanted to show me something special. And promised me delicious food and cold beverages.

After I broke down, I ended up falling asleep. I'm not certain what time it is or how long I slept, but Flynn got approval to miss his class and for me to skip my group therapy today. He said it was something already in the works and my group therapist approved the lesson. What I experienced for my day on Otium wouldn't have been beneficial for the group, anyway.

Sometimes it's nice to have special treatment here.

"I'm exhausted," I answer, leaning toward him in emphasis. Everything is tired. My muscles, my mind, my throat. I don't feel good or free or light yet. Just tired.

"Is there anything you want to discuss about that lesson, or would you like to close that for now and move on?"

I see a rock ahead of us large enough to sit on. I walk us off the path and take a seat, pulling Flynn down next to me.

"Why is it my responsibility to educate people who don't deserve it? Like awful humans. I have the power to grow and evolve, and that suddenly makes me responsible because other people can't do it on their own?"

"You aren't growing and evolving on your own, Theo. You're getting help."

I sigh, running my hands over my face. "That's not what I mean." I tangle my fingers into my curls. They are still matted down from the sweat before my nap.

"Is everyone awful?" he asks, and I reluctantly shake my head. "Not everyone has access to the same resources. The correct and credible ones. There is a lot of misinformation out there, skewed for people to believe them. You are privileged enough to have grown up in a family with access to accurate information. From my understanding, your uncle did not have the same upbringing. Therefore, he has other beliefs."

"Right. But why is it my responsibility to educate him?"

"Your focus isn't on the generations before you. Your focus is on your generation and after. If change happens to the older generation, great. But we are focused on the long-term goal of Otium, and that means everyone below you. Though, sometimes that does mean educating through decades of misinformation in some family lines."

I shouldn't have stopped. The lesson before took all my energy, and I'm in desperate need to regulate my blood sugar before I get hangry.

"What Otium is asking is not easy," Flynn continues. "However, it also isn't asking much different from what you already did on Earth. You are just educated that there is something to fight for. You're getting therapy to work through your own trauma. You're leaving here healthier. You are given skills that'll benefit whatever path you choose to take. We don't know what you do in this future, Theo, nor do we know the future of any other mentee. But we are confident in every mentee's ability to go back to Earth fighting stronger and harder with less burnout. Doesn't it help in the slightest to have hope? Before, you fought to try and make things better for Earth, to try and change a damaged planet. Now, you're fighting to improve people's ways of life so that when they come to this planet, they have less of a chance of damaging it."

I tug at the end of my curls, feeling the burn at my scalp. It's all so. much. work.

"Can I just be plain old Theo right now? The Theo who isn't going to do anything outstanding? Just the Theo who wants to hang out with the boy he likes and eat some food?"

"Yeah," he breathes, smiling wide. "Let's go." Flynn jumps off the rock, jerking my body forward. "We're almost there."

As we get to the edge of the Forest, I breathe in. My lungs take in the salt as it wafts through the breeze. My fingers tighten around Flynn's hand, a pool of sweat forming inside. It's humid as hell, but I can't believe he's kept this from me.

"This is the beach."

We reach the opening, and the light of vita causes me to squint. The grass intermingles with the sand, and before I know it, my shoes are filled with sand. I let go of Flynn's hand, take off my socks and shoes, and dig my toes into the different particles. This feels unreal.

Kneeling, my fingers lift and sprinkle the sand, watching as the breeze allows it to travel behind us.

"You've been holding out on me," I say as Flynn squats beside me.

I use a sandy hand to cover above my brows so I can take in the way he gazes at me. His glowing eyes and big, bright smile. His right hand reaches toward me; his fingertips combing through my curls rest at the base of my neck.

I lean in, and his other hand cups the back of my neck. His thumbs massage gently. My heart races at his touch. I tilt my head back, working the massage deeper into my muscles.

"That feels so good," I whisper, tilting my head forward. I want to lean in to kiss him, but the forward movement causes my body to sway, specks interrupting my vision. "I need water." Closing my eyes, I try to regulate the wooziness. I gather saliva in my throat to swallow. It's been so long since I had a sip of water.

Flynn unzips his backpack, and a bottle is up to my lips in seconds. He helps me take a few sips before he drips some of the water over my face.

"When you're ready, put your shoes back on, and let's get some food."

I nod, slipping my shoes on but shoving my socks into my pockets. Socks and sand are an immediate no for me. But with the heat that's coming from the vita, I can only imagine how hot the sand is.

Once ready, I stand up, stumbling a bit. Flynn interlocks our arms and steadies me. I won't be 100% okay until I can get food and maybe soak my feet in the ocean.

A brand new ocean on a brand new planet. The thought has me smiling, and I almost want to dart to my right and examine it. I bet the ocean is fresh and clean and clear.

We arrive at a tiki bar. A few people are scattered

around the area—some sitting at the bar and others are sun-bathing. There's a handful of people in the ocean as well, surfing, it seems. Despite the gorgeous day, it isn't heavily populated. Even my small lake about an hour north of me has more people than this on the coldest day of the summer.

"Where is everyone?" I ask as we make our way to the bar. I take the first empty seat I find. The roof of the bar shields us from the light, allowing a brief moment of relief.

Flynn fills a glass with water from the communal pitcher, handing it to me before sitting down. I chug it all in one go.

"This town isn't heavily populated. What helps keep things this calm is the fact that there are many beaches. This entire location is sandy. Basically, the town is almost all surrounded by water. So those who have chosen to live here have also chosen their space."

"Hey guys, what can I get for you this afternoon?" the bartender asks us. He immediately refills my water glass and hands one to Flynn before giving us a smile.

I down another glass of water, and Flynn somehow just takes a sip. The humidity increase from the coolness of the Forest seems to have put me into overdrive. Flynn is breaking a sweat, but I suppose he didn't also just break down.

"Two watermelon cucumber juices, please," Flynn orders.

"Watermelon and cucumber? What?" I scrunch my nose at the suggestion. I *hate* cucumbers.

"Trust me." Flynn winks, and I'm grateful for the shiver that passes through me. "It'll be great for hydration."

The bartender makes our drinks. I'm not sure about this at all. The substance gets darker as he mixes it. Once the juices are handed to us, the liquid is this weird, dark pinkish color. A lime sits on the lip of the glass, and some mint is in it.

"Can we also get two orders of the Mediterranean shrimp orzo salad?" Flynn orders.

I don't know what he means by delicious food. I imagined some comfort food that could put a bandaid over my traumatized heart. Not a salad and fresh-pressed juice.

"Not a problem. Will you be eating here or at the beach?" the bartender asks.

"Over in the alcove, if that's available," Flynn says, tilting his head back to, I assume, point at the alcove.

"Not a problem." The guy nods and jots something down in a pad similar to Corie's in therapy.

Flynn takes his phone out and scans the points for our meals before I can even process paying. I don't know what was just discussed.

"Awesome," the bartender says. "We'll bring the food to you. Feel free to add to your order whenever." With that, the bartender then walks away to another customer.

I don't see a kitchen here. There's only a bar that's stocked with different beverages, fruits and vegetables, and mixes, and then there are tables and chairs.

"Let's go," Flynn says, grabbing our glasses of juice and hopping off the bar stool. "I've got a really cool spot I like."

Once we leave the bar, the vita shines down on us. I wish I had my vitaglasses. I haven't really used them since I could see the violet sky, but the way the vita reflects off the sand and water is nearly too much.

"There's an alcove down over here. We are protected from the vita and we have our own private spot to put our feet in the water."

"Sounds great," I say.

We head down toward the water, veering right, so we

are near the edge of the Forest. Our sand becomes a little rocky before we're literally climbing down some rocks. Soon, we are in our own little square of smooth sand with some tree coverage. Waves come in over some small rocks.

"When the tide is high, this doesn't exist. But it's my favorite place here. The beauty of the beach, but with silence."

"Have I told you how much I like you? How much you get me?" I ask, grinning widely. This is exactly what I need. Maybe not whatever drinks and food he ordered, but sand, water, warmth, and silence. Real silence in my head and in person.

I sit down right where the waves end. I take my shoes and backpack off, tossing them further up in the alcove. Sinking my feet into the wet sand, I exhale as a wave crashes over them, and the sand continues to bury them.

Flynn sits next to me, bumping my shoulder, and hands me one of the glasses. It's cool on my palm and already condensing.

"Trust me on this. If you don't like it, no worries, we can order something different. But try it."

I raise my brow as I put the glass to my lips, taking a sip. The cool liquid is welcome on my lips and tongue. It immediately brings relief. I don't want to admit that it's actually quite delicious. It's so refreshing and a nice change from water. I take tiny sips, admiring the horizon.

"You're so stubborn," Flynn laughs. "You fucking love it; just admit it."

I turn away from him, taking a few gulps as laughter barrels out of him; the sound settles me. My shoulders relax, and I stretch my legs out.

This is joy. This is freedom from my mind.

"Why would I possibly give you something awful?" he asks, still laughing.

He wouldn't, but it's so nice messing with him. Hearing his laugh, knowing how it feels against my body when his chest rumbles. His laugh is light and airy, like he hasn't experienced hardship. Like he doesn't know what tragedy is. I want that. I want a laugh that makes me feel like I'm floating.

For now, I'll take little doses of joy.

I place the empty glass beside me, facing him, and stick my tongue out. "You love my stubbornness," I joke.

Honestly, I'm not sure anyone does. And when his laughter stops and his bright eyes widen, I think maybe I could be totally wrong. Maybe it's actually annoying.

"Theo," he whispers.

A tingling sensation consumes my nerves, traveling through my body and out of my fingertips.

Flynn's hand caresses my cheek. A smile forms on his lips as my body caves toward him. I reach my sandy hand up to grip his cheek and pull him forward. I connect our lips, tasting the watermelon sugar on him. Flynn wraps his arms around my body, swooping me over and onto his lap. I let out a giggle at his soft wince, but soon, his hands tangle in my curls, pulling me closer to him. His lips are desperate, and my hands grasp the back of his neck. I want to be closer. I need to be as close as I possibly can to him.

My entire body is electrified at his touch. I can feel sand caking to my skin and on my face and dripping from my scalp. His hands travel down my hair, over top of my chest, and all I want is to lie on him, shirtless, breathing in time.

So I do. I push him back, hovering over him with my hands planted in the sand beside his head. I reach to unbutton my shirt, trying not to break the kiss. My elbows waver, and the unsteadiness separates us, my curls dropping sand on our faces. I roll off Flynn as we both cough, trying to spit the sand out.

"Flynn Thomas?" We hear from above.

Phew. I breathe.

Flynn jumps up and jogs over to the rocks. "Hey, dude!" Flynn greets.

I glance over, and a person around our age grins at him, leaning down with a woven basket. "Hey, Flynn, I have your lunch," they say. "Can I get either of you guys anything else?"

"Is there water in here?" Flynn asks as he grabs the basket.

"Always." They nod.

"We're great. Thank you." Flynn waves and jogs back over to me, placing the basket in the sand.

"What service," I say, reaching over to open the basket. "This would be some expensive treatment in America."

Flynn locks eyes with me, placing his palm on my shoulder. "Welcome to Otium." He winks and then sets off on getting the food out of the basket. Our salads are each in a glass dish. The water inside the basket are individual glass bottles, quite similar to our takeaway margaritas the other day.

"Are these bottles returned too?" I ask, taking one out.

"Yup. Everything is reusable. They give out a ton of water at the beach, always complimentary for your time here."

"Most beaches near me, it's like four dollars a bottle. And it's always the crappy water."

"Crappy water? What do you mean?"

"Some water is just not filtered well, or they put crap in it like salt."

"Salt?" He scrunches up his nose. "Like we're talking about the condiment that we put on roasted vegetables?"

"Yes." I laugh, and his face contorts further.

"You have got to be joking. Why in the world? That would make you more thirsty."

"Exactly. Money-making scheme. The thirstier you are, the more you buy."

"That's bullshit."

"Welcome to America." I wink. "The land of disaster."

He throws his head back with a laugh. My insides warm, and I lean into Flynn, resting my head on his shoulder. His head lies on mine for a few moments.

"Thank you," I whisper. "I'm really grateful I met you. It's really cool that people I love so much have you in their family."

"It's really quite bizarre when you think about it."

I laugh. I try not to think too much about it. I like to believe the separation between us isn't grand. But in reality, there are generations and light-years between our times.

"It is," I agree.

The two of us eat our shrimp-whatever, and what a freaking surprise, it's delicious. I mean, I don't think I'd order it again. It's not really my cup of tea, but it is tasty and does hit the spot. At least enough that I think I'll be able to get back to the apartment.

"Do you think today's lesson was helpful?" Flynn asks once our meal is done and packed back up in the basket.

We settle, so our feet submerge in the oncoming waves, and we're lying down, our elbows nestled in the sand, lifting us.

"I think so," I say softly. A part of me is afraid to jinx it. If I think too hard, is all the anger going to resurface? "I feel peaceful."

It's stunning here, looking out at the horizon. The water is naturally a deep purple that lines up with the violet sky. As the ocean becomes more shallow, the vita reflects lilac, instead of aqua, over the ocean floor. Somehow, the hue calms me even more than the blue sandy beaches at home.

If I move to Otium with enough time to enjoy it, I genuinely don't know where I'd create my home.

"Are the locations really all that close? Otium is quite massive, right?" I ask, thinking about how we've been in three locations, all by bike, foot, or a short train.

"Kinda, yes. From Olive, we can reach the Valley and the Oceanic locations. However, you've only seen fragments of each location. We have a prime location. When NASA originally did research, they found that where Olive is located is the thinnest part of the Flatlands. This gives leaders of each location the ability to meet easier. Each leader lives in the main city of their location, both of which border Olive. However, if you'd like to get lengthwise from one end of a location to the other, it would take quite a bit of traveling, and a lot is still untouched."

I nod, thinking of how my past self on Otium chose the Valley. It's a nice thought to live in an area just like home with the luxury of being able to travel to a beach faster than in my actual hometown.

Flynn's fingertips start to play with my own, reigniting my passion from before, but there's a time and place for that later.

"I want to meet my family here," I say, and his fingers instantly stop.

"Theo," he breathes. "We've talked about this."

"I know, and I've talked with Corie too. I don't care. I need to know who I was to determine who I can become."

I've thought long and hard about it since the day I found

out my parents didn't originally die. I came here not knowing if I wanted to continue to fight, knowing my entire identity was about making the world better. It was my parents' future. But to know my parents could have had a future, and their time got cut short? I have to continue the fight. To do so, I want to know where I originally ended up and how I can do better.

"I don't know who I am in the future in order to change my outcome," Flynn points out, and yeah, yeah, sure. But he also doesn't have a future to go to. Mine is only a few miles away.

"Let me rephrase." I sit up and turn toward him. He follows suit, so we are nearly at eye level. "I am going to find my future here. You can come along with me, or I will do it alone. Either way, you're an accomplice, because you can track me." I offer him an awkward smile. I'm not sure I'm joking, and the way his eyes narrow, it's clear he definitely doesn't find this funny.

"It's breaking the rules. They are made for a reason." His hand doesn't leave mine, but his voice tenses.

I lift my brow, crossing my arms. "Your mom broke the rules to get me here. I deem that means the rules don't apply to me. I am confident that meeting my family on Otium will only motivate me further. I need to know what I accomplished with my parents' help and figure out how to do that *and* more. If they died because of the initiative messing with the timeline, then I need to make sure they died for a good reason. Everything my future holds has to be for my parents' legacy."

His eyes search mine as I wait in silence. I know I'm good. I've practiced telling him this for a few days. That is, after running through every negative scenario that could happen if I potentially ruined a timeline. But it's impossible for anything negative to happen.

My future family knows about the Otium Initiative. They know I have a history of activism. Therefore, showing up shouldn't be a surprise. Their timeline on Otium doesn't get affected by how I live my life on Earth.

"What if you love your life here, and then you search desperately for that while on Earth, and somehow it doesn't end up the way you envisioned or even experienced here?"

"You told me my purpose was to heal myself," I say instantly. "That my real purpose here wasn't saving Earth. In order to help myself, I need to know what I was capable of. If my life changes, it's okay because that means that the family here still has memories of their life how it was. No harm done."

"Except to yourself."

I shake my head. "You're not understanding, Flynn. I would have all the information here. I don't lose this information when I go back to Earth. If anything, it makes me more powerful."

He eyes me and then sighs, focusing on the water. A massive wave crashes up against the rocks surrounding us, spraying specks of water in our direction. The droplets immediately dry once they hit my skin.

I really don't want to do this journey alone. I'm not even sure how to find my family. I haven't come across a directory on my phone, and there isn't anything like Facebook here. I'd likely need Flynn's expertise or have to randomly ask people in the Valley if they heard of my name and what they might remember.

"Two conditions," he says softly. His fingers carve in the sand, lift the particles, and he watches as they drift away.

"Anything," I say, and I think I almost believe that.

"You read Sam and Ellie's letter first. Learn what your future could be before you go messing with what has been."

My breathing constricts just slightly as he makes eye contact again. "And?" I whisper.

"I will break the rules," he says slowly, and I let out a breath. "But I choose how we do so and when."

I nod over and over, reaching out for his hand. I interlace our fingers and squeeze them. "Thank you."

Thirty-Two

Flynn switched up our schedule today. He sent me a message at six in the morning to let me know that he thought it would be a good idea to rework today's schedule. We'd eat breakfast, I'd read Sam and Ellie's letter, I'd process it with Corie, and then we would see where we went from there. The only thing I liked about the schedule was skipping school work for the time being. Each day on Otium, it becomes less important to me.

After only stomaching a few sips of my chai at breakfast, Flynn guides us back to my room.

"Would you like me to stay?" Flynn asks, standing in my doorway.

I glance at the letter sitting on my desk. I tore it out of my backpack this morning. It's dusty, one corner is ripped, and the other corners are bent. I'm lucky the important parts are intact.

"Would it be weird? They are your great-grandparents," I say, but he's quick to shut the door behind him.

Flynn's hand falls on my lower back, his fingertips

pressing into my skin, gently pushing me forward. "It'll be okay," he whispers.

I take a few steps before I hold the envelope in my hand. This could be nothing at all. I could have worked myself up over something silly. Or this could be my next piece of healing.

We make ourselves comfortable on my bed. Flynn has his back against the wall, and I'm leaning into him, our legs stretched out. His feet extend a few inches further, nearly reaching the end of the bed.

I trace Ellie's handwriting on the envelope a few times before I take a deep breath in. Flynn kisses the top of my head, and I sink into his embrace with a huff.

"Can you read it?" I ask, handing the envelope over. "I don't . . . I need to hear it all the way to the end, and if it isn't what I want to hear, I won't finish it."

"Of course," he exhales.

Before I can even process a change of heart, he's pulling the letter out and unfolding it.

Theodore,

If you're reading this, Andrya must have thought it was time. Sam and I don't even know where to start. Another world, how crazy is that? And our family? Our family helps lead a new world? It's all overwhelming. We can only imagine how overwhelmed you are, too. Which I guess leads us to, we are so unbelievably sorry and heartbroken for how we handled this past year. We can recognize how it needed to happen for Sam and me, but we should have never let it happen to you. We made a promise to you and to ourselves that we would always be by your side. That we would never abandon you and that we saw you as our own. Theo, honey, we are sorry we failed you. We do see you as our own, but we got scared and took the easy way out. For that, we understand you may never forgive us.

The moment we found out we were pregnant, it felt like we were about to see another disaster. We had no hope this time. We didn't even want to tell your parents until the first trimester was over, but well, the protest was scheduled and we were supposed to go to it. I think you understand now why we didn't. None of us understand what happened that day. But suddenly, our best friends died, our own support system, and I wanted to run away. I didn't know how to handle anything without my mom. All of a sudden, I was becoming a mom, and the world was a terrifying place that I had to raise a baby in, and we ran.

It wasn't until we got to Colorado that I truly recognized what we had done. I was so selfish searching for my support system that we forgot we were your support system. Before we could get our act together to get back to you, Andrya and Jay came. Andrya had convinced us that you were doing okay, and we followed her lead. When she left, that's when I started seeing what you were doing. I started following your movement. Sam and I had our world even more rattled with Andrya's appearance, that because we saw you up and out of bed, we decided to take the time to work on ourselves and work on what this new future meant. The damage of us leaving had already been done. The least we could do was start to heal ourselves, to be there for you.

I don't know if you know this, but we constantly communicated with Alejandro's parents. They were our in for the agency and fundraiser, but also, they told us they were making sure you were okay.

I don't know if Andrya mentioned it, but we did go to Otium for a few weeks. We stayed in the Oceanic. Please tell Flynn that we hope one day we get to meet him. We hope that he's a good friend for you. It sucked knowing we were so close and we couldn't meet him. The goal for us being there was to recognize it existed, to know how it came to be, and to learn how to support you.

In order to support you, we are stepping back into the role of your second parents. We will be at the portal to pick you up. You'll be living with us, and then at eighteen, if you don't want to be around us, you can leave. Otherwise, your home is with us. And if you choose, we would love for you to shower our baby with love and Marvel. Sam's nudging me right now, wanting me to let you know that he found the first edition Spider-Man and Captain America comics you've been looking for. They are yours. (Yes, we are bribing you.)

We love you so much, Theo. We can't wait to see you and talk more through together. This time, we're here until the end.

Love, Sam and Ellie

Flynn drops the letter onto his lap before he tightens his grip around me, pressing my head against his chest, letting my tears soak through his shirt.

I don't know how to start processing. My tears aren't even sobs, just silent rivers down my cheeks. It's everything I wanted, and also not at all, wrapped into one. I hate that doing my own growth allows me to understand their perspective. I hate that I want to be angry and push them away, but know to my core I can't . . . and shouldn't. A part of me wants to fall back into their arms like no harm was done, and the other wants to act out. Not giving them the satisfaction of moving in, but that only harms me and forces me back under a roof with my aunt and uncle.

"That's really freaking cool that my comic books are actually yours. Also, very weird." Flynn breaks the silence, and I can't help but let out a breathy laugh.

That's all I can do, though. I feel trapped in my next steps. Any word spoken feels like a significant step forward or backward.

"I really hope I do get to meet them, though. I'm not sure how I feel about the fact that they were here and my parents were with them. It kinda rattles me. I suppose this might be how you've felt or are feeling. All I've truly known is Otium, but now we're intermingling."

This is my chance, my moment to push for making our timelines intersect. "This is why Otium should time travel everyone to this timeline. We all intersect. You and I will be the same age. You'll be able to meet Sam and Ellie . . ."

"And we'll be the selfish ones potentially messing up the entire initiative plan because we want to stay together."

"No," I say, sitting up and wiping my cheeks. My hands are soaked, and more tears are coming, but I think my hurt is slowly being healed with each stream. "No, time-traveling everyone here within the next few years helps the most people. It helps my people not suffer through the tragedies that no doubt haunt Earth. Natural disasters are not getting better. Earth is getting warmer and more polluted. Each moment on Earth is a moment lost here. I'm not saying that this happens in the next five years, but maybe ten or fifteen? A hell of a lot sooner than thirty."

Flynn's silent as he processes my words. I lean against my window, sideways to Flynn. I take the letter and put it back in the envelope, tossing it aside. I need alone time to process those words, but this, right here and now, is crucial to my fight.

"I can't go back to Earth knowing that at any point in time, you have the ability to extract me from Otium."

"No, I can't," Flynn interrupts, and I eye the black watch on his wrist. He has worn it every single day since I've been here. Even on our movie nights when he's in sweats, he has his watch on.

"You can, but you don't because it's against the rules. But you have the power right on your wrist; the technology exists, and you don't need a higher up to open the portal for me. We could open a portal right now and meet Sam and Ellie."

He gazes down at his watch as if he had never thought of the possibility before. Now that I mention it, heading to Earth for a quick moment to talk to Sam and Ellie sounds brilliant.

"We can't do that," he says, making eye contact with me now. His palm covers the watch like just the sight is now too tempting.

"I'm not asking you to. What I'm saying is that there is the *ability* to. Therefore, knowing that the technology exists and being on Earth, if devastation arises and my people aren't making moves to Otium yet, I think whatever happens will be unforgivable."

"There are rules and regulations in place for a reason. We aren't ready yet. The initiative just started. And when we get people here, they have to go through their own set of classes and therapy. It's a lot of work, Theo. You only know a portion of it."

"And so do you. You only know what you're told. You can't even confirm we come back in the same timeline. We need to talk to your mom."

His eyes bug at the thought. He pulls his legs up against his chest, resting his chin on his kneecaps.

"If we ask your mom, and she doesn't give us the truth, then I learn to deal with it. But if I can get that information, maybe we can also help speed up the process. Get the other mentees involved, and past ones. No one seems to know the answer, and no one seems to be fighting for the answer except me. If I'm being brought here to make a change, the change can start on this planet."

Flynn focuses on the wall ahead of him. I don't know if he's listening, but I've made the decision myself. I'll ask Andrya on my own if I have to, just like I'll find my family here. They can teach me how to heal, but I can put myself first, too.

"We aren't talking to my mom," Flynn says. He holds up his hand as I go to interject. "I'll find the information about your family, and we will go from there."

I grin, leaping back over to my place beside him. I pull his arm around me and cuddle back into his side.

"Let's change the world together, Flynn Thomas."

PART THREE

Thirty-Three

The next few weeks flew by. Flynn and I suddenly had a mission that wasn't just about healing me. We were working collectively on something, which only brought us closer while we spent less time together. Between our regular schedule, Flynn was searching for information on Earth and my family, and I was traveling around different locations. I promised Flynn that I wouldn't ask about my family in my travels until he finished his part, and I made true on that. Instead, I went to the beaches on my own and hiked through the mountains in the Valley. I reread Sam and Ellie's letter over and over, each time focusing on a different section, reflecting on how I felt about it. I had asked Corie to give me space on healing from the letter. Instead, we focused on healing my "inner child," as she liked to call it. Focusing on why I spent so much time helping others versus helping myself and even those closest to me. While we didn't talk about Sam and Ellie, we worked through what abandonment was and how I related to it, and how I could learn to heal that part of myself even if I didn't fully let Sam and Ellie back in.

I knew deep down that Sam and Ellie would be my family. That I would stay with them for as long as I wanted or needed. Of course, I'd be a part of their baby's life, especially now knowing the future. But I didn't have to like how they handled everything, and I didn't have to forgive that right away or if ever. At least, that's what Corie told me today in therapy when I finally opened up to her.

My feelings are valid, and just accepting something from them doesn't mean they are forgiven. It's living simultaneously, working forward while healing the past.

I like the thought. Makes me feel I can implement that with my friends too. Alejandro and Jonah don't have to forgive me for how I've treated them in the past, but maybe we can all move forward as we work through things. Maybe that's how you heal. Maybe it's how you remain friends after a breakup.

Over the past few weeks in group, I offered the bare minimum while I listened and dissected what everyone's plans were when they went back to Earth. Some did question if we'd time travel or not, and the therapist did sidetrack that conversation, but no one seemed to push the issue. My plan is to get all the information I can before I go to the mentees for help.

No one questioned my minimal involvement in the group because of my different program, and I still hung out with them while we waited for Flynn after class, and we still all got dinner afterward. It's just the main schedule that changed was instead of hanging out with Flynn, both of us would go our separate ways after dinner. He'd go do research, and I'd reflect. We'd then come together late at night to watch something, usually Marvel.

When I woke up this morning, there was a message from Flynn telling me to do my normal schedule without him, and then after therapy, I had a message telling me to come to the cave on my siesta. He asked me to bring lunch too.

As I'm lighting the last candle in the cave, Flynn tumbles in, two bags on his back. He's breathing heavily as he strips the bags off. Immediately kneeling and pulling a small blanket out of one.

"Okay," he huffs as he spreads the blanket out. "I think I found everything I can. But this has to be top secret for now until we come up with a plan, okay?"

"Yes, absolutely." I grab the food and drinks, setting them on the blankets before taking a seat. "I can't wait."

Flynn flips on two small white lanterns that he unfolded from a bag too. They instantly give us enough light to see each other and likely read whatever is in his bag.

Flynn's face is soaked with sweat, and his hair is matted against his skull. He was on a mission. A smile graces my face. I reach over and take his hand in mine, pausing his chaos for just a moment. He's on my team. We're a team.

"Thank you," I say softly. "I know how this made you feel, and I just want to say that I appreciate you doing this."

Flynn sits, settling into a cross-legged position. His blue eyes gaze into my own, his skin wrinkling just slightly. "Thank you," he whispers, squeezing our hands. "These lanterns are vita-operated and fully charged, so we should have a bit of time. The documents will be stored here. If we want to look at them in the daylight, we can, but they will not be returning to Olive. Do you understand?"

I watch as he wipes the sweat from his brows, and suddenly, I'm unsettled. My stomach twists as his breathing slows. His hands still shake as he reaches for the next backpack.

"I rarely break the rules, Theo, and this is a lot. I got a

lot. I broke into my mom's devices, sometimes while she was sleeping, and other times, stealing the actual device altogether. Some things had so many passcodes to get through. But I think I got it all." He pulls out stacks of paper, tossing them onto the blanket next to us.

None of it looks organized, as if he found bits of information here and there and just half-hazardly printed as he could. My suspicions are confirmed when I start to look through the papers, and some only have a couple paragraphs of information while others are filled to the brim.

"Most of this is the start of the Otium Initiative and the Thirty-Five-Year plan."

My heart sinks. That confirms it. Their plan was always going to be waiting until the very last second. A part of me doesn't even want to see the details they wrote out. None of it is as well thought out as it could have been.

"I found a little bit about your family," Flynn continues, and my eyes dart over to him. "I do have an address, and I have reached out to them. We will only visit them if they give consent, do you understand?" Flynn lifts his brow, and heat rises to my cheeks. It feels like a lifetime ago when I asked him about consent and if he understood what he meant. Now I'm trying to rework an entire system this planet created over the past sixty years.

I blink, slouching as the idea consumes me. Who do I think I am to try and rework their system? To think I can possibly have any single idea of what the founders of Otium went through. Only one version of me experienced it.

"Theo, do you understand?"

I blink again, refocusing on him. "Yes, I understand."

"Great, now let's eat." His laugh is airy, still riddled with nerves. His trembling hands reach out for a container of tacos, and he's diving into the food before I can lift my container.

I may be in over my head. I may just have to sit with the fact that while I am fighting for a new world, there will be losses. There are always losses in any situation like this. That's part of the fight, part of the journey.

The two of us sit in silence, eating our lunch. Flynn scatters some papers out as he eats, doing some sort of organization. I don't even know where to begin. And now that the reality is in front of me, do I really want to know who I've become?

"What do you want to start with? The info I know about your Otium self or this plan?"

I place the lid back on my empty container and take a few sips of water. My lungs get heavier with each inhale. I want to know everything and nothing at all, but I can't have both in this world.

"Do you know if I lived a good life?"

His smile is warm, and he interlaces our fingers again. "Yes, you lived a very good life, and you helped a ton of people."

I nod, scattering papers with my free hand. "Okay. I don't want to know anything else unless my family wants to see me. I think it'll be too hard if I know and they don't agree."

"Okay, then just give me a moment." Flynn searches through the bottom of the pile and pulls a tiny stack of papers out. He shoves the stack back into his bag. "Okay, nothing else should be about you here. Let's begin."

The two of us read through every single document we have. Sometimes silently, other times out loud. The pages are not much different from reading a bill or law from the United States Government. A lot of legal jargon that goes over my head. We're able to piece together information that we do understand. This plan isn't complete, which is why it isn't public knowledge yet. One document we look at has legal terms, and the next looks like someone opened up a blank computer document and just started typing away ideas.

The gist is that they do plan to time travel people here. They estimate quadrupling the population here, which is still a shit-ton of people left on Earth. They plan to start bringing people to Otium in twenty years. It'll give them ten years to bring a mass group in, train them on the world, set them up with therapy, and let them settle before another mass group comes in. In the next five years, they plan to quadruple the number of mentors they have trained. With the start of the new year, the initiative expands. Each semester, in all three locations, will have at least twelve people instead of six. Semesters will overlap too. Six weeks into the semester, another semester will begin. It ensures that all mentors they train always have work, but also allows them to train people at a faster rate. This Flynn knew, but it was news to me. In just a year, they'll have trained nearly one-hundred new activists to go back to Earth, instead of this year being just twenty-four.

The numbers still seem so low. I can't help but think this could all be done at a faster rate. I understand work-life balance here and the idea that you also don't have to work, but when humanity is at stake, it seems relaxation is a waste of time.

For the mentees who go back to Earth, they don't want us talking about Otium for another five years, at least. This isn't confirmed, and each mentee leaves Otium with the knowledge that Otium will reach out when it's time. Instead, they want us to work on community levels. Spread more kindness, help others out, make changes within our community, and help build bonds. The bigger the impact we make, the more people trust us, the better chance mentee will have to convince people to join Otium when the time is right.

"This planet sounds like a cult." I laugh as I read through the potential dialogue they want us to use to inform people about Otium. I only laugh because I'm kinda uncomfortable with how this might play out. I understand how someone can create a following and have people blindly follow them; I feel like I had that with my social media back home, but it doesn't sit right with me now.

"Each mentee has to do what they need to do in order to convince the largest group of people that this planet exists for them. You'll be backed by scientists by this point, too, it seems," Flynn offers like it's any consolation.

"I don't want to wait five years before I start talking to people about this. At least my friends. I think the more people I can convince early on that this is real, the better. Plus, I'll have Sam and Ellie on my side."

"I think we have to discuss that with my mom."

"And tell her that we stole her plans?" I raise my brow.

His eyes close, and he lets out a long sigh. "No, no. You're right." Flynn lays back on the blanket, covering his face with his hands.

I move some papers so I can lie down beside him, curling my leg over his, resting my left hand on his stomach. My hand rises and falls with each breath he takes. Flynn's hand caresses my shoulder.

There has to be a way to get more people to Otium. There will never be enough mentors to train enough activists at the rate they are going. For a planet that focuses on bettering humanity, they aren't taking enough risks.

"Let's have dinner with your parents. It'll be casual, but maybe we can interlace some questions that just seem like my curiosity," I offer, my voice semi-muffled from his shirt.

"So we tell them we are dating, while also admitting that we broke into her device, while also breaking my mom's rule of no work during family time?" His tone is neutral. It almost feels like he's joking, but I'm not sure anymore. He's been so tense and overwhelmed the past few weeks that it was hard for him to relax even in our good moments.

"I just thought dinner would be less threatening. Maybe if I'm just your boyfriend at the dinner table, it can be a more casual conversation, like 'Hey, so what are your thoughts of me going home and immediately telling my friends where I've been?'"

His chest rumbles beneath me, his breath ruffling my curls. That's the sound I love. "Not exactly how I envisioned it, but I understand your reasoning." Flynn's fingertips creep up into my curls and start massaging my scalp. I breathe out, sinking further into his side, my eyes fluttering closed.

Thirty-Four

My past self chose to live on the outskirts in the town of Laurel. Close enough to the shops and civilization but far enough out that not a lot of people have surrounded the home I had built. It's a lovely two-story cob home with a back porch. The outside remains the reddish clay. Large windows make up most of the first floor. Clearly, I needed as much vitalight and alone time as I could get.

It's been a few days since Flynn and I got approval from my family to visit. They asked if we could wait until the weekend, and here Flynn and I are, hopping off our bikes and laying them gently in the front yard. Like most homes, there is no fence in the front yard, but the landscape is filled with the vibrant wildflowers. I bet past me was just as entranced by them when his vision adjusted. They surround the pathway to the front door, expand around the front of the house and run up against the back fence.

A stunning middle-aged woman opens the door as Flynn and I walk hand-in-hand toward it. She has long, wavy maroon hair. Her smile is wide with thick lips. She's smiling so bright that it nearly takes up her entire round face. As we get closer, I see she has light green eyes, no competition to my family of brown eyes. Flynn had told me that Kira was my daughter, but I didn't want him to tell me anything else. I thought it would make more sense coming from the sources with the memories.

"Welcome! I'm Kira." She holds out her hand, and we each take a moment to shake it.

"I'm Theodore, and this is Flynn." I offer her a small smile. My body feels jumbled, filled with nerves and excitement, and even caution.

Kira tilts her head just slightly, her eyes soft. "I'd recognize you anywhere, Da-Theodore." She corrects her mistake, her olive skin blushing.

It hadn't occurred to me that she'd be reconnecting with her father. That *I* was a father.

Flynn lets go of my hand, placing his on my back. He rubs small circles as I blink, trying to focus my mind. Maybe this isn't the best idea. Do I let her call me Dad? Is it weird for her to say my name? I wouldn't want to talk to my mom and dad by saying their real names. I shudder for a moment before smiling down at her. I hate that I feel like I'm slightly older on the single fact that I'm taller.

"Let's go out on the porch. Amir and Josie are out back waiting. Our children aren't here, nor grandchildren. Our children are old enough to understand, we just didn't think it was appropriate to reopen that grief for them if we aren't sure what the future holds. I hope you understand," Kira explains, but I can't get over the idea of them having children *and* grandchildren. I have great-grandchildren in this life.

I'm only seventeen years old. Flynn is my second boyfriend. I don't even know if I want a husband *or* kids. I haven't even graduated high school.

My balance wavers, and Flynn's fingers carve into my hip, steadying me.

"Are you sure this is a good idea, Theo?" he asks me. His hand turns my head toward him as he searches my face. "This is your last chance."

I slowly nod. This is weird and uncomfortable and strange. But I felt like I had to do this for a reason, and I can't back out now. Kira mentioned grief in the idea that I was a part of my grandchildren's lives. That I meant enough to them that they'd be heartbroken with me weirdly being alive. I like to believe it's just as strange and complicated for Kira. If she's my daughter, she might be battling grief too.

I don't know how I'd react if my parents were suddenly in front of me.

"I'm good," I say softly. "Just please be patient with me." I look at Kira, and she nods with a smile.

"Of course. All we ask is for you to do the same."

Kira leads us through the home, and it's so similar to what I love about my parents' home. I don't have enough time to inspect the decorations, but I suspect there are some artifacts I brought here. I wonder who lives in this home now if I've passed. A giant picture in the living room catches my eye right before we head to the backdoor door.

I break away and walk toward it. It's a painted family portrait. As if we stood still long enough for someone to paint us. Shivers run down my spine as I inspect my old age. I didn't age well; I fought through hell, I'm sure. But I'm surrounded by Kira, who I recognize, and a gentleman and another woman. In front of them are three girls and four boys. They range from a toddler to teenagers.

"We had that family portrait done right before our Theodore died. He was eighty-five. The littlest one in the picture is now sixteen. It's wild how time has passed, and here you are now, a part of the initiative. It's incredible, really." Kira breathes out, her eyes are glossy.

Weird *and* incredible, alright. A sharp pain shoots through my heart. I don't know these people, but they knew me, loved me, and they may never be a part of my new future.

They may not want *to be*, I remind myself.

"Let's go outside," Kira says.

Flynn helps guide me to the backdoor. We step outside into the bright vitalight again. The backyard is entirely fenced in, and it's quaint. The back porch is nearly identical to my childhood home with the bench swing Jonah and I loved. A few bicycles of different sizes are lined up against the fence. A volleyball net is centered in the grass past the barbecue area where there are four loveseats arranged in a square. The carved wooden loveseats have vibrant turquoise cushions. A gentleman and a woman, similar ages to my parents, are seated on one. They immediately stand up, grinning.

"Wow. This is unreal," the woman says, rushing over to me. Her blonde curly hair bounces as she moves. "May I hug you?" she asks.

I glance over at Flynn, and he shrugs. "Sure," I say softly.

"This is Josie," Flynn says before he nods toward the guy. "And that is Amir."

Josie's arms envelop me in a hug, so similar to my mother's. Just her presence is radiating warmth. When she pulls away, a single tear rolls down her cheek.

"Sorry." She laughs, wiping at her face. "It's just, not every day you get to see your father again."

I nod, glancing between her and Kira. Amir is still at the loveseat, but he's dabbing his eyes. I definitely didn't think this through. I was selfish and wanted answers. Sometimes it feels like Otium is still all a dream as if this isn't a real world with real people who have real feelings.

Kira clears her throat as she walks to the seats. "Let's go sit. You're here for answers, and we are ready to give you what we know."

She sits next to Amir. He looks distinguished with his perfectly crafted beard and combed back, jet black hair. All he does is offer me a wave as I sit down across from him.

"Do you mind if I sit next to you?" Josie asks. "I don't want it to be weird, but it's just—"

"Of course." I smile, patting the seat next to me. Flynn sits on an empty loveseat by himself.

I try to put myself in Josie's shoes, imagining what it might be like if my parents—even if they were a teenager like me—came to talk to me. How would I react? What would I want to know or relive in this moment? If she needs the comfort of her "father" sitting next to her, it may be the least I can do.

"So, what do you know?" Kira asks.

There's a coffee table between us with what looks like two photo albums. All I really want to see are those pictures. Who made it throughout my life? Who did I marry? Despite them all looking different, are they my biological children?

"Everything and anything. I only know your names," I say.

Amir's eyes shoot up, connecting with my own. They immediately glaze over.

Kira takes a deep breath and exhales, leaning forward and opening one of the photo albums. "This is the album you cherished. It's a mixture of pictures that represented your life on Earth and some of your life here."

She pushes the album toward me, and I'm immediately introduced to my childhood. I must have collected pictures here and there to condense what I brought to Otium. There are pictures of my parents and me protesting. There's a picture of the three of us the day we were awarded the plaques from New York. I didn't think there were many photos of my parents, brothers, and me, but somehow I found enough to cover a few pages. In every single family picture, we seemed to be laughing or smiling big cheesy smiles. Seeing these pictures . . . I don't remember them or understand them. I barely have happy memories looking back on all of us together. I always thought my brothers were unhappy children. I soon reach the picture of Jonah and me that was taken before my parents' deaths.

I gasp, reaching out to touch the photo. I'm not sure I recognize the Theo looking back at me. He's happy, for sure. But it's a different happiness from what I see staring back at me here on Otium.

"You always described that as one of your happiest days," Josie says.

"May I look?" Flynn asks quietly.

I jump at his voice before glancing over at him. Honestly, I forgot he was here. I nod, and Josie scoots over a little, so Flynn has room to sit next to me too.

"This is Jonah," I tell Flynn. My eyes become cloudy as I trace the photo. It doesn't seem possible that just a couple months ago we were in his bed, reminiscing about this photo. While the photo holds happiness, there's a dark cloud interlaced with the memory of our bad day.

"You guys look so happy," Flynn says, his shoulder leaning against mine.

"We were. This is the day before my parents' died." Flynn's hand shoots to my lower back, rubbing circles as our knees touch. I glance over at Kira, who's watching my every move with a confused look. "Did my parents—"

"Your parents didn't die."

I inhale, and Flynn's hand provides pressure on my back. Andrya was telling the truth. They lived in this timeline. The Otium Initiative has messed up *my* timeline.

"Your parents didn't make it to Otium, but they fought until the very end," Kira continues.

"So why was this one of my happiest days?" I question; my voice barely a whisper.

"You always said it reminded you about the happiness of your first love instead of the heartbreak," Josie offers.

I guess it wasn't just grief that tore Jonah and me apart.

"You worked at With Love for a while after high school," Kira continues, but now I'm even more unsure of if I want to know this life. A life completely unattainable. "Then you started working hands-on with adoption agencies that worked with With Love," Kira says.

"My parents still operated With Love?" I ask. I know it always broke my heart to see children in the foster system who never found forever homes, but I didn't expect it to become my passion.

"Yes, alongside Samuel and Ellie. Rosalyn volunteered and worked there too, similar to what you said you did as a teen," Kira says.

"Rosalyn?" I question, looking over at Flynn.

"My grandmother is named Rosalyn?" he questions, looking over at Kira.

She nods. "Yes, Samuel and Ellie's daughter. Andrya's mother."

Flynn's breath catches, and I lean forward, covering my face with my hands. Taking a deep breath in, I let out an exhale slowly. They never mentioned a baby's name in the letter. Tears escape my eyelids as I squeeze them shut. My breathing starts to heave.

"Theo, are you okay?" Flynn's hand trails up and down my back.

"T-that's my m-mom's name," I breathe, my voice slightly muffled. Flynn's hand pauses for a millisecond before he continues to soothe me. With his free hand, he finds mine and interlaces our fingers, squeezing tight.

"Keep going," I whisper, keeping my face covered. I need information in small doses, I think.

"Your mission was to make sure that children were placed in safer foster homes, and you put more focus on making sure children were adopted too. All throughout New England. When a future on Otium became possible, you doubled down, ensuring that every orphan in New England was adopted by a family coming to Otium. Amir, Josie, and I were the last ones, and you chose to adopt us." I sit up as Kira says this. My heart rapidly beats in my chest, forcing itself against my rib cage. "I was fifteen, Josie was seven, and Amir was three. You protected us, loved us, built us this home, and made sure that we had everything we ever needed. None of us ever knew what a home was before you." Kira's eyes are glossy, and Josie leans into my shoulder.

"You're the only parent we've ever known," Josie says.

I take a deep breath in. I can't align any of this. Yes, I'm passionate about With Love, but I never even knew if I wanted kids or if I'd adopt, especially after my experience with my brothers. I'm almost afraid to ask if my brothers made the trip. How did I even know how to be a father to children at various ages?

I lift the photo album off the coffee table and place it on

my lap as I lean back against the seat. I skim the rest of the photos in it that I can pinpoint together. There's a photo of Alejandro, Jonah, and I all smiling, similar to the pictures that are hung up in my apartment back in the Flatlands. There's a graduation picture of Alejandro and me, but no Jonah. A graduation picture with me, my parents, and my brother. That photo alone nearly stops my heart. There are a few pictures of me with a baby; that same baby is with Sam and Ellie, so I can only assume it's Rosalyn. The baby grows up throughout the photos of different events and festivals . . . Majestic Park is a park and not a factory. There's a picture of Alejandro getting married; I'm his best man. A picture of me and presumably my plus one at the wedding. As I age in the photos, the less I can pinpoint who these important people may be. Likely new friends and friends with kids. But there aren't any other photos of me with another guy. Or photos with Jonah. The last picture in the album is of me holding Amir, with Josie and Kira on either side of me, with my aged parents on either side of Josie and Kira.

"This was the day you adopted us. A few days later, we traveled to Otium," Josie says.

I trace the picture with my parents, tears streaming down my face, but quickly flip back to the last picture I remember. The day before my life changed forever. This future is lovely—a dream, really—but it'll never be my future.

"Do you guys know who Jonah is?" I ask, flipping back to the picture of us on my parents' back porch.

"Your greatest regret, you said," Kira offers. Flynn's hand tightens on mine. "We never got details, but every time you looked at that picture, you said you could never forgive yourself for how you treated him and how it ended.

You never found out if he made it to Otium. You refused to."

I trace the photo again. I guess our crash and burn was inevitable. I hope my leaving for the Otium Initiative helped put a pause to our tragic end this time. Now I can go home and civilly talk to him since I know our history—or I suppose our future. Maybe we just remain friends. I wonder if that's part of the benefit of time traveling or if it's the detriment of knowing your future.

"Did I ever marry?" I ask, taking it upon myself to pick up the next album.

"No, you were too focused on your career, you said. But you slowed down when you got to Otium. Instead of trying to take a leadership role here, like Rosalyn begged you to do, you spent time with us and gave us the best life," Josie says. "It took us a while to all mesh and click, but you never gave up. You made it your mission to understand each of us and give us all what we needed. We may be an odd pair, but we're also the closest family."

As I open the second album, I'm graced with polaroid-type film. "We brought some instant cameras with us because we wanted to document the trip and have instant evidence. There aren't many photos before technology was built here because we didn't want to waste film," Kira says.

And she's right. It's only the first couple of pages that are polaroid films. But there's a picture of the four of us in what looks like the space plane that brought us here. I'm middle-aged, holding on tightly to all three of them. We don't look like we all belong with one another, but somewhere along the line, I became a support system.

There's another picture of us in front of what looks like this empty lot. A few pictures of our surroundings, with no homes built yet, just the wide-open valley. When the polaroids disappear, they're replaced with thinner paper with high color concentration. There are pictures of all of us swimming in the river and the beach, all of us building this home, Amir on a bike, likely learning to ride for the first time. A lot of photos have Amir and me bonding, which makes sense as he had no memory of a life before me. For all he ever knew, I was his only parent.

I glance over at him, and his eyes are locked on me, but he isn't making eye contact. All he knows is Otium, just like Flynn. He likely doesn't remember Earth, just knows that he had a father that looks like he loved him and that father passed, and now that father is sitting in front of him as a teenager.

I break off to look over at Kira and Josie, both are watching me too. These pictures are everything I imagined a family would be like if I did have one. All just without someone. These adults in front of me are all different and came from different backgrounds but could bond over one thing—they needed a family, and I could create that for them. My parents must have been proud.

As the album ends, and it's clear I'm aging, more people are added to the photos, and babies come into play. There are even a few pictures of Alejandro and me scattered throughout. One last photo of us was taken at our old age, sitting a back porch swing.

"Alejandro lived next door. He passed away a few years before you. His son's family lives in the house now," Kira says.

I smile, thinking that we made it through. My best friend stood by my side every step of the way.

"Why did Rosalyn want me to lead?" I ask after a few minutes of silence.

Kira shrugged. "Not sure. Didn't really matter to us at

the time, and I never looked into it because it became irrelevant to our life. Rosalyn and her boyfriend moved to the Flatlands, even though you begged her to stay with us. Somewhere along the line, her daughter became the leader of the Flatlands. Rosalyn was still a part of our lives, though. We saw her every few days, and she treated us like family. We aren't as close as we used to be after you passed, but we still check in every so often."

"Rosalyn is still alive?" I turn to Flynn, furrowing my brows. I can't even do the math in my head to process it.

"Yeah, she's eighty," he says. He seems wrapped up in his own head, eye scanning over the open photo album. Maybe it's too weird for him to be here, hearing about how truly connected his family is to my own, with people he doesn't know.

"Was I happy?" I ask softly, making eye contact with each of them. Amir is still shying away from my eye contact.

"Yeah, I think so," Kira offers. "You definitely had your sad moments, and there were times you wished you did way more on Earth. You weren't satisfied with how many people didn't make it here. And leaving your parents and Samuel and Ellie took a toll, but overall, I think you were happy."

We socialize for only a little while longer. I ask them about their lives, but they respectfully decline, saying this meeting was really just for me, and they didn't need to share their lives with another version of me when they had the real Theodore. Amir barely says goodbye to me, but Josie sobs as we leave. Kira was the one to explain that I couldn't get any more information.

My mind races in every different direction as Flynn and I bike away. I need to connect the dots of what I know, what

I've been told, who I am today, who I possibly could be, and who I want to be.

I don't know if it was a good idea to have done that. I don't feel any more settled. Can I be as incredible as I seemed despite grief now in my timeline? Even better, maybe? Is it possible to help as much as I did *and* focus and value myself? Is it possible to have Jonah in my life? Or have I ruined that beyond repair? Could his smile have been fake on the picture of us from the fundraising event?

I don't remember getting back to the Flatlands, climbing on my bed, or staring up at the ceiling. I'm not sure when Flynn left my side or if he muttered a word on our journey back.

I do know that I'm not any closer to clarity.

Thirty-Five

"Holy shit," I pant, gazing at the vast ocean in front of me. Little islands are scattered in the distance to my left. Most of the water is relatively untouched, with no end in sight. The sky is lighter up here as the vitalight tries to obscure our view.

"This is the highest peak we've discovered," Flynn says, gasping for breath.

And it is high. We're miles from the ground, one slip off the cliff, and I'd be done for. The minuscule islands have to be at least a few miles long and wide. Though I can cover them with my thumb from where I'm standing.

My morning started with Flynn knocking on my door, asking me to go on an adventure with him. He said that we both needed a breather from the onset of information and to disappear for a bit. That he felt unsettled with what he now knew and had done, and he couldn't begin to fathom the chaos in my mind.

I couldn't even argue when he showed me his backpack filled with breakfast, lunch, and a ton of water. He's right, I did need to escape. After a sleepless night, I could feel my mind teetering to hole myself up.

I didn't know our plans until we took the train to the Valley. Instead of getting off where we usually do, we stayed on for another thirty minutes or so. We had plenty of time to eat breakfast and caffeinate before we reached the entrance to this hike. The highest peak here; surpassing the Northeast mountains. Definitely the most I've ever hiked.

My body would agree that this is the most physical thing I've ever done. My lungs burn with each inhale, and my muscles feel ready to cramp at any given moment. However, my mind shut off the moment it had to fight to survive.

"Let's stretch a little before we sit and take it all in. I highly recommend it," Flynn says.

I don't want to take my eyes off the view, but I'm certain I won't make it down this mountain if I don't take care of myself now. We hiked uphill for over three hours.

Neither of us spoke the entire hike, aside from Flynn warning me of loose rock or uneven ground. We had small talk on the train, like what things I still wanted to experience with my time here and if my breakfast wrap was good. All of it felt insignificant to the bombshells dropped on us.

Flynn leads me through a series of stretches that feel like my muscles may snap at any moment. Searing and fizzing with each movement. He walks me through some breathing exercises to help regulate our breaths, and when it doesn't feel like my lungs are being sliced with each breath, I take a few gulps of water.

Flynn grabs a blanket out of his backpack and spreads it out on the rock surface. It's the smallest overlook spot, with just a slab of rock before trees and bushes surround us on all sides. Most of the hike was cleared; some of it, Flynn had to move branches, or we had to step over numerous logs and boulders. We had split our food up into two bags, so I place my own bag next to his before we sit.

"I don't do this hike often as it's pretty killer," Flynn starts, "but I do it every time I need to escape and clear my head."

The ocean sparkles various shades of purple, depending how the light touches it. From up here, we can't even see the Oceanic location. We are just surrounded by water. It's the literal perfect escape.

"When have you needed to clear your head?" I ask. I try to keep my mind neutral because it's hard to remember that bad things happen here. Flynn can also be in pain and experience hurt. His stress levels over the past few weeks are enough to convince me that this society is just like mine. My mind just can't process it completely.

"When Remy broke up with me. I had heard of this hike before, but never did it. It felt rigorous enough for my mind to stop a bit. I ignorantly stumbled my way up here. Without food, water, or a friend. Had to call Mattis to come help me as I neared the bottom. I blacked out before he got to me with fuel."

I glance over at him. Sounds like something foolish I'd do.

His eyes squint toward the ocean, but his hand reaches out for mine, interlacing our fingers. I give our hands a gentle squeeze even though our hands are clammy, and it increases my body temperature.

"May I ask what happened?" I ask softly, giving him the privacy of watching the small ripples in the ocean.

"I'm not the greatest at balancing my schedule. I kind of hyper-focus on what's in front of me and what excites me."

Each day it seems he's more like me. His crystal eyes are

intense as his body turns toward me. I follow suit, and he takes both of my hands, resting them on his lap.

"My advising training picked up. My mom started focusing heavily on your case and reminding me of my studies and why I needed to work as hard as possible so I could mentor you. I felt all this pressure, and I took my studies so seriously that I studied every waking hour that I wasn't being actively trained with a mentee. I tried my hardest with each mentee I was co-mentoring, too. I started running myself dry and snapping at Remy when they asked to hang out or whenever they told me that I no longer made them a priority. They ended things, and my life clicked back into focus. I feared losing them, more so as a friend, that I learned how to refocus my time and attention.

"And then, just as I was healing things with Remy as friends, my mom called me in a panic, telling me that you were coming to Otium. Months ahead of schedule. It felt like everything might crumble again in my life. Before completing my checklist for you to arrive, I came up here again." He squeezes my hands, continuing to keep eye contact with me as my heart accelerates.

I know I'm a special case, but it's weird to know how much I affected his life before I even knew of Otium.

"And then I came again when you went back to the hospital. I feared that I might have failed you. That if you never came back, everything I worked so hard for would have disappeared. I wasn't sure how my mom would react or feel toward me; if she'd blame me, if I'd still be a mentor."

My eyes blur as his grow cloudy. He pauses for a moment, and the oxygen is sucked dry between us. I underestimated just what Flynn was going through—what he does go through. We aren't that different, just teens trying to find our way in the next phase of our life. Different planets, laws, and lifestyles separate us, but our feelings are the same.

"And then the final time was just last week, the morning we met in the cave."

I gasp, and he stops speaking. I had assumed he was in the middle of still pulling files that morning. But he sat on them for a few hours.

"I started traveling here before it was light outside. That's why I was a hot mess when I arrived at the cave. I panicked. I didn't know what I did. I had read bits and pieces of your life and Otium's plan. I couldn't balance what needed to happen with what was going on between us and this life we've created. You're going home soon, and I don't know what I'm feeling or how to process anything. Us dating isn't against the rules, but it's advised to not become too close with your mentee for fear of losing focus. But I can't help wondering if our meeting, of us taking this journey together, if it was meant to be somehow. Does it have anything to do with your mission, with your healing, with the greater purpose Otium is trying to achieve? Is it possible that we are meant to shake things up together? We're meant to break the rules and think outside the box? Or is it all just in our heads? Convincing us that we should be doing it all because love is blinding us from reality? Like if we believe that we are meant to work through this together, there may be hope we can be together?"

A few tears trail down my cheeks as he finally pauses. His grip on my hands is so tight, and I'm afraid if he lets go, it might suffocate my lungs.

"And then there is Jonah," he whispers.

I choke on an inhale. The filing cabinets, in my mind, try to sort through how Jonah could be an issue. How can

Flynn be talking about a love between us and then mention an ex.

Holy shit, Flynn said, "love."

"Seeing that picture of you and Jonah," Flynn continues, "it hurts. Because you get to go back to him. Live a life with him. All the work you and I have done together can help you create a stronger relationship with him, and selfishly, I hate that. I don't want Jonah to get what I have. To reap the benefits."

I let go of his hands, pushing myself off the blanket to walk a few feet away. I lean forward, taking a deep breath in and letting it out until I'm gasping for another breath.

"I'm not a project, Flynn." My voice cracks as I speak. "Who I am and who I become is because of the work I've done. You don't get to claim that, nor could Jonah."

I find a boulder to sit on, keeping the space between us but allowing my legs to rest.

"That's not . . . that's not what I meant," he whispers. I can barely hear him over the breeze that passes through. He doesn't stand up, though. He gives me my space.

I wipe my tears as I sort through his words. We're both just scared of the unknown. This feeling between us is grand and intoxicating. It's a comfort I fear I might not experience again. I have proof that my past self never valued a relationship after Jonah, so what happens to me now? I proved I didn't need anyone, but will I want someone?

"I don't want to go home and date Jonah, Flynn," I say, glancing toward him. He's wiping his eyes, sitting up a little straighter. "I want to be friends. I don't want a future where he isn't a part of my life. But I don't think any amount of healing on either of our ends will set us up to date. I think it'll just solidify our differences that we can have as friends but not as partners."

He reaches his hand out in the distance. Wincing, I stand up and make my way back to the blanket. He lays down, and I cuddle against him, resting my head on his chest as he holds me tight. We breathe in and out together.

"I am choosing to believe that you and I have a greater mission," I say. "Whether or not your mom was hoping it would happen, I think our brains, history, and connection open up doors for us that we need to take. Otium's plan isn't perfect, and it never will be." I lean up, looking down into his eyes. "I think we can make a pretty powerful team if we work together. I don't know what that means or how it looks with us being in two places, but it isn't impossible. It may break more rules. But the big question is, are we willing to take some risks in order to better humanity?"

His eyes search mine for a moment before a smile consumes his face. "Yes, I think I am," he breathes, reaching his hand up to comb through my sweaty curls.

The feeling of his fingertips nearly has my eyes rolling back into my head. A calm wave glides through my body. I hover over him before crashing my lips onto his. His fingers grip my curls, and I straddle him, cupping his cheeks in my palm, drawing him in.

Flynn's hands travel over my body, tugging, massaging, gripping wherever they can, frantic to be closer to me. He flips us in a swift motion, careful to place my head on the blanket. As my hand travels up underneath his shirt, goosebumps spread over his skin. He pulls away just slightly, a grin consuming him.

"Theo?" he breathes. I inhale slowly, the pressure of his chest weighing me down like a weighted blanket. "I love you."

His body sinks at my exhale as I pull his mouth back to my own, savoring his oxygen. A few salt tears mix between our kisses before I separate us just enough that he'll be able to feel my lips with each word.

"I love you too, Flynn."

His grin melds with mine, and we tangle ourselves up, itching to memorize every part of each other. Something aligned us to meet, and I don't give Andrya all the credit. In my timeline, I was meant to meet Flynn, for him to teach me about love and communication. For us to break up, planets apart, in order for me to build myself back up again, better and stronger.

We separate a few minutes later when our stomachs growl. We both groan before laughing and pushing ourselves up on the blanket to grab our respective lunches.

"Why did you bring me here?" I ask, taking a bite of my sandwich.

Flynn looks over, his mouth already full. He gives me a closed-mouth smile, brushing a few curls away from my face. When he swallows, he gives me his full attention, his fingers grazing my chin.

"I want this place to become something meaningful to me. It's way too stunning for me to keep using it for my problems. I thought maybe instead of running away in frustration, I could run away with you. Now, if I ever come back here, for whatever reason, I'll have this memory."

Tears cloud my vision, and I gaze down at the sandwich in my hand. Our separation starts to weigh on me. I'll have our memories in my mind, but Flynn gets to have places he can travel to; that we've been together. I don't get that on Earth. No one knows who Flynn is at home. If Flynn is sad about us and wants to talk, he has people, especially Mattis, who knows me well enough. I have to use the tools I'm learning here to heal myself of a heartbreak from a boy that doesn't exist in my timeline.

"Talk to me, Theo."

"I'm terrified to go back home. To lose you. To have to move on from you. I can't run off to someplace that reminds me of you." I look up at the sky, trying to keep the tears at bay.

"There will be places that remind you of me . . . there will be people you'll have. The reminder will be the greatest and worst thing we both experience. I wish I could explore some of Earth with you, but I think it'll be easier for you to move on without my memory haunting you." He pauses momentarily. "Theo, you've been to all my favorite places; if I let the heartbreak consume me, I'll need to find new places."

I glance over at him, and his thumbs come forward, brushing beneath my eyes. There's a part of me that loves how much I may haunt him here. I don't want either of us in pain, but if he is, it just means that I made as much of an impact as he has.

"I believe people come into our lives for a reason," Flynn says softly. "And just because they have to leave, it doesn't mean that their purpose wasn't significant. You and I are both going to be better than we were before we met. You and I are going to come up with a kick-ass plan for you to return to Earth with. And if it's meant to be, you and I will meet up again, someday in the future, and reminisce about our adventures. Maybe we have families, maybe we don't, maybe we never see each other again. But we've made an impact on one another that'll, in turn, create a butterfly effect. That I'm confident of."

I lean forward, giving him a quick kiss before I breathe through a sob that's trying to escape. I try to focus on the sky turning deeper violet as we rotate around vita. I haven't spent nearly enough time admiring the calmness this sky can bring.

My brain starts to map out plans as we finish our sandwiches in silence. At the end of the Otium Initiative, every mentee has a meeting with their mentor and Andrya to map out their plans for what they want to accomplish on Earth. My plans can be more personal, but with all the information I have now, I don't want them to just be about healing myself. Yes, it is going to be extremely difficult to create a space for the new version of me, and even harder to not fall back into my bad habits or fall into the heartbreak and grief, but I think a solid plan focusing on how to get back to Otium will give me the drive and motivation I need.

As Flynn and I stumble off the trail in the late afternoon, walking toward the train station, the thought hits me like a chaotic burst of energy.

"What if I create an Otium Initiative on Earth?" Excitement courses through my bloodstream, firing up my nerve-endings just at the single thought, but Flynn's furrowed brows and immediate halt in his step start to simmer it.

"Like before you can speak about Otium, or do you mean, trying to get it started for when you can talk about it?" he asks, using his forearm to wipe the sweat from his face. We are in desperate need of showers. I thought the day I biked my ass off to the cave was the grossest I could be. The only benefit of today is that I dressed appropriately. But it doesn't stop the clothing from trying to absorb into my skin.

"I don't know. I mean, if I can talk about Otium in five years, I likely can't get everything situated by then, anyway. But regardless of the planet's information, what if I can create a series of workshops similar to here? Maybe I can get some counselors and therapists to help, too? My parents' agency works with some therapists already. And we already get donations and funding. What if I can create an affordable program—maybe even free, so no one gets left behind—that helps my community grow and evolve, so when it is time to step foot onto Otium, they are already sufficient?" I say. The thoughts scatter through my head a mile a minute. I can barely focus on one before another idea shoots forward. This is honestly brilliant.

"Wait, wait!" I jump up and down for a second, grasping Flynn's shoulders, shaking them forward and back. I break through his seriousness, and he lets out a laugh.

Flynn shakes his body out, runs his hands over his face, and centers himself in front of me, bouncing left to right. I follow his rhythm, grinning as the energy has space to flow out of its clustered ball.

"I apologize," he pants. "You caught me off guard." He massages his scalp and gives me a goofy grin that does wonders to the flutters in my stomach. "Our Greater Mission is now activated in my mind. You're speaking with Flynn the Risk Taker; how may I be of service?" His tone sounds like Jarvis from Marvel, and I can't help the giggle that escapes my lips.

"What if I can create a program good enough that all the people who go through my program only have to learn about Planet Otium when they time travel? They can bypass the workshops here that are lined up for them. This could bring more people over faster. Right?" I'm strictly running on adrenaline.

Flynn slows his bounce, nodding his head. He focuses behind me, his eyes circling in their sockets, no doubt running through options.

"That's an interesting thought," Flynn says, but his enthusiasm doesn't match my own.

I bounce a little harder, trying to maintain my enthusiasm. "This plan could work. Well, if it's established. It needs a lot of effort, but I think it would be cool if we could work on it together. What if we spent the next few weeks creating these plans? Something that quite literally works off the initiative itself? It doesn't have to be mentioned in my plan with your mom yet. That can be something brought up years down the line if it's sufficient, but it's a plan that even if it fails, I still impact a large number of people. Because if I can get it to work in my town, and then region, maybe I can also expand it further. I already have resources within my parents' agency. I'll have Sam and Ellie on my side, who have more experience in this business. When I left Earth, I had quite a following on social media that I could work in my benefit. . . . What do you say? Will you try and work through this with me?"

Flynn's hands cup my cheeks, steadying my body. A smile slowly breaks out wide enough that his eyes crinkle. "I think that I'm in love with a really brilliant person."

I rush forward, connecting our lips. He separates us after a breath, and my adrenaline starts to fade.

"With that said," he continues, "if you want this to work, in a way that could potentially bypass the initiative here, we have to work really hard to get this plan solid. There are things that I can do here to help further the plan, but you will be in charge of most of the groundwork. If we solidify it here, as much as possible, you can actually take information from the initiative."

"Look at you breaking more rules." I grin, embracing him. His head rests on top of mine, and we breathe in deep, syncing ourselves together.

WE DECIDED THAT IF WE WERE GOING TO BE WORKING around the clock to create this plan, we needed to rest tonight, and we'd start tomorrow. We couldn't use much of the initiative time because I still had the program to complete. However, we could take notes from the rest of my lessons, I could learn more about the other mentees' experiences, and then our nights would be dedicated to this plan.

On our way back to the apartments, we stop at communal dining and shove pasta down our throats before we head home. The battle between renewed energy and physical burn-out is more extreme than I've ever experienced.

"Want to watch some Marvel?" Flynn asks as he opens the apartment building door.

"I'm happy to try, but I need a shower first." My body is itching to peel these sweaty clothes off of me. If I didn't have the new idea focusing my mind, I would have stripped everything ages ago.

"Me too." He yanks my hand to a stop at the staircase landing, where we would make our separate ways. He takes a few steps forward, and I lean back against the wall; a shiver runs down my spine as my thoughts freeze. Flynn presses a gentle kiss to my forehead. "Would you want to join me?" he whispers.

I inhale, squeezing our still-interlaced hand. My heart accelerates when his lips hover over my own, our oxygen blending. His free hand trails up my arm, over the crevice of my collarbone, and grasps my curls at the base of my neck. He ignites my nerves, a tingling sensation under each touch.

"Y-yes," I breathe, connecting our lips.

We fumble our way upstairs, taking mini-breaks, alternating pressing each other up against the wall. Behind closed doors, we peel our clothes off, heading toward the shower, both breathing heavily, gasping and gripping onto skin as we try to keep our lips locked.

We're in the shower before the water turns on, Flynn's chest pinned against mine, his knee between my legs. The cool clay wall is a welcomed surprise, balancing my over-heated state. One of Flynn's hands reaches in the distance as his mouth nips and kisses my neck. I let out a soft moan, arching toward him. Water suddenly hits us, freezing cold, causing us both to yelp and jump apart. The water warms, but we stand on either end of the small cubicle. We're both panting, eyes searching one another, as the space between us diminishes the moment.

I don't know what I was doing or what I was about to just agree to, but the memory of Jonah and me in the shower hits me like a tidal wave, and I sink to the floor, letting the water hit my head and drip down my body.

"I'm sorry." Flynn rushes over, sitting beside me. He taps a button on the wall, and similar to my own shower, lavender and eucalyptus filter in.

I breathe in the calm, leaning my head on Flynn's shoulder. "You don't need to apologize. I wanted . . . want . . . "

Flynn grabs my hand, rubbing his thumb back and forth on my palm.

"I've never had sex before," I whisper, and Flynn's head rests on mine.

"We don't need to. We shouldn't anyway," Flynn says slowly. He brings our hands up to his chest, kissing them. "I would love to have that connection with you, Theo. But I really don't think it's smart. I got caught up in the moment, but—"

"But leaving will be too hard," I finish for him. I can't

have that experience with Flynn. My feelings are already too strong. The last thing I need is for him to hold that first memory of mine forever.

"Exactly," he exhales, lifting his head.

I look over at him, and I peck his lips. "I love you."

"I love you too, Theo." He kisses me one last time before lifting us both up. "Let's shower and watch Marvel?"

I smile, tugging him into a hug underneath the waterfall. My body screams at me to reignite what we had, to be irresponsible and go all the way, but as the shower starts to countdown to shut off, we both race to wash and rinse before stepping out into the cool air.

When we make it to the couch, I bury myself in Flynn's bigger sweats and nestle into his side. As the Marvel animation logo begins, my eyes drift off to sleep.

Thirty-Six

There are T - 4 days until I walk into a portal and return to Earth with the hopes that I will make it back to Otium at some point in the next thirty years. Flynn and I have worked tirelessly to develop a plan to get more people prepared for Otium without breaking *too* many rules. Our regular schedule remained intact, and our planning for the future fit into pockets of free time. Our Marvel marathon was pushed aside right before we started *Infinity War*. We have at least four more movies to watch to make sure we experience *End Game* together. I already told Flynn I wasn't entering a portal until we watched it.

We worked through my last bit of bias, talked through the anger that still settled deep in me, prepared conversations with those I love, broke through some fears of mine, and helped prepare me with more confidence. In therapy, I learned new techniques and skills to work through my anger, dug a little deeper into who I wanted to be, who I wanted to be for my parents, who I wanted to be as a brother, and whether or not they all aligned. Each session, especially as the end of the program neared, we tore my entire being apart before molding the pieces back together. Each night for weeks, I battled between exhaustion, wanting to give Flynn my entire attention, trying to create a plan for Earth, and just wanting to *be*. Some days, Flynn and I worked through plans until the middle of the night; other times, we fell asleep in each other's arms and started over again the next morning. Ever since we said "I love you," we haven't spent a night apart, and we've also made good on our promise to never go further.

My plan for Earth is pretty solid, and my meeting is scheduled for tomorrow morning with Andrya. Flynn recommends we meet at the volleyball match after his class to avoid me ripping the entire plan to shreds with my nerves. Today's volleyball match is supposed to be intense. Apparently, this has been a series of games, and tonight is the final one.

The rest of the mentees decide they are going to do the same after our last group therapy. The next two days consist of a series of tests on what we've learned, and we will have our individual meetings. Then we get two days to just explore Otium as we see fit. It's also in those two days that if we don't pass the program, we may have to stay behind. There's nothing I want more than to fail, but my tests are on my mental health and personal issues versus saving the world, and frankly, I don't want to fail those.

"What are your plans for going back to Earth?" I question Zhang and Amalia as we walk toward the gym where the game will be. We all briefly discussed how we were feeling about our plans in group, but we weren't asked to go into detail.

"I plan to create a system to get more people informed and aware," Zhang says. "I want people to be able to access information that isn't censored by the government. I was starting to do this back home and have a few people working with me who are awaiting my return. It's a grassroots production."

The three of us head toward the bar. The line is already pretty long as everyone finishes their day.

"I really want to work with high school students," Amalia chimes in as we wait. "I think I'm old enough for some authority, yet young enough to still remain cool. I travel a lot, but I want to go back home and work in my hometown. I plan to start getting into high schools, where I can host a workshop that discusses emotional, physical, mental, and spiritual health. I've been working with my mentor on it. I will then be able to travel to other high schools. My goal is to remain in France for a while."

"What about you?" Zhang asks.

I take a moment to decide how much I want to share. Flynn and I have it all mapped out on what I won't share with Andrya tomorrow, but if Zhang, Amalia, and I are all going to be on Earth, maybe we can team up somehow.

"Promise to keep it quiet until we get back to Earth?" I look between the two of them as we move up in line.

Amalia's eyes sparkle, and Zhang elbows her side gently. "Don't look so excited about a secret." Zhang laughs, then she looks over at me. "But yes, of course. Let's grab our food and get some privacy first?" she suggests.

I nod. I may not have spent as much time with them as I normally would have in this situation, but they have been supportive of my different program and have gone out of their way to include me.

"Can we stay in touch when we all get back?" Amalia asks.

"If you like my idea, yes, please." I grin, and then step up to order myself a pretzel and cider.

The two girls follow suit before we wait.

"I think there's an Otium network for past mentees so we can all coordinate together," Zhang offers. "It's likely for when we have to spread the word on Otium, but I think we're allowed to stay in touch. I heard that we all get packets to go home with, outlining everything we can and can't do?"

"We do. I think that's where all of our Earth contact information is, and then it'll have reminders from what we learned here," I say, grabbing my pretzel and cider. Flynn and I had discussed hiding the material I'll need in the back-pack I'm given for my journey home. It was the perfect setup to be able to take tangible materials from Otium to Earth.

Zhang and Amalia find a spot on the ground, and I grab us blankets and pillows. Once we're situated, Mattis and Flynn shout and wave over to us. They are waiting to grab their own orders at the bar. I glance over at Amalia, who waves back at Mattis. Her eyes are glossy, and she takes a gulp of her cider.

I reach over, placing my palm over her hand on the blanket, squeezing it a little. She smiles, blinking away some tears.

"We'll have each other back home. We're all just one message away," Zhang offers with a smile.

I've been so busy planning for my meeting with Andrya that it's been a nice distraction from thinking about leaving Flynn. But my heart has been heavy all morning, and I know it's going to take all the energy I have to push through and be present for the next few days.

"So, what is this plan of yours?" Amalia asks, forcing a smile.

I take a sip of my cider and sit up straight. "I am going to create the Otium Initiative on Earth. It may never make it out of New York, but I am going to create a program similar, with the hopes that the people who attend my program can immediately be let into this society without having to go through the initiative. I'm aiming for it to increase the number of people we can bring to Otium. I have some connections back home, and my parents have an agency that already raises money. So I'm hoping if I market it correctly, I may be able to get donations to offer the program for free."

Amalia's face lights up. "Wow. That's so cool. Maybe we can all try and team together when you get it established to bring it to our communities?"

"That'd be amazing!" I beam.

It may not be possible, but this program is all about hope. Hope that there may be a better future than so many have experienced. It'll only act as motivation for me to get my act together if I have the potential to get the program to Hong Kong and France.

All of a sudden, Flynn's arms wrap around my waist, his cider sloshing slightly in his cup. He presses a soft kiss on my neck, and I squirm into him with a laugh.

"Remy and Ryleigh are competing against each other today," Flynn says, nodding toward the court, but no one is up there yet. I had no idea either of them played. Though, I'm not big on sports. Otium didn't change that about me.

"Do you ever compete in any of these events?" I ask him, watching as the rest of the mentees set up blankets beside us. Zhang joins in a conversation with them as Amalia and Mattis whisper to one another.

"Nah," Flynn answers. "I prefer my solo hikes or bike rides or chasing my boyfriend through the Flatlands as he has a mental breakdown." He's smirking by the time he finishes talking, and I jab him in the stomach with my elbow.

"Jackass."

"You love me and my ass," he whispers in my ear. My arm hair stands at attention as a shiver passes through.

While I definitely felt jealous seeing Flynn with Remy at his sister's barbecue, I can now confirm that the jealousy doesn't exist, at least in a romantic fashion. I am completely jealous that Remy still gets to see Flynn whenever they want without light-years in-between them. And that Remy gets their best friend to cheer them on. I'd give so much to be able to have Flynn motivate me through this new journey.

"There has to be a way we can still see each other when I go back to Earth. You have a portal . . . right there." I point to Flynn's watch as we walk back to the apartment building.

The game may have gone on longer than I anticipated, and I may have had three ciders instead of my occasional one. But the conversations drifted to Earth, and with just one look shared between Amalia and me, we both had excused ourselves for another cider. And then another before Flynn and Mattis separated us.

I'm leaning against Flynn as we walk. The only problem with our entire plan is that we haven't figured out a way to communicate with one another. He has a set list of objectives, and so do I. He's convinced we don't need a connection to be able to make them happen, but I don't agree.

Flynn sighs. "It'll be too hard to coordinate our lives for the portal to work. You know time operates differently. It's the end of the twelfth month on Earth and the beginning of the eleventh here. Between us trying to accomplish our objectives and figuring out our timelines, it'll be too chaotic."

I stop walking for a moment. *The end of the twelfth month? Did I miss Christmas?* Not like I have a family I want to celebrate with. My aunt and uncle had taken my brothers with them to go visit my uncle's family last year. I had been "invited," but it wasn't a real invitation. Instead, Jonah's and Alejandro's families had made the holiday special for me. Alejandro had brought me into their Christmas Eve traditions, where they baked cookies and opened a few gifts. They had all their family over too. And then I slept over at Jonah's house on Christmas Eve and spent the holiday morning with him and some of his close relatives. It wasn't perfect, but I was kind of hoping it would become its own tradition.

"Have I missed Christmas?" I ask, trying to do the math in my head, but I'm only fooling myself. I haven't been able to keep track of the timeline this entire time. Flynn isn't wrong; if we can't have constant communication, I'd never remember when I needed to be back at the portal.

Flynn clasps our hands together as he looks at me. "Christmas is this Saturday for you. Is Christmas meaning-ful? Would you like to do something special? I apologize. It really didn't occur to me to celebrate the holidays. I kind of lost track of time."

"Do you celebrate holidays here?" I ask. "Will there be a Thanksgiving or Christmas in the next few months?" There's a sharp pain in my chest at the thought of these celebrations existing and not being able to celebrate with Flynn.

"We have our own holidays mixed in with Earth traditions. Some fall over the next few weeks when the Otium Initiative is shut down for a break. That's when schools will also be on break. We don't celebrate Thanksgiving because of the origin. We do have Otium Week, which is similar in a sense; it's all about being grateful we exist on this planet. It starts the day the first astronauts arrived here and falls in month six. But we have some people who still celebrate Christmas, Kwanzaa, and Chanukah. We have more mini-celebrations throughout the year because we are still so grateful to have been given this chance. Therefore, we make more time to celebrate the little things."

I smile at that. I imagine the little celebrations are about genuine time spent together versus a Hallmark holiday.

"For Christmas this Saturday, can we get tacos, non-alcoholic margaritas, and some peanut butter chocolate for dessert? And finish whatever Marvel we still need to?"

I discovered a couple weeks ago that the chocolate shop made peanut butter chocolate bites. They've become my downfall, solidifying that nothing on Earth would satisfy me as much as the food here.

Flynn wraps his arms around my neck, leaning his forehead against mine. "Absolutely. That sounds incredible."

I seal it with a kiss, swallowing the onset of emotions.

I can do this.

Thirty-Seven

Flynn failed to mention that I would be on my own for breakfast before my big meeting. He only let me know as we were falling asleep in my tipsy state. Apparently, before my meeting with Andrya, he has to meet with her and Corie. If I take a step back and see his role as a mentor, it makes sense. This is his job, and he is being evaluated as well. But it does royally suck trying to stomach food when I've never felt nerves this intense before. I'm confident I won't fail my tests, but for some reason, this feels like Doomsday. And I definitely didn't get a wink of sleep after Flynn dropped the bomb on me.

I'm a shaking, nervous wreck when I knock on Andrya's front door. Lana leads me to her office. Inside, Corie and Flynn are already sitting, electronic pads on their laps. I knew Corie had one, but it's weird thinking that Flynn had one this entire time, too. I'm not his boyfriend *or* his friend here. Whenever he had work to do in my presence, it was always his studies, never his initiative work. It made it easier to forget he was always evaluating me.

They both offer me warm smiles, but I'm glad I tossed

my food instead of eating. I'm certain it would cause me to hurl. Corie and Flynn are both in dress pants with collared button-up long sleeve shirts. Not a single piece of hair is misplaced in Corie's curls, and Flynn's hair is freshly cut and styled. Not long enough for my fingers to grasp anymore. I'm grateful I decided to wear my own nice jeans instead of just shorts. Flynn might be on my side, and he's my advocate, but we are not a team in this office.

Andrya stands behind her desk in a sleek maroon power suit. Her devices project in front of her, but with a solid back, so I can't see anything.

"Good morning, Theodore. It's lovely to see you again," Andrya greets, and my smile is weak.

Flynn and Corie are seated in the corner. Another chair was brought in for me on the other side of the room. Once I'm seated, Lana excuses herself from the room.

My heart pounds in my ears. I wipe my sweaty palms on my jeans, trying to calm myself. I'm already starting off with limited lung capacity. I don't know why I'm so nervous. The worst thing that happens is I'm shipped back to Earth. She can't touch me there.

But she can forbid you from coming back.

All of the files and research we've broken into flash through my mind. The memory of meeting my family, knowing their names, seeing my photos, learning my story. My stomach gurgles, and I grip the sides of the chair. I glance over at Flynn, and he looks like a ghost. I feel similar as the blood drains from my face and my blood sugar plummets.

I hope nothing has come out about what we know so far, but I hate that I put him in this position.

"Alright," Andrya starts, and I jump. "Theodore, you can relax. This is a happy meeting. No need to fret."

I nod and force a smile, but it's all happening so fast and too soon. There are plenty of reasons to fret. I want to leave this room, but I don't want to leave Otium.

"Let's start with the basics. You will go back through the portal this Sunday, and the portal will bring you to the hospital where you and Lana last entered. Lana will already be there on the other side, waiting for you. She will direct you out of the hospital, and Sam and Ellie will be there to pick you up."

Right. Cool. We are starting off real slow. Nothing like an immediate forced interaction with them.

"You will be staying with Sam and Ellie for the foreseeable future. They've arranged an agreement with your aunt and uncle. When you turn eighteen, you then get to decide where you live."

I inhale for four seconds, pause, and exhale for four seconds.

"Now," Andrya continues, "I want to tell you how proud I am of you." I swallow the bile that rises. I don't need her praise. "I know we met each other under tough circumstances, and I know you aren't happy with me, but I do hope you've come to peace with your time here. You've exceeded all of my expectations. I have no doubt that you have an incredible plan to tell me about. Corie and Flynn are both very impressed with what you've accomplished as well."

I glance over at both of them. Corie grins, and Flynn smiles, but it isn't my smile. It's the professional smile he gave me the day we met. I only want his praise. No one else's opinion matters.

"When you leave Otium, you will be given a backpack filled with materials to aid you in your journey back on Earth," Andrya continues. "It'll have the contact information of your fellow mentees as well as a link to the social media app we've created to connect all of the mentees. We will notify you through that when it is time to start introducing Otium to your community. When we notify you, we'll be in constant contact with specific instructions on how to implement the information. Tomorrow, on your last day of testing, you will be required to swear and sign that you will not speak of Otium until we give notice. You will only be allowed to discuss this trip with Sam and Ellie. If we get word that you have spoken to any other person before the time, then you may not be allowed to rejoin Otium. Do you understand?"

I gulp, swallowing the definite vomit pushing its way up my esophagus. Flynn warned me a few times throughout our planning that I could not tell Jonah or Alejandro under any circumstances. But he never mentioned that I might not make it back here because of it. That I'd have to *swear* on it. I twist my fingers tight in front of me to avoid looking at him.

"You will be assigned a therapist on Earth who will also know about Otium. You may speak with this therapist about the planet; it's a secure line. These sessions will be conducted through video chat, as this therapist counsels multiple mentees throughout the world.

"Every two years, you will be in contact with me. You will receive notice through the app on when we will talk. This is the time to bring up any concerns you may have and to let me know how your plan is being implemented. Other than that time, you will not have contact with Otium." Andrya's eyes dart over to Flynn and then back to me.

I force a swallow at the lump in my throat. Inhaling, I hold for six, pause for six, and exhale for six. My shirt is attached to my sweaty pit. I blink a few times, trying to keep the room from closing in.

"You will come back to Otium in thirty years after we have secured everyone we can from Earth. You will time travel to this timeline."

I figured that the mentees would be the last to travel back. It makes sense as much as I hate the idea. But that wasn't disclosed to me. What happens if the plan doesn't work and some of the mentees don't make it back? What if I spend thirty years making sure everyone else has a safe future, and I get left in the dust?

I want to get up and run. Maybe get lost on this planet and start fresh. Break the phone with my tracking device. But my legs are definitely jello, and if I stand, I'll either pass out or vomit.

"If any unforeseen changes do happen, you will be notified. Now, you may present your project whenever you're ready." Andrya smiles as if everything is bright in the world, and this is the most successful meeting she's ever had. Her world is fucking bright on her throne of this planet. It doesn't really matter to her life if I succeed or fail. It only matters to mine.

I don't think I can speak. My jaw is tight, and the thought of opening my mouth feels like a signal for my body to betray me. It should be easy to tell her my plan. It's in my head, memorized down to every comma and period. But this is just for show. She already knows my plan; I had to send her a digital copy. It's likely something she discussed with Flynn and Corie this morning.

The room starts to speckle as sweat rims my eyebrows. I know if I sit up, my shirt is soaked to my back. The pounding in my ears increases, and my body begins to sway.

Cool, clammy hands cup my face, gently maneuvering me forward, resting my head between my legs. I gasp as my oxygen is restricted. I can't see; my world is black. My ribcage expands and deflates in rapid succession against my thighs.

"Theo, I'm right here," Flynn's whisper travels through my heartbeat and clogged ears. "Theo, follow my voice."

His fingertips massage my scalp as he works his way to the base of my neck, massaging the tight muscles. My vision comes and goes until my body starts to cool.

"Theo, you're okay," he breathes.

Light trickles back in, and I focus on my breathing. I still want to run, escape from this. As my breathing starts to regulate, Flynn lifts my head slowly and with control until we are at eye level. I can't face Andrya now. It's been weeks since my last attack.

"Hey," he whispers. His eyes are warm and a little glossy. "Let's get some air." Flynn doesn't wait for permission; he just lifts me up by my sweaty pits, wrapping one of my arms around his shoulders.

I close my eyes, regaining equilibrium.

"Flynn, what are you doing?" I hear Andrya ask.

"We are done here. You've already approved Theo's plan. I'll take it from here."

My eyes dart open, and Flynn starts to walk us to the door.

"Flynn," Andrya's tone has shivers running down my spine.

"Thank you. You have given my mentee all the important information. Your job is now complete," Flynn says.

I don't know where his confidence came from with his ghostly features before, but he leads me out to the fresh air, where I proceed to fall to my knees and empty the contents of my stomach in her wildflowers. Flynn brushes my hair away with one hand and traces soothing circles on my sweaty back with the other.

After a few minutes, I sit back and lean into Flynn's solid frame. My body shakes. Likely for a variety of reasons. I know there isn't anything left to throw up as I haven't eaten in hours, but the walk back to the apartment sounds like a nightmare. Really, anything other than climbing into bed and succumbing to the darkness sounds awful.

"Let me carry you. Get on my back," Flynn says, squatting next to me.

He lifts me with ease, and I rest my head on his shoulder, closing my eyes.

I'm a zombie as I go through the motions of showering and redressing. We function in silence; the only words spoken were Flynn telling me he wasn't going to leave me alone. While the silence is heavy, it beats trying to put into words how I'm feeling. I need to start processing the next steps and coming to terms with my new life. The finality of possibly never seeing this place again. But at the moment, in order to get through my days of testing, I need to put one foot in front of the other and keep my head down.

Thirty-Eight

My two days of testing were the longest, most grueling, and fastest days of my life. Flynn calmed my nerves after the first day of testing, letting me know that he squared away everything with his mom. He explained my panic attack had to do with me heading back to Earth and the uncertainty of it all. He told her that I was anxious to see Sam and Ellie and felt so much pressure from my created project that I felt like I might fail.

Flynn isn't lying. I do feel all of that, and I'm grateful I bypassed my speech, but it also isn't comforting that it was my excuse. I think some of my panic stemmed from Sam and Ellie, but a majority had to do with all the lies I was keeping from Andrya, what I had dragged Flynn through, and knowing that my project was only half-true.

Andrya only thinks that I want to further my work with the agency, focusing on children in foster homes who can't go to Otium unless they have a family present. I'll never know if she knows that I met my family here to get that idea, but it doesn't matter. Flynn will be walking me to the portal, and I won't have to see Andrya until our two-year meeting. Which was news to me *and* Flynn.

After my first day of testing, Corie came by to check in and see if I needed one last therapy appointment. I declined her offer, thanked her for everything, but wished her the best.

Now, the hours are nearing to close out Saturday, and Flynn and I are gripping onto every minute we have. We're finishing our Marvel experience with *Spider-Man: Far From Home.* The last movie in phase three. It kills me to see the next few phases of Marvel on the app, but I haven't experienced them on Earth yet, and if I am really going to be living with Sam and Ellie, watching those movies in real-time with them feels important. Flynn can carry on this experience with someone else, even if my heart starts to break at the thought.

His promise rang true, and before we started our Marvel marathon, we traveled to the Valley one last time. We grabbed tacos and non-alcoholic margaritas, and to soothe my emotions, we even picked up my favorite peanut butter chocolates.

As the movie ends, the two of us are cuddled tight on the couch, watching the credits pass as if it's the most interesting part of the movie. Each minute is sacred.

"Oh my god!" Flynn exclaims as he watches the end credit.

I chuckle against him, knowing my reaction to it as well. When it finishes, I shut the projection off. A silence overcomes us. Usually, this is when we would talk about Marvel theories, and I'd hint at what is to come. But I don't know what's to come in anything at the moment. We can discuss future movie theories, but thirty years is a long time away to then talk about whether or not we got them correct.

Maybe there's a future where we reconnect. Maybe we can watch Marvel all over again. Maybe if Sam and Ellie make it here, he can watch it with his great-grandparents. Or maybe, worst-case scenario, there is a future where the two of us end tomorrow. Just a moment in time, a blip in the universe.

"I can't keep you a secret," I whisper. Too much silence has passed; my ears have started to ring.

His body shifts to look at me; his face straight. "You have to. You heard my mom. You could risk not being able to come back. It's not worth it."

I trace my fingers down his cheek, smiling as he shivers. "Flynn, walking through the portal tomorrow is going to break me. This," I gesture between us, "is going to break me. You have friends here that know me. I won't have anyone."

"You have Sam and Ellie," he rushes out, and I lift my brow.

"Yes, but would you want to talk to your aunt and uncle or your parents about your heartbreak?"

He shakes his head, pulling my hands toward him, burying them against his chest. "I'm scared," he admits. His eyes gloss over.

"Me too." I squeeze our hands. "But I need Alejandro and Jonah on my side. I need to tell them about this and about you."

He tightens his grip, head down. "They aren't going to understand."

"Flynn," I breathe, "put yourself in my shoes. I am being asked to go back to Earth to make these massive changes for a new outcome. Without even the guarantee that I'll be back. I am going to need all the help I can possibly get. I need people on my side who aren't a part of the Otium Initiative. So I have to tell people I trust. I need those people I love to be on my side when I start to make some strange decisions in my life. I am going to need people to help keep me focused when our love crushes me. I cannot, and absolutely will not, lose my people in order to help the greater good. If I lose them on my account, that's fine. That's my fault. But if I lose them on account of Otium and their rules, that won't be okay."

He sighs and nods. "But what if you scare them away?"

I hold back a smile as I defeat him. This isn't the time for a victory dance. This isn't him agreeing with me.

"That's a risk I need to take." I sit cross-legged, leaning toward him. "If I'm going to be better at being honest, I cannot lie to my best friends. If they walk away from me, at least I can say I was honest."

His lips twitch at that. All his hard work is coming to fruition.

I end the conversation with a kiss. His lips devour mine, sitting up and pressing me forward, into the couch. We spend the next few hours kissing, touching, embracing, trying to memorize every portion of each other.

And when the vitalight starts to shine through the window, we cry ourselves into a restless sleep.

Thirty-Nine

Flynn and I walk to the portal instead of taking bikes, so we can hold hands and let the time draw out a little longer. His grip is tight, and it only gets stronger the closer we get. There isn't a specific time I need to jump through the portal, but it does need to be within the next hour.

We slept for as long as we could, clutching onto each other for dear life, knowing the inevitable was soon. We both chose not to grab any food. I'm not certain anything would stay down, anyway. The last thing I needed was a reminder of how delicious chai lattes were here. I have a feeling I'll be needing a comfort drink to soothe some heartbreak on Earth and I'd like not to hate it.

A cool breeze brushes across my bare arms. It's just getting cool enough here for maybe a long-sleeve shirt, for a portion of the day, that is. The vita is high in the sky, burning bright as we walk. I'll miss the violet skies and stunning rainbow of wildflowers through these fields. Out of all the times we traveled to the Valley, it still doesn't feel like enough.

"I wish I could jump in the time portal with you. Live

with you, Sam, and Ellie. Experience Earth and then come back with you," Flynn says.

I suck in a breath at his words. He's spent so much time telling me it isn't possible. I can't fight it anymore, though. He's made the decision, whether or not I agree, that neither of us can cross through the portal until our designated time.

And after signing the dotted line and swearing away my life, I'm already going to be challenging Andrya's word by talking to Jonah and Alejandro. I can't risk too much more.

I wrap my arms around his waist, closing the space between us. As I rest my head on his shoulder, he envelops me in his arms.

"I wish it wasn't this hard. I just started loving you. I'm not ready to stop," I whisper, trying to swallow a sob. I need to make it back to Earth before I collapse. But our sleepless night and my emotional state are not a good recipe.

"I know," he whispers. His fingertips glide through my hair, massaging my scalp. A tingling sensation courses through my bloodstream, calming me from head to toe. "But we both have to kick-ass with the motivation that, in the future, if it's meant to be, our paths will cross once again."

I give him a meek smile as some tears trickle down my cheeks. I've been hoping for a lot lately. Our potential reunion almost seems too good to be true and potentially too damaging to hope for if I need to heal.

Flynn pulls away first; my tears have soaked his shirt. I know I'm supposed to be on top of the world, and I'm this new, incredible person, or so they say. But fuck, if it isn't hard to walk away from one of the most extraordinary experiences that has ever happened to me.

Flynn places his hands on my cheeks, lifting my face up slightly to meet his gaze. "Go see Jonah. Go be his best friend again. Show him what you've learned and mend that friendship. Then start to conquer the world, okay?"

He's so genuine and sincere. His smile glistens from his tears. But now I see the difference in him. The difference for him. We may love each other. We may have seen the most intimate parts of ourselves. He may be broken-hearted from this goodbye, but he also recognizes his accomplishments. His job. His proof that he can be a mentor. He has to be the bigger person here because I'm barely holding myself up.

I fall back into his arms. I need to memorize the way my head nestles in the nook of his neck, his head gently laying on mine.

"Thank you," I whisper. "Thank you for being the best mentor anyone could ask for. Thank you for calling out my shit. Thank you for helping me become better."

"Thank you for loving me," he murmurs in my ear.

A sob rips through my throat at his words, and I clench my eyes shut. His arms tighten around me, holding my head against his chest as I shake.

"Things won't be easy going home," he says. "This isn't a cure-all place. You will have down days—remember, though, that it is all within you. It was always within you, Theo. You just need to tap into it. Try not to run from what scares you, but instead, jump ahead full force. I've seen you do it. Go make me proud."

I laugh. Spit and tears betray me as they hit his shirt. I wipe my face free of snot with the back of my hand. We both know I don't jump well into fear.

He lifts my chin so he's looking directly into my eyes. "I love you, Theodore Montgomery."

"I love you, too, Flynn Thomas."

I stand on my tippy toes and connect our lips in a snotty

last kiss. His palms force the back of my head closer to him, and his lips remain stagnant in an intense peck. We don't kiss passionately or erratically. There isn't any tongue. Just the commitment of our mouths on each other, frozen one last time.

As we break away, I take a few steps back. If I don't, I won't ever leave. In a blink, he opens the portal. Just as I'm about to step through, he reaches his hand out for one last squeeze. Our eyes connect, and I hope, beg, plead to whoever may be listening that this isn't the last time I ever see him.

Forty

Sam and Ellie respect my space as my brain tries to compute what's happening. They tried to talk to me on the car ride home, but I began to shut down as we traveled through snowy streets and neighborhoods with Christmas decorations. I didn't prepare myself well enough for this moment. Hell, I didn't even prepare for winter.

I had envisioned either falling into their arms when I first saw them or being reserved, but at least speaking. Turns out I can't find my words. I lost them the moment I fell through the portal and collapsed in the hospital, sobbing in a fetal position.

When we step into their one-story, three-bedroom, two-bath home, they introduce me to Rosalyn. I still can't find my words. All I can do is sink into their couch, hold their eight-month-old baby, and cry. Rosalyn smiles and giggles through my tears, squirming to try and move around. She has Flynn's eyes, a gut-wrenching reminder of what I've lost.

I try reframing the words in my head, trying to absorb

Rosalyn's happiness. I lost Flynn, but I'm supposed to gain so much more here.

When Rosalyn, or Rosie as they call her, falls asleep in my arms, Sam and Ellie show me my new bedroom.

I have the bedroom on the opposite end of the house from theirs and Rosie's. It seems like the master room as I get an attached bathroom. It's way too much. Though, it'll offer me some semblance of privacy. They even managed to pack up my old room and set everything up almost perfectly.

I manage to find enough words to ask for privacy, and I close the bedroom door behind me. I worked through re-establishing my presence on Earth with Corie and Flynn. We had scenarios that we role-played through. But I never considered that I was taking advice from people who have never left their planet. I never considered the true shock I'd experience going home.

The air is thick, like I can feel the pollution caking my skin. Even though there's crisp white snow, an unpleasant fragrance takes over Creston. One I hope is either temporary or one I get used to. I didn't even realize how strange it would be to sit in a moving vehicle after three months. I don't even want to imagine trying to drive anytime soon.

But the most crushing feeling is still being able to taste and smell Flynn on me, still feel his hand on my own, feel the way his chest rose and fell as he held me. I don't have photographs to remember us, though. Or any videos or voicemails to replay his voice and his laughter. He may just become a figment. A love I might be able to convince myself I dreamed of.

I make it over to the bed before I lose my balance in my new reality. Laying down, I grab my phone that's charging on the bedside table. When I turn it on, I'm bombarded with notifications. My phone tells me I have 99+ for all texts, social media notifications, and emails.

As tension creeps up into my shoulders, my breathing at least settles into familiarity.

I click through my social media accounts. I have nearly eight million followers. I left Otium at just close to five million. Not a single person left my side. Instead, my goodbye video blew up, and after clicking on a few posts, it looks like so many of my videos have been shared. Alejandro even posted a few compilation videos from the protests on my page. I want to watch them to re-experience that life, but I'm terrified it'll suck me into the deep end before I can establish new roots.

Instead, I search for the one video I've been petrified to see. I click on it; the cover photo is my arm wound back. My lungs constrict as I hit play. As if on autopilot at the verdict, I jump over the rope and confront the police officers. I'm shouting something incoherent as the crowd is rowdy behind me. I swing not once, but three times before I'm yanked away by another police officer, and my body collapses. The video shows Alejandro and Jonah screaming, but it also catches Sam collecting my passed-out body from the officer as EMTs arrive. The video cuts off. The internet has different versions of the video. I'm at different angles, and the lengths of the videos vary, but I click off the page. One is enough.

Alejandro and Jonah both replied to my last text messages to them, both wishing me the best and telling me they loved me. Early this morning, messages came through telling me how proud they both were that I completed grief counseling and to let them know if or when I was interested in seeing them.

Instead of answering, I put my phone back on the side

table. As I'm about to curl underneath the sheets, I catch sight of the backpack from Otium. The only piece of evidence I have proving it was all real.

I grab the bag before climbing back into bed. The Otium Initiative folder that I was promised is in there, as well as the packets of information Flynn and I prepared for my Earth Initiative. Tears brim my eyes. It was all real. Just as I'm about to toss the bag on the floor, I see a rectangular package. It's wrapped in simple brown paper with just a heart written on it. I breathe in through a sob that threatens. Unwrapping the gift and lifting open the box, I'm greeted by a picture of Flynn and me. Mattis took it the night of the volleyball game. I'm sitting between Flynn's legs, back against his chest. Our hands are interlocked on my stomach. The light in my eyes surpasses any single happiness I had in my last future.

I lift the photo, and beneath it is a vertical bar necklace with the word "Ubuntu" engraved into it. The cardboard it's attached to has a definition.

Ubuntu

(n) the belief that we are defined by our
compassion and kindness towards others.
"I am because we are"

My fingertips graze the necklace as tears stream down my cheeks. I immediately take it off the cardboard, clasping it around my neck. I then toss the backpack off my bed and clutch the photo of Flynn and me. I curl underneath the blankets and fall asleep, stroking the necklace. A part of him will always be with me.

THE SHRIEKS OF GIGGLES WAKE ME UP IN AN INSTANT. Rolling over, I rub my eyes and check the time. It's the following day, just after eleven in the morning. It must be cloudy, as my room is still dark with the curtains open.

Suddenly, I hear Jonah's voice coo, and Alejandro makes some weird, deep voice. Another shrill of laughter comes.

What in the world?

I have a text from Jonah that was sent a couple hours ago.

Jonah: *Hey, you. Sam and Ellie asked if Alejandro and I could come over. I know it isn't approved by you and I don't want to overstep your boundaries. So if you see this and aren't ready to see me, please let me know and I'll leave.*

My heart warms as an onset of tears overwhelms me. I definitely need more sleep, but no matter how hard I try, I won't be able to avoid everyone. It's better to choose to rip the bandaid off than to be forced to.

I'm grateful to have the bathroom attached, though, so I have a moment to freshen up. Time travel doesn't suit my appearance well. I text Jonah that I'll be out soon, just in case he's ready to leave. Once sent, I climb out of bed, catching sight of the photograph falling off me. I forgot. I reach for the necklace, grasping it as a flood of emotions rushes through me.

One foot in front of the other.

I put the photograph on my nightstand before allowing myself a mini-breakdown in the shower. I get dressed in my favorite yellow and blue checkered flannel and my comfortable dark blue jeans. As I ruffle some hair product through my curls, I stare at my reflection. I remind myself that the people outside of my door love me, want the best for me, and hopefully, can't wait to see me.

They will accept the new me. What they may not accept is my fresh, tanned skin, in the middle of a New York winter when, you know, I was supposed to be in a dingy hospital psych ward.

Though, it's a nice reminder of my time. I barely noticed on Otium. I always tan in the summer, so when I started to tan, it all became relative to my location. Now that I'm not stark white, it'll instantly confuse Jonah and Alejandro. Maybe a step in the direction of them believing I went to another planet.

As I open the bedroom door, Rosie's giggles fill the silence as Sam, Ellie, Alejandro, and Jonah all lock eyes with me. Like I thought, Alee and Jonah share a confused look, but it brings a smile to my face.

"Hi," I greet with a weird, awkward wave.

How do you greet your best friends after a secret, life-changing experience?

Alejandro runs toward me, enveloping me in a hug. "It's so good to see you. You look so good. Did they have a tanning salon in the hospital too? Is it some new self-care practice?"

I chuckle, and I hear Sam and Ellie laugh. They understand. I wonder if they had to sign a waiver that said they wouldn't speak of Otium too.

"Not exactly," I say as we part.

I cross into the living room, and Rosie crawls toward me, handing me some squishy giraffe. It's bizarre to see her as a baby here, identical to the pictures from Otium. She can't even walk yet, and her future is already so bright.

I lift Rosie, and she squeals as I hug her tight. "Hey,

little girl." Her crystal eyes cloud my own. She watches me intently as if, on some level, she understands who I am. "You and I are going to have some pretty cool adventures. I'm going to be the best uncle I possibly can be. We'll kick some ass and change the world together, okay?" She grabs at my chin, and I kiss her little fist. "Oh, and we're going to talk about how you cannot just give away first edition comic books without letting someone know they need to be properly stored."

"Wait, what?" Sam chuckles and his eyes dart over to their bookshelf.

I remind myself to check over there for the comics. Another reminder of Flynn. He was right; I'll find him around me.

"Are you talking about Spider-Man and Captain America?" Sam asks.

I smile over at them and nod. "I'll explain another day." I look back down at Rosie. "But Rosie needs to know it's never too early to learn proper Marvel etiquette."

Ellie rolls her eyes, but she and Sam look at me like they understand I know something they don't. It will likely be a strange transition with them, but even if Alejandro and Jonah don't believe me, I'll be able to connect with my new family over Otium. Today, and for the rest of our lives.

I set Rosie down on the ground, and she crawls over to Alejandro, who wiggles his fingers at her, and she squeals again.

I look over at Jonah, and he stands, opening his arms for me.

"Hey," I whisper as I pull him into an embrace. We don't fit together like Flynn and I did. We aren't each other's missing puzzle pieces. But he smells of cinnamon and bacon, and I inhale his familiarity. "We have a lot to talk about."

"I know," he whispers back. "But we have plenty of time. I'm just happy you're home." Jonah kisses my cheek before he pulls away, creating a distance that I think will forever remain. My heart doesn't shatter at the thought, and no tears brim, nor did his lips elicit shivers down my spine.

I sit back on the living room carpet, looking over at the five most important people in my life in *this* timeline. Eventually, I'll have to reunite with my brothers, form a new relationship with them, and hopefully get them to work with me. But for now, I like my small cluster. We've never all been together like this before, no doubt a new ripple in the timeline, but I'm confident it's for the better.

"So, I have some news," I start.

Sam and Ellie glance at one another but thankfully don't disrupt. Jonah and Alee look nervous, sitting up straight at my words.

"I have a new plan to help save humanity."

Jonah's face drops as if weeks of his anticipated hope in me diminishes. "Theo, don't you think you should take a break?"

I shake my head. "Trust me, Jonah." I look over at Sam and Ellie one last time. Two small nods give me all the confidence I need. "You all are going to want to listen to this incredible, unbelievable story I have to tell you both."

Author Note

Holy smokes. I made it.

In my career, I feel like there will be books I write, and then there will be books I *write*. The ones that take every fragment of my being, consume my mind, stress me out beyond belief, and have my heart in a death grip.

Theodore's Work in Progress is one of those books. It started as a thesis novel for my MFA at Southern New Hampshire University. The original plot of this book is entirely different from what is published on these pages. But the chaos I've gone through while writing this . . . spoiler: there is no world without chaos.

I started this book pre-pandemic and am writing this on the 3rd anniversary of the pandemic.

Oscar Wilde said, "Life imitates Art far more than Art imitates Life."

I didn't find that particularly true for this book when I first started it, and then 2020 hit, and I felt myself racing the clock to get this novel out. If you've read the novel, you know that nothing is specific to what has happened in the past few years. I purposely kept dates out for a reason, but the realities of certain situations are realistic and/or have happened in some form.

We only have one Earth. We may not ever see a future planet where we can escape.

I urge you to be kind, compassionate, and loving. Life has been hard. Harder for others than some. Sometimes it feels like we can't catch a break. But we can do something to change our outlooks. We can choose the foot we put forward each day.

While we can't all be protesting, we can all be making small changes that result in butterfly effects on a greater scale.

Don't wait for the world around you to change. Create your own opportunities to change the world that surrounds you.

Acknowledgments

A book can take a village to write, edit, and publish. Some books more than others.

First and foremost, **Brittany**, this book wouldn't be complete without your invaluable suggestions during beta reading. This cover wouldn't be so breathtaking without your incredible graphic design skills. I'm thrilled I got to work with you on this book, and your services have been incredible. I can never repay you. I'm also so grateful that I get to call you one of my closest friends.

Kevin, thank you for believing in me and my dreams. Thank you for giving me the opportunity to write and edit full time. This book would likely be left in a Google Doc to age if I couldn't work full-time on it. This took every ounce of energy I had some days.

Michelle, thank you for beta reading for me and always being my soundboard. You don't always know what I'm talking about, but you respond with enthusiasm and pretend you do.

Michelle and Caitlyn, thank you for being two-thirds of the Babbling Bookies. Thank you for being readers of mine. And thank you for always being excited when I told you I finally finished this book—no matter how many times I claimed that. But hey, I FINISHED THE BOOK!

Jamie N., thank you for always being enthusiastic about my writing and for jumping at the chance to beta read each novel! I hope you like this version way more than the original.

Tiffany N., thank you for believing in me as a business and trusting me with your own work. I'm so grateful we've gotten to know each other. With that said, thank you for listening to me during *your* business call and flipping my entire world upside-down with your novel questions. I sincerely think it improved the book.

Professor Clayton, thank you for your inspiring words, commitment to my book, and motivation. Thank you for reading more than you ever had to. Your passion for teaching and critique of this book have made me a stronger writer.

Readers, thank you to each and every one of you who has supported me. Your reviews of my past work have meant the world and have been my motivation on the hardest writing days. I hope you enjoy Theo's story, and I'm grateful you're along for the ride.

Also by Chelsea Lauren

Novels:

Underneath the Whiskey

Simply An Enigma

Novellas:

'Tis The Effing Season

Short Stories:

"You Matter, Marley Mae" and "Happy Ex-Max" from Winter Neverland: An Anthology

"All A-Boat You" from Because of You: A Represent Publishing Anthology

About the Author

Chelsea Lauren is a YA and NA contemporary fiction author. Chelsea has been writing ever since she had vivid dreams in middle school. The only cure was to write them down, and only then, did Chelsea realize she could become an author.

She's an upstate NY native, establishing roots in her hometown with her partner and St. Berdoodle, Kaiya.

Chelsea is the founder of Represent Publishing, a self-publishing company dedicated to helping authors strengthen their writing, edit, and publish their novels. Her passion lies in helping others accomplish their dreams.

When Chelsea isn't writing or working on her business, you can find her devouring books, snuggling with her pup, camping, or having game nights with her friends.

9 781732 464384